Also by Lorene Cary

BLACK ICE

The Price of a Child

The Price of a Child

———— A Novel ————

Lorene Cary

Alfred A. Knopf New York 1995

THIS IS A BORZOI BOOK
PUBLISHED BY ALFRED A. KNOPF, INC.

Library of Congress Cataloging-in-Publication Data
Cary, Lorene.
The price of a child : a novel / Lorene Cary.
p.   cm.
ISBN 0-679-42106-8
1. Afro-American women—
Pennsylvania—Philadelphia—Fiction.
2. Women abolitionists—Pennsylvania—Philadelphia—Fiction.
3. Freedmen—Pennsylvania—Philadelphia—Fiction.
4. Philadelphia (Pa.)—Fiction.
I. Title.
PS3553.A78944P75   1995
813'.54—dc20   94-24667
CIP

Manufactured in the United States of America

First Edition

For Laura Hagans Smith

and

Zoë Drayton Smith

Freedom lurked around us and I understood, at last, that he could help us to be free if we would listen, that he would never be free until we did.

James Baldwin, "Sonny's Blues"

Jesus saith unto them, "Did ye never read in the scriptures, The stone which the builders rejected, the same is become the head of the corner: this is the Lord's doing, and it is marvellous in our eyes?"

Matthew 21:42

ACKNOWLEDGMENTS

I am especially grateful to Phil Lapsansky, Research
Librarian at the Library Company of Philadelphia, for
leading me to the story of Jane Johnson in William
Still's *The Underground Railroad* (1872), available in
reprint from Ayer Company Publishers, Inc., in
Salem, New Hampshire.

The Price of a Child

One / Crazy Hope

When Ginnie looked at Jackson Pryor she thought of nothing but how to leave him, like she'd thought of now for two days on end. She expected it to leap out of her throat: *Run, run, as fast as you can. You can't catch me, I'm the Gingerbread Man.*

Each time Ginnie thought of running away she hid the thought. He'd see it in her eyes. She tried to force it deeper inside her, but it lay just under the skin. Stubborn. Her eye was jumping.

She'd sprinkled herself with orange water Suzy had given her, and now she stank of rebellion.

He threw another of his pointless compliments her way. "You smell nice," he said.

I've run away from a little old lady and a little old man, and I can run away from you, I can.

They used to make gingerbread all the time, little brown men with raisins for eyes. Children bit off the heads. Raisin eyes winked at her from the cookie pan in her mind. Gingerbread men grinned, plump and shiny.

I run, I run, I run my best. I run pretty close to a hornets' nest. The p'trollers run. They run their best. They run right in the hornets' nest.

. . .

Worse yet, she'd dreamt of the gray cat, and she couldn't shake off the shadow of the dream. Like that's what she needed: to dream up the gray damn cat. It had been a childhood nightmare, stalking her imagination and hissing in her sleep when she was seven or eight and her mother, Lily, was loaned out to another farm to sew for a big wedding, leaving her alone in their lean-to cabin. The cat came back to frighten her after her mother, bitter and almost crazy, had coughed up blood and died. Ginnie hadn't seen the cat since she'd taken up with Coop, almost fifteen years before. Like real cats, like Coop, it came and went as it pleased. Its appearance in her anxious sleep felt like a warning, or maybe as if something bad had already happened.

"I want to travel with my children," she'd told Pryor, and he'd agreed. Then The Bat found out, as she would, of course, since he kept her calmed about the Nicaragua trip by telling her everything, or close to everything. The Bat had said no, no children. So Ginnie made her own fuss.

"I'll be no good to you without 'em."

"Don't threaten me, Ginnie."

But he did go to The Bat and make a deal; and he came back and plopped their deal in Ginnie's lap. The two older children, but not Benjamin. So there.

"Suzy'll watch him," he said.

Ginnie could hear The Bat in that scheme. Always planning out somebody's damn life. What they'd eat, what they'd wear, where they'd sleep, and who they'd lay. Always trying to direct what happened when she was out of earshot. Nicaragua was out of earshot, so The Bat would keep Bennie.

Watching Pryor's back all those years had made her shrewd.

She made it worse with that pie-faced lie about how they

wanted to let him go, wished they could, but how Ginnie couldn't do the work Master Pryor required—now could she?—with three pickaninnies in tow.

She liked to lie was all Ginnie could figure. She must have stayed awake nights figuring how to look folk dead in the eye and say words that sounded like one thing and meant another. Ginnie knew what damn work the master required. His requirements gave her two children.

Why, shucks, The Bat said, if Ginnie took three children, then they'd have to send somebody to take care of her. Hah-hah-hah. Now, that was some funny shit there: somebody to take care of Ginnie.

She'd been having nosebleeds since they had left home. And dreaming: of the gray cat and yams and teeth.

Pryor looked hard at her. "We'll only be here for a few hours," he said, as if apologizing. He frowned and squinted at his pocket watch and ran his fingers through his hair.

"You must be hungry," he said, "you and the children. Mattie-boy, you hungry?"

Pryor's father-in-law had told him not to bring Ginnie.

"Jackson," he'd said, "you could not do a worse thing."

"You always traveled with Mammy Rae."

"That was twenty years ago. This is 1855. Things have changed."

Pryor pouted and smoked his segar. "Ginnie wouldn't leave me," he'd said.

Now, as she later had cause to remember, he was on her heels every minute.

"Yessir. I is," Mattie answered.

Pryor was an intelligent man, educated in the North, a stickler for hygiene and manners. He'd taught her to speak, because it offended him to hear her go too wrong, and he taught her her ABCs, because it amused him and he saw no harm.

"I am," he corrected.

Ginnie had heard it coming.

"I am," Mattie repeated.

Pryor wrinkled his nose and made a smile at Mattie. It was his best smile. He called him Mattie-boy, the baby Bennie-Boy. He spoiled them with pennies and candy. Then he turned and wiped the rest of the smile on Ginnie.

"Cat got your tongue, Gin? Huh?"

"I suppose."

"Traveling will tell on you. Keeps me wound up."

Wound up: she knew what that meant, but he was too proud to do anything to take his comfort on the road. He didn't want Northerners to know that he bedded his black servant. So he hired separate rooms while they traveled and locked her in at night. Nobody seemed particularly interested in their evening arrangements, as far as she could tell.

That morning as she'd lain in the last inn, head propped on her hand to keep the stink of mildewed ticking out of her nose, she'd wondered whether the gray cat had been sent to warn her away from escape—or to trick her out of trying. She couldn't tell. Her neck was stiff. She'd been straining to do something in her dreams.

Crazy hope rushed through her like water. The muscles under her eye kept jumping. Blip, blip. Like chipmunks peeking out of their holes. Blip.

Pryor was watching her, staring at her as if she weren't herself. She wasn't, of course, and he could see. He studied his pocket watch some more. "We all need to eat, I think. That's what we need." He laughed a little. "Least that's what I need.

"I surely had hoped that we would make Philadelphia in time for the regular New York steamer, without all this foolishness about takin a ferry and then gettin on more railroad cars, and then ferrying into New York. . . . Not to mention this waitin around and whatnot."

He sighed and shrugged at her, as if the two of them were real companions, old partners journeying together, as if Ginnie gave a good shit how they traveled to New York City, or who they might meet on the way, or how fast they got to Nicaragua so he could start working over them ignorant people down there for their land. Had to be land in it or money, or both, or why else would he be going?

It didn't matter to her anyway. Why should it? Why should she care a damn what advantages he was traveling such a far distance to secure? Travel fast; travel slow. So what? And besides, Jesus have mercy, she just might not go along.

Run right next to the hornets' nest. I run, I run, I run.

She'd been waiting for this stopover like a cat waits under a bush for a dove. She'd been waiting quiet for years and very still.

"So, I'll go on down now and get a bite, nothing heavy. We don't want anything heavy."

Ginnie managed not to look too desperate, but she could not speak, either, naturally. She saw the damned cat in her head. The devil was a busy man.

Ginnie's first attempt to slip out of slavery had been twelve years before. Cooper and his brother Singin Sam had planned it for themselves, and then, when she popped up pregnant, Cooper figured a way for her to go too. It still made her catch her breath sometimes, as if she were eighteen again, thinking herself a woman grown, finding out that "her man," as she called Willie—Walleye Willie, Willie the cooper, Coopyman, Coop—was planning to go and never a word. That taught her something about thinking she knew somebody, and about how far to trust the tingling in her thighs and the itch at the bottom of her belly.

The plan hadn't worked for her. She never made it to where

they were supposed to meet, because she was missed sooner than she expected and they sent someone out to look for her.

She walked back to the Pryor place behind the horse of the overseer's helper. Cooper was gone, and she was hungry. She never forgot the sour hunger on that walk back, or being so sleepy that she could barely move her feet.

Jackson Pryor did not punish her for sneaking off, although it was clear in the next few days that Cooper had escaped, and Cooper had been her man. Pryor prided himself on his leniency, as he said: he let it be known that he would not suffer a pregnant woman to be whipped. He did remind her, however, that Cooper had gone with his brother and left her; he mounted a campaign to domesticate her. She'd been a yard dog. Now he'd burn off the ticks and bring her indoors.

She prayed that she would not begrudge Cooper his freedom. Cooper and his brother couldn't take bondage. It was that simple. People always said it of them. Some people just couldn't, the way that some women couldn't take childbirth. Cooper couldn't take the driver's contempt or the overseer's authority or the master's mastery. He couldn't take knowing that the strength in his body fattened another man's belly. He had always wanted to be free; he and his brother, he told her, had wanted to run since they could walk. And when he'd said it she had recognized what she loved in him: he refused to settle. She loved the part of him that resolved, when the overseer threw a melon rind and spoiled his hat, to leave at any cost. She was the cost. Their daughter was the cost. Life together, for however long they might be together, was the cost. They paid.

You don't just run. First, you make up your mind.

Her father had been like that. After a particularly bad flogging he decided never to let himself be whipped again. Virgil was a big man, with a deep, sharp voice like the voice of God, who let her stand on his foot and hold on to his thigh as he walked. His leg felt stronger than anything.

After the whipping, Lily washed Virgil with water and turpentine. The next night, as soon as he was able to walk, he ran away to the woods and stayed for a month, long enough so that Jackson Pryor's father decided to call back the patrollers and send instead a black man to negotiate Virgil's return. In the meantime, the overseer was fired. Virgil came home again to live with his wife and family.

He came back changed. He was thin, and his skin and breath smelled like earth. Lily slumped into his arms and wept. Her body heaved with each sob. While he'd been gone, Ginnie's older brother had died of a fever. Lily and Ginnie cried off and on through the night. Virgil held them on the pallet and rocked them in the dark.

"Hush, hush, hush, now," he said.

The husks made dry groans under them; they breathed in the new smell of him and cried some more. Later he told them how he had escaped from a forest fire so hot that he could hear the pop of rocks cracking open behind him. He figured he'd been in the fire the same time that his boy, Ginnie's brother, had died.

Virgil was with them another eight or nine months. Then Master Pryor died. In January, the farm had an old-fashioned settling. Traders' wagons rolled up without warning on the first day of the new year. They'd been told about Virgil. They came for him first, grabbing and shackling him fast, so that he could not run. Lily cried and cursed and screamed and ran after the wagon, and Ginnie ran after them both. Virgil shook his head and shouted no, don't make it no worse. Lily stopped in the road. Virgil had made her promise never to forget him and never to let them make her crawl.

After Virgil was gone, Lily made it a point to tell her daughter several times that Virgil had made her able to walk right. She said that when Ginnie was born her toes were stacked one on top of the other, so that she could not have stood straight. Virgil held the little foot on a board with the toes flat, and he'd tied them down tight so that they would grow straight. "Think of your daddy," Lily said, "every time you run."

Ginnie thought of her father the day they brought her back from trying to run away with Cooper. Jackson Pryor had the overseer's helper bring her into his study. He didn't ask her whether she'd tried to run, but he did say he was going to watch her. He also told her that she was too smart to make her life more difficult than it needed to be. She was eighteen; he was forty.

Ginnie had always figured that he didn't know as much as he thought he did. But she'd been a young fool, paying more attention to what Pryor didn't know than to what he did. He knew plenty. He'd been raised to make money and take comfort from black people. She sat before him, her big belly, his profit, between them, filling the room, pushing aside the memory of her father's resistance. She wasn't running now.

"How're you gonna go, Ginnie?" he asked her. "It's not just you. You'll have to take care of your little baby soon, won't you?"

He'd have it from her own mouth.

She knew something else, now, too: that knowing made no difference. Her daddy may have run, and Cooper and his brother may have run, but, to her shame, she couldn't. At the end of the day, pain shot through her buttocks and down her thighs; at night, her calves bunched like fists. She wished she could spit in Pryor's face. She could not. She wasn't running; she was sitting, and pitifully glad of it.

Lily used to argue with Virgil, after he was gone, as if he were still lying next to her. "You say they can't make you do nothing but die. They can't make you crawl. But everybody ain't like you, Virgil."

Ginnie had been ashamed of her mother. Now she was ashamed of herself.

"Just like you say, sir," she said.

"Good."

Ginnie was moved from the washtub to the kitchen. There, she was apprenticed to Suzy, who had taken her in as a girl after Lily died. In a few years, Ginnie had learned enough to cook in

Washington when the Captain went on government business. His wife did not always accompany him.

Suzy saw it coming, and warned her. Ginnie saw it coming, and it came. Pryor told her that he'd been on the lookout for a girl like her for some time. He wanted her to be discreet: only in town and when his wife stayed home in the country. That worked out to once every couple months or so, and usually when he'd been drinking, so it didn't take long. He wanted a gal who wouldn't preen. Ginnie didn't tell him she had nothing to preen about. He wanted his comfort, nothing more or less, was how he put it to her and to himself, as if he were on trial.

"He lets you take Etta when you go now, huh?" Suzy asked.

Ginnie couldn't answer except to nod her head. Suzy had taken her in; she'd cared for her like a mother. Ginnie stood embarrassed before her as she would have been before her own kin. Quite suddenly her eyes were wet.

"Please don't shame me no more."

Suzy cried with her. "I'm not fault-findin. I know you're doin what you think is right."

"What else can I do?"

Unlike some owners Ginnie'd heard tell, Pryor would not have whipped or thumbscrewed or tied her hand to foot and raped her had she tried to refuse him. But he might have sold her.

"I'd've been change in his pocket, Aunt Sue," she said.

"I know that, Ginnie. You know I know."

"And you'd've got Etta the same way you got me. That's if we was lucky."

Ginnie told herself she was fortunate that in these, his middle years, Pryor had moderate habits and little passion. He was clean. And to keep peace with The Bat, he behaved, most of the time, as if nothing ever happened between them. He didn't come at her in the kitchen or swagger and wink. When she got pregnant, the household behaved as if it had just happened on its own, like a haystack catching on fire, or the Virgin Mary.

"I been needin a gal like you for a long time." What he'd meant by "a gal like you," she began to realize, was someone who'd make no demands.

"Couldn't I be free? It'd be like it is now, only I'd be free." She whispered it, offhand, casually.

"Well, then, what would be the point?"

She brought it up periodically, no more than a couple times a year. He'd look thoughtful and surprised. He'd tell her that she was a handsome girl, an excellent woman, that she was comfortable, that he was certain she could run a fine home of her own in a place such as Washington—as if she were in doubt—and that he would free her one day but couldn't part with her yet.

"I need you here."

He said it the way children say they need a doll baby or a lump of sugar—because they will not be denied. What you need is a smack in the ass, old people replied.

"You don't need me," she said.

"Surely do."

The children, she'd say, and he'd nod his head.

"The children, of course. In time."

In his way, Pryor showed favor to Mattie and then to little Benjamin. The children, he'd say, he would surely free. "Surely" was his favorite word. Ginnie could not be sure of anything. Sometimes she believed him, because it helped.

Then came Nicaragua. The Bat wouldn't go because of the climate. And Ginnie found herself pulling out seashells that Cooper had given her twelve years before. They were purple and white, and smooth on the inside. She took to carrying them in her pocket. She knew that folk had smuggled themselves onto trains and ships out of Baltimore, that they walked the woods to Pennsylvania, rode hidden in carts and crated up in boxes to Philadelphia. Each story fed her hope. The whole system of states and laws and slavery leaked like old women sneezing, like old men bleeding into their bowels. They tried to keep it secret, what with the laws and passes and patrollers, the lies on top of lies and shows of force. But slavery leaked. On the one hand it held; on the other it leaked.

She might be put in the way to escape; or not. She might get the chance to run and miss it. She might realize her loss that moment, or never even know it had come and gone. She might never, ever get the chance. She might try and fail. She might die trying. She might lose the children if she tried, or lose them if she didn't. Who knew?

Her mind was making itself up. It clackety-clacked like a wagon full of broken hoes. She could hear it, storing up resentments and hope. Bits of songs, sarcasm, and bitten-off butt ends of rage littered her head like the tips of segars around a porch. She sang deep and rough to herself like she'd sing to a colicky baby. Her time might appear on the Nicaragua trip. She came to believe that. She might recognize it; and it could be in her nature to act. She began to accept the uncertainty of it, and the costs; and when she could, she felt as clear and as strong as a waterfall pouring over sadness hard as bone.

By now her eye was jumping something awful.

"I'm going down to the dining room for a bite to eat," Pryor said again. If he didn't stop repeating himself, Ginnie thought she would scream. Either that or she'd reach over and grab him by the collar that she'd laundered and ram him up against the wall.

"I'll have them send a meal up for you and the children. Do not leave this room." He said it quietly and firmly. "Ginnie, you hear me: you and these two children"—he pointed his finger and smiled at them—"do not leave this room."

Chastising Ginnie in front of her own children was the sort of insult that Pryor generally spared her, but he was nervous. She should not have felt as if he had slapped her face, but she did.

It would not pass. Ginnie could not distract herself: not

here in Philadelphia, where black people went about their own business—*their own business*; hadn't she seen them?—wearing tidy bonnets and leather shoes. Frozen out of the infant manufacturing industries, they made their living on the fringes of the industrial boom. They were barbers, dress and shirt and shoe and hat makers, pastry cooks, brick makers and layers, carpenters, coopers, dentists, domestic servants, cracker bakers, cabinetmakers, schoolteachers, sail makers, drivers, housepainters, and tanners. They turned up everywhere. Handsome Negroes. Well-spoken Negroes. Negroes carrying kid gloves at the train station, speaking better English than white folks at home. She had imagined escape, but she had not imagined such a place, such a world, as this. Here, she could not let Pryor's words pass through her as if she were a grazing animal, sucking up slop from the trough, crapping out pits from rotten leavings.

"These two children" was a threat—Ginnie recognized it, of course, as he meant her to do—reminding her that Benjamin had stayed home. She knew damn good and well where he was. Too far away to visit on Saturday-night roads crowded with black men on their way to visit their wives, carrying with them their dirty clothes and parcels of food. Hadn't she asked to bring him? Hadn't she risked arousing suspicion by pressing Pryor on it even after The Bat had told him to make Ginnie leave Bennie home?

Ginnie bore it like a champion, though, like fighters who'd take a hit to the face and keep on standing. Or wives. She didn't flinch, even though she knew they were holding Bennie-boy for surety. She saw the chance of a chance to run—and its price. Ginnie disciplined herself. She let maybe be maybe until she could get close enough to see for sure. In the meantime, she wouldn't flinch.

"You all sit tight right here. Y'hear me?"

Ginnie avoided Pryor's eyes. Her temples burned. The arteries and veins in her neck stood out; she could feel the blood surging through. She was breathing too hard. Her jawbone ached with holding still to keep in her voice.

"You hear me, Gin?"

She nodded, and he left.

With Pryor gone, six-year-old Mattie began to gallop about the room, playing horsie. Ginnie turned toward him and put a finger over her mouth. He didn't mind fast enough. She strode across the room, grabbed him by the arm, jerked him hard enough to make him cry out, and then steered him to the wing chair where Willietta sat, silent and scared. Etta's frightened eyes angered Ginnie as much as Mattie's antics. Mattie squirmed in her grip. Ginnie slapped him, and as soon as her hand hit his arm, she felt a muscle snap in her back. It coiled up under her shoulder blade, the place where Suzy said wings would sprout in heaven. Ginnie snorted at the thought. The pain was on the right side. So she used her left hand to grab the material in the front of his shirt and lift him off the chair.

"Make me speak to you again," she hissed. "You just make me and, so help me God, I'ma whip the black offa you."

She banged on the side of the chair to keep from hitting him again. "I'ma hurt you, boy."

She could feel it, the pounding inside telling her to get him right, get him right, so he wouldn't misbehave again. Who knew what would happen to them in the next few hours?

"I'ma hurt you, Matthew. I feel like tearin somebody up. Can you see that?"

"Yeah."

"What'd you say?"

"Yes'm."

"Who you think that gonna be?"

He mumbled.

"What you say?"

"Me."

She dropped him into the chair beside Etta. He pulled the edge of the cushion between his legs and rocked, pouting and coughing. He had a cold.

"Did I give you a kerchief before we left?"

"Yeah."

"Use it."

Ginnie stepped to the door that opened onto an ornamental balcony. Below her clamored the city, where even the stables were built of brick and stone. Philadelphia had grown in thirty years from a town into a big city; its population, swelled by thousands of immigrants from Ireland, Germany, and Italy, had doubled in the same time and would soon reach half a million. Horses' hooves clopped on cobblestone streets; and wagons, hand-pulled carts, and shiny black cabs, clattered and jostled and rolled. Philadelphia overflowed with noise and smells. The grid that William Penn had begun two hundred years before repeated itself west and north and south from the Delaware River. Block after block sprouted rows of red-brick houses, and in the oldest sections, shacks, shanties, and backyard houses squeezed between the rows in the damp, airless alleys and courts without privies or hydrants, with neither sun nor wind to refresh the inhabitants.

Immigrants, minorities, political groups, charitable and social societies, founded clubs to give them the companionship and services that the old town had once provided. They formed closed-off social knots of like people, who wrapped themselves in identities as narrow as the alleys. And the neighborhoods sprawled on, planned not according to the social needs of its citizens but the real estate agents' profits. Visitors from Europe found the sameness dreary and the insularity confusing. After an hour's walk in Philadelphia, Charles Dickens claimed he would have given the world for a crooked street. But to Ginnie, the spreading anonymity looked like hope. She and her children could slip into those streets and disappear.

One brown-skinned man with a wavy black queue bobbing

out from under the back of his hat was selling oysters from a cart on the street. He spoke to passersby in a nasal twang, casual and familiar. When no one was buying, he sang out, as if to keep himself company: "Oysterman. Oysters, clams." He shook his bottle of red sauce and polished glass salt and pepper shakers, which caught the sunlight. He sharpened his knife. He had a spry body and deft hands. Above him, above his customers and the rows and rows of straight-up-and-down brick buildings, the sky stretched clear and blue. Ginnie had never tasted an oyster. Suzy had always wanted to try one.

Ginnie whirled to face her children. The room was spacious and bright; but it was a pen. They were penned in like hogs. Ginnie made a grunting noise in her throat. For a moment, the children stopped and looked at her. Then Mattie began to whine. Etta cuffed him. Ginnie went to them. She took their hands and spoke quietly. She told them that they'd have to be a little man and woman and sit still. She threatened Mattie with another whipping and went to the door. Mattie lay back in the chair. He tried to suck his thumb, but his nose was too clogged for him to suck and breathe at once. So he sulked even more.

Then Ginnie cracked the door. From the hall came the sound of a woman humming to herself.

Jackson Pryor saw how agitated Ginnie had become now that they were waylaid in Pennsylvania. His father-in-law had warned him. Still, at fifty-two, Jack felt that he was entitled to a few comforts. He'd be in Nicaragua who knew how long, and although he was a man of moderation, he wanted his gal around. A little brownskin now and then calmed nervous tension. It balanced the manly fluids and kept him vigorous. Jack didn't want any nasty old whores and foreigners. He liked his gal. She knew him. She was clean. She cooked to his liking and kept his clothes.

He told his wife, who had pouted, and his in-laws that Ginnie wouldn't run. She was well cared for and obedient. He'd had her since she was a girl, and if loyalty wasn't sufficient, she was smart enough to see how slim were her chances and how much she stood to lose. Besides, he'd scheduled carefully to keep them moving once they crossed the Mason-Dixon line. Ginnie would be with him on the steamer from Pennsylvania to New York.

Joellen had put the cap on it, though, when she insisted that they leave Bennie-boy home. Jack had argued against it. Bennie-boy was his favorite. It was a shame that his only sons had to be by Ginnie and not Joellen, but there it was. Sons of his old age, both healthy as foals and sharp as tacks. Bennie-boy particularly. He laughed and cooed and talked. He sang songs; sing him a song, and the next day he'd sing it right back. He'd cut teeth early and crawled early and he ran around on his toes, delighting everyone who saw him. Ginnie kept after Jack to free the boys, and although he hadn't told her, he'd already made out a portion of land for them in his will. They could share it, the L-shaped corner of land near the creek. Joellen wouldn't like it, but she'd have to keep still. Jack Pryor wasn't like some swine who'd sell their own.

So no harm in leaving Bennie home. It would keep Joellen quiet, and just in case Ginnie got ideas, it would keep her in line. She'd be back to Bennie in a year or two, when Jack's commission ended.

But as Jack sat in the dining room of Bloodgood's Hotel, sipping a glass of ale and waiting for his soup, he could not help being disturbed by Ginnie's obvious excitement. He remembered how each Christmas and Easter she'd come sidling up, worrying him about why couldn't she be free, and wouldn't he free the boys? She had sense enough not to talk about didn't he care for her and whine and cry like some gals would, but damned if she wasn't persistent. Water dripping on a rock. You could set your calendar by her, come to think. Twice a year every year, like the equinox.

Oh, well, he thought. Another two hours and they'd be on the ferry, on their way to New York. Surely. Then to Nicaragua.

He'd chat her up and send the food. The two hours would pass, and he could rest easy. Two hours wasn't long. Besides, she had two children and no money. How much trouble could she get herself into?

"Ma'am. Excuse me, ma'am," Ginnie whispered. "Over here."

She was a black woman with leathery, oatmeal-colored skin and a wide face. She wore an apron. From the doorway, Ginnie motioned for her to come into the room.

"You need somethin?"

"Please step in."

The woman came warily.

"My children and me are on our way to New York with our master, and I'm tryin to get free." She whispered the whole story about how Master Pryor was headed for Nicaragua, where he'd be the U.S. ambassador, and about how they were taking the boat that afternoon.

Ginnie spoke as nice and congenial as she could, knowing suddenly that she had to make this woman her friend. It made her talk too much, too crazy, too fast. What'd the woman care for Nicaragua or New York or ambassadors? The point was that Ginnie needed to get sneaked out of the hotel. The woman squirmed and looked away. What could Ginnie say to make them seem like decent people deserving help instead of good-for-nothing gimme-niggers crying please, please, please, and never no nothing in return?

"Can't you help us? Gotta be a back door. What steps do y'all use?"

Finally, she shut herself up. It was too late. What steps do y'all use? The woman looked as if she'd been slapped. Fifty wrinkles turned into a hundred and fifty.

"I am so sorry for you. I am," she said. She made a sorry face. Impatience peeked through.

"But I wouldn't know how to begin. . . . I wouldn't know

where to take you or nothin. There'd be no hope with me, none at all."

She sounded determined to put Ginnie off.

"I'm working now." She backed out of the room and closed the door.

Ginnie sat down on the side of the bed. She was breathing as fast as if she'd toted a load uphill.

"Bitch," she breathed.

The knot in her back balled up as if on purpose to break her spirit, like that big-face woman had been sent to break her. The children stared at her, eyes wide and terrified. Ginnie felt dizzy, and her heart flailed around in her chest.

The door opened. Pryor appeared, asking whether or not their food had come, and whether or not she needed anything.

Jesus, God, he'd come close. She felt as nervous as if she been laying up in bed with another man. He wore the same falsely bright face he'd worn when he'd left.

"Naw, sir. No food yet. I heard somebody in the hall just now, and I looked out, but it wasn't nobody but the cleanin woman."

"Well, let me just go on and see what's holding it, shall I?"

"Uh-hunh, I'd appreciate that, thank you."

Then he left.

Ginnie watched the children's faces. Etta tried to mask her alarm; Mattie, who did not quite understand what was going on, fidgeted as usual. Against the striped green damask upholstery, they looked small and dirty. She turned away, hating herself for seeing them that way; hating the colored woman who could back out of the room into her own private life; hating Pryor with his two-faced concern; hating God for letting them keep Bennie in Virginia; hating the call inside to give in: she could feel it coming on from somewhere inside, cramping, threatening, like a miscarriage.

They done broke you now.

"Hope you don't never have to trust no white folk nor depend on no niggers, neither." So Ginnie's mother used to say with a bitter bark, and squinch her beautiful almond eyes at Ginnie, who knew, when her mother looked at her, that she appeared every bit as wretched as her own children looked now.

"Goddamn," Ginnie whispered to the ceiling. Enraged tears pricked hot behind her eyes. They held back despair that waited patient as death in the corner of her soul.

"I could go find somebody," Etta said. She was beautiful, as Lily had been. But unlike Lily, Etta toted her beauty skittishly, like a poor man out on the road carrying too much money. She'd been all right at Pryor's—Pryor had no teenage sons—but she wouldn't have been all right for long. Look at Ginnie, and she wasn't nearly as pretty as Etta would be.

"Mama?" Etta spoke haltingly to Ginnie's back, because Ginnie was staring at the doorknob. It was an exquisite piece of work, the doorknob was, round and smooth, the brass polished to a shine. Goddamned doorknob. Ginnie heard her daughter's voice but could not take in her words.

"Say again, baby."

"I said I could go for you. I could slip right out and find a man, a colored man, out there, maybe. . . ." Etta had seen them too, riding in, the stout and handsome colored people, looking for all the world like prosperous cousins preparing their welcome. A mischievous, twinkling-eyed man at the train depot had tipped his cap to Ginnie. Etta gestured toward the window and stopped in midsentence, because imagination had taken her no farther than finding someone to help.

"Find a man," Ginnie repeated absently. She humphed down deep in her chest.

Ginnie turned to look at her daughter. Although she favored Lily, Etta had Cooper's mouth and his smile. Neither of them smiled often.

Ginnie remembered making Cooper laugh at night in the cold cabin; she remembered his hands wrapping around her waist and scooping her toward him on their pallet; she remembered the warmth of his chest against her back, the backs of her legs against the front of his; the comfort and the bullying of his body. She recalled his touch with leisure, as if she were not a terrified woman trying to run away in broad daylight in a strange city, where she had no family or friends, but some dotty white lady sitting plump and naked at her vanity table, filling the time, pretending to be good-looking, and pretending that because she was white, good looks could do anything for her besides get her big and pregnant like a horse with a bellyful of grass.

Ginnie used to joke like that with serious old deep-running, still-water Willie the Cooper. It was about the only time he ever laughed. She'd do voices and pretend to be different people. She'd mimic how the white grandmother in the house would sit looking at herself like there wa'n't squat to do in the world except sit and wait for some nice nigra to come get you for your next hot meal. Ginnie would sit on the side of their pallet, legs crossed under her, combing and braiding her hair. Every few minutes she'd turn to Cooper and ask, with a faraway look and a breathy voice: "Is it time for supper yet?"

Then she'd answer brusquely, like Suzy when nobody was around: "No, ain't time for no supper yet. You know you just had your dinner. Live to eat."

"Oh, I see. Well, how about tea? I could almost swear for teatime. Now, don't tell me no. You run along and go see."

Coop would laugh until tears slid out of the corners of his eyes to his ears.

It had been a long time since Ginnie had made funny.

"She kicked my ass, that old white lady did. The grand-mother. Kicked my ass." Through the years Ginnie said it with feeling as she rubbed the shiny scars on her buttocks and the backs of her thighs. "Of all the people there, it was the old grand-mother beat the hell outta me."

One day The Bat would be an old grandmother, and she'd beat some poor child, no doubt. It wouldn't be Bennie, though. Pryor set great store by that little boy. But did he love him? Did he see himself in him enough so that he wouldn't sell him? Would he let Suzy bring him up and then settle something on him, a few good acres or enough money to let him start a business or go to school?

Thinking, thinking, thinking.

"Mama, I'ma go." Etta stood.

"No, you don't have to go."

Ginnie's mind rushed like water downhill.

"Sit down, Etta," she said.

Ginnie's mother, Lily, had gotten mean at the end. She held her up by the hand and beat her so bad that she wrenched the girl's shoulder right out of the socket. They came and picked Ginnie off the floor and dragged her mother outside, and old Homer took his big hands and snapped Ginnie's arm back into place. She observed the moment in her mind, saw herself howl and shake as Homer came toward her, talking about, "Hold still."

Thank God for Uncle Homer, she thought. Thank God for Suzy, who took her in the night after Lily died and now cared for Bennie. Before they left, Suzy had looked at her tearily—she'd always been a big crybaby—produced two tarnished dollars and said: "Just in case."

Ginnie had tried to make excuses.

"Well, now," Suzy said, "if you don't need 'em, you just bring 'em back."

Maybe the chambermaid had been a sign.

Ginnie looked again at the children. How could they not be shabby and thin? Ginnie watched Mattie squirm. He was going to be sure enough trouble one day. Not Etta, but Mattie would. They'd want to knock the piss out of him, and they could likely kill him in the process.

"No, Etta, you not gonna find nobody. We'll stay together unless I say different. You hear? Could be patrollers in this city. You know who I'm talkin about?"

Etta nodded her head. Sure she knew. Etta was kind-hearted. She was thinking about Bennie-boy too. Ginnie could tell.

"Etta. I'm doing the best I know how."

Etta's eyes were sad and afraid. She nodded.

Ginnie went to their chair. She bent down and put her arms around them. "Y'all with me? You gotta be with me. Listen to me: If I hold my breath, you hold yours, you hear? If I look surprised, you look surprised. You know what I'm trying to do?"

Mattie looked confused, but when Etta nodded, he nodded too.

"Did I say it's gonna happen?"

They shook their heads no.

"But I said I'ma try. God as my witness, I'ma try." Then she smiled, suddenly, sincerely, and rubbed the smooth skin on their cheeks. The feel of them gave her courage.

If worse came to worst, Ginnie thought, she might have to send Etta after all, but not yet.

Nig-Nag saw the new chambermaid go into the room. He heard what the women said. It made him scared to hear. He had to tell somebody. He had to tell one of the Vigilance men. He had to tell them, but maybe he couldn't. He felt the tickle in his throat just before it began, the neighing and snorting that erupted from him like a hiccup and lasted as long as it would. The chamber pot sloshed. He steadied it against his body and hurried down the stairs and out back to empty it into the big privy. George was there too. Nig-Nag tried to explain about the woman upstairs, but he couldn't get it all out, because the neighing was too bad. George got the room number, but not much else, before the boss called him come quick, back to the kitchen. Nig-Nag was scared. George could write. He could write notes, and he knew the men to give them to.

"You go on," George said to him, under his breath. "You go.

You seen what we do. Talk to her. Find out how long she'll be here and where she's goin. Ain't nobody gonna miss you. Then come on back. I'll write you a note for Mr. Still—you know him, right?—and Mr. Williamson."

George had gotten work at the hotel for Nig-Nag because he felt sorry for him. The young man lived in George's alley. He was an outside boy, and for a few days in winter, George had let him sleep on his floor. But George and his wife had just one room of a two-room house, and Nig-Nag barked and twitched so bad that when the weather broke, Marie put him out. He took up with two men, Jack and Bo-Bo, in a rougher, poorer court nearby. George suspected them of an unnatural affection, but Marie would not have Nig-Nag back. Besides, they looked after him, and he wouldn't freeze to death. In any event, he'd stayed. But he still came around hungry. George would not give him money, but when he could, he found him a day's work and a plate of food.

"Go on, you," George said. He took off at a trot toward the kitchen, stopped suddenly, and turned. "Then come back to me and let me know what happened. I'll tell you what to do next. Go on, now. Good boy."

Nig-Nag ran upstairs. He began to hiccup.

"Breathe, boy. Breathe, goddamn it. Or else lay there and die." Nig-Nag's uncle's voice commanded him from the grave. He, too, had had the malady: the uncontrollable noises and cursing and coughing that erupted from inside him. He'd died drunk, in the shed above the stables where the two of them had lived together, having suffocated, during an attack, on an apple stolen from the horses' barrel.

Nig-Nag reached the top of the stairwell. The empty chamber pot dangled from his hand. He stopped to breathe nice and easy. Then he tried to move the fluttering down somewhere where it wouldn't do any harm. He pushed it to his feet. Nig-Nag felt clever to have quieted himself. Now his toes jerked, but it was better than neighing. Sometimes Nig-Nag thought that other people, smart people, could not do what he did inside his body.

He was sharper than they knew, plenty sharp, and a lot of stupid bastards could talk pretty and make money and poke women, and he couldn't. It made him want to go to Juniper Street and get some whiskey from the whores. That's all they'd sell him.

A white gentleman was backing out of the room. "I've had a word with them, and the food'll surely be here in a few minutes. Y'all just stay put," he said.

The white gentleman closed the door and stood by it a moment like he didn't want to leave. Then he walked down the hall to the front staircase. He did not notice Nig-Nag, who watched open-mouthed from the rear staircase, polishing the chamber pot with a rag that hung from his apron tie. When he heard the gentleman's footsteps on the treads, Nig-Nag walked to the woman's door, but he couldn't bring himself to knock.

Ginnie heard his step and opened the door. Nig-Nag bobbled the chamber pot. She pulled him into the room and closed the door behind him. He was a smooth-faced boy, with an odd, but appealing, face. His mouth hung open.

"Listen," she said. "Listen to me. I need help. Look at me. You know the kind of help I'm talkin about?"

He grinned because he knew that already.

She frowned at him. "Can you help me?" Her voice became sharp. "Can you show me how to get out? Is there people near here who could help us? Can you go get somebody else?"

Two children stared at him from a large chair across the room. Nig-Nag nodded yes and then shook his head no. He started to hiccup and put up his finger.

"I know somebody," he said.

The woman's master was taking her onto the next ferryboat to Camden. They'd missed the noon steamboat from Philadelphia to New York, so he'd determined to cross the river and catch the train. In New York, they were scheduled to board a ship to Nicaragua, where her master would be the United States ambassador. Nig-Nag knew that he had heard as much as he could remember. He wanted her to stop, unless what she was saying would change his instructions. He still had to go to George, and George would send him to Mr. Still and Mr. Williamson. Much as she might go on at him, that's what he was still supposed to do.

Nig-Nag put his finger to his mouth to tell her to be quiet. But she kept talking low and fast into his ear. Her long fingers wrapped tight around his arm. The children stared at him. He noticed the stink of his apron and the grime crusted on his palms.

"I heard Pryor say," the woman told him, hissing even more than before, "that the ferryboat leave at three o'clock. That's no more than an hour now, I figure. That's all the time we have. Do you hear me, boy? Don't need to go get somebody. We don't have time for that. Just sneak us out the back."

Nig-Nag shook his head violently. She talked on. What was she talking about?

"No," he said. "I can't." He hiccuped the word "can't." It erupted with a spray of spittle in her face.

Ginnie's head snapped to the side. She swore to herself under her breath. Nig-Nag cringed.

"Oh, Christ," she said to herself. "Oh, Jesus, I can't stand no more of this."

Nig-Nag grinned at the woman. She did not smile back.

"You can't hardly talk, can you?"

He gave a sheepish shrug. He could talk, but she was scaring him. She looked to him as if she were going to beat him.

"Don't hit me."

"Don't hit me, you say." Ginnie looked from the children to the idiot and back again. Come to think of it, she did feel like giving him a slap. Might do her some good.

"Ain't nobody gonna hit you."

Ginnie slumped against the arm of the chair. For the moment, she gave up. She could almost taste relief at the back of her tongue.

Bennie.

Then Nig-Nag neighed. He hit himself on the behind, gave a little hop, and scampered out of the room on jerky feet.

Ginnie stood by the door, her hand on the beautiful brass knob. Maybe she would just walk out. She'd go down the back staircase, out of the hotel, and into one of the alleys. Then what? Under a bridge by the river? In the alleys? An outhouse? A stable? She'd find a stable and get into the loft with the children until dark. Or else she might leave Etta in one stable, or somewhere else they'd never find her, or maybe with someone, like that oysterman, maybe, not him, but someone like him, a Negro woman with children of her own. Then she'd take Mattie with her, 'cause she sure as hell couldn't leave him anywhere alone.

This time, the knock did not make her shriek. She was too worn out. She was crashing down from crazy hope into desperate certainty. They'd go out and find a stable to hide in. Now that she had a plan, Ginnie was able to calm herself. She opened the door to a round-faced young black man, carrying a tray of food.

George waved his hand at her with authority. She closed the door and stood with her back to it. As he put down the tray and laid out the food, this new man asked whether or not she was the one he was looking for. He had an accent that she'd never heard. She nodded, astounded.

"And how long you be stopping here at Bloodgood's, ma'am?"

No one had ever called Ginnie ma'am. "Not long."

"Have you any idea how long?"

"Till a quarter to three."

"The ferry to Camden, ma'am?"

"Yessir. I suppose so."

The young man looked at her for a long while. He was memorizing her, she knew. The smell of cooking grease wafted off his clothes and skin.

"There is a committee of men who watch for fugitives. They call 'em Vigilance. I will get them word. But the only thing is that you cannot move. You cannot give away what is to come. They will find you."

He took a deep breath. "Truth is, of course, and well you

know it, there's very little time. But if we cannot move fast enough, they will telegraph New York for you. If no one approaches you here, then you look out for two men to meet you there and take you with them.

"Either way, we'll come for you, you understand?"

Two / **Stand**

Nig-Nag danced into William Still's office and thrust George's notes at him. Although he had been chairman of the Vigilance Committee for some time, Still felt excited each time someone new came to the office with a note. He never knew what circumstances would be described, or what he was about to thrust himself into: gunplay in a barnyard in New Jersey, live cargo in a box at the wharf, children, pregnant women, women dressed as men, and at least one man dressed, quite convincingly, as a woman. Still took both notes eagerly, the one with his name written on it and the one addressed to Passmore Williamson in the hand of George the Haitian. He was about to give back Williamson's note, when he saw that the young man appeared feebleminded. Still read his note:

> Dear Mr. Still, sir—Will you come to Bloodgood's as soon as possible, as there are 3 fugitive slaves here who want their liberty. Their master is here and on his way to New York on the 3 o'clock ferry to meet the cars.

Still knew without looking that Williamson's note would say the same thing, in the same hasty scrawl.

"I'll save you the trip to Mr. Williamson, boy. But I'll give you another errand in exchange. Can you remember it?"

Nig-Nag grinned confidently.

"Do you know Mr. Quick who runs a stable in Rodman Street?"

Nig-Nag nodded. "His brother is my landlord. You could say."

Still worked his brows. Emmanuel Quick rented some god-awful hovels as well as a few decent houses. He turned George's note over and wrote, asking Quick to send one of his carriages to Bloodgood's immediately.

"I want you to take this to Mr. Jeremiah Quick. He's the hackman with the stable."

"Yes, sir."

Still reached in his pocket and handed Nig-Nag a few pennies. "That's for your good work, eh?"

He winked at Nig-Nag, who grinned, hit himself on the buttocks, and jumped over the threshold and out the door.

Still put on his hat to go to Williamson's office on Arch Street, shaking his head to himself about the strange business they were in. He had absolute faith in the idiot who had just left, more faith that he would do his part to help the fugitives than in many so-called men of quality. The Vigilance Committee had requirements: money, transportation, safe havens. But first it depended on the character of the men and women involved—and the judgment of the men who engaged and directed them. Still trusted his intuition. George, the freedom-loving Haitian at Bloodgood's, would not have sent Nig-Nag if he could not be trusted. He was a good choice; a simple boy like that could slip into and out of anywhere and people would never notice—never remember he'd been. Still told himself to keep him in mind.

Williamson could see from Still's attitude that the matter was urgent. He read the note standing up.

"I'm afraid I'm to go to Harrisburg, William. I'll have to leave you to take care of this one without me."

"Quite sure?" Still made a disappointed face. He genuinely enjoyed working Vigilance with his white counterpart.

Williamson shrugged. He felt obliged to take care of business. "Must support my committee work."

It was Still's joke—that they worked only to pay their Underground Railroad expenses.

"The fact is, William, you may not have enough time to manage all the details before they're to leave. If it were I, I'd find out the owner's particulars and then telegraph our people in New York, so that they might meet them there."

"I thought of that."

"Yes?"

"But this one intrigues me."

"This one?"

Still had assisted or directly handled more than a hundred cases. They all intrigued him. He kept careful records of each transaction, as well as his subsequent correspondence with the fugitives. Committee members implored each other to destroy evidence as a matter of course, but Williamson knew that Still never would, even though he was aware that if records were discovered, the entire Philadelphia Underground Railroad would be badly compromised.

But Still, the son of a self-purchased freeman, had had an experience that none of the other members had: his own brother, who had been kidnapped as a child forty years earlier, had made his way north and found him. After that meeting, after watching his brother and his mother embrace, Still knew he must keep records. Who else, he asked Williamson, could help fugitive families reunite? And who else would tell the stories of their struggles to their posterity? As *Freedom's Journal*'s editors wrote in their inaugural issue, and as Still was fond of repeating: "We want to plead our own cause. Too long have others spoken for us."

"I'll go see," Still told his partner. "I may end up wiring New York after all, but at least I shall not have let the opportunity pass without a glance."

"Something else: a writ of habeas corpus would be the most certain way to secure their release."

"But there's no time."

"No." Williamson pressed his lips together. They disappeared into a straight line. "You've thought of it, of course."

"Yes." Still drawled the word thoughtfully. His hat was on again, and his hand was on the doorknob. "But just consider for a moment: what if I didn't bother with the writ? What if I deal directly with the fugitives and simply tell them that they are free to walk away?"

Williamson smiled. "To walk away?"

"That is the law."

"Pennsylvania law would allow them to walk away."

"Or ride. I sent a note to that Quick man we've called before for a carriage."

"So much the better. I hope you succeed. Take care, Still."

"And you on your Harrisburg trip."

Williamson went back to his books. In ten minutes, he called his assistant. "Telegraph Mr. Satterfield in Harrisburg, Joseph, and let him know that I'll be arriving late tonight on the cars."

Then he hurried to Bloodgood's to catch Still.

Della Quick shouted at Nig-Nag from the kitchen.

"Not today, y'hear? Go on, now. Shoo."

Della was a round woman. Her face was round; her nose was round. She had a round mouth, round elbows, round hips and belly. Her husband, Emmanuel Quick, was tall and big-boned. Manny stood just inside the door of the shed kitchen, a wooden addition to the back of the house, trying to take off his pants and having a hard time of it. He raised puffs of dust from the dirt floor as he stamped his feet.

"Jack Sprat. Sprat. Sprat." Unless Nig-Nag concentrated, it popped out each time he came to the back door.

"Out, Nig-Nag," Della called. "Go."

Manny had fallen the day before. He was sore. Besides

being sore, he was angry. Since his seizure the year before, it took all his will and all his might to walk to Rachel's house every couple weeks; it took all his cleverness to keep from his son Tyree just what money he gave Rachel; and it took all his patience to live the week through till he got to her. He'd been accustomed to stopping in whenever he wanted for thirty years. He'd taken her every way to take a woman. He'd supported her; he'd bought a house for her, although he sure enough held on to the deed; and now, since the goddamn seizure, he could barely shuffle through the streets to get a bit of pokey once a fortnight.

He hated the falling. This time he swore it had been the fault of a German boy who'd run by him too fast and knocked into him. Otherwise, Manny told himself and his family, he'd never have toppled. Now his hip hurt through to the bone and something in his chest stabbed at him when he breathed too hard; and he always breathed too hard these days, because every movement was so damned difficult.

Nig-Nag was staring at him.

"Get out of here!" Manny yelled. "Go 'way! Go! Go!" His voice no longer thundered. He held on to the words he could say fast, without having to think, and chewed the meaning out of them. "Go!

"Gimme some damn help," he shouted toward the kitchen door.

Nig-Nag stepped into the shed kitchen and craned his neck to see Manny's half-naked body. He made an O with his mouth.

"Black and blue," he said, pointing to the long, purple bruise on Manny's hip.

"Get this nigger outta here," Manny shouted as loudly as he could.

Nig-Nag shrank back toward the door.

"Did I say come in?" Della had to holler over Manny to make Nig-Nag hear her. "No, I did not. You see Mr. Quick there waiting for his bath? You see him there, fool? You just step back, boy, and say what you have to say so I can get on with my work, now, you hear me?"

But how could they hear him? Besides Manny and his ruckus, there was the kitchen, overflowing with people and talk and food preparation for the annual pilgrimage to the grave of Zilpha, Emmanuel, Jeremiah, and Beatrice Quick's father. Each year, on the anniversary of his death, they packed a picnic, which grew more sumptuous with their increased prosperity and numbers. They went now in light hacks instead of the colored car of the streetcars, or by foot, as they had for years when they were young.

So Nig-Nag shouted over the din, and at the end of his diatribe, no one had heard a word.

"Nah, nah. Listen, boy. You go away. What happened to your job? You still workin? You didn't get yourself fired, did you?" Della looked up.

Nig-Nag shook his head and tried again to talk.

"I got no time for you today. You can see we're taking a trip, can't you?"

He began to sputter and bark.

"Ah-ah. Don't you start with me." Della waved a fillet knife, shiny with grease, toward the back door.

Nig-Nag lived in the worst of their shanties, in a closed court next to Juniper Street. Nasty house. Nasty court. Nasty poor people bunked four and six and twelve to a room for half a dollar a week. They came and went, and nobody even knew their names. Nig-Nag had made the court and the alley next to it his home. From time to time since his uncle died, various kind souls had taken him in, but no one could stand him for long. If the barking didn't drive them crazy, his occasional bouts of drinking did.

Nig-Nag lived by his wits, and he must have them, everyone agreed, because he stayed alive. He was in the habit of coming to the Quicks', where their lodger, Abby Ann, gave him scraps of food and parcels of clothing that Manny no longer wore, now that he was at least partially confined. And when Nig-Nag didn't get his handout, he'd been known to throw tantrums.

Once, he'd come wearing a painter's cap and claiming to need money for clothes to start his new work. When Della refused him, he ripped his cap off, threw it on the ground, and stamped on it. During his drinking periods, he'd appear with elaborate, feebleminded lies and tears, wanting food, pennies, or a warm floor to sleep on at midnight. Abby Ann would let him into the shed. If she let him into the house, he'd steal.

Now Della pursed her lips at Abby Ann. "You started him with this. Mighty free with charity. Charity begins at home, I say."

It was a familiar argument: that Abby Ann, who had not a pot to piss in or a window to throw it out of, loved nothing more than to play benefactor to any Negro who happened along with a sad story and an empty belly. Abby Ann had grown up with Della's daughter-in-law, Blanche. When Blanche married into the household, Abby Ann had moved in too. Despite the one's marriage, the girls had remained inseparable.

Now that Abby Ann was engaged to the young Episcopalian priest (a victory, Tyree said, of good color over good sense), things were changing. The girl who had stomped sullenly into Della's home changed her opinion of herself. She took on affectations to display her new class and her piety. She batted her eyes to express several different emotions. She began to wear a hat everywhere, because, she said, her husband-to-be told her that ancient Hebrew women covered their heads at all times, except in the company of their husbands. Della thought the idea ridiculous. They covered their heads, she answered, because they had lice. No matter. Abby Ann wore hats now—across the alley to Aunt Bea's for a paper of pins; into the backyard to feed the dog; to the privy; in the house. Blanche, who did millinery piecework, made little indoor bonnets for Abby Ann out of felt. Silliest damn thing Della had seen.

"See," Della said, pointing at Nig-Nag, "you've given him a

taste for begging. They get trained to it, you know. It's easier than doing for themselves, isn't it?"

Abby Ann rolled her eyes but kept her head bent over her ironing. She was assigned to iron Manny's clothes and the children's. Della's daughter, Harriet, had ironed everyone else's the night before, as soon as she'd arrived from teaching at her school. Her sister-in-law, Blanche, had worked right along with her, until she'd begun shaking with nervous exhaustion. Blanche had always been that way: went right to the edge of collapse and then keeled over. "Oh!" And she'd drop in her tracks. It drove Della crazy. Didn't she always say so?

Harriet continued to work that night until finally she burned her hand. That had been practically inevitable, stiff as she was from rheumatism, which she'd developed in a stunning attack at age twenty-four, just as Della had done exactly twenty-four years earlier. Manny had written it down in his diary in the section where he kept facts about numbers, all sorts of numbers that he found significant.

Now, as Abby Ann sprinkled and ironed, the smell of old wool, old cotton, old sweat, and dried sweet bush puffed up into her face. Clouds of steam caught under her bonnet—she was wearing it indoors, of course, cocked low and a little to one side— and rolled over the brim in one smooth motion like fog. Harriet sat next to her, shining shoes with one hand.

"What's he saying?"

Abby Ann shrugged.

"Go on, boy. Go on, now." Della waved the knife to dismiss Nig-Nag. "Go on and eat at the hotel. . . . Of course you know," she said to anyone who might be listening, "they probably don't feed 'em anything that's not already rotten through."

"Uh-huh," Sharkey said idly. He'd gotten his nickname as an infant, when he got into the habit of biting to defend against his overpowering brother. Sharkey sat in a chair; he was still coughing with the exertion of dragging his older brother down the stairs. Not only was Manny taller than six feet, and nearly fourteen stone, but he'd fought the whole way, insisting with each step that Sharkey had helped him enough and was now a hindrance.

"Hotel people probably feed their workers worse than we feed the damn dogs."

As if in response, Nig-Nag stepped across the alley and whistled to Manny's and Sharkey's sister Bea's dogs. They whined and jumped against the fence that Tyree had built for her. Nig-Nag reached into his apron pocket and threw them a couple of lumps of sugar.

Manny saw Nig-Nag throw the sugar and yelled at him. "Stop."

He called into the kitchen: "Dogs gonna get worms."

"Stop that," Della said. "Don't let me see you throw any more of that over there."

"Aunt Bea spoils Nig-Nag too," Abby Ann said. She pouted.

Della frowned at her. "I am too tired for your sass, Abby Ann, and I am too busy to have to keep correcting you. I've been correcting you and your devilish mouth ever since you were thirteen. You're going to be a married woman soon. Believe me, your husband will not put up with it like we have."

"Bea spoils everybody," Sharkey said. "Ain't that right, brother mine?" Sharkey shouted toward the shed kitchen.

" 'Cause she so black."

"He can say that, can't he? Nigger can't say nobody's name clearly, but he can talk about his own sister like a dog. Suppose it had pleased the good Lord to have made you black and her mean. What do you think then? Do you think you'd spoil people too? Or would you just be black and evil?"

"Go to hell."

"Go to hell? Did you say, 'Go to hell'? My God, what verbal prowess. You stand right there with your drawers off like a bad boy. I'll come help you into the tub in a moment. Lemme go and see what this poor child Nig-Nag wants."

"Get him away from the dogs," Della called after Sharkey. "He'll get fleas and spread 'em all over the alley."

"That alley got fleas'll eat these little fleas for breakfast, Dell."

Sharkey went out the back door and talked to Nig-Nag. In two minutes, he came inside, throwing open the door.

"Hey, Ty," he called.

"Sir." Tyree called to him from the basement, where he was making an inventory of dry goods and ale to distribute the next day.

Sharkey went to the steps and spoke to him. "Listen, Ty. Nig-Nag's been sent here on Railroad business. Now, he doesn't seem so clear on who else is coming or what's required. The Haitian down at Bloodgood's sent him, or else Still—I can't get it straight from him but the note here is from Still, with George's note crossed out on the back. I figure they need a carriage, but I don't know if they want someone to go into the hotel or what. So, Ty. Will you run to the stable and get a carriage? Tell the Tobies that I require it directly. I'll find a hack on Walnut and go to the hotel."

Sharkey argued briefly with his brother and sister-in-law, until it was decided that he and Tyree would come meet them at the cemetery.

Tyree took shortcuts through the alleys to his uncle's place. In the hot October, everything stank: beer joints, disorderly houses and their diseased young women, privies, people, a cat and rat, bloated and rank where they'd fought to a draw and died. Filthy black and white children ran shouting around Tyree's legs in packs of six or eight. Some were no more than two years old; all were barefoot. From inside the dark houses came the stench of old cooking, rancid oil, and turpentine. Only here and there was there a greasy stain to indicate that someone had had the decency to throw a splash of dirty wash water around a privy or on the steps. Tyree held his breath. Consumption and cholera and scrofula lived here. Children died as soon as lived, and old people with no money for doctors lay out of doors to perish with creepers in their legs.

The Quicks owned three shanties this bad, and Tyree knew that if he was to keep the business going in good faith, he'd have to repair or rebuild them. One was the shack that Nig-Nag lived in with Bo-Bo and Jack. No wonder he barked. Tyree strode so fast that Nig-Nag had to trot to keep up. A filthy white woman with a black eye spat at them as they passed.

Spread in a line along the alley, like a parody of an opera opening night, stood three carriages waiting to be mended by Sharkey's favorite freelance carriage restorer, Peter, a Dutch-speaking black man from New York. He was good, but he was also old and failing. The carriages clogged the alley on the residential side, the street side being left clear for traffic. Children had climbed the kneeling rig of a rusty trap, where they fought for a chance to sit in the driver's seat.

Tyree could smell the stench of horses. In front of the stables, the aroma was complex and appealing: leather upholstery, oil for gears and for polishing, horses' bodies, and fresh hay, and, behind those smells, the urine-soaked hay and rich manure. In the back it was simple: piss and dung, heat and stink.

Tyree went in. Nig-Nag, who was afraid of Sharkey's regular employees, twins called the Tobies, stayed by the door. The Tobies nodded at Tyree and pointed toward Nig-Nag. His sudden movements made the horses nervous.

"Stay outside," Tyree told him. Nig-Nag rolled his eyes at the twin men and stepped back into the alley. They could hear him neigh.

Tyree told the men what Sharkey had said, and they rigged a horse to a covered carriage silently. They worked slowly; nothing could make them hurry. He watched them as he had since he was a boy, fascinated by their likeness. Tyree himself had a twin, a sister, but they looked no more alike than other siblings. He found Harriet's company more comfortable and familiar than anyone's, but they had never, except perhaps when they were babies—and this he knew only from his mother's say-so—they'd never made their own world, like these two men, excluding everyone else: other family, friends, lovers. He wondered what one Toby would do if the other died. They did not even have separate names.

Tyree's older brother, Roland, had died violently, and he had probably asked for it. Now, eight years later, Tyree found himself waking from what felt as if it had been a dream: married to Roland's widow, raising Roland's child, and overseeing the family's businesses—which was to have been Roland's work. Tyree had planned to teach at his academy with Harriet and stay a bachelor like Sharkey.

The rig was not especially fancy, and it was old, but Sharkey kept it impeccably maintained. It was outfitted with leather rigging and generous springs that made for a spongy ride. Tyree hadn't driven one of these for some time; it felt rich. Once out of the stable, Tyree turned the corner and motioned for Nig-Nag to jump onto the runner but not to get in. Then he headed toward the river and Bloodgood's Hotel. He hoped the Tobies' unalterably slow pace hadn't made him too late.

George saw him from the window. After he'd sent Nig-Nag for Sharkey, George had made a show of dispatching another boy to follow him and see to it that he brought fresh oysters. It gave him an excuse to keep checking the windows and doors. He'd already spotted Still and then Williamson and directed them to the dock. The older Quick gentleman had come, too, and told him to expect his nephew, driving a carriage. Fortunately, George thought, the nephew had Nig-Nag with him, but the boy'd come back without one oyster to show where he was supposed to have been. George sighed. He'd given him too many tasks at once. He covered his biscuit dough with a linen, looked into his stew pot, and stepped out the back door, exclaiming loudly that if Nig-Nag wasn't back this time, they should get rid of him.

"Quick, sir. Mr. Quick!" George had to shout to summon Tyree before the carriage turned the corner. He waved, and with the uplifted hand made a subtle motion to beckon Tyree.

"I see you've brought back that worthless boy. I thank you, sir, for your time."

He rushed over to the carriage, grabbed Nig-Nag by the arm, and yanked him from the runner. Then he pulled a slouch cap from his apron and slapped Nig-Nag with it a few times, berating him for having forgotten the oysters and for shirking his work. Then he spoke quietly to Tyree, who bent low to hear.

"They're gone over to the ferry, Mr. Quick," he said. "Mr. Still and the other one, the white gentleman, too."

"Williamson?"

"I expect so, yes, sir. The two of them come and gone already to the river. I told them; I tell you. The person in question is a woman. She is tall and well formed, and her color is medium brown. The owner-man, he's right with her, and she brung her two children. They've gone to take the ferry to Camden. There's a carriage stand just south of Dock Street, and I believe you can see the boat from there."

Tyree squinted in disbelief at the round-faced young man. "All of them gone to the dock?"

"Yes, sir. I told them; I tell you. The woman went, as I have just told you, and the men, they say they're going too."

Tyree could not imagine what they might do there. He'd expected someone to give him a message to meet them at a corner, or the back door to a church, but what could they do at the docks? How could anyone be secreted from the foot of Walnut Street in broad daylight?

"Thank you," he said.

"You're quite welcome, sir."

Before he had driven the carriage away, Tyree heard George yelling at Nig-Nag again.

Tyree guided the horse to Delaware Avenue, the newest and broadest street in the city. Five years before, he would not have been able to make it to the ferry in time. Along the bank of the Delaware River, where William Penn had envisioned a tree-shaded promenade for the health and exercise of Philadelphians, early lot holders saw opportunities for making money. As early as 1700, they'd erected so many vaults, storehouses, primitive manu-facturing huts, and houses that the city required them to build a street. It was cheaply done, narrow and irregular. By the 1840s, Water Street had become so jammed with traffic that business at the wharves suffered.

Then it happened that Stephen Girard, the wealthy China merchant who established a college for the education of needy white boys, also left the city a half-million-dollar bequest, whose interest went to buy up Water Street's hovels and build a widened Delaware Avenue. It was generally believed among colored Americans, although no one had proof (rich men were too clever for that), that Girard's great wealth came in part from "holding" six million dollars for Haiti's liberator, Toussaint L'Ouverture, and neglecting to give it back to the Haitians when Toussaint died. Tyree relished the irony that in 1855, Girard's Delaware Ave-nue was making freedom possible for a black woman.

At Delaware and Dock Streets, the thing was in progress, and it was no mere quiet, secret, scuffling sneaking away, such as Tyree had helped in before. This escape was a public exhibition.

From the driver's seat on the carriage, Tyree could see the dock and the ferry. A group of onlookers had already gathered at the wharf. Sharkey stood among them. Dockworkers had left their cartons of freight and were standing under the CAMDEN AND AMBOY sign on the warehouse. White smoke curled from the chimney behind the ferry's waterwheel. Up on the hurricane deck was William Still, the black cochairman of the Vigilance Committee. He stood motionless, with one arm outstretched to beckon a tall, brown-skinned woman, who sat a few feet in front of him. A girl and a boy huddled on the bench to her left. A well-dressed white man sat on her right. Still reached out to the woman as confidently as a gentleman ushering his lady into a coach. Downstream from the ferry, the Dock Street sewer spewed filth into the river. The stink of it clung to rotten holes in the wooden wharves, which sanitary commissioners had for years urged owners to replace with stone.

"Madam," he said, "I believe you are the woman we are looking for."

Passmore Williamson stood next to Still and spoke in a sharply enunciated tenor:

"You are entitled to your freedom according to the laws of Pennsylvania, having been brought into the state by your owner. If you prefer freedom to slavery, as we suppose everybody does, you have the chance to accept it now."

He stopped for a moment, while the white man to the woman's side made some objection. Then Williamson continued, speaking loudly and with confidence:

"Madam, act calmly—don't be frightened by your master. You are as much entitled to your freedom as we are, or as he is."

"Ginnie, we have no idea who these persons are." Pryor waved his hand dismissively.

"Madam," Williamson continued, "you know who we are, I'm sure, and why we are here. Please be assured that the law will protect you."

"Get out of here. You don't have a ticket. You're harassing us. And you have no idea who I am."

"But remember, if you lose this chance you may never get such another."

"Listen, I've had enough of this meddling," said Pryor. "She knows about the law. Believe me, she knows the law. What she may not know is the mischief you people make—pulling in nigras who know no better, and then, a week or two later, the marshals of the United States of America have delivered them back to their rightful owners. Isn't that so?"

Ginnie did not move, although her upper body seemed poised to rise and her eyes moved from William Still's face to Passmore Williamson's and out to the onlookers.

"Madam," Still said, ignoring Pryor, "you may be certain that judges have time and again ruled in favor of cases like yours."

"I suspect you even turn a profit doing this," Pryor said, sounding at once confident and irritable.

To contradict him, Still looked at the woman and shook his head in a slow, deliberate motion. The Dock Street sewer belched out a load of filth. The plopping and trickling made an obscene noise in the unnatural silence on the wharf.

Tyree saw the woman's eyes travel up the dock. There was something magnificent about her stillness, something terrible about her utter isolation from them at that moment. He invited her gaze. If only she could know that they stood with her. If she could know that escape was possible, that it could happen if she would have it.

Stand, he thought, as if he could communicate with her. Only stand and you'll have it.

She looked his way. Her eyes were fierce. Tyree felt revolt inside him. Who, in God's name, would hold this woman? He examined the white man next to her. How did they dare?

For a moment, Tyree let himself feel his desire to wrap his arm around her shoulders and show her a safety she'd never known. Freedom was part of that safety, the most rudimentary safety, from men like the one who sat next to her, imperious. Freedom meant safety from whatever treatment he and his agents meted out, but, beyond that, other assurances: safety from being ogled as if the cords of vein, the muscle in her neck, and the depth of fear in her eyes were public fare, available free to passersby, as the sweating brown haunches of a horse were public or the udders of a cow, because horses and cows had no shame; or the fountain in the park, because fountains had no sense. Hungry hod carriers and stevedores gorged their eyes on her riveting fear. Even a dog would look away if stared at so long.

Tyree wanted to give her a life with curtains around it that she might close at will, so that these gathered people could not lick their lips with the excitement of her predicament or the exquisite sweep of her bosom. He wanted to keep her safe from the fugitive officers and kidnappers who came in the night.

But he wanted her freedom to mean more than that. He wanted it to show her how full of promise and delight, how colorful with passion, a life lived free could be. Sitting in the sun, with sweat gathering in his armpits and under his hat brim, Tyree found himself full of yearning. Had he ever thought to imagine his own life as he had just imagined a free life for her?

Perhaps he had. He'd known it vaguely when he was fifteen years old, when he had worked weekends with his father from dawn to dusk. That had been an experiment at first, to prove that he could match the old man job for job on holidays home from the academy. But before he'd become Manny's mule, then helper, and, finally, replacement, before his ascension into the tiny club of well-off colored men, those strange, resented, and, perforce, resentful creatures making quarter-fortunes on the fringes of the modern manufacturing that had just begun to churn—before all that, for a moment, he had been a strapping boy-turning-to-man, with a molasses voice and ambition for his own burgeoning manhood.

The yearning threatened to spread into a woozy melancholy, unseemly for a man of Tyree's station and responsibilities. Instead, he made of the woman and the ferry; of Still, with his outstretched hand, and Williamson, finger in the air like a politician; and of the curling white smoke, a perfect daguerreotype, the colors turned to gray and the fugitive's dark-eyed fierceness at the center. It helped him to quiet the yearning and keep himself patient.

Having made their first audacious display, Williamson and Still seemed content for the moment to let the drama mount. Tyree marveled at the daring and genius of it.

Passmore Williamson stepped forward. The black rescuer, William Still, maintained his distance, as if they had decided ahead of time that a free and sturdy man of color ought not move too close to the owner of slaves.

"Madam," said Williamson, "we will see you through this. We will not abandon you partway."

"This woman is going to New York," Pryor bellowed. "New York, y'hear? And you have no idea of her circumstances. No idea."

This he shouted at her, right in her face, so that it made the onlookers jump: dockworkers and hewers and carriers, servants and employees of makers of candles, shoes, textiles, nails, and pins. Most of them had known the terror of bellowing parents, had been beaten and cuffed with rods and brushes and belts and belt buckles; they'd been dragged and scraped and slapped and burned; shut up in coal holes and cellars and chests; locked alone in the dark at night to wait and wait and cry to God for mercy and the dawn. They were working people, trained by fear to work and obey. When Pryor shouted, with rage in his voice, they winced together.

He continued as if he'd won: "Now. After her visit to New York, she wishes to return to her child, whom she has left in Virginia, from whom it would be hard, so hard, to separate her."

He turned and looked at the woman, with a face both desperate and smug. She stared back. Tyree wondered how they two could look at each other like that. What did they know that free Northern onlookers could not guess?

She was going to lose her baby boy. Ginnie knew it again. This time the knowledge came suddenly. It came like the devil and sat on her chest. Right in broad daylight. She couldn't breathe.

She was giving up her boy, her best baby, easy and fat. People loved Bennie. They cooed at him and held him and pulled faces to make him laugh. Oh, Jesus, her best baby.

Behind William Still's sedate and handsome head and Passmore Williamson's curling whiskers, Ginnie saw the blue sky: a fine blue sky and white, drifting clouds, lazy and fat, nothing to do but drift. Ginnie's head was fit to burst, and her temples rushed so hot she thought she would explode, and she could barely catch her breath. Her best baby.

Please, old master, don't whup me, Whup that nigger behind the tree.

I run, I run, I run.

The clouds above so lazy, nothing to do but drift. And the sky blue behind them. She almost floated up out of her body like in a dream, into the blue sky that didn't laugh or cry, to kiss her baby's fat cheek and hold her lips to the corner of his mouth and smell his breath, sweet like milk. But she held herself in; she held fast to the boat and these two children and the bench she sat on and her sore feet in her ill-fitting shoes. Goddamn Pryor.

She could not run or fly or float, but she could stand. It was all she could do. Etta trembled next to her.

Ginnie stood. "I am not free."

Her voice ripped up the silence. Excitement shot from behind Tyree's navel into his chest. His head pounded in the sun under the sweaty hat.

Raspy and shrill and scared, her voice erupted again. He could hear it, just barely.

"But I want my freedom. I always wanted to be free. I always wanted to be free—"

Hers was an accent such as Southern Negroes had, and

not at all remarkable, but the edge of her voice was ragged with emotion.

"But he holds me."

She spoke to William Still, and then to Passmore Williamson.

"That's enough of this. That's enough! She b'longs to me. She b'longs to me, do you hear? This woman b'longs to me, and there's an end to it. She is perfectly free with me. I intend to grant her her freedom when we return. Grant it completely."

Who was he telling?

Then, the bell: it tinkled from below, on the bottom deck. It caught them unawares, as if they'd forgotten that they sat on a boat for carrying passengers across the water. William Still touched her arm.

"Come."

She stood. Behind and nearby her, people whispered: "Go. Go along."

Three or four passengers touched the children from behind to urge them along. William Still stepped cautiously backward, his hand barely touching the underside of her forearm, his eyes combing discreetly through the crowd for Railroad men.

Pryor jumped to his feet and grabbed for her. Tyree could see that. Then Williamson stepped in the way. Pryor raised his arm and pushed him back. Williamson's slender shoulders listed to one side. Colored porters appeared; Tyree had thought them on the lower deck, but they now surfaced suddenly, like genies from make-believe, to restrain Pryor. With astounding gentleness, they took hold of his arms.

One white man, whom Tyree took to be another slave owner, shouted: "Let them alone; they are his property."

The mere sight of their grasp on the slave owner's coat, black and brown hands controlling a white man's body, made the crowd shiver. It was taboo.

The colored porters said nothing.

The woman's little boy looked over his shoulder to see the

men lay hold of Pryor. Startled and frightened, the child began to scream: "Massa Jack, Massa Jack."

Jack Pryor's head swiveled to watch them go. Mattie's voice pierced him. It happened so fast, and damned if they weren't walking away. Big as life. Ginnie never looked back. And five niggers had hindered him from grabbing her back.

"This is outrageous. Outrageous. You've abducted her."

"No, sir. She's gone of her own will. We have witnesses."

"Witnesses? They've witnessed larceny. That's what they've witnessed."

"They've witnessed freedom, sir, guaranteed by the laws of the Commonwealth of Pennsylvania."

"Don't you lecture me, you pompous son of a bitch. What is your name?"

"My name is Passmore Williamson, sir."

"Well, Passmore Williamson, you are going to be sorry for this nasty piece of work here today, do you hear me?"

Williamson stepped aside, and the porters loosened their hold on Pryor, who started down the steps. The conductor ran to tell him that the boat was leaving and to remind him, in a fussy manner, that they could not be expected to honor his fare on a later ferry. Jack Pryor poked his finger in the man's shoulder.

"You just hold this damn boat. You hear me? I've got business abroad for the United States, and I said hold the boat."

Tyree saw the child's mother jerk his hand; and, surrounded by supporters, the fugitive family descended the stair. On the street, Sharkey had stepped to the front of the crowd. Tyree could see he was preparing to help run the fugitives through, in case the crowd turned into a mob.

"Knock 'im down. Knock 'im down."

Didn't Tyree feel it too, the obscene excitement? Knock him down. For a moment, he could envision the man on the ground, eyes rolling with panic. He could see him gulping air, his nose dripping. You could see the boy then. In the man's shame you could see the boy he was.

Tyree shifted to readiness in his seat. It didn't matter what they did to the owner. It was time to take the woman away.

In fact, no one took up the cry. No one raised a hand to hurt Pryor or Ginnie or the children. Instead, a tiny group stood together to protect the woman and her two children as they walked down the steps from the upper deck, across the boat, and onto the plank. Pryor followed; the crowd hampered him. He pushed and waved his arm.

Still looked at Sharkey and Sharkey nodded toward Tyree. He drove to the dock and sat picking his teeth. Tyree could see that Pryor detoured to catch the attention of a policeman, who stood watching, but not moving, half a block north of Dock Street. The two men were still talking, Pryor pointing and motioning, the policeman nodding his head, as William Still led the woman to the carriage. Still put out a hand to help her in. Tyree wished they would hurry. Pryor and the policeman had begun to walk toward them. The woman nodded but turned first to her son. A colored porter was holding the child on his hip. The boy had stopped screaming; now he sniveled loudly and coughed.

"You are a fool for crying so after 'Massa Jack.' A fool, you hear me? You better pray God he never catches you, 'cause he'll sell you for sure. And he'll sell me and your sister too."

Then she turned, grabbed her skirt, and put out her hand for William Still. Tyree felt the carriage dip to the side. He felt her weight as she sat in one corner. The girl climbed in, and the porter plopped the boy in after. William Still mounted the steps coolly. He looked over the crowd, his face unsmiling but triumphant. He caught the eyes of several people, nodded to each one, and, having concluded the business as publicly as it had begun, he closed the door. On the other side of the carriage, Sharkey quietly let himself in.

Once the group was safely in the carriage, the policeman stopped. He turned to Pryor and shook his head. Pryor argued,

but it was clear to the officer that there were too many sympathiz-
ers. He could not compel them to give up the woman, and he had
learned early in his career not to intervene when he could not
prevail.

"They are stealing them away."

Jack Pryor could not move the policeman. "Isn't this
kidnapping?"

"Looks mighty like to me."

"You won't pursue them?"

"Sir, you've got a crowd here. Maybe you people down
where you come from have never seen a riot, but we have, sir. I
won't risk it, sir."

Pryor watched Still flash a smile at the porters who had
held him.

"What's his name?"

"Who, sir, the colored man there? Name's Still. Vigilance
men is what they call themselves."

"And them?" He pointed to the porters.

The policeman just made a barely audible snort of impatience. "Those are porters, sir."

Pryor ignored his impertinence. "This whole crew will hear
from me. And your name?"

"My name is Officer Robert Brown."

"I'll remember that."

Then he walked back to the ferry that was waiting for him.

Ginnie looked north from her carriage window along the broad
street. Brick buildings, some four and five stories tall and as wide
across as three houses, squatted in rows. Horses and loaded wagons were hitched next to them or off to the sides of intersections,
where they'd be out of the way of traffic. In the middle of the
stone road, dusty streetcar tracks reflected the sun. To the side
was a pile of stones where men had opened the street and dug a
hole, in which they were working.

Signs were painted on the side walls of the buildings: NO. 2 CHAINS; IRON AND METAL; TAVERN; SEGARS. She read them again and again, but she could not make them make sense. Nor could she stop her hands from trembling or her eyes from darting—from one word to the next, to the children, to Still, to the plush upholstery.

"Madam, listen to me," Still said. "I know an old midwife. Quite good. Superb black. Are you listening?"

Superb black. Ginnie had never heard the phrase. She looked vacantly at Still. Superb.

"This woman tells me that when women are distressed, one must remind them to breathe. I think you must breathe now. Do you hear me? Breathe deeply. There. Now. Blow out slowly."

Ginnie breathed. She stopped whirling. Then she put one arm around each child and squeezed their shoulders.

"Children, you heard what the gentleman said: Breathe."

Three / The Quick and the Dead

Tyree and Sharkey let William Still out at his office and said good-bye. He was leaving the fugitives in their care, and they decided to take them along to meet the Quick family, according to plan, at the cemetery.

First, Tyree and Sharkey stopped briefly at Sharkey's stable and traded the carriage for a wagon, which would be less conspicuous. They sent the Tobies down the street to fetch a new wineskin from the Italian leather dealer, and then they changed vehicles cautiously, at the back of the stable, with the carriage shielding both wagon and fugitives from view from the street. Although the wagon did not have a false bottom, there was a square lower compartment that Sharkey used to transport his brother's ale to fancy houses. In that compartment, he and Tyree spread horse blankets to cushion the ride. They coaxed the woman and her children to lie down on their sides, back to belly, like spoons. Over them they spread a ragged quilt, and over the quilt a layer of hay, thick enough to obscure the curves of their bodies but not so thick as to smother them. They gave Ginnie a stick so she could lift the quilt to let in air. Tyree encouraged her to try the stick a few times to make certain that it worked. Up close, her tilted eyes were wary. She worked the stick with fingers as long and square as his own. She was handsome, bigger than she'd seemed from a distance—her features, her body—and animated by a watchful intensity. Tyree smiled to reassure her, and she nodded. They exchanged names. The bloodshot eyes were taking his measure.

When the Tobies returned with the skin, Tyree filled it with fresh water. They looked puzzled at having been sent to buy the thing, and a little put out. Sharkey joked that he hoped that by the time they took the first sip, the water would have turned to wine. The Tobies, who started their days with twin mugs of ale, laughed heartily.

The wagon was on its way when Tyree asked: "How long they been working for you?"

"Thirty-some years. Your father hired them before I took over the stable."

The Tobies had killed their master years before in Delaware. That was common knowledge.

"I'd hate to have my life depend on those two."

Sharkey laughed aloud. "Well, that's it, isn't it?"

He looked sideways at Tyree and made a face of grim amusement. "I'll tell you what they told me twenty years ago. They worked for me for five or ten years before I had the nerve to ask them about it. They said the old man was sick and wanted to ease his mind, so he told them where their freedom papers were, and how he had loved their mother, and all this horseshit."

"Boy oh boy. That was a big mistake."

"Why'n't he just say: 'Shoot me, boys'?"

"Why'n't he just shoot his own damn self?"

They shouted with laughter. The horses picked up their pace, and they laughed some more.

"What *did* they do to him?" Tyree asked more seriously.

"Held a pillow over his face, that's all. The way they tell it, they waited till he was asleep. They were eleven or twelve at the time. When your father met 'em, they were thirteen or fourteen, I think, scroungin for food, runnin errands for scraps. They were skinny and pitiful. Manny said they looked like rats, with that black hair and little tiny eyes, and just the way they act now. You know what I mean?"

"I know just what you mean." Tyree bared his teeth like they did. It was their one movement for smiling and laughing and for communicating the ironic contempt in which they held most of humanity.

Sharkey nodded. "Uh-huh."

"Daddy hired 'em because he figured he could—what?—make them his creatures? That it?"

"And two of 'em for the price of one."

Tyree pursed his lips. "And he was right, wasn't he?"

For years Manny had hired them to collect rents from his alley houses. No doubt they resented Tyree's decision to do his own collecting. Occasionally they let slip some word of disrespect for Tyree's dead older brother. Roland had been planning to leave the United States for Africa. For a time after Roland died, Tyree had wondered whether or not the ubiquitous Tobies had had something to do with his death. After all, despite their years together, Sharkey still did not trust them with Underground Railroad business. But no, Roland had earned his own bad fortune. Roland the golden boy, the spoiled older son, Roland the grand.

"You know, Uncle Sharkey, that the Tobies go to African colonization meetings? I've seen 'em a couple times."

"No. Do they? They some sneaky niggers. Maybe I'll look up one day and they'll be gone."

"It costs a fortune to pay the fare and make a claim."

"Besides, I don't think they'd leave your father, not that they can do anything for him, but I'll bet you they'll be there when we close his eyes."

"Even though—"

"Even though he's never gonna die."

Tyree stared ahead, seeing not the road but his father, the right side of his body slumped since his seizure, hunched over his strongbox, counting over and over again, drooling onto the papers he took out to read and reread every day, while Tyree repaired their houses and collected rents, while Tyree helped his mother cater the big white households and ran liquor at night to restaurants and whorehouses. It galled him. The family's money was the most closely guarded of his father's several secrets.

Money, or, rather, the family's need for it, was Manny's objection to Tyree's working too much or too conspicuously with the Underground Railroad, and especially their Vigilance Committee. Like other educated freemen of his generation, Tyree wanted to participate in the furious political action. His parents begged him not to work so publicly that he offended their proslavery white customers—the best-paying people in the city.

"If we had to depend on your radicals for our catering business, we'd've starved twenty years ago."

In this, as in every other business detail, Della and Manny Quick worked together according to rules that they both knew and agreed on but would have denied had they been asked. Until recently, Tyree hadn't known this. He hadn't known it when he stood between his parents and promised his father that he'd never let him hit his mother again. He hadn't known it until, two weeks later, when Manny collapsed over his papers, Della blamed Tyree and blamed his brother Roland for dying on them when they'd had such plans for him, and blamed Blanche for trying to run away from Roland years before, and blamed Beatrice, Manny's sister, for drinking and living off them, and blamed Zilpha, Manny's older sister, for hovering over their lives like a sign. Tyree wouldn't have believed that his mother would close ranks with Manny and against him, despite his work to hold their businesses together, despite the clear fact that there was no one else to do for them what he was doing, and the even clearer fact that Big Manny Quick, who did not, on the whole, like women, or whites, or Negroes who were too black or too white, treated his wife shabbily, and always had. So Tyree had begun to attend Canadian emigration meetings. More important, he took up Railroad work, attending with Sharkey a few meetings in the Anti-Slavery rooms and volunteering himself as one of those people, as the charter stated, "who could be relied upon to act systematically and promptly and with the least expenditure of money."

Sharkey looked thoughtfully at his nephew, seeing in his fine eyes and brow the boy who had escaped to his stable as if to a refuge, crying because his father had beaten him. Tyree had even lived with Sharkey for a year. Now Tyree talked occasionally about moving to Canada.

"Say, Tyree-ree," he asked, using his childhood name, "how much money is Manny making?"

Tyree pursed his lips. Old, old arguments rankled among his uncle and his aunts and his father, inevitably underpinned by money. They'd started out catering together before Manny and Della had married. When they'd made a little money, Sharkey went to hacking with a trap and an old nag, and Manny bought a house and rented it out to as many people as would stand to live there. Transients, runaways, Irish immigrants, poor black people, paid him by the week, and within two years he had enough to buy another house. In the backyard behind, he built a two-room shack with no privy; families of eight begged to hire it and rented a space on the floor to the occasional single man. In twenty years, he acquired six three-room houses and the back alleys behind them, and three six-room houses a few blocks away. He had sold Bea her house for one dollar and, as the deed said, "the promise of eternal love." He referred to the transaction as "the swindle." Bea claimed he wouldn't give her the deed and that he only gave her the house when its backyard shack was on the verge of collapse. (In fact, it did fall down six months later.) He maintained that she'd get drunk and ruin catering jobs. Bea countered that he worked her into the ground for years and never shared the profits. Manny and Bea continued to argue. Sharkey kept his business separate. All three occasionally talked to Tyree confidentially about one another. At twenty he'd been flattered. Now he knew that they only used him, like a liver, to absorb poisons that ran

through the family. He no longer listened to everything they had
to say, and he no longer told everything he knew.

In answer to Sharkey's question, Tyree shrugged and
opened his palms.

"I know this," he said. "I know that *I'm* working, and *he's*
making. I know that I turn over the money to my mother and him,
and they sit together over the strongbox, like they always have. I
know that I get paid, just like the Italian who brings us tomatoes.
I know that Daddy takes the better part of a morning to add a
column of figures, and that we keep handing them over to him to
add. But do I know what the totals are or what I would do if he
were no longer at the head? No. . . . You regret having asked?"

No one had expected Manny Quick to live after his seizure,
but he lived. No one had expected him to sit up, and he sat up; no
one had expected him to walk; and now he was walking, and, with
ruthless determination and a slight slur, he was talking too. His
hair had thinned, including his mustache, but he had Della draw
whiskers on his face with a charcoal pencil. So maybe he would
come back, full force, looking smug as a cat with his painted
whiskers and licking his lips.

"What does Della say?" Sharkey asked.

"Mother? You know Mother. She says just go on doing like
we've been doing. We'll be holding the place for him until we see
whether he's coming back. That's what she says to me."

"Can you?"

"Can I what?"

"Can you go on like this, you doing the work and him
counting the money?"

"Till when?"

"Well, that's part of the question, i'n't it?"

"Uh-hunh."

"Can you?"

"I can."

"Are you willing?"

Tyree snorted a laugh. "Am I willing? For the time being, I suppose. What else shall I do? Go off to Canada and write long, lovely letters? . . . You know he fell again the other day."

"He's taken a lot of falls."

"Well, he will walk by himself, and go out when no one's watching, and then slip back in."

"Serves him right. He still go to the Shed Kitchen Woman?"

"I do not have the time to check on him, Uncle Sharkey."

"Serves him right. Do'n't it? You're mighty quiet."

Tyree turned on the bench and looked at his uncle. "Well, if my mother tolerates it, what business is it of mine?"

"None," Sharkey said. "None of mine, either."

Just before the bridge to the western section, they pulled to the side of the road. Tyree jumped down and tapped on the tip of a stick poking out. The stick moved just barely in response. He watched suspiciously as a white farmer rode by in an old Conestoga wagon and stared at him. Tyree pulled on the ropes as if checking them. He shouted, "All right, now," to Sharkey. Then he jumped back up, and they drove on.

Just across the river was the university, and near it, near enough to smell the slops and the shit, was a piggery. The two men wrinkled their noses and rode the rest of the way in companionable silence, raising their chins to direct each other's attention to the mansions that rich men had built on gentle rises for themselves and their families. Here and there, whole blocks had been laid out with row houses like the ones that lined the old city by the Delaware. More houses would be built, no doubt, now that tracks had been laid for streetcars, but most of the land along the Lancaster Road was still open and green, not yet worth enough for the owners to begin carving it into a grid and selling lots as small as the city would allow.

It was cooler here than in town. Red-brick houses did not hem in the sky, and the air did not stink of people and horses and waste. Still, the road was rutted, and it was a warm day for October. Tyree took off his hat. The wet straw in the crown smelled to him like summer. The fugitives, he thought, must be having a hot damn ride in the wagon.

Ginnie felt the ruts and the heat; her clothes were wet through with sweat. In her children's hair and on their skin she could smell the horse blankets and the mildewed quilt. Somehow Mattie had fallen asleep, and Etta lay quiet and afraid. Ginnie could feel her daughter's fear as sure as she could feel the sun. She could smell it sharp and metallic over the horse and mildew. She patted Etta's arm now and then when she thought of it.

> *Come, day*
> *Go, day*
> *God send Sunday*

All her life she'd been singing for life to pass on. Hurry up. Move along. The only thing that sped up was her own mind. She flew about in her own head and body like a bird in a barn. The wagon bucked on the road, and the wood under her paddled the muscle that had coiled along her spine that morning. A few times her back began to shake uncontrollably, making the ball of muscle coil tight and hard. Pain seemed to have been there all along, under her wing buds: impatient wings, no longer willing to wait until she could bear to feel it. They'd held back until she was free. That's as much as she'd get.

Finally, Etta fell asleep too. The wooden wagon banged against Ginnie like her mother's bed when old Romey with one arm and hush-your-mouth pennies came and slapped himself on top of her in the dark lean-to, trying to sneak and get some before her mother got home, but missing his mark and his timing, so that Lily came flying at him with firewood as a weapon and opened a gash over his eye.

"You don't remember nothin. You don't know nobody's

name. Do you remember this, old man. You remember to keep your one arm and your three legs away from my girl, or I'ma kill you."

Then she'd stumbled back against the wall and coughed up blood.

Crazy as she was, Lily had done her best to protect Ginnie. Who would protect Benjamin?

Ginnie trembled, convinced of one terrible thing after another: that the free black men on the driver's bench, despite their handsome faces and fine clothes, were going to turn her over to the patrol; that they were good men, but the catchers were riding them down on swift horses and would force them with guns to hand over her and the children; that Pryor had canceled his trip and was personally overseeing the hunt for them, that he would rip off the mildewed tarp and appear standing over her, too soft and white and good to dirty his hands with her punishment but aiming to sell them cheap to people who would value their lives accordingly. At the very least, her children would be gone. These two she had left, gone. And despite her resolve never to be whipped again, she'd be tied up and beaten like a dog.

She could just lie there and wait for another miracle like the Virgin Mary. Ginnie imagined Mary as she always had: lying on her back on an inky-black hilltop in Jerusalem, with her heels up to the sky, shimmying up her skirts to a heavy red-and-gold moon, groaning as the beams came on down into her, hard as moonlight and cool as night.

"God Almighty," Ginnie prayed, "help me."

Virgil said religion was a cheat, an elaborate lie the whites made up to keep black people looking toward heaven.

After Lily died, Sue took her to prayer meeting on a big farm an hour's hard walk east from their place. A dozen and a half people met behind wet quilts hung on purpose to drown the sounds of their voices. The leader said that night that he did not know how folks faced this evil world without Jesus. She didn't, either. She'd fallen on the ground and writhed. Words bubbled out of her mouth that night that she'd never said before or since, and they said it was the Holy Ghost coming out of her like tongues of fire. They told her after that that she had life and death in the power of the tongue, but what did it mean? She'd been saved. That was all. Still, her parents' disbelief had preceded her faith and made the prayer pictures in her head, like her image of Mary, irreverent.

She tried not to dwell on Benjamin, but how could she keep from moaning when she felt his absence next to her like an open wound? And there was no help for it. No golden beams from heaven, no Holy Spirit blowing, no forgiveness like a cool stream or forgetting like death.

Giddap. In her mind's eye, she saw a mule cart and herself standing on the board. She was the driver and the cart and the mule. She was the yams in the cart. She was the dirt under the wheels and the water in the puddle next to it. She was the mule wanting to stay home in the barn with the other mules, and she was the whip. Giddap, mule. Move ass.

"Oh, God Almighty," she prayed, "what else could I do?"

She sucked in the hot, stinking air in gulps. Her heart rattled against her chestbone with dread before a God who, if He was there, was sure to be almighty and was damn sure keeping account.

She'd left her baby.

She couldn't bear to think too long on his face, or on how he'd root around at night for a suck.

All gone.

All gone.

White folks threatened it all the time. Even the nicest ones—butter wouldn't melt in their mouths—they'd sell black folk in a minute. Any Negro, any minute. If the time required, if the price was right. They couldn't help themselves, unless they freed their slaves and gave 'em a wage, like Mr. Rhinehart in Upper County had done. The Bat called him Swinehart because he lived with a black woman and did not keep her hidden or enslaved. Just coupled up with her, like it was half her house too. The only such pair Ginnie'd ever heard tell of. Otherwise, they had the devil's own power, and it made them devilish.

"I can feel you in my pocket, nigger." Pryor's father, the old man, used to say it and pat his thigh. Jackson Pryor was too discreet to put on such a display, but that's how it was. Nobody forgot just because he didn't mention it. Her baby boy could be spending change.

All gone.

"Oh, God," she prayed. Better not to pray for anything. God didn't have time for niggers crying and whining and asking for shit. The devil was a busy man, and if God was God, He had His work cut out for him.

"Jesus, help me."

They'd tried to hold her by holding Benjamin, but she'd pulled free anyway. Wasn't that what Virgil had shown her? And Willie? Wasn't that what Lily had taught her with her crazy spirit and her hopeless hope? Ginnie would never forget the sky over the ferryboat, blue and clear as treachery, with a wind as soft as Judas's kiss. Pryor had her caught in a trap but promised to let her leg go and put her in a box. A hawk would tear off its whole leg to get free. Even a scruffy old raccoon would have the dignity to chew off a toe if need be.

So. So did she.

As a healthy boy whom people loved, Benjamin had a better chance than most. If Pryor had the balls and the decency to fight off The Bat, who would want to sell him, Benjamin would get as much love from Sue as Ginnie had. The love he inspired in people and the love she'd give—they'd give him a fighting chance amid so much hate.

So much hate that Ginnie was swollen with it. Hate like pus. Hate jammed up her most private places. No wonder black women lost so many babies. Steady hate. No wonder a man could drive for his owner for thirty years and then one day slit his throat and throw him, still shaking, onto the road. Hate in the care of fat little babies. Dripping into their milk.

Run, run, as fast as you can. You can't catch me, I'm the gingerbread man.

They told the story in cheery voices to little white children when the grown folk were out of the room, and the children clapped their dimpled hands and begged for more.

When had Ginnie not wanted to be free? When had she not wanted to join Virgil in the forest where the fire burned so hot that rocks cracked open with a pop, and he hunted and fished with sticks and ate berries still warm from the sun?

She'd get to know the people who'd secreted her away. She'd get to know them and earn their trust. Could be they could help her steal Bennie out too.

"I've run away from a little old woman and a little old man, and a cow and a farm full of hands and the man who made me whore myself, and I can run away from you, I can."

The Catholic Cathedral Cemetery, with tombstones gray and white like teeth in the afternoon sunlight, marked Tyree's turn. Crosses rose up at intervals. In the tallest and most elaborate gravestones were carved small shelves, protected from the weather, to hold flowers. Those were few. Mostly the family names were crowded onto thin slabs of mottled granite, just like the people themselves had crowded into hired houses, just like the children and grands still did—just like Negroes, in fact, except that Negroes stayed black, whereas the Irish lost their accents.

Tyree maneuvered the wagon carefully. The turn was sharp and the horses were tired; foam dripped from their mouths over the bits. Their sweat soaked the reins to black. Olive, the colored cemetery, lay ahead. Its pointed tip of land aimed at them like an arrowhead. The familiar white and blue-gray stone markers gave a silent welcome. They were always the same. There was a comfort in that and a threat too. Children hoped for their parents' rest, and they paid money to the stone carvers, as if carving it might make it so.

Tyree could just barely make out his family, picnicking. He and his uncle sighed at the same time. They looked at each other and laughed softly, confidentially, together. They'd made it without incident, but they felt brazen and conspicuous. In a year or two, the woman and children they were transporting would have friends and a community to protect them and make it too costly and difficult for the slave catchers to bother to steal them back. But now they were freshly outlawed: flagrant and subversive. Damn the law. That's what their escape said. To hell with the United States government and its collaboration with the death-dealing slavers.

"I love Vigilance," Tyree said.

Elegantly, with the simplicity of action, they had accomplished so much at once.

Tyree drove to the end of the cemetery in order to park the wagon next to his father and mother's old carriage and another raggedy wagon, which they must have got from the carter on their street.

Now that Manny's walking was less steady, Della insisted that the family drive in their own conveyances, but Tyree thought of how much more frugal it would be to visit the cemetery on the streetcars.

"It never fails, does it?"

Sharkey's voice brought him out of his own thoughts with a start.

Tyree looked about him and knew what Sharkey meant. Olive never failed to comfort and disturb his aunts, his father, and his uncle. It never failed to inspire them to retell old stories. Sharkey would inevitably tell how he ran errands for the old Mr. Dandridge for a penny. Manny would snort contemptuously. Zilpha, the older sister who'd raised them, would tell them to be grateful they had had parents, which was more than a lot of colored people then could have said. They'd argue, sometimes good-naturedly, sometimes with rancor, and resolve to agree that things were better now.

His grandparents' graves never failed to stir Tyree, either. When he'd been a child, Olive had been his favorite place in the world, as if they'd come to a location his grandfather had prepared for them, a green hill where they brought food and drink and a brown rubber ball to kick down the slope and race to the creek. Once, after several drinks, Manny told his sister Zilpha that dying and leaving them money was the best thing his father had ever done. Now that he was a man with a wife and children, Tyree was beginning to understand the older generation's numb bitterness and the sudden rushes of gratitude that shot through it like pain.

"Looks the same," Sharkey said. "Smells the same." He inhaled deeply. "Let's see how our passengers've made out."

Sharkey pulled back the quilt. The woman sat up first. Her face and neck shone with sweat. She squinted against the light. When she opened her eyes wide, she looked expectant and exhausted and dazed.

"You've got to be wore out," Sharkey said to her. He put his arms up to assist her.

Tyree helped the girl climb down. Then he got into the wagon and lifted up the boy, who was sound asleep and sucking his two fingers. All three of them were slick with sweat. Ginnie watched him come down. He held the boy in one arm and the side of the wagon with the other. Mattie looked safe. Ginnie breathed in the smell of fresh hay and woods. Up the hill, well-dressed Negroes approached, waving.

"Madam," said Sharkey. "My name is Jeremiah Quick, and my nephew Tyree and I had the privilege of being present when you stood and claimed your freedom. I want to tell you it was a moment I will not forget."

Sharkey held her hand, palm down. Tyree watched him

stroke it gently, respectfully, as he would stroke the hand of a mourner at a funeral. Ginnie's bloodshot eyes raked across the hillside. She looked at Sharkey and then at Tyree. From a distance he had thought her older than she was. Now he saw that she was his own age, thirty-two, give or take a couple of years: a handsome woman, people would call her. She stood still. So did the children. They heard the others coming closer.

She put out her arm and pulled her daughter to her. Sharkey made a little bow and stepped back. His formality gave the occasion a feeling of ceremony. Tyree thought of the clothbound book of prayers they'd read from each morning at his academy. In it were prayers for rising, prayers for study, for friends, for grieving, but none, of course, even in an academy that admitted black students and preached abolition, not one prayer to acknowledge the fugitive. The whole business, underground by necessity, trickled like groundwater, and the white world seldom took notice—of those escaping or of those captured and dragged back to bondage. The play within a play unfolded, born-and-bred Americans crossing the land, on foot, on boats, on trains, parcel post, looking for freedom—and hearing the desperate whispers behind the curtains, America hurried past. Who sang their songs? Who wrote their romance?

Hundreds and hundreds came through. He himself had helped plenty of them, forced to scuffle on dry feet in the sheds and basements like rats, forced to beg help and then move on with no thanks, leaving only a child's bowel movement bundled carefully in hay and set apart in a corner.

But this woman had stood up in the open air, on the top deck of the ferry, open to the sky, insistent and straightforward and clear. What could convey their admiration? How could they tell her that even though they hadn't known her before that very day, they'd been preparing for her, and that she was helping to prepare the way for others?

Sharkey's formal bit of speechifying, Tyree knew, his stiff-shouldered bow, were rituals borrowed from other ceremonies of celebration and awe, words and movements to reflect the magnitude of her transition as well as their own participation—the Quick family and others, people in the crowd who were going home to describe to their families over cold suppers and watered ale the miracle they'd witnessed. Tyree watched the woman standing before them, her eyes darting covertly from one face to the next. Her nostrils flared as she sucked the air and held back her tears; sweat dried on her skin, leaving powdery salt tracks above her brows. He was as thrilled by her now as he had been in town; he knew suddenly that this one escape would reverberate through their lives.

The Quicks surrounded the woman and her two children as if they were long-lost family members and walked them toward the maple grove where their picnic was laid. They stopped to show her Gabriel and Rebecca Quick's gravestone, which the children purchased when Gabriel died to mark his grave and honor their mother, Rebecca, who was buried in a churchyard in the countryside. The headstone was made from local marble quarried twenty-five miles out of town, the same stone used for steps and sills and lintels, grayish white and streaked with blue. The headstone stood waist high. Next to it rose a thin gray obelisk that read: ROLAND QUICK—SON, BROTHER, HUSBAND, FATHER. Tyree and Harriet had bought it at their mother's request. It wasn't as tall as they'd have liked. Manny had refused to help pay for it.

On the other side of the grandparents' grave was a modest square that lay flush with the ground. Ginnie asked about it. They told her that it was the stone Gabriel had ordered for his mother years before, even though no one knew where her body was.

Ginnie shuddered as she read it out loud: "Mary Quick: Never Forgiven."

"She was part Indian, and she had an Indian name, but her husband called her Mary. 'Mary Quick: Never *Forgotten*.' " Tyree corrected her gently. "You read."

Ginnie stared at the stone. She saw the word correctly and sighed with relief. "Not so good. . . . Your grandparents," she repeated, pointing. "And your great-grandmother. And your brother."

Ginnie looked from the gravestones in front of them to the others in groups across the green. "This whole cemetery is for black people?"

They nodded.

"Black people own the land?"

Ginnie's voice sounded whispery to them. She patted her toe on the earth and turned in a circle, surveying the triangle of well-maintained grass and stone and trees.

Tyree's aunt Beatrice led a group of children toward them: Tyree's son, who looked at him carrying the sleeping boy with a mixture of curiosity and resentment; their friends, who'd been invited to join the picnic; and Bea's boarders, two sisters, ten and twelve years old, whose parents had sent them to the city to work and attend school. Tyree could see that Bea was preparing to be expansive. The other women stayed behind at the picnic site preparing food.

"This is my aunt, Beatrice Quick. We call her Aunt Bea, and sometimes we call her Little Aunt Bea." Tyree smiled blandly at his aunt, who stood shorter than every other adult in the circle around the headstones. "You can see why."

"They call me other names too, but no need to trouble you with that now."

Tyree sighed impatiently. From her childhood, Beatrice had also been called Black Bea or Little Black Bea. When she got drunk or felt ill used, she referred to herself as poor ol', soggy ol' Black Bea.

"What can you be thinking, dear," Bea asked, "when these men whisk you off to a cemetery, of all places?"

"This is a beautiful place," Ginnie was moved to say. "I was thinkin that y'all must be proud."

Tyree and Sharkey looked at each other.

"You are so right," Bea said. "We should be proud."

The truth was that they were not as proud of Olive Cemetery as they might have been, though they knew it to be greener and bigger than some cemeteries for Negroes in town, or public graveyards for the poor and the unchurched. They did not feel true pride for Olive, because of the tall shadows cast by the Cathedral Cemetery across the road. But none of them elaborated.

Bea went on breathlessly, her wig shiny and thick under her hat, her false teeth looking uncommonly real to any but her closest family. Despite the consumption of more gin than she could remember, she was still "black but comely," as her father had called her whenever children teased, and as she described herself with a bright, artificial smile that ruined her extraordinary looks.

"Well, I just cannot get over how collected you are, my dear. And self-possessed. Isn't she, Tyree? Completely self-possessed. Sharkey, isn't she magnificent? I mean, just a few hours ago—think, just think—you were still in slavery, and now you stand here chatting to us like an old friend. Old Friend—that's just what I'ma call you."

Tyree could not keep from half-smiling and nodding. His aunt was showing her most diverting face to their guest. The fugitive woman stood up well under flattery. She seemed mildly curious about Bea.

"Were all these people freeborn?"

Aunt Bea twirled the black curls at her temples and answered, "Oh, no," as if she were sharing a delicious secret. "Oh, no, no. Gabriel Quick"—she pointed to the stone—"was born into slavery. He told us how there used to be a special pen where they kept people fresh from Africky. Remember," she asked her brother, smiling, "he used to call it Africky?"

"Um," Sharkey responded.

"He used to tell so many stories. He told one about a party for the British during the Revolutionary War. They occupied the city, and they were thick as thieves with the best white families.

"For this party, anyway, they spread a table as long as this cemetery, and all the military men attending the party dressed up in their best uniforms and sailed on boats on the river, and then they paraded up Walnut Street to the Wharton estate. Oh, it was a big estate, that's all you need to know.

"And when they all sat down, they were served twenty courses of food—can you imagine?—by slave boys. Daddy was one of them: all dressed up in blue-and-white satin drawers and sashes, with no shirts, and wearing hats like Turks. Can you imagine?

"Daddy said they looked so handsome. You know we hesitate to wear bright colors, but Daddy always said that he'd never seen Negroes' true beauty until he saw all those beautiful young men done up in blue and white that day."

Sharkey pursed his lips. "Daddy also said that they looked like trained monkeys. We needn't keep pulling out that old story as if it were an heirloom, Bea."

"It is an heirloom. Our daddy was there at the Revolution. He saw the British march in, and he saw them march out. What's wrong with that?"

"And wore a hat like a monkey, and served them a feast. Bea, please do not argue with me any further. They were not monkeys."

"Except for the tails, which the British thought they had anyway. . . . He was my daddy too, Shark."

"You remember him," Sharkey said. "When Manny and I were young, he was out to sea most of the time."

"Well, my dear, what am I to do about that?" Bea pouted. Her old face fell into a girlish look. "I recollect," she said, "that when he came home from sea he brought me a puppy. And Zilpha got rid of it when he left."

"My sister Bea and her dogs." Sharkey said it with a wide smile at Ginnie. He was trying to move the conversation along. "You've heard enough, I suppose, about our family now."

It made Ginnie feel at home to watch them together.

"The shorter answer to your question, madam," Tyree said, "is that many of the people buried here were slaves. Most black people came to freedom here some time back, but Pennsylvania did not abolish slavery completely until just eight years ago."

The Quicks pointed out to her some of the other people buried nearby, relatives and friends of theirs. In the quiet, they heard birdsong.

"Mockingbird," Sharkey said, scanning the tree branches. "Where is he?"

Tyree said, "On the fence."

They watched as his beak and throat changed with each counterfeit song.

"Why?" Sharkey said. "Why, with all the bounty of nature, does such a bird exist?"

Tyree and Ginnie answered at the same time:

"To devil the other birds," she said.

"To mess 'em about," he said. "Make 'em mad, that's all."

They laughed at the joke, and at the grand mischief they'd made that afternoon. When they looked up, the young Reverend Ephraim was coming toward them.

"Well, Ty," said Sharkey, "thought we could sneak in a moment of, uh, secular reverence without a formal prayer, but here he comes, Bible in hand." He turned to Ginnie. "For your sake, madam, I do hope you are a Christian."

Ephraim came upon them and grinned all the broader to share in the joke he hadn't heard.

Sharkey clapped him on the back. "Where you been, Reverend?"

Sharkey asked it in a voice that held the threat of sarcasm. It was the voice he always used with Ephraim, the young Episcopal priest who had been his nephews' playmate, and he used it especially now that Ephraim was courting Abby Ann.

" 'Vanity and vexation of the spirit,' boy," Sharkey had warned when Ephraim had first come courting.

"Don't tell him anything," Tyree had said. "Ephraim thinks he can handle it. We told him how she is. But he's a big man."

Tyree's twin sister, Harriet, had gone further. "He sees what we all see. And he likes it."

Della had told her daughter not to say again what was so obviously and embarrassingly true. Under her self-righteous religiosity, Abby Ann oozed sex and seduction. It sat in the tilt of her bonnets and beckoned from the taut cords on the nape of her neck, which she exposed by keeping her bun pinned just above her hairline. It swung in her swayback walk, pert and emphatic. And it shone out of her irreverent brown eyes. Harriet noticed, of course, because Harriet was as big and brown and plain as a turtledove. She'd studied men's looks and the women they desired.

"He wants to make her better."

"Well, then," Sharkey had said, "if he thinks that, he's a fool."

Tyree did not enter too enthusiastically into the family's glee. His own marriage made him humbler than his uncle on the subject of other men's marital errors.

As a bachelor, Sharkey taunted the young man mercilessly.

"This is our Reverend Ephraim Johns, miss," Sharkey said. "We had hoped that he'd be here to bless your safe arrival into liberty, but he was otherwise occupied. Glad you made it back, Father."

He had seen Ephraim and Abby Ann coming back to the cemetery from a walk around the neighborhood before Ephraim headed toward them and Abby Ann went to help the other women. He was a handsome, brown-skinned man, with eyes that looked as if they'd been drawn with black charcoal pencils. She had a plain face, a voluptuous figure, and looked nearly white.

Ephraim pursed his lips. As he assured Abby Ann, God had given him the ability to bide his time.

Abby Ann was Ephraim's mission and his temptation. He knew that. She unleashed in him a lust that made him have to leave the room sometimes at the very thought of her. She peopled his nights and dreams. Over and over again, he undressed her in his head and bade her stand before him. In his dreams she stood or sat nude—skin, buttocks, legs, breasts, neck, shoulders— awaiting his touch. Just as she had brought his body to life, he would bring forth the hidden beauty in her soul. It had to be there; how else could he love her? She could be a vain and mean-spirited woman. Ephraim knew that, but his desire felt more powerful to him than her faults. Moreover, she herself had chosen to put her life in his hands. What more proof did he need of her wish to be good? Because Ephraim believed Abby Ann sufficient to stand, he no longer saw her as she was but, rather, as a chrysalis, whose future beauty only he could predict.

"You're going to see this thing through, aren't you?" Sharkey asked.

"I have no idea, sir, what you're talking about."

"You have an idea. You just have the wrong idea."

"You, sir, are a bachelor." Ephraim was beginning to have suspicions about Sharkey's manliness. He decided to start mentioning it to see whether the older man betrayed any fault.

"That I can always change if I choose. But once you marry the Princess, boy, you in it for good."

Ephraim nodded. His grin slid down to half a smile. Then he turned to Ginnie and Etta.

"Excuse me," he said, waving his hand toward Sharkey. "In order to welcome you, madam, I have chosen a text—"

"Not a text, Ephraim. Not an entire text, surely," Tyree said. "We're not in church, after all."

Sharkey rolled his eyes.

Ephraim ignored them. Tyree wanted to box his ears, as they'd done when he was small. He'd never had brothers to protect him. Now he had the Lord God on the throne.

"You won't mind, miss, will you? A short reading? I've thought about it ever since we heard."

"No, sir, I don't mind."

Tyree pantomimed exasperation.

Ephraim opened the Bible and began thumbing pages. "The text is from First Peter, the second chapter:

> Wherefore also it is contained in the scripture, Behold, I lay in Sion a chief corner stone, elect, precious; and he that believeth on him shall not be confounded.
>
> Unto you therefore which believe he is precious: but unto them which be disobedient, the stone which the builders disallowed, the same is made the head of the corner,
>
> And a stone of stumbling, and a rock of offence, even to them which stumble at the word, being disobedient: whereunto also they were appointed.
>
> But ye are a chosen generation, a royal priesthood, an holy nation, a peculiar people; that ye should shew forth the praises of him who hath called you out of darkness into his marvellous light:
>
> Which in time past were not a people, but are now the people of God: which had not obtained mercy, but now have obtained mercy.

An old priest had once told Ephraim to use the passage whenever black people gathered together, and he didn't know what else to use. It always worked.

"Let us pray: Father God, who has brought this woman and children safely out of the mouth of bondage and oppression, and gave us Jesus as our cornerstone, use us for your good work on earth. We pray to be worthy. We celebrate the mighty hand that accomplishes more than we dare to ask. Grant us strength and courage to love and serve you with gladness and singleness of heart, through Jesus Christ our Lord. Let the people say: Amen."

"Amen."

" 'For in time of trouble he shall hide me in his pavilion: in the secret of his tabernacle he shall hide me; he shall set me upon a rock.' "

"In the secret of his tabernacle," Ginnie repeated, "he shall hide me."

" 'Once you had not received mercy, but now you have received mercy.' "

"Amen."

Four / **Mercy**

In future years, Ginnie would remember how protected she'd felt that day, surrounded by the Quicks and the headstones and the other picnicking family across the green lawn at Olive Cemetery. She'd remember the richness of the fabric of their clothes, Manny's drawn-on whiskers, Bea's luxuriant black curls, and the orange glow of the sun on the polished marble stones. They made her and her children safe by surrounding them, and they asked nothing in return. These were her first impressions.

Later she learned more. She learned that the function of the Quick family was to make money. Manny had decreed it long ago. The reason, he said, ought to have been self-evident: "You'd think that niggers would know what they're up against," Manny said. "More than anything else, the white man in America wants us to make money for him. Failing that, he'll be satisfied to keep us poor forever."

They joked about how the wealthier whites in their neighborhood had moved out in the forties, leaving poor whites and Negroes with money as home owners and renters. And as the city's population doubled in midcentury, bringing waves of desperate Europeans, the Quicks, along with a handful of other black neighbors, became landlords to Irish tenants. ("You think the widow MacNamara said to herself back in Ireland: 'Well, I think I'll sail five thousands of miles with four little babies and have one die on the way so that I can arrive in America and rent me a house from a nigger'? Hell, no. That was not her original ambition.")

They joked about black men dead in the alleys behind whorehouses, because after eight years, the Quicks were still stunned that money and education had not saved their oldest son, Roland, from being one of those. Roland—handsome, funny, spendthrift Roland; unpredictable Roland, who'd get drunk and set the privy on fire, or tack the chess pieces to the board from underneath; nasty Roland with his temper, slapping Blanche, quarreling with Manny; Roland, who never accepted being a colored man in America and wanted to go to Africa; lazy Roland, who thought making money over there had to be easier than here.

"So many niggers stuck up back in that court, they don't even notice when one of 'em's missing." They laughed until tears ran out of the sides of their eyes, because it was too wretched and inevitable to bear, as if men of color had no will, as if, unlike everyone else in the world, they alone had been made free to fall but not sufficient to stand. Ephraim said it all the time: sufficient to stand, yet free to fall. He said it to show he could quote Milton. He used their words to try to contradict them. What other words did he have?

Slavery was gone from the North, but its lies had become flesh. Old Negroes who remembered the auction block still called each other Nickel, and now and then a young black man would beat another to death to settle whether Paris was in France or France in Paris. The Qüicks had to joke about it, or they'd lose their minds.

"I told you that France was in Paris," Manny would say whenever his family pressed too close, and then he'd leave through the back door and return in the morning. Paris and France and London and New York and America had their own places in the world and their own profits sucked out of Negro bodies. And what did Negroes have? Slavery breathed in by the grandparents infected freeborn grandchildren with stigma and shame. They petitioned Congress for the franchise and built colored reading rooms and staged Shakespearean productions.

So Manny Quick made money. He said it was the only answer. When, at twenty-eight, Roland got himself shot clean through, as the family came to say, the Quicks adapted. They worked harder, more efficiently, to keep functioning and bury their rage. Tyree put aside his teaching to shoulder family business. After attending the radical white Thetford Academy on scholarship in Vermont, he had begun his career teaching at the Institute for Colored Youth and then founded, with Harriet, the Quick Institute for Elementary Education for Boys and Girls. Soon, to his family's (and his own) surprise, he married Roland's widow and inherited the child Roland ambitiously insisted on naming Africana. Later he and Blanche produced a boy, Cyrus. The family continued to do what Manny had decreed it must: they made money.

Now, despite his stroke, Manny still worked. He called every member to account. Della pushed the catering business forward. Tyree maintained the rental houses, delivered food for his mother, and occasionally, much as he hated to, helped her serve. Moreover, he had just revived a lucrative service that his parents had stopped rendering after the riots of the forties: the delivery of beer and ale from a colored brewery to wealthy customers and other caterers. He also delivered to a few fancy houses, a practice he did not talk about, but his family knew, and only Harriet disapproved—and he never dealt with the cheap drink-and-poke hovels behind which his brother had been shot.

Abby Ann remained self-absorbed and lazy, but Della did squeeze some work out of her, and besides, she was soon to be married. And Blanche, who had seemed so idle when Tyree married her, now conscientiously sewed pelts into hats. No one particularly liked the fur business; they complained that the arsenic in the hides was unhealthy. But Blanche proved willful about the furs, and the family agreed that it was better for her to sew pelts

than to do nothing. She kept her new business to herself, therefore, eventually turning Tyree's and her bedroom into a shop of
sorts, where he seldom slept because of the dander.

Bea, who had for years taken in laundry and boarders, now
took in girls from the country who came to be educated at the
institute. Zilpha, who had left her house on the grounds of a
wealthy estate in West Chester, Pennsylvania, in order to nurse
Manny for most of the past year, was going back to do nursing
and act as companion for the ill and elderly of a few favorite families in her neighborhood. Zilpha said that she loved her own family best when they were not sitting up under her.

Aside from Sharkey, the Quick clan had never done much
fugitive slave work until Harriet and Tyree got into it. Sally, who
rented their Waverly Street trinity, three small rooms stacked one
on top of the other, liked to put people in the basement there,
and they'd given their tacit permission. But Sally had become old
and careless, and the word spread. She received few passengers
now. Manny and Della breathed relief. They had watched the
race riots of the twenties and forties: roving white bands had set
upon other black caterers and restaurants while police looked on.
Now they rented houses to poor and resentful Irish tenants. No
need to push your luck, they said.

Della felt vaguely guilty for their lack of contribution to the
cause. She claimed that if they were in a business with more con-
venient hours, or if they had more money, they would do more.
Each year, she attended the anti-slavery bazaars and bought merchandise ostentatiously. Each season, she purchased cloth at the
free-labor cotton shop. She'd come home saying that she didn't
mind if the texture was a bit more coarse, or the cost more dear;
she was glad not to wear on her back fabric that had been "com-
pelled from enslaved hands."

Manny snorted. "I am not giving my money away to no
damn body. I am not takin up my good time to sit around and talk
about the downtrodden colored race. Preachers say slavery degraded Africans. Well, this African is *up*grading. All my life I

been upgrading. I'm making some damn money. I am proving that colored people are not unfit for freedom. The race don't need the vote. The race needs to eat. The race needs land. When we own enough, believe me, we won't need to be runnin around, kissin up to white men, signin petitions for the legislators."

They ignored the fact that their older son, and now their younger, showed interest in emigration schemes. They ignored any behavior they did not approve—and waited for it to pass over like weather. They were proud of what was now Harriet's school, with its write-ups in the Negro papers and its neat rows of insect collections and animals jarred up like pickles, but they ignored, for the most part, her anti-slavery societies and associations. They treated Sharkey's long-standing Vigilance as a self-indulgence and an expense—not his own expense, as he maintained, but family expense, since that money of his was not coming back to the family, to the children's education or expanded family property—for which they had only intermittent patience. If he noticed his family's political work at all, Manny only mumbled that a man shouldn't educate his children too far beyond himself. It was a good thing, he'd mutter sarcastically, that he'd ruined his health with work to educate his children just so they could take up costly hobbies such as adopting runaway niggers.

On her first day of freedom, in Olive Cemetery, Ginnie knew only that she felt their power. They surrounded her—with food; with their voices and their ideas; with the ghosts of their ancestors and stories about them. Ginnie felt safe amid their freedom and wealth, among the tombstones of their dead and the pretty groves of hardwood trees turning red and yellow and brown. Olive provided a safe haven from the old city's painted advertisements and clattering cobblestone streets, where poor people's laundry hung on clotheslines strung diagonally across windows and banged against filthy shutters in wind that reeked of horseshit.

Here, the Quicks were able to protect the fugitive, like a lover who lies on top of his woman's body and pulls the cover over them both to keep out the cold.

The children played. Africana allowed Etta to tag along next to her. Mattie attached himself to Cyrus. Like Mattie, Cyrus was not a well-broken boy. When Mattie refused to speak to him at first, Cyrus roared and tackled him. The women looking on gasped. Mattie roared back, and the two boys wrangled in the grass. When they got up they were laughing.

"See that, Mama," Tyree said to Della. "That's what that boy needs. That's what Roland and I did."

Della rolled her eyes.

Ginnie asked, "You want me to make mine stop that rassling?"

"No. No," Tyree said. "Mama's trying to make poor old Cyrus into a girl."

Watching the boys play, Sharkey nodded toward Mattie and said with satisfaction, "There's a boy gonna grow up a free man." He shook his head. "You all make three more they done lost. Hah."

"How many you figure a year, Uncle Shark?" Tyree asked.

"Hundreds?" Della ventured an estimate.

"More than that," Sharkey said. "You just think: from the Atlantic Ocean, now as far as the Pacific. I think it's more than a thousand. Just look how many Africans and West Indians live in Canada now."

"Nobody gonna miss'm." It was the first Manny had spoken since the fugitives arrived. He tipped his cap to Ginnie and said something through barely opened lips.

"What do you mean, no offense?" Della huffed. "This child here has gone through God only knows what, and look, Sharkey gave us a chance to be part of it. Now you just stop."

The old man looked mean to Ginnie. It seemed clear to her that he did not particularly want her there.

"They'll miss me, sir. You can believe that." Ginnie did not want to be disrespectful—it was his table she'd eaten from—but she could not bring herself to leave him unanswered.

He said something back. Della asked him to repeat it, and then she paraphrased what he said. "He's not saying that you personally won't be missed, my dear, but that with all the Negroes they've got left, the South doesn't hardly miss the people who run away. In other words, they have women enough to replace one who gets free, you see?"

"You been saying the same foolishness for years, brother man," Sharkey answered irritably. "I tell you these fugitives are bleeding the South. They're embarrassing it, and they're bleeding it."

"It's gonna fall."

"Ain't nothing gonna fall. Folk gotta pull it down, same as you pull down an old house."

"Time for a drink," Manny said.

Ginnie studied his face. She'd noticed the strange whiskers, but now they seemed to command her attention.

"What drink?" Della shouted at him. "Nobody brought any drink."

Manny grinned. He pulled a thin leather flask from his breast pocket and dangled it.

"Who got that for you?" Della asked. She squinted at the family members assembled on the blankets on the ground. "Who?"

They all pulled their mouths down at the corners and shook their heads.

Manny laughed and took a swig. A thin ribbon dribbled from the side of his mouth onto his collar. He wiped his mouth with the back of his hand. A few of his whiskers smeared. He saw the smudge on his skin.

"Damn it," he said.

"Oh, Mr. Quick," Della said, addressing him as she sometimes did, the old people's way, "you can't drink if you're going to drool." Della got up and took the flask from him.

"And you can't sit there and not offer anyone else a drink."

She wiped the top of the flask with a napkin, and with the same napkin, and aggressively raised eyebrows, wiped the other side of his upper lip, thus evening his mustache.

Ginnie stifled a gasp when she saw his facial hairs suddenly altered. Tyree and Harriet shook their heads and looked away.

"Here."

Della began pouring whiskey into the empty lemonade cups. Manny protested. Della insisted that Tyree and Zilpha and Ginnie take cups.

Bea protested. "You haven't given me a taste."

"No, Beatrice, I haven't. You don't want none o' this old poison," Della said cheerily.

"I most certainly do. Specially if my brother's havin' some."

"Well, it's no good for you at all." Della said, "You haven't touched any for months, and I just won't have it."

Bea pouted. "I don't see what a taste would hurt. I haven't misbehaved myself in months, just as you say."

"Harriet, I know you won't have any," Della said, with her back turned to her daughter.

"Well, here," Bea said. "I'll have Harriet's portion."

At the pouring of whiskey, Ephraim and Abby Ann went to the carriage to fetch a pack of cards. Unlike Della's Methodists, Ephraim's Episcopalians didn't mind cardplaying, so long as no one gambled.

Bea held out her lemonade cup. "Don't pass by your sister-in-law again now, Della."

Della pivoted and splashed a few drops into Bea's cup.

Bea looked into the cup, pursed her lips, and then swallowed.

The whiskey burned Ginnie's lips. It burned her tongue coming in, and it burned her throat going down.

"Y'all ever made liquor?" Manny asked. After a few swigs, he seemed more interested in her.

"Who, white folks?"

"No, the colored."

"No, sir. Didn't have time to make whiskey."

"Oh," he said. "I see. So what's your name?"

"Virginia, sir."

"So tell me, Virginia, what are your plans for freedom?"

"My plans, sir?" She tried not to stare at the little black mustache, now shorter than his wide top lip, which was overlaid with a few wisps of gray and black hair.

"Plans," he shouted.

Ginnie could tell that he had to work hard to talk. His words slurred, but she could understand him.

"Lotta Sambos just outta the South," he said, "think they'll get free and everything then will be splendid: nice house and streetcar rides and rainin money every Sunday afternoon. But I'ma tell you, you've got to earn a living now, Virginia. You've got to feed those children."

"Well, Daddy, don't you think that'll do?" Tyree asked, interrupting his father.

"No, I don't. You knew those fugitive niggers over by Mole Street."

"Hicks Street."

"Oh, dammit. Mole or Hicks or one of them. Didn't work longer than it took to earn the next meal. Then they took to stealing—and there ain't nothin lower'n a thief. Then there's that sneaky boy, sneaky-ass ginger nigger. What's his name, Dell? What'sa name? He was a runaway too. Said he was tryin to raise money for relations who were on the run. He was lyin. Took good people's money and bought his black behind some new clothes."

Ginnie took a moment to understand him. "That's about the lowest thing I ever heard," she said when she'd taken it in.

Tyree smiled at her shock. "People do some low things, miss. In fact, for a time there, one of our magazines, *Freedom's*

Journal, used to print the names of blacks who informed on others' freedom plans."

"Oh, my Lord."

"Now, like I was sayin, we know you wouldn't do a thing like that. I'm just sayin—"

"I don't know what my father's saying, but whatever it is, it's plenty," Tyree said. "Aren't you ladies about due for a walk after your meal?"

He motioned to his wife, Blanche, to come from across the green now that her companion, Abby Ann, had left with Ephraim again. He felt irritated with her for staying with Abby Ann, who'd begun to shun her in favor of Ephraim, and vexed with his father.

"Miss Virginia doesn't need a walk, Tyree," said his mother, Della, waving a cracker at him.

"I could walk just fine, Mrs. Quick."

"Oh, no. You are going to sit here and rest."

Ginnie would have liked to stretch herself. She satisfied herself with getting up to replace her cup in Della's basket. Blanche approached.

"This is the first drink I ever drunk," Ginnie said. "And if it's all like that, I reckon this one'll do me for some time."

Blanche spoke to the family as if Ginnie were a child. "Well, that's no way for us to take care of her on her first day of freedom."

"I read in Mr. Douglass's *Narrative,*" said Harriet, "that the colored people where he lived down South were given whiskey on Christmas, lots of it, and they all got terribly drunk, and then the master told them, 'See? See what whiskey does to you people? Aren't you glad we protect you from it year round?' "

Suddenly Ginnie remembered Virgil's telling about similar Christmases at the place where he'd grown up. She hadn't remembered the story until just now. In her mind, she could see him lurching and weaving, talking about "Happy, Happy, Hap-Hap-Happy Christmas," and dropping to his knees to retch.

At the thought, Ginnie threw back her head and laughed.

She laughed because Virgil had looked so funny, and she laughed with the joy of rediscovered memory. The others laughed with her, more tentatively. "Folk sick as a dog: did he write that in a book?"

"Sick as a dog, yes," Harriet answered.

Tyree watched tears collect in the outside corners of her eyes. Virginia's entire body laughed, and not for the first time that day, Tyree found himself seeing in these public actions intimations of how she might appear in private. Some years before, his cousins had had a baby whom everyone wanted to hold, because when they held her, she seemed to radiate calm from her tiny little body. Holding her, as Shakespeare wrote, would "gentle their condition." Tyree suspected that holding this woman would be a powerful sensation too, not calming, but what? What did he think she would give him? What could seep from her into his arms? Or was it that her proximity would release something in him, as heat released from some chemicals properties that stayed locked in them in the cold?

Ginnie looked up and caught Tyree's eye. The power of his gaze surprised and touched her. He looked away from her to the children, whom he dismissed to go play. He reminded Africana that she'd brought her needlepoint sampler and suggested that she show her work to Willietta. Then he reached into his pocket and pulled out a lump of rock candy wrapped in noisy paper.

"Now," he said, with mischief in his eyes, "now that those greedy children are safely gone, a grown man can have a bit of candy."

"You and your candy," Della said.

"Anyone like any?"

"Nobody wants your old candy, Tyree."

"Miss," Tyree said, holding out a paper-wrapped piece as big as a knuckle, "would you care for some?"

"Yes, thank you. I love me some candy."

While Tyree and Ginnie shared candy, and with the children out of earshot, Della said to her husband: "You hear that,

Mr. Quick? This girl here was sent here as a warning to you. Old John Barleycorn isn't kind to people our age. You ain't got no white people to protect you from yourself."

"Yep," Manny said, as if Della had not spoken, "nothin lower than a thief."

Ginnie sucked her candy and suddenly felt girlish. Manny was looking at her. "Beg pardon, sir?"

"I said nothin lower than a thief is what I said. I once stole two dollars from the teacher at my school. You know what my father did?" Manny waved his arm in the direction of Gabriel Quick's headstone.

"I'll tell you what he did. He come to school and told the teacher to dismiss the class so that they could stand outside and watch him beat me. Two dollars, mind you. And he would have done it for two bits. And some ginger-color, ex-slave, big-lip nigger gets away with twenty-five dollars at a time from idiots with soft hearts."

Della turned away from him. Bea got up, nodded at Manny, as if to underscore what he'd said, and then, when he turned his head, picked the flask out of his hand and splashed herself another drink.

"Oh, here," she said when he began to protest, and shoved the flask back into his hand. "So selfish."

On the green, the boys were joined by three or four others, from the picnicking family on the opposite side of the cemetery.

"Those are the Rawlinses, aren't they?" Della asked Harriet.

Because of her school and anti-slavery activities, Harriet knew most of the colored people of quality in the city. Since Tyree had turned over the school, Harriet had been obliged to reassure her students' parents by giving them confirmation of her learning; in a week, for instance, she would give a talk on anatomy. People required a colored woman to provide more proof than white teachers or black men, she'd found—and more services too. Today she'd brought four students who boarded out during the year while their parents worked in wealthy homes, something no one had ever asked Tyree to do. So she went abroad in colored Philadelphia and knew most everyone to whom a decent woman could go to raise a dollar for her school and for abolition.

"No; they look like them, don't they? That's Mr. Fletcher and his new wife and her children."

"Well, they all wear spectacles like the Rawlinses."

Ginnie took the rock candy from her mouth and replaced it in its wrapper.

"What's the matter, Old Friend? Too sweet for you after while?" Bea asked.

"No, ma'am. I'ma save some for the children."

"Aw, no," Bea said, waving her hands. "Aw, no. You like your candy. Tyree. *Tyree.* Call 'im over here. He'll give you some more."

"No, please don't do that."

"Leave 'er alone," said Della. She broke a claw off the last crab, put the torn end into her mouth, closed her eyes, and pulled the meat out in one piece with her teeth. Then, eyes still closed, she savored it.

"No, I want my old friend to have her candy."

"Aunt Bea, please." Harriet frowned.

"Well, why can't she have some candy? Woman just escaped from slavery can't have a piece of damn candy to herself?"

Feeling embarrassed to have caused such a fuss, Ginnie unwrapped the candy again and popped it into her mouth. "There. See? Them old children'll get candy again 'fore I will, I know it."

She turned to see what the children without candy were doing. The boys had organized themselves into a game of ball. Off to the side, Africana worked on her sampler. Etta sat next to her, watching her fingers move. Etta had her grandmother's fingers as well as her looks. Ginnie knew that by the end of the day, Etta would be able nearly to reproduce Africana's labored stitches.

Except for Mattie, the boys wore dark trousers, with black

shoes. Their feet moved over the grass like a flock of birds settling in a fallow field to pick worms. Ginnie wondered as she often did whether Virgil was alive. She wondered if she'd know in her heart when he died, and if, by then, she'd be settled somewhere with the children and making enough money to lay aside a portion to buy even a modest little stone for him, like the one Gabriel Quick had bought for his mother, Mary the Indian.

Tyree threw a brown rubber ball to the children. He threw it high, so that they had to look into the sky and zig and zag, trying to be where it would drop to earth. They fell in a heap, trying to catch it. Mattie joined in the scramble. He fell down among the free boys with their dark trousers, and he got up, slapping his thighs with laughter. Tyree called for them to throw the ball back. He looked at Ginnie and waved his arms. She sucked contentedly on her candy.

After the Quicks had fed and petted Ginnie, the women told her their names again, because she had trouble remembering who was who. Harriet, the schoolteacher, was her favorite. Then there were Della, her mother; and Bea, Manny's and Sharkey's sister; Blanche and Abby Ann, the inseparable cream-colored cousins, one married to Tyree and one betrothed to Ephraim; and, finally, Zilpha, Manny's and Sharkey's and Bea's older sister, a tall, thin woman with straight black hair, who told Ginnie to drink more water to flush herself clean of poisons.

A long, slow twilight bled across a sky of deepening red and purple, like wool in a dyer's kettle. From over the hill, Ginnie heard a train's whistle and felt the heavy momentum as the locomotive dragged its cars along the riverbank through the city. Food was in her belly now, and she felt dreamy. She shook her head and yawned. When she put her hand to her mouth, it smelled like the papery flesh of crabs and peppers. Ginnie apologized for yawning. Etta opened her eyes wide at her, as if to compensate for her mother's sudden exhaustion.

Tyree returned from playing with the boys and threw himself on the grass.

"You gonna change your name." Zilpha said rather than asked it.

Ginnie nodded. She hadn't thought about it, but the moment Zilpha said it, she knew that she must have been waiting to do so for some time. "I expect I will."

"It's the safest thing to do. And if safety had nothing to do with it, she'd still want her own name. One she picked herself and not somebody gave her."

"Have you a name in mind already?" Harriet asked.

Everything in her homely face reminded Ginnie of Tyree, but plainer, like a female cardinal next to the male. Harriet smiled as if they were plotting something together.

"You have a new name already. I'd wager it."

"We always changed our names," Zilpha said matter-of-factly to the younger women. "Everybody when I grew up—everybody that was free, that is—had two names. Daddy kept Gabriel, but he took his own daddy's given name, Quick, for his Christian name. Name were Quickie, really, but who want to call theirself Mr. and Mrs. Quickie?" Zilpha never tired of telling this. "I don't know one person kept they old name just as it was."

"Tell Ginnie your mother's name, Zilpha."

"Nothin I can say that this one don't already know." She looked at Ginnie with small, hard eyes.

"What was you mother's name, ma'am?" Ginnie asked as gently as she could. The older sister was brittle and gaunt. She had spent the day in attendance on her brother. Now he sat dozing on a folding chair. At intervals, she'd taken water to Manny so that he, too, could flush his body, but he said that walking to the woods to pee every half hour was too hard on his bad leg. She continued to offer and he to refuse. Each time, she'd come back and sit on her own folding chair, next to the women on the quilts on the grass.

"My mother's name was Big Miss Take. How about that?

Little teeny baby, never did anything to anybody, somebody calls her Miss Take." She sighed. "I don't like nicknames. Nickname is for a damn horse."

"Isn't that what you all worked for, so your children could have some"—Harriet searched for a word to soothe her aunt's irritation—"some more leeway?"

"Don't need no leeway. And I don't like nicknames. You all can use'm, but I don't like'm, is all."

Della jumped in. "You never know how your children gonna take what you give 'em." As always, Della's voice mixed equal parts good humor and bitterness.

"Look at this child here," she said, gesturing toward Harriet, "a *Quaker*. I remember when them pious old thees-and-thous used to make my girlfriend's mother sit on a bench at their meeting all by herself. Bea," she said, talking faster and breathing hard, "you remember Emeline I went to grammar school with?"

"Sure do. I remember her mother, too, and all her Friendly ways." Bea chuckled to herself.

Harriet took a deep breath. She knew everything her mother was about to say, and she knew that hearing her mother say it would confirm her guilty feelings about attending meeting. No American organization honored the sons and daughters of Africa as the black churches did. But Harriet so loved silence and light.

". . . and now, this what they did," Della continued. "They would put one Quaker on each end to keep Friends from sitting too close. Lord, save me from that sort of friend. I never, ever thought my child would go running up to be with them."

Della wanted Ginnie in the conversation on her side. She shook her head at Ginnie and waited for an answer. None came.

"Now, Mother," Tyree said from where he lay on the grass, "I don't believe that you've heard from Harry what it is that she has found in the Society."

"I'm not a Quaker," Harriet said, lifting her chin. "I'm an attender."

"Why?" her mother asked pointedly. "Won't they let you join?"

"I haven't chosen to join." She looked out toward the tumbling boys. "For some of the very reasons you've mentioned."

"They got no music; they got no preaching; dry as dust—"

"Mother," Harriet said, suddenly breaking her schoolmistress mask in a look of supplication. "I don't like everything these people do, but I went to them because they understand, Mother, that God did not stop talking to mankind eighteen hundred and fifty-five years ago. They believe that God is still speaking to us now. He can talk to me. Right now, in the nineteenth century, He can talk to a plain colored woman—"

"Oh, Jesus, Harriet." Manny Quick looked up from where he'd been dozing over his flask.

"Shhh. Every time you get to talkin about it, you get your father going. . . . Now, we raised you to be a lady, and these old saggy, baggy white people trying to make you a fanatic."

"Well, sister, I like to hear you talk about God talking to men, and colored men into the bargain. The way Harriet tells it," Tyree said to his mother, "is wonderful to hear. Maybe I'll go join up too."

"God ever talk to you?"

"No, ma'am," Tyree answered, smiling. "Not a word. Not yet."

"Well, there." Della nodded her head in triumph.

"God doesn't talk to me," Blanche said suddenly, "but I feel His presence with me sometimes. A few times, as if our Lord were sitting next to me."

"He's telling you to stop sewing those poisonous pelts, Blanche," Tyree said quietly. He said it not with humor but with gentle earnestness.

"Blanche, please don't start. First Roland went with the back-to-Africas. Then Harriet with the Quakers. Tyree, you start up with Canada. You're the only one helping me keep my right mind. Maybe I shoulda had more children. Manny, why didn't we have more children?"

Bea answered. "Well, you know what they say: Children on the farm make hands to work; children in the city make mouths to feed."

Ginnie looked at them. She had noticed before that nobody in the group and no one, so far as she could see, in the other picnicking party, not one, was pregnant, and it had struck her as strange.

Manny said something. He was getting drunk. They questioned him, and he repeated himself three times before they understood.

"Emmanuel says," Zilpha translated, "that after Harriet and Tyree were born, Della, *you* swore you'd cut your throat before you had any more children."

Della pressed her lips together. "Why do you always tell that story, Mr. Quick? My Lord, I was young and silly. Besides, the twins almost killed me. You don't know. I almost died.

"Bea's right about children," Della said, returning to the original topic and turning to Ginnie. "You mark my words, my dear. Keep your eye open. Because up here, and especially in the city, there are any number of influences on your children."

Ginnie looked serious, even severe, despite the hint of a smile on her lips. "I'ma watch 'em, God willing."

Zilpha gave an amused humph. "What you say? At least you'll see 'em goin wrong, eh?"

"Yes, ma'am, that's it."

"But what about your name?" Harriet said. Her voice was mild, soothing, as if to calm them all and return the conversation to something other than themselves. "Perhaps you want to keep it after all."

"My mother named me. She named me when she first felt me move. She told my daddy she wanted to name me Virginia so I'd never be sold out of state. My daddy got sold off himself, and my mama died."

The Quick family women watched her. They watched her brows quiver and frown. Her eyes darted about as if she saw something in her mind's eye that troubled her. She was a powerful woman; untutored, for certain, but intelligent. She sighed.

"I'm sorry," Harriet said. She knew that they'd insulted her by assuming that a master had named her. "But now you've left Virginia."

"Yes, I have." Ginnie nodded.

Virginia was the wrong name now. She thought for a moment to change it on the spot to Philadelphia, but she didn't know how long she'd be here, and besides, unlike Virginia, Philadelphia was not a proper given name. The old lady Zilpha was right: some names were for horses.

Ginnie wondered if there wasn't a name that she'd given herself without knowing it. Under her wing bud, the coiled ball of pain pressed hard. She began to sweat again, and she was embarrassed, because she knew she had the stink of old sweat on her and that goddamned horse blanket.

"You'll think of something, Old Friend," Bea said cheerily.

Harriet wasn't satisfied. "Dreams. Have you any favorite dreams, or did you ever have dreams that told you this would happen?"

Ginnie thought. She was surprised to feel the give in herself. Where she had been wary and hard, she now felt softness spread in her belly. She took in their ideas and their chatter. Harriet's question about dreams had done it. Ginnie thought of the gray cat that had reappeared just the day before, like a childhood disease. It was gone now. Funny how she knew it had gone, back to wherever it had been for twenty years. She could not call it up. Instead, she simply remembered it, saucy and blue-gray like the marble in Gabriel and Rebecca Quick's headstone. The lazy violet twilight settled in around her, and the name suddenly pinged in her mind solid as the drop of silver money.

Ginnie looked at Harriet, and Harriet waited, smiling mildly. It must have been how she was with children in class. She looked patient and respectful, as if she had nothing more important to do in the meanwhile.

It was a merciful look. Ginnie had not earned it any more than she'd earned the day's fortune. She hadn't chosen it any more than she'd chosen the psalm Ephraim had read, although it had felt like choice in Bloodgood's, and it had felt like choice on the boat. Mercy had come down and passed through her, like light through the window. Mercy shone through those men who'd appeared and spoken to her with kindness and learning. It had shone through the men who'd held Pryor back. Mercy had given her the strength to stand. Mercy would forgive her, if there was any forgiveness in the wide world and mercy enough in the heart of God, for leaving Bennie. Mercy had brought the gray cat back to her to help her keep all the craziness in one place, and mercy had freed her from it again. And hadn't the young priest said it? "Once you had not received mercy, but now you have received mercy."

"I got a name. I did have kind of a daydream from when I was a little, little girl," she said, "and I almost forgot. So I'ma take my last name from that."

"All right, Old Friend," Bea said, her normally dramatic speech made lush by whiskey. "This dream, this daydream of yours: what'd it tell you?"

"Told me my name is Mercy Gray."

Five / **Family**

M ercy," Della said in the dark intimacy of the carriage on
the ride home. She poked out her bottom lip and sighed,
as if finding words were a burden. "It sounds like a . . . like some
kind of made-up name."

"It is a made-up name," said Zilpha with a snort of
amusement.

"Oh, Aunt Zil," Harriet breathed. "What a thing to say."

"This woman understands me. We get along fine."

"Better she hear it from us first," said Della.

Ginnie laughed. "I don't mind a made-up name."

"You need a"—Della spread her hands wide in front of her,
as though she were holding something large—"a bigger name.
More of a name. That's what comes to me."

Harriet said, "Mercer. How about that? Remember my
teacher Mrs. Mercer Johnson? She was a dear lady."

"Mercer." Della repeated the new name appreciatively.

"Mercer suits you. It's elegant, really. Isn't it, Mercer?"

Ginnie humphed gently.

"Let us welcome the newly baptized," said Beatrice,
clapping.

Harriet clapped with her. "Is that your name now?"

"I'll take it."

"Tell you the truth, I have been thinking this past hour of

inviting Mercer to come speak to our female abolition society,"
said Harriet. "You have an excellent voice," she added.

"That's kind of you to say."

"Surely you've been told that before."

Willie had liked her voice; so had Pryor.

Mercer pulled her arm tighter over Mattie's shoulders. She
thought of Pryor's long fingers, and how she hated him to touch
her breasts. Why her breasts? That had always been hard, just
getting past that part. Especially when she was pregnant or,
worse yet, nursing. She could wall off from the waist down and
make herself not mind so much. Maybe her breasts were too
close to her head. She couldn't wall off from the neck down,
which is what she tried to do. Why this thought led her mind to
the hotel chambermaid, she didn't know, but she saw the
woman's leathery face in her mind's eye, fearful and resistant,
backing from the room and apologizing, trying to keep out of trouble. It made Mercer sigh.

"Not in so many words."

"Now don't get discouraged now," Della said, patting her
hand. Della's clothes and hat made noise in the carriage, and because of her weight she breathed hard, even when she was resting, which seldom happened.

"I like my new name," Mercer said.

"Good," Della said quickly. She had not finished with the
business about speaking. "What kind of people would she speak
to? I just wonder. You deliver your lectures, but you're an educated woman; you're trained to it. Mercer may not wish to speak
in public, and before men."

"This would be the Ladies Anti-Slavery Society, Mother."

"And what does that *mean?*" Having riled herself by talking
about Harriet's Quakerish leanings, Della became angry at the
very mention of the Ladies Society, in which Quaker women
figured prominently.

"Means," said Zilpha, before Harriet decided how to answer, "they all bleed, Della, and they all bear children in pain—

although I expect not so much pain as they say. Mine wasn't never so bad. I believe young women now are inclined to whine more than they need to do."

"I don't know, Aunt Zilpha," Harriet said. "I've never had a child, but I was there for Blanche having Africana."

"Africana. Now, why doesn't somebody change that child's name?"

"I was there for her birth, and honestly, I thought it would kill Blanche. It did almost kill her."

"Almost everything almost has."

Harriet shared the family's general impatience with Blanche and felt sorry for it and sorry for Blanche these days. Abby Ann was poised to fly off and play priest's wife; already she was making it clear that she no longer wanted a confederate. She'd even signified that she would rather Blanche had ridden in the carriage with the other women. Blanche would be lonely in the Quick house.

"She had terrible headaches that whole pregnancy," Harriet recalled. "Were you here, Aunt Zil? It was dreadful. She'd see little floating specks, she said. Then the pain would move up and down her side. Then what happened? Oh, then she'd get violently ill. She's still affected, you know, though not half so much as before."

"Well, then, if she so fragile, why she keep sewing those furs? How many times have we told her about the devilish arsenic in 'em?" Zilpha said. "I say young women have their health all wrong. Work with things that'll kill 'em, and whine and cry about something God meant for them to do."

"With all respect, Zilpha," Della said to her sister-in-law, "I think that women who have an easy time of it with babies can say some terrible things to make other women out to be liars. Woman worked for us had eight children, and she used to always say"— Della mocked her in a high-pitched singsong—" 'Why, it ain't no harder than your daily constitutional.'

"Idiot. She'd say it around women; she'd say it around girls; she'd say it around other women's husbands."

Zilpha said, "They tell us that black women in the fields work up to the day they deliver, and then they drop 'em and keep right on going."

"Well," Mercer said, "they lie."

"Do you like Mercer, honestly? Does it feel as if it suits you?" Harriet asked.

"I like it just fine."

"Oh, I had a terrible time keeping my babies," Della said. "They tried to come too early. I lost the first two, you know, when I was right about six months gone. So from then on, when I started to show, they just put me to bed, and that's where I stayed. That's how I got so stout. But I kept my babies."

"You was stout before, Della," Zilpha said.

"Well, I was stout, but—"

"When my mother had me," Zilpha said, "she tells me she had a ring of bumps right the way around her belly. And under the bumps was some awful kinda pain. She said it were like a ring of pain. The bumps or whatever they was disappeared eventually, and she thought no more of 'em. But lo and behold, Bea was born, and didn't they come back and kill her dead? . . . You know what it was? Death came for her once, and then she got a reprieve."

"Is that how she saw it?" Della said.

"No. She thought it was me again. Said it was me killing her."

Bea held Harriet's hand and patted it. "We shall live to be old women, Harry," she cackled, " 'cause we don't have to put up with that."

Harriet smiled in the dark at her naughty little aunt. Now thirty-two, able to read and write Latin, accomplished in anatomy, arithmetic, geography, history, and literature, Harriet Leigh Quick Wilson had been married for two years and widowed for eight. She did not want another husband. She did not want children of her own or a pinched little row house, so hot with the new anthracite to keep the babies warm, full of coal gas, windows coated with the greasy steam of bacon and cabbage. Harriet could do without.

She'd had one husband with his bull neck throw himself onto her and ram and sweat every night, even when she'd begged him for decency's sake not to. Every night God sent. Every night, like a prison sentence. He was as proud of his prowess as he was of his gray eyes and curly brown hair. To whom could she have complained of such a thing? And whom did he tell? She'd wondered. It would have been impossible that he would have bragged to no one.

How she escaped without a baby, Harriet couldn't tell. But she never wanted another man to suck on any part of her body or dribble tobacco juice into her mouth and down her belly. Thank you, no. Harriet had had quite enough marriage, although she was genuinely sorry for Wilson that he died early from a bad heart. Aside from his carnal obstinacy, he'd been a good man. She kept to herself the mean-spirited suspicion that voluptuousness had contributed to his early demise.

So. No more marriage. Harriet loved her schoolhouse, with its open windows for ventilation, its neat rows of desks and books, and its catalogued collections: rocks, insects, mammals in formaldehyde. She took rooms in the house her parents had rented for years to the Beckers. Now Mrs. Becker was widowed and glad of company. Harriet had the late afternoon sun to read by. All alone, and nice and quiet.

Bea patted Harriet's hand companionably and breathed warm puffs of whiskey breath at her. "Of course now, they'll only call you a widow, and that's not so bad, but me, I'll be an old maid."

"You been an old maid for twenty years," Zilpha said. "And if you keep drinkin that stuff you and your brother drink, you won't make it to be a older maid."

"Listen to your sister, Bea," Della said, "if you want to make it to her age. We got to make it to be like Zilpha."

"Zilpha's gonna live forever," Bea said, with a pout in her voice. "And who'd want that?"

"No one lives forever," Zilpha said.

"You see, Dell," Bea answered, "so I shan't worry about it."

"But, Harriet," Della said, pulling the conversation away from Zilpha and Bea, "where was it you were thinking of inviting Mercer? I do like that name, Mercer. Where to?"

Mercer looked up when she heard her new name. She'd been remembering how much she had bled after she'd had Benjamin, and how weak she was. She remembered that the tiredness would not lift as it had the first and second times. For months she took to sitting down every chance she could, even to chop an onion.

"Yes, I said that," Harriet said, "but it was thoughtless of me. Mercer's likely going to move on tomorrow."

So Sharkey had said. He'd told them that he thought it safer for Mercer to spend the night with them and then head north the next day. She was worried about Pryor sending private bounty hunters after her, so Sharkey himself would take her to New York, where he'd see to it that she and the children got on the train cars to Boston. He'd wire friends of their committee to meet her. She might well stay in Boston—it would be harder for the kidnappers and slave catchers to find her there, if they were looking, he figured—or she might go elsewhere in New England or to Canada.

With these words in her thoughts, Mercer Gray tucked her children and herself into Bea's four-poster bed. After a brisk debate, the Quick family had decided against putting them in the shed kitchen of their Waverly Street house, because Sally could no longer be trusted not to brag; and when Manny had suggested the basement of their own home, Tyree argued against it hotly on account of the rats.

Bea volunteered to keep them in her house for the night. She gave them her own bed, on the understanding that it was only temporary.

It took some effort to get to sleep after all. Beatrice's house had fleas.

"I didn't mention them, did I?" she asked.

"Course you didn't," said Zilpha brusquely. "You all had better brush off your ankles and rustle your dresses. Rustle 'em hard till they snap. Snap 'em. 'Cause if you don't, it's a misery."

"And now I'm giving you my bed, so whatever you do, please, please, please wash your feet before you get in," Bea added.

The fleas came from the dogs, who were in the backyard, barking at the newcomers when they arrived. Their job was to keep out rats. Old Standby, Bea explained, was an excellent ratter. Simple Simon, the new dog, was simple, and good mostly for attracting fleas.

Bea's bed was soft and wide. She had linen sheets and feather pillows with embroidered cases on them. The whole thing smelled faintly of lavender and hair oil, like the woman herself. Mercer made sure that she and the children washed well before getting into the bed. Mattie, who had slept on the ride home, cried about washing. Mercer bathed him anyway, vowing that she did not want to be remembered as a mud stain and a patch of stink on Little Bea's bedclothes. Then she rubbed her hands up and down the children's legs before they jumped in, and did the same for herself. The bed was very soft. They rolled into one another, laughing and rubbing their itchy ankles with the soles of their feet. Then, with Mattie in the middle, they fell asleep, all of them, instantly.

Mercer was dreaming straightforward dreams about the events of the day when Mattie woke her with his heaving. She reached under the bed for the chamber pot she knew would be there and shoved it under her son's chin.

As soon as the first episode subsided, Mercer collected
Mattie in her arms to take him downstairs and outside. Etta came
behind Mercer with the chamber pot, unable to keep from catching her breath in her throat each time one of them tripped or
bumped in the dark. The staircase turned a corner in the tiny row
house; each tread gave barely enough room for their bent feet.
The fleas bit freely. Try as they might to keep quiet, they awoke
the household: Bea bustled sleepily behind them, demanding to
know what was happening; the boarders came to the top of the
stairs, calling, "What is it?"; Zilpha stood in the entrance to the
front room like a haunt.

As Etta stepped into the backyard, Standby let out a growl
and leapt at her. Etta screamed. Mercer swung Mattie over one
shoulder and used her free hand to grab at the door and pull it
closed. The dog's head caught between the door and its jamb.
The dog writhed and growled and whined.

"Oh, shit," Mercer muttered.

Bea caught up to them. Her curls were gone. Gray fuzz like
mold covered her head.

"What are you doing to Old Standby?" Her voice accused
and blamed. "Jesus have mercy. You'll kill my dog."

"The dog's trying to kill my child."

"Oh, move. Move, move over," Bea said. As she passed,
Mercer smelled liquor. It seemed to be coming from the top of
her bald head. She moved unsteadily.

Mercer felt new flea bites. She cursed again.

"Standby," Bea shouted, and grabbed the door.

Mercer let go of the door. Bea dropped onto the dog and
held him tight around the neck.

"Stop it," she screamed. "You stop that."

The dog shut up. Etta whimpered and sniveled in the sudden quiet. Mattie burped and choked loudly. In the melee he had
vomited on Mercer's shoulder and down her back.

Outside, the night had turned cool. Above the alley, blurry

stars shone just behind the low-hanging mist. Bea passed Mercer
a small washtub and sent the boarders up the alley to fetch water
in an old leather fire bucket that hung on a hook in the shed
kitchen.

"Here, give him this." They made Mattie gargle with salt
water. He was moaning and hot.

"He's burnin up," Mercer whispered to no one in particular. Her voice was swallowed by the mist. "He's burnin up."

Zilpha hoisted her nightdress and tucked it into the tops of
the boots she kept by her bed. She walked to them and put her
hand on the back of Mattie's neck. "You better sponge 'im down."

"With what?"

"Cool water, right here. Bea, you got a rag handy?"

"Maybe I do better just to wrap him up and let him sweat,"
Mercer said.

Zilpha ignored her and slapped at her ankles. The smell of
turpentine wafted from her. It made Mercer remember home:
Sue swore by turpentine. When Mercer gave birth, Sue had
mixed it with lard and smeared it onto her with a rag to keep her
from tearing. They used it after beatings too.

Bea answered dizzily, as if she hadn't heard Mercer, that
she had most anything they could think of in the shed kitchen.

"I believe he'll be all right if I just wrap 'im up and get 'im
outta the night air," Mercer said again, stomping her feet.

Bea handed a rag to Zilpha, who handed it to Mercer.

"The boy is burning up," she said. "Cool'm down, I tell you."

Cold water had to be flirting with death. Mercer said again
that she figured Mattie would be better in the morning, now that
he'd cleaned himself out.

Etta stood beside Mercer, bouncing nervously on the balls
of her feet. Mercer pursed her lips and frowned at her daughter
through the darkness until she stilled herself.

"Aw, come on, child," Zilpha said into Mercer's ear. The
old woman's voice was almost as low as a man's. She sounded

impatient. "Come on. The boy's burning up. You been living in a shack all your life, just like I used to. You think you know ever'thing there is to know? Just do like you're told."

"Ma'am," Mercer said through her teeth, "I been given a lot of orders in my life. You understand what I'm sayin?"

"Uh-huh. But this here is your son. His life could depend on whether or not you know when to listen. This is what I do, you see. I nurse people. You know that?"

Mercer felt hemmed in. The rows of brick houses with their crazy, tilting lean-to sheds and backyard shacks cut off the low-slung sky. She felt hemmed in by her jittery daughter and this frantic freedom and dogs and fleas; by Little Bea's gawking boarders and her liquor breath; she felt hemmed in by Zilpha's strange medicine and death's-a-comin old voice.

It began to rain. Mercer dipped the rag into the leather bucket of water. She'd never seen a leather bucket before. It gave a slow rock as the water sloshed. Zilpha took the rag from Mercer's hand.

"Hold 'im up, like this."

Mercer held him with one arm around his back and one under his buttocks. His body stretched along hers, and his skin burned through Bea's thin cotton gown. Zilpha began to sponge him. Water splashed on Mercer's belly. She felt the heat of her son's body and the cold slap of water between them. Mattie moaned, and Mercer prayed that she was doing right. Raindrops plopped on their faces and on the ground.

In half an hour Mattie had cooled down. Mercer was soaked and shivering. It took all her strength to carry him back up the winding staircase, wrap him in a piece of sheet, and lay him in bed again next to Etta. She took off her nightdress, soaked with water and vomit. Bea gave her another threadbare gown. She put it on, brushed her legs, and lay down.

Too tired to sleep, she lay listening as her children scratched their ankles. She heard Mattie's ragged breathing and felt Etta twitch in her sleep like a puppy. Rain thudded on the flat roof. She wondered when Mattie would be well enough to travel, and whether she'd be able to wait until he was. She wondered about Boston and Canada and New England. How could she tell which place would be better, when she knew nothing about any of them? She wondered what old Pryor would do once he got to where he was going. She wondered about the slave catchers and kidnappers, and how they could find people, and how a body could hide from them.

Tyree Quick came into her mind too. Mercer watched him laughing and throwing the ball to the children. In her mind's eye she marveled again at the wholeness of him: eyes, skin, fingers, thumbs, teeth. This man wasn't missing anything. He wasn't pockmarked. Her mind rushed to admire him, whole and free. Not free issue or manumitted or half free or on loan, but truly free. His freedom let her admire him without reserve, without calculating in the back of her mind and with shame how much profit his strength would provide for someone else, or how many of the master's problems his agile brain would solve.

She thought of Tyree's wife, Blanche, who had stayed the better part of the afternoon with the vain woman the minister was courting. She could see the two of them sitting under the tree, with their matching bonnets and bangs and their skirts spread around.

Mercer felt mean toward them. She probed the meanness as she would a bad spot in a tooth with her tongue, to find where it hurt. They'd looked so comfortable; that's what stuck in her craw, so cocksure that their men would protect them, that their dead would rest in peace, that they'd have sweet lemonade to quench their thirst, and that their children would have rubber balls to throw. They looked like freedom too, and instead of admiring them, she resented them for it.

The rain stopped. An ivory haze of moonlight seeped into the room and shone on Bea's dark furniture and white linen. Mercer turned her new name in her mind like fresh-minted money.

Always wanted to be free. Well, she'd said it; she'd said it and sold her own baby boy down the river with a mother's tongue. Now she understood the desire and what it took to let it loose, big like the sky and liable to strike lightning. But lightning struck any-time; and the cost of freedom was no dearer than the cost of bondage could be.

Now you free.

Tough titty, she told herself. Gotta suck it.

Cats in the alley began to yowl. Some poor cold pussy, Mercer thought, was trying to keep old Tom from giving her a litter she couldn't keep alive. The yowling went on and on and on, like a baby crying from far away.

Mercer prayed for Benjamin. "Light like a garment." Sue would say it again and again, just that phrase, picked up from her prayer meetings held at the farm five miles away. In her mind, Mercer wrapped her son in a soft white coverlet that gave off a glow like moonbeams.

"God keep us while we are absent, one from another." There was no one to say it with. She said it alone. The time will come, Mercer told herself, when Suzy will teach Benjamin his prayers and he will lie on his cot and say them into the dark. She'd pray the words with them, and—it came to her like inspiration— she'd pray somehow to get him back.

Pryor would try to get *her* back too. Mercer knew it. He would pity himself that he'd been so ill used. He would remind himself of everything he had ever given her—every yard of fabric, every strip of bacon, every scrap of learning. And after he'd fin-ished, he'd roll his sorry up into an angry ball and hurl it at her. What a nice man he'd been, what a decent fellow. Could've done her every whichaway, and slapped her for crying, but he never did. That's what he'd think.

He'd call her an ungrateful black wretch, whispering through his teeth while he was alone: while he shaved or used the commode or took his comfort in his own cupped fist at night. She who had never stayed in his bed longer than a quarter of an hour—with her head wrapped and towels under her to make sure that she'd leave nothing and depart laden with his sweat and slime and seed—she, the newly named Miss Mercer Gray, she would linger in his head day and night.

He would come after her surely, surely. She crossed her arms over her breasts and burrowed into the bedclothes. This new freedom was a shaky proposition, and it had cost her her son. She would never go back. If Pryor wanted to come after her, well, then, let him.

They did not leave the next day or the day after. It was dangerous to stay in Philadelphia, but Mercer could not take her unwell child on the road. Mattie returned to health only slowly. At Mercer's insistence, they moved out of Bea's bedroom onto pallets in the shed.

Tyree built them wood platforms out of crates to put the pallets on. He got the crates from a tobacconist. They advertised a plug tobacco called Wedding Cake, made by a company in Richmond, Virginia. As he was constructing the platforms, Tyree asked Mercer whether she wanted "Virginia" turned down.

"Leave it up, please," she said. "I want to see every day that I ain't there."

Bea made Mattie a drink from sweet green syrup mixed with water. She brought it to him in a ceramic cup in the shape of an elephant and with a quill to sip through. Its trunk formed the handle. She told him about a real elephant he could go see for a quarter on Market Street, and that she'd take him when he got well. Mattie asked each day if the elephant was still on Market Street, as if he knew where Market Street was. When he worried about the price of the ticket, Beatrice put a quarter under his pillow and told him that it had come from the fairies. Mattie liked to hold his coin in his hand or in his mouth.

"Take that outta your mouth," Mercer told him. "Money is filthy."

"This money," he said, grinning, "is clean."

Harriet took to visiting each afternoon, with offerings from a secondhand store called the Clothing Cellar and invitations for Mercer to accompany her to the lectures and meetings she attended in the evenings. She brought a picture book of United States scenery for Etta and Mattie to look at and a volume of her journal to show to Mercer. In it were psalms, Scripture passages, and poems by Browning, Macaulay, Wordsworth, and Longfellow. Harriet also pinned articles cut from newspapers or copied in her small, oval hand.

Mercer turned the pages to take in the sheer mass of it. Pryor collected guns and tiny toy soldiers. This compilation made sense to Mercer. She stopped at one page that caught her eye and asked Harriet to read it to her.

Harriet cleared her throat and began in a pleasant, practiced voice:

"Be ever gentle with the children God has given you. Watch them constantly; reprove them earnestly, but not in anger. In the forcible language of the scripture, 'Be not bitter against them.'

"'Yes, they are good boys,' I once heard a kind father say; 'I talk to them pretty much, but I do not like to beat my children—the world will beat them enough.' It was a beautiful thought, though not elegantly expressed.

"Yes, there is not one child in the circle around your table, healthful and happy as they look now, on whose head, if long spared, the storm will not beat. Adversity may wither them, sickness fade, and a cold world frown on them; but amid all, let memory carry them back to a home where the law of kindness reigned.

"I have put the article in a frame and hung it on the wall in our schoolroom," Harriet said. "And I'm afraid more than one parent has taken me to task for it."

"I'm sure they has. It makes you ashamed. What'd it say? 'The world will beat them enough.' We always say we're gettin 'em ready. Read that last part again, please."

" '. . . but amid all, let memory carry them back to a home—' "

" 'Let memory carry them back to a home . . .' "

" '. . . where the law of kindness reigned.' 'Reigned' meaning ruled," Harriet said.

" '. . . where the law of kindness reigned.' "

"The parents tell me, in so many words, that schoolmistresses without children of their own ought to confine their lessons to children."

Mercer smiled. "My father never hit me. They said I was spoiled because he never hit me. Just this minute is the first time I ever heard anybody say different. . . . What else you have in there?"

Harriet turned to the back of the journal, where she'd written short stories for her children at school. She wrote them herself so that her pupils would have stories to read about other colored youngsters. One story featured Negro missionaries with two sons who go to Africa and convert people to Christianity. The boys make friends, and the friends take them to see a herd of elephants.

"Elephants," cried Mattie in a hoarse voice from his bed. "Like the elephant on Market Street?"

Harriet called back to the shed from where they sat in the kitchen: "Just like the one on Market Street, only bigger. Don't strain.

"I dictate these to the children," Harriet continued. "Then I have them draw pictures about the story and take them home and read them to their parents. I'll give Etta one of the girls' papers to copy, if you don't mind. Do you think she'd like that?"

Etta appeared in the doorway, grinning and looking adoringly at Harriet. "Yes, ma'am."

"Speak up," Mercer said. She took care to say it gently. The article had chastened her. It made her want to defend herself to the writer of the article. She knew good and well why parents at Harriet's school did not like to have the thing framed and beaming down on them. It made you want to shout at it: "I am doing my level best. What else can you ask of me?"

Harriet had brought something else too: a *Wilson's Primer* for Mercer to study.

"Only if you like, of course, but I see how you've taught yourself so far—"

"Nah. I didn't teach myself. But I would like to work, since we are here and you willing."

"Excellent."

Harriet's homely face fell into happy lines. Mercer supposed that it was how she looked at school when the children pleased her. Harriet pulled a copybook from her leather pouch.

"Here's one to start." She took a pencil from the bag and wrote on the first page: "Verbs, Irregular. Copy fifteen times each. To be: I am, you are, he, she, it is, we are, you are, they are."

"First lesson. And oh . . ." She pulled a matching copybook and a piece of paper out of the pouch. "Etta, here's a copybook for you and that story I told you about. This was written by a very nice girl in our classroom named Sarah. I hoped to bring Africana's paper for you, but it contained four errors, and that's no way to begin. Besides, Africana's hand is terribly sloppy. . . . Now, don't mind that you won't understand it all. Just copy, and copy carefully."

"Guess you got us occupied now, Miss Harriet," Mercer remarked.

Harriet flashed a smile. "Yes. I see you are mocking me just the littlest bit, and I don't care. Work, write, read." She laughed out loud. "New students, and fugitives. There's nothing I like better. Etta, you must study hard and write me beautiful letters one day from wherever you go, so I can put you into one of my stories."

Etta squirmed happily and fingered her copybook. As Harriet expected, the two began their work within minutes after she left.

Harriet came the next afternoon and the next, bringing more lessons and another invitation, this one to a lecture she was giving on anatomy in the Quicks' parlor. Mercer accepted.

Bea sent one of her boarders over early to help clean, and Mercer went with her. They beat the carpets, dusted and polished the pianoforte, mahogany sideboard, card tables, and mirrors. They brought wooden folding chairs from the basement, dusted them, and set them in rows in the parlor and back into the dining room.

The audience came to the house on Pine Street promptly at seven and consisted of colored people of quality, as they called themselves, mostly women and a few men. They were well dressed, perfumed and pomaded. Mercer worked alongside Della, and no one thought anything except that Della had hired her to help. When she brought a chair in from the kitchen and sat at the back of the room, only a couple of people bothered to turn their heads.

Harriet's musical voice practically sang the long, Latinate words. Who knew how much the audience grasped or how many of them merely sat back admiring the learning that one of their own had achieved? Crowded with so many bodies, Della's prim parlor warmed considerably. The audience fanned themselves and seemed not to mind. Harriet, who cared for their children by day, who led up their minds, through Nature, to Nature's God, was leading grown minds this evening through the science of anatomy. Why, they would gladly have sat sweating and fanning and listening to her pronounce those unpronounceable words till sunrise.

Throughout Harriet's talk, Della baked lemon cakes in the kitchen, with Abby Ann pressed into service as helper. The cakes had been ordered for a ball, but Della made extra. When Harriet finished, she sent Africana and Etta into the dining room with trays of little cakes and put Abby Ann at the end of the table to pour tea. Then Della herself swept in, to collect compliments on her daughter's erudition and her home, her eighteenth-century English soup tureen in the shape of a red hen, brought out specially for the evening and perched on the buffet, and her cakes. She promised faithfully to pass each comment on to Manny, who had not come downstairs, she said, because he didn't feel up to it. They knew about his seizure and made sympathetic noises.

A handful of people refused to leave. They stood about the dining room table munching and sipping and talking. Having found that Harriet could not be stumped by their questions, three men who considered themselves science minded now stood in a clump, arguing with a fourth, who claimed that according to Lamarck's theories, black people who lived in the north would eventually lose their color, because dark skin gave no biological advantage in northern climates and, certainly, as any fool could see, no economic advantage, either. A group of five women stood on the other side of the room, gossiping quietly.

"Well, gentlemen," Tyree said, "I thoroughly expect to stay black until I die." He put his arms out as if to direct the men to the table where they'd laid their hats.

"But if I see any folk starting to turn, I'll let you know."

Della walked the ladies to the door.

When he heard the doors close, Manny called Tyree to help him down the stairs.

"What'd you do, invite every Sambo in Soapfat Alley? I heard Tyree. Had to beat 'em out the door. Harry, you got the riffraff this time. You know not one of those niggers had any idea what you were saying."

Mercer could not help laughing.

"No, lookit," Manny said. "These niggers ain't quality."

"Who's quality, Daddy?"

"I'm quality. That's who's quality."

Manny poked his chest with his thumb and turned a frown on the room, resting on Mercer.

"They looked like they was listening, Mr. Quick."

"Hah. Lemme tell you. All they did tonight was keep up appearances. Dressed up and came out and sat there with their faces screwed up like they thinkin. 'At's all. How many did you have?"

"I'ma say three dozen," Della answered. "She did give an excellent talk, Father. Everyone said so."

"Thirty-six people?"

"More or less."

"Why didn't someone count? Don't you count, Harriet? Or can't the schoolmistress count and talk at the same time?"

"There was thirty-two people who came," Mercer said.

The Quicks turned to look at Mercer.

"You counted?" Della asked.

"I didn't think much about it."

"Thirty-two. Same as Tyree's Harry's age." Manny said this to Mercer, as if, because she had counted, she'd be interested, as he was, in the coincidence.

"Well," he asked Harriet, "did any of them sign up new students for you? Paying students? No? Did they eat up the cakes for the Logans' ball? No? Good. They do warm up the house, though. Ought to have 'em all back for another lecture in January. Geography, maybe."

"So, Daddy," Harriet said, "I see you're happy to have your house empty of guests." Her voice sounded tired.

"I hate a houseful of strange Negroes, you know that." He looked at Mercer. "What made you count?"

She shrugged. "Don't know, sir."

"You should take her on tour," he said. "Dress her up like a lady. Nobody'll know the difference."

Harriet pressed her lips together. "Thank you," she said to Mercer, "for not taking offense."

Mercer's mouth slipped into its half-smile. "No, ma'am. Least Mr. Quick thinks I could pass off as a lady. He must be takin to me."

Tyree laughed.

"Take her on the tour," Manny said. "Let her see what real quality looks like, not these pompous old Negroes sittin around in my parlor like a bunch of crows on a chimney."

"When we were small," Tyree explained, "my father used to take us around the city, showing us all the colored businesses. He would walk us up and down street after street, telling us what each man did and how he started and what he owned now. And he always ended up on south Broad Street to show us the lumberyard of Mr. Stephen Smith, the richest Negro in America."

"We should take Mercer," Harriet said to Tyree. "Perhaps you'll make it through this time."

"What do you mean, make it through?" asked Abby Ann.

"Without getting smacked," Harriet said. "Daddy would be telling us how this one began with nothing, or how that one bought himself out of slavery by paying his master a dollar a week for ten years—"

"And ended by buying the master's shop twenty years later—"

"And Roland and Tyree would giggle—"

"Or fight."

"And then Daddy would box their ears."

"I'd show you a lumberyard built by a colored man, a man who owned fifty brick houses, and one of you would stick your foot out to trip the other." Manny sighed.

"Mr. Smith was very generous to charitable causes for our people," Harriet said meaningfully to her father.

"When I finally met him," Tyree said, "I'm afraid I was disappointed. He didn't look so very rich."

"Well, and how would rich appear to us, eh?" asked Harriet.

"The man moved lumber on the rails, I tell you," Manny said. He was standing next to the shelves he'd built into the wall in the parlor to display his ships in bottles. "Oh, get me a rag," he said.

Mercer did not know whom he was talking to until Della shuffled into the kitchen and back again to get a rag for her husband.

"He gave generously to our organizations," Harriet said again.

Manny called Mercer to see the ships as he polished them. He told her the number of sails and the height of the masts and other numerical details she did not understand and could not remember. The ships themselves appeared perfect to her, and yet she had no interest in them whatever. Besides, she did not like collections of things, although she'd have been hard pressed to say why.

"Oh, he was the most boring little man," Della said, "with those cheap spectacles. And he was just losing his hair in tufts."

"Yep," Tyree said, laughing. "Money will not buy you hair."

"It bought Aunt Bea some hair," said Abby Ann.

"Be still," Della said.

"Well," Tyree asked, "we fixed him, didn't we? That'll teach him to be so black and so rich. . . . So, having heard the grim history, Miss Gray, would you like to go stand outside Smith's mansion and kick shins with us so that you, too, can come home and say unkind things about our betters?"

With sudden seriousness, Mercer turned from the boats in their bottles and said: "I put my education in your hands. Now I gotta go back and sit with Mattie."

Blanche had stayed upstairs that night, saying she was indisposed, but at Harriet's urging she and Abby Ann came to call for Mercer at Bea's the next day. They walked around the block to the front door, rather than go through the alley, to avoid Old Standby and Simple Simon.

It was a short visit. When Mercer asked after Ephraim, Blanche clapped her hands.

"We haven't invited you to church, have we?" she asked.

Zilpha snorted.

"You must come." Blanche became winning and willful. "It's St. Thomas African Episcopal Church. I was raised Catholic, but"—she sighed—"Mother Dell won't have it, you know, and Daddy Quick is Episcopalian, or he was, at least, and that's where they've agreed on, so I go." Her voice trailed off.

"And Ephraim is a priest-in-training there," Abby Ann said.

"Well, he's a deacon, actually. He'll be ordained into the priesthood, please God, next year."

"I'll come. Thank you for asking me."

"Oh, you'll love it," Blanche insisted. "Saint Thomas was started by a slave. Did Harriet tell you that? Absalom Jones. It took him something like fifteen years to earn himself out."

"And then he stayed working for the same man for wages."

"He said that colored people had to 'throw off that servile fear, that habit of oppression and bondage trained us up in.'" Again Blanche smiled winningly. "This'll be an excellent place for you to bring your spirit."

Mercer felt irritable after they left. She didn't need Yella One and Yella Two lecturing her about shaking off servile fear. But she'd go to church anyway.

The following Sunday, Mercer found herself sitting at the end of the Quicks' pew in St. Thomas African Episcopal Church. A young man who carried a gold cross walked down the aisle first. Then came another, this one swinging incense in a metal latticework box. The box hung at the end of a long chain, and the young man swung it in wide arcs on either side of his body. Through the smoke he was as beautiful as an angel and as worldly as a dancer. The smoke rose in swirls to the ceiling and burned the insides of her nostrils. It smelled hot and dry and rich. Here in church, where Mercer had expected her soul to spring to life, her body came alive instead. She wanted to be made love to and held. With the feeling came tears, and an acid wash, only as much as she could bear, into the raw places inside her, the places of shame and rage.

Behind the young men came younger boys, very serious, as if they were marching at the head of an army, strutting and bouncing under the weight of their banners, ready to make themselves men. Then followed the choir, singing elaborate and beautiful music about joy, and Ephraim, wearing a white robe trimmed in green, and behind him, similarly robed, but much older, the priest. Tears trailed down Mercer's cheeks. She did not sob or tremble, but the tears ran freely, and she could no more stop them than she could stop the procession down the center of church.

The priest, a small, grandfatherly man with white hair to his shoulders, told them in a resonant voice: "Stand fast in the liberty wherein Christ has made us free." Mercer repeated the phrase. She would write it in her copybook.

When the congregation went forward for communion, Blanche told Mercer not to take the bread and wine, since she hadn't been baptized, but to cross her hands over her chest to receive a blessing. She did. The minister looked compassionately at her red eyes and touched her head with cool fingers. At the end of the service, the organist played more of his complicated music. Parishioners stood to leave or else knelt on the low benches in front of them. Blanche knelt. Not wanting to speak to anyone, Mercer knelt beside her and closed her eyes.

When she opened them, acolytes were snuffing the tall candles. A woman dressed in well-made but threadbare clothing walked to the high altar, after some bowing and curtsying, followed by two small boys who favored her. Mercer assumed that they were her grandchildren. The woman handed each of them an ornate item from the altar. She bowed to them, and they bowed in return. They were impossibly well behaved and beautiful, with wide eyes, fat cheeks, and clear faces. These people took care of their own. Mercer felt pride and envy.

Next to Mercer, Blanche stayed on her knees. She asked Jesus to help her to embrace the suffering of her life. She wanted to embrace the exhaustion of her headaches, because she knew they would bring her closer to him. In her mind, she prostrated herself on the cold floor. And in her mind he smiled at the sacrifice.

After that, Mercer agreed more often to travel abroad in the city with her adopted family. They called her Cousin Mercer. During the day she nursed Mattie and cleaned for Little Bea. Harriet began taking Etta to school with her as an assistant. She assigned her niece Africana the task of visiting Mattie each day and reading a story to him. And in the evening she took Mercer out to learn abolition. They attended one meeting after another, sometimes alone, often with other family members. Most of the speakers were white, occasionally accompanied by a Negro, who came onstage to display scars on his back or to testify about the evils of slavery. Only once did a former slave take to the podium to give the talk, and that was not at one of the halls but in an African Methodist Episcopal church.

The speaker looked nearly broken; he spoke in a flat voice that seemed separate from what he said:

"They's a game that some of the overseers likeded us to play, and it went this-a-way. When a slave got hisself caught in the wrong, they would call the other slaves together and give everyone a switch, a green switch, and cause 'em to stand in a circle. The one what's in trouble, he stand in the middle. Then they give the command to start the whuppin. That's the game.

"That's the game."

As he spoke, he waved in the air a nubby right hand on which the thumb and all but one finger had been cut off at the knuckle.

THE PRICE OF A CHILD

"Now, can you fine peoples tell me which is worser, gettin the whuppin or givin it?"

The colored people of quality shook their heads together. They talked back to him to give him their earnest sympathy.

"My Lord," one woman shouted.

"Dear Jesus."

"Since I been up North, I heard people talk about what they woulda done if they'da been a slave, but I'ma tell you this one thing: I don't care who you is or how old you is or how big and strong you think you is—huh, slavery could break anybody."

Mercer left the slavery talk feeling anxious and weary. She suddenly feared that Pryor might be waiting for her at the bottom of the steps. She could see him in his two-tier gray winter cloak. He had once flung it around her shoulders. She could still remember the weight of it. She'd never even imagined a wrap so warm. No wonder Negroes were always sick. No wonder that man in the pulpit looked twenty years older than he said he was.

"Gonna fix for a rain," she said. It made no sense, but the cold drizzle cheered her, as if a man with a two-tier winter cape would be daunted by bad weather.

An old woman next to them waved and spoke loudly, as though she were hard of hearing: "Tyree Quick? That you? How're your parents? Who's that? Harriet? Hello."

She pushed toward them across the milling people on the steps. Behind her, Mercer heard Abby Ann sigh impatiently.

"Hello, girls," she said to Abby Ann and Blanche. "I tell you one thing, children, and it's the truth before God. I bought myself out of slavery, and there's no one can *ever* buy me again. You hear me what I say? Who's that with you there? Hello."

Mercer broke into a smile. "How do?"

"Who's that?"

"This is our cousin Mercer."

"Didn't know you had no cousins. Where's she from?"

"Mother said to give you her best if we saw you."

"Same to her."

She pushed back the other way.

"That's all that woman says, every time I ever see her."

"Get used to it," Tyree said. " 'Cause she's going to live to be eighty-five, and she's going to keep saying it."

Harriet waved goodbye to her. "That was something, wasn't it?" she asked. "That old gentleman was magnificent. There's no other word."

"There are other words," Abby Ann said.

"I say that old man has seen some things," Tyree said.

"And I say, Lord, please don't let him get up in front of no hall full of white people."

"Oh, Abby Ann, shame on you."

"Oh, stop it, Harriet. You know it's the truth. You heard him. It started off bad and got worse and then it got—worser."

"Shame on you," Harriet said.

"I thought unfortunate brethren brought out charity in you, Abby Ann."

"Only when they beg, I think, Tyree," Harriet answered.

Abby Ann turned and spoke directly to Blanche in a whisper: "And waving that awful stump in the air—that's bad luck, isn't it? Don't you have to throw some salt over your shoulder if someone waves a thing like that at you?"

Blanche giggled.

Tyree frowned at her. To Abby Ann he said, "That's enough of your meanness. You sing a different tune when Ephraim's around. I suppose that means we ought to bring him everywhere with us, God forbid."

The drizzle accelerated into rain. They walked fast to keep warm.

"All that whipping," Blanche said soberly, as if to atone for her giggle. "All that whipping. It would break me. He's right, there. Why, I suspect I'd just lay down and die."

"No, you wouldn't," Mercer answered her. "You just find a way to keep from being beat."

"Is that what you did?" Abby Ann asked.

"You ever been beat?" Mercer asked her. She wanted to smack her herself.

"I don't see what that has to do with it."

"If you had been beat, you'd try not to get beat again. That's all."

Abby Ann did not answer. None of the others said anything. They did not have the heart to tell someone outside the family the stories of how Abby Ann's mother beat her until she ran down the street to Blanche's house, how she'd spend the night, then days, and no one would ever come after her.

"They cannot break everyone, though," Tyree said. "I was sorry to hear him say it."

Mercer said, "My daddy was like that."

"Virgil?"

"Yes." Mercer smiled suddenly, because he'd remembered. "Is he still alive?"

Harriet sucked her teeth. "That's none of our business."

"I don't know. When I was younger, I always thought I'd be able to tell if he died, but that's just being young."

Mercer found herself remembering a Sunday evening when Lily was young and strong, before the fight in her had turned inward. Lily had made corn bread and traded some of it for stolen coffee and sugar from old Pryor's driver. The corn bread had a crust on the bottom, and the coffee was sweet. They'd sat together, and something Mercer said made her mother laugh. Mercer remembered with sharp longing, because she so seldom could make her mother laugh. Lily's laughter filled their ugly room. When they'd finished laughing, they chewed the crunchy crust of the corn bread and drank the sweet coffee and sat up most of the night watching the stars and the moon move across the sky. Two stars that night shot down through the sky, trailing icy blue-white tails, and Lily absently told her the story of the gingerbread man.

"Why'd he run away?"

"*I don't know. Maybe the people beat 'im. Maybe he was wicked.*"

Tyree watched Mercer's face. "Are you tired of meetings yet?" he asked. "You must tell us. I'd hate for you to go to your bed each night praying God to deliver you from *us*."

"No, sir," she said.

"Good," he said. "In that case, I think Uncle Sharkey and I'll take you to one of those Africky meetings, as Uncle calls them."

"You know you don't want to go to Africa," Blanche said.

"No, I don't, Blanche. You know where I'm thinking about."

"Canada."

"Yes, Canada. But the Africa-emigration men say sensible things that few other Negroes are willing to speak aloud. Besides, Silver's giving a talk soon, and he's been my good friend since we were boys."

"You haven't spoken about Canada for months," Blanche said.

Tyree continued: "They say that butterflies in Africa fly in such numbers that they turn the sky to pink."

"Pink?" Mercer asked. The idea made her laugh.

"Yes, pink, like a rose."

Mercer laughed harder. "I don't know why those crazy old butterflies just hit me funny."

"Well, Mercer, it's raining, and we are all standing here in the rain getting our feet wet." Blanche sounded angry. Mercer felt like a naughty child.

"I'm sorry."

"And next to this alleyway to boot." Blanche's irritated whisper caused the others to look into the alley. Standing at the end of the slanting lamplight from the curb stood a black man holding an umbrella and propping up an older white man, who was wobbling and urinating onto both their feet.

Tyree sighed. "Makes those pink butterflies sound appealing, doesn't it?"

They took Mercer to Bea's and then went home. Sharkey was waiting for them in the kitchen.

"Where's Mercer?" he asked.

"We've just taken her to Aunt Bea's," Tyree said. "What's wrong?"

"Well, perhaps it's better that I tell you first."

"Have they put out an advertisement?" Tyree asked. He had not read the paper that day. Nor had he gone to the post office where runaway notices were posted.

"No. Actually, it's worse than that, I think. They've arrested Still and the porters for assault and battery."

"No one assaulted him. They touched his arm. They held him."

"And riot."

"Riot? It was the most orderly transaction I've ever seen."

"Riot. All six of them. Still posted bond, of course, and three of the others. That means two men are in jail. The Vigilance Committee, I believe, will find funds to give to their families to post bond for them, too, as soon as possible. Those men cannot afford to lose a day's work."

"And what about Williamson? Or are they only arresting Africans?"

"To the contrary. Because Williamson is a white man, and because her owner figures that a white man must be in control, you see, he's charged Williamson with larceny. They served the papers when he was out of town on business, and his father—you know his father, don't you?—brought them round to Still and told him: 'Passmore's gone to Harrisburg. Thee had better attend to it.'

"So Still has their anti-slavery lawyer go to court and tell the judge the same thing. Then Williamson comes home, goes to court the next day, and is told to produce Mercer. He can't do it, of course. Doesn't know where she is. So the judge puts Williamson into prison too, for contempt of court."

"But if he doesn't know where she is, how can he produce her?"

"That's what the lawyer said."

"What was the answer?"

"I suppose the judge figures he's lying."

Six / Happy Few

At breakfast the next morning, the Quicks argued about what to do with Mercer. Tyree joked that they'd become as sentimental and as meddlesome as Gertrude Wren, the Vigilance Committee's old white widow who wanted fugitives brought to meet her before they were sent on their way. She cherished their stories. She wept over their sufferings and laughed at the ruses they used to escape. Then, gleefully, she reached into her purse for a gold dollar coin to put into each palm.

"They tell me," Tyree said, "that she folds their fingers over that piece of money, and then she just holds 'em like this." He pantomimed pressing the dollar into Africana's palm, closing her hand into a fist, and then cupping his two hands over hers.

"Or like this." Then he pulled her to him and smashed her face into his chest.

" 'Oh, oh, oh, my dusky daughter,' " he said in falsetto, " 'my sable son. Oh, you faithful black husband and wife. Together you escaped, together, after all! And with children. Tell me again how the wind howled.'

" 'Well, it howled, all right, ma'am. Didn't it howl? Howled somethin fierce.' "

Manny grumbled that Mrs. Wren had an ample supply of gold coins. "Kinda money she has grows by itself," he said. "And every mornin she wake up, she got more."

"And where's it come from?" Sharkey asked rhetorically. "Her bankers probably invest in the very land that those same poor wretches escaped."

Having received Tyree's attention, Africana smiled. She'd adored and feared her father, Roland. Now she was warned not to be like him. Harriet wanted her to be more studious; Della wanted her to work harder in the house; her mother wanted her to be quiet. She tapped Tyree's sleeve. He patted her on the shoulder and turned to Sharkey.

"We've got to move them north," Tyree said. "Any white man who'll take the trouble to prosecute Williamson will see to it he hires better slave catchers than the government's half-wits."

"All the more reason," Della countered, "to have them here where we can keep our eye on them."

"No," Manny said to his wife.

Della sucked her teeth. "I'd just feel better if I could keep an eye on 'em."

"You keepin an eye on 'em won't keep 'em safe," Sharkey said.

"We really must fetch Mercer if we're going to discuss her welfare and the children's," said Harriet. No one objected when she left to get her.

"We should ask Mr. Still what to do," Blanche said. She watched her daughter pick through embroidery threads for a new strand.

"Blanche, please talk to her," said Della.

"Africana," Blanche said, "do one color at a time."

"Now, Blanche," Tyree said, "what were you trying to say?"

Blanche looked at the floor and mumbled. "I said maybe we should ask Mr. Still about it."

Harriet came into the kitchen. Mercer stepped in behind her.

With uncharacteristic gruffness, Sharkey said, "Mercer, that man you were with on the ferry . . ." He wouldn't call him her owner, and she appreciated him for it.

"Jackson Pryor."

"Right. Jack Pryor. . . . Why do you smile?"

"He wouldn't like us all to call him Jack." She had called him "Sir," and nothing else, not Mister anything, never Master, and nothing at all, no name, no words, nothing, in bed.

"I cannot stand a noisy woman," he had said. She was silent, and it suited them both.

"He's a Jack-ass for what he's done. He's accused Williamson of larceny, and he's charged Still and five good men of assault and battery and riot, for God's sake. They shoulda took Jack-the-Ass and threw'm overboard. Can he swim?" Sharkey asked.

"I wouldn't know."

"And now Williamson is in prison, because he's claiming, quite truthfully, that he doesn't know where you are and therefore cannot produce you in court, as he's been ordered by the slavery-loving judge."

Tyree asked, "How well do you know Pryor?"

Mercer shrugged.

"You know 'em like you know people when you're in service, Tyree," Harriet said.

"Will he go through with this campaign?" Tyree asked. "Will he back off?"

Mercer shook her head. "No, sir. He won't back off. We'll leave y'all now. We should've gone earlier, but we'll head on north now, I guess up to Canada. That'll be best, don'tcha think?"

Della said, "That boy of yours can't travel yet."

"I expect he'll have to."

"My mother's right, Miss Mercer," Tyree said.

"We can't stay here."

"I don't see why we can't talk to Mr. Still," Blanche repeated. She had earlier suggested that they take Williamson a basket of food. No one had responded.

Tyree closed his eyes and rubbed them. There was Blanche again, looking for someone to take care of things. He'd told himself not to take it personally, but it irked him. It had to be why his brother had slapped her down and shouted, "What *I* say goes."

Tyree wouldn't hit her. He'd promised himself never to hit a woman when his father had knocked his mother into the lamp for nagging him, and she'd caught on fire, and they'd had to hold her on the floor and roll her in the rug while she screamed.

This time, Sharkey frowned at Blanche. "No, my dear. We do not talk about this to Mr. Still, and he does not talk about this to Mr. Williamson. And we do not talk to Mr. Williamson. The only thing saving both of them right now is the fact that they can honestly say that they do not know where Mercer is. Giving them that knowledge would be a great disservice."

"Oh." Blanche looked hurt. In a few moments, she slipped upstairs. Africana followed her. After a time, Tyree went to find Blanche in her room, where she was sewing with her daughter.

"Why is she by the window, getting the best light, and you're here on the bed? Africana, go around and collect Etta and get to school. Your aunt Harriet has already gone."

Blanche got up off the bed and sat in her customary chair.

"Besides, if you sit up on the bed all day, your back will give out. You know that."

"I'm a ninny," she said.

"No, you're not, Blanche. To the contrary. You are willful in the extreme, and once you've insisted on your own way, and someone pushes back with equal force, you go in the corner and cry."

"You always call me willful."

He raised an eyebrow.

"How was I willful, Tyree? Stupid, maybe. I see that now. Uncle Sharkey showed everyone how stupid I was," she said bitterly, "but how willful?"

"I told you that it wouldn't do to talk to Still. You tried to override me."

She kept sewing.

"What is it?"

She cried silently and sewed.

"What?"

"Now you're angry at me too." She stopped sewing and gave herself up to weeping.

"Yes, now I am."

"I'm not a good wife. I'm not a good mother. I know that."

Tyree refused to reassure her this time. He was tired of reassuring Blanche.

"Africana's a lazy little girl," she said.

If Tyree did not console her and make up to her, she'd drag out every failing in her life and the life of anyone she could claim.

"She's not little anymore, Blanche."

"And I cannot make her better. And Cyrus would rather be with you. He'd rather be with anyone. . . ."

"Blanche, why don't you give up these damn furs? Aunt Zilphie's right. I think they're affecting you. They are making you morbid."

"Please don't take away my business, Tyree."

"We'll start you in another business."

"I couldn't do anything half so well as I do this."

Tyree found it hard to argue with Blanche on the subject of the furs. It was the only endeavor she'd ever pursued diligently, and she did indeed make her own money. He had stopped wishing Blanche were other than she was, and he had stopped rehearsing her few virtues to himself. He'd made a mistake. He'd married with his pants instead of his head. He'd snatched her up, thinking that the years of coveting his brother's wife signified more than mere covetousness, and supposing that he would find pleasure in trying to make up for his brother's mistreatment of her. He'd learned that Blanche had not been miserable because of Roland, although Roland had done her ill. Her innermost core held a puddle of misery that never dried.

"We do the best we can, eh?"

Tyree passed his fingers under her chin. Then he left, grateful for sunshine and a chilly blue sky.

He headed for Waverly Street. Sally had taken ill and moved in with her brothers, so her house had come vacant. Tyree decided to enhance it by digging out the cellar to make another full room. Sally's husband had left her enough money to keep the house by herself, but Tyree could charge twice the rent—and provide decent accommodations—by housing two or three families in the house, with the basement addition. Manny had suggested putting on a shed. Sheds were fast to build, but they took weather badly, and were cold in winter.

He began to shovel. It was harder than he thought, because he could not stand up until he'd shoveled down a foot. He knelt and shoveled into a bucket. Then he dragged the bucket to the window, which was at street level, and dumped it. When Nig-Nag grinned into the window, asking for work, Tyree accepted. Because Tyree could shovel faster than Nig-Nag, he set up a system that let him move dirt from the back of the cellar to a mound at the front, where Nig-Nag shoveled it out the window. They tied handkerchiefs around their faces to keep out the dust. They did not talk.

Before the arrests, Tyree had toyed with the idea of installing Mercer and her children in this house. He liked her near him. He knew good and well that he wanted her and that if she stayed with them, he'd try eventually to have her. Tyree had kept his marriage vow. But he had entered his thirties now, and it was beginning to look as if he'd be shoveling clay in rat-pissy cellars for the rest of his life, married to a woman who would never be a partner. The abundance of feeling he'd had when he'd first seen Mercer had not diminished. He thought of her in the mornings when he awoke and in the evenings when he had eaten and washed. And he felt a rich joy in her presence, as he had now and then as a child with a special friend. He'd never felt quite so much for a woman before. Of course Jackson Pryor wanted to get her back. The son of a bitch. Why wouldn't he?

The work was dirty and repetitive and hard. The soil in the cellar was damp and heavy. Tyree thought about the arrest of the porters who had helped Mercer escape. He remembered the gentleness of their restraining hands. He could not help but think about the more famous cases he'd followed since the enactment of the Fugitive Slave Law in 1850. Anthony Burns had been arrested in Boston and marched to the jailhouse by federal officers. The plan to liberate him from prison failed, and he was impounded by the government, like so much freight, and sent back. And then there was Solomon Northrup, a freeman, who wrote a book that described how he was stolen, sold into slavery, and worked for twelve years, until his wife and friends in the North were able to track him down and free him.

Harriet and Tyree and Sharkey had worried about these and other cases ever since Mercer's arrival, and yet scores of escapees lived in their midst, in the Cedar ward, in tree-named alleys like Juniper, where Nig-Nag lived, renting half a room and hiring themselves out for dirty and dangerous work where nobody asked their name or where they'd come from. Others moved to the countryside and slipped into the quiet lives of other Negroes or of white Quakers and Presbyterians who were happy to acquire good workers cheap and to give a principled discretion in return.

Tyree stepped out of the basement into the October afternoon. He washed his hands under the pump in the alley and cajoled Nig-Nag to do the same before he'd share his lunch with him. They didn't bother to wash their faces, so the two of them sat opposite each other with striped mugs as they gulped their food. When Tyree took out the boiled potato that Zilpha had packed for him—she refused to eat Della's rich cooking—he got an idea: Mercer could stay in West Chester with his aunt. The boy, or maybe both children, could stay with the Quicks, and with their group broken up like that, they'd be harder to spot. The more Tyree turned the idea in his mind, the more he liked it. By the end of the afternoon, he was stiff and tired, but happy. It occurred to him to stop on the way home and buy her something.

. . .

At first Zilpha refused. She'd been with the family in Philadelphia since Manny's last stroke, and she'd looked forward to returning alone to her cottage. Finally, frustrated by her aunt's resistance, Harriet asked whether Zilpha wanted them to pay her a lodger's fee on Mercer's behalf.

"I wouldn't give that"—Zilpha snapped her fingers—"for your fee. But now that you've made me appear mean, I'll take her till Christmas. So you'd better hope they get things resolved, because you'll have her back for the new year. And no children."

They made arrangements quickly. Mercer agreed that breaking up the family group described in the newspaper account would help confound any spies. Etta would continue her studies and live with Bea. Mattie would stay in Tyree's household and go to school with Cyrus. Mercer would live and work with Zilpha until she could secure a situation of her own in the country and send for the children. As always, they'd watch for events and write in case of any change. Who could tell how their lives might be altered?

Once she had packed her few things, Mercer took a tray with supper to Bea, who was sewing in the late-afternoon light of her bedroom. Mercer waited as Bea put aside her work and fussed with her napkin. She liked being waited on.

"What am I going to do without you, my old friend?" she asked.

Mercer smiled and went downstairs to her children, who were waiting by the stove in the kitchen. She told them the latest plans. They were both quiet, at once fearful and expectant. Then she served them bowls of bean soup and a biscuit. They were handsomer children than the two frightened urchins she had brought into this house. In only three weeks they had taken on the sharp-eyed look of their new, free peers. Mercer reached around the table and rubbed first Etta's cheek and then Mattie's.

"I'ma make us some money while I'm away," she said. "And then we can find our own house to live in."

For reasons she could not fathom, Mercer felt trust, tentative, temporary, but comforting as the fire in the stove. She did not want to leave them, especially not after these weeks that had been more tender than any they'd had together. But she could do it because she believed her own words.

"May we go now?"

Earlier, Cyrus had come to tell the children that Della was making pudding from the bread and cakes left over from last week's catering. Before they ate, however, the children were required to do their lessons and chores. They went with Phibbe and Jane, the young boarders. Zilpha got into bed, as always, promptly at seven. Going upstairs to fetch Bea's tray, Mercer smelled Zilpha's pipe smoke. Bea had fallen asleep in her chair. When Tyree came upon Mercer washing up in the kitchen, she was alone.

He had brought a small trunk and a traveling bag and a covered bowl of pudding. The bag was made of brown cloth, with wide leather straps that had darkened and softened with age.

"You don't have a proper valise, do you?"

Mercer laughed out loud. She'd packed her things in a bleached tea crate. "No, Mr. Tyree, I didn't bring me a proper valise. I did have a trunk like that—well, not so fine, but that size—for my things and the children's, but as you know . . ."

"You did not have time to collect it at the docks. Yes, I recall you were in a hurry."

Tyree took his time to study her face up close. She was not pretty, as people used the word. Instead, her face looked taut and powerful. "In my family," he said, "I'm afraid there's not much time just to be nice and quiet like this."

"Did Miss Blanche help you pick this out, or Miss Harriet?"

"No."

"Your wife—"

"My wife sends her best for your journey, and she'd agree

with me that we couldn't let you go with your things stuffed into a tea crate."

"No, sir, your wife don't care a damn if I go or if I stay."

He looked into her eyes. She did not shrink. He threw back his head and laughed. "Well, truth to tell—"

"Truth to tell, she'd just as soon I go."

"Not without reason," Tyree said.

She turned her head away from him. Her hair had been pulled back hard into a bun. It made tiny waves from her temples, like an ocean at night. Tyree would bet that she'd never seen the ocean. It pleased him to imagine taking her to Cape May in the summer and kissing her under the black sky while the black ocean made shiny black waves next to them, like her hair.

Mercer felt Tyree brush his fingers over her head and rest them for a moment on the nape of her neck.

"I love this family like a child would love a family that took her in out of the cold, Mr. Tyree. What you do is your business, but I don't want to do nothin to hurt anybody here."

"We're not hurting anybody."

Slowly enough that Mercer saw it coming, Tyree turned her toward him, bent his face toward hers, and brushed her mouth with a kiss. Had he done more or done it with force, she would have pushed him away. But he hadn't. He'd gone nice and slow, and she'd met him halfway.

"This i'n't right," she said.

He looked at her steadily. He hadn't thought about Pryor until this afternoon, when he'd admitted to himself that he wanted her. He hadn't wished to know. He didn't like to think what she'd done before him, even though he was a grown man and she past the first bloom and a mother. Mattie was a honey color but not too, too light. Maybe nothing had happened. But why else would he have let her bring her children at all?

"A lot of things aren't right, but we all do them, don't we? We do them because we tell ourselves we have to, or we do them because we don't know any better."

"Yep."

The more he wanted her, the more he knew that Pryor had been there first. Black man can't have anything to himself. He yearned to push back her past, just roll it away and have all of her, pure and smooth as skin, for himself. If he could get ahold of Pryor, he'd grab him by the lapels and ram him against a wall, just ram him, just ram him until he had quenched his thirst for injury. He felt like shaking Mercer and screaming at her for letting him do it, for not refusing, for not saying she'd rather die than submit and bear little honey-colored babies. Tyree dropped the hand he'd been holding and sucked in his breath.

"Thank you for the bag," she said. "Thank you for the trunk and for everything you've done for me. I owe you . . ."

Poor Merce, he thought. Did she think she owed him? He was sorry that that bloody-mindedness had rushed in to spoil his precious time with her.

"I owe you," he said.

He left. Instead of going home, he turned at the end of the block toward Sharkey's, to tell his uncle that he'd like to drive to West Chester.

Mercer's presence, from the moment he'd seen her on the ferry-boat, had disturbed his brain, the way a September storm would make rats leave their tunnels and scritch crazily in chimney walls.

She'd disturbed him. She'd upset his careful life and his disciplined contracts with everyone around him. The events of Tyree's life cut loose like fighting cocks, and memories flew up in his face, looking to draw blood.

Tyree remembered his father taking him and Roland—just the boys, although Harriet stood at the door and cried to go—to the place where the Wissahickon Creek emptied into the Schuyl-kill River. He remembered how he and his brother would wait at the mouth of the creek while Manny swam out to the rock in the middle of the river. The boys splashed up the backwater, looking for beavers, or they swam out into the river just six or eight feet, which was as far as they dared.

In the long minutes when his father disappeared behind the rock, Roland would get right up to Tyree's ear and hiss the unutterable—"Maybe he's drownded"—and they'd fix their eyes on the east side of the rock, where the tide caught in a smooth V. They watched, terrified to think of Manny dead, and terrified to know their own titillation at the thought. Then their father's head burst through the surface of the water, orange and brown in the sunset, and when he snapped his face upward to suck at the air, they could see a swirl of water and the glint of his teeth. Tyree sighed relief and Roland tripped his tongue each time nature failed to rid them of their father. Sure enough, Manny would return, so vigorous and self-satisfied that Roland would inevitably sulk, and Manny would inevitably beat him. He'd beat him with a green switch in the water, where it would sting. Roland writhed and thrashed but refused to cry; and Manny would lay on quick, hard strokes. They churned the creekbed to a muddy brown. Tyree ran and held on to his brother, and Manny would beat him too.

Then they'd dress and walk to town, where Manny would leave the boys with Little Bea, who'd assure him that she was not drunk, and that she would not get drunk, while Manny went down the block to his Shed Kitchen Woman. He'd return in an hour, trailing a vague patchouli smell and promising Bea something for her trouble.

On each occasion, scores of them, Roland had wished his father dead. Now Roland was dead. Tyree did not know why, but Mercer's coming to the Quick household, Mercer's leaving, brought it all back to him fresh.

If she asked about his brother, Roland rose up sulkily by his side. If she asked about the way north, he thought about his trips to Thetford Academy in Vermont, where they'd been kind to his brother and himself, and where he'd learned algebra and geometry, Latin and French, science and English literature.

She'd asked one night what he'd liked best in school, and he'd recalled learning monologues and reciting them at the Philadelphia Library Company of Colored Persons, where he and Roland had first met Blanche. He remembered seeing his effect on the people in the audience and feeling his own new manhood, reflected bright as sunlight. He'd been seventeen.

" 'We few, we happy few—' " he began, and then let fly his fluid voice and warlike hope. The recitation stayed in his mind, each word remembered.

> *. . . we band of brothers:*
> *For he today that sheds his blood with me*
> *Shall be my brother: be he ne'er so vile,*
> *This day shall gentle his condition.*
> *And gentlemen in England now abed*
> *Shall think themselves accursed they were not here;*
> *And hold their manhoods cheap, whiles any speaks*
> *That fought with us upon Saint Crispin's day.*

Words about ragtag adventurers who'd lived and died centuries before seemed fresh and new when Tyree spoke them, as if they'd been written on purpose to describe the free colored people of Philadelphia. Black Americans who'd lain abed, figuratively speaking, in the mid-1800s would wake up one day, and like Britons of the Middle Ages, they would "hold their manhoods cheap," because they had not been part of the advance guard, fighting, organizing, petitioning, meeting, working, conniving, to rid the United States of slavery's canker and to cheat America of every red cent they could steal away from the slave trade and its sleek profiteers.

Mercer's smile, like her resistance at the dock, called forth in him long-neglected passion that had once told him who he was. The old people had a phrase: naturally manhood. That's what they'd said he had: not just usefulness or cleverness with his hands, not a smooth, sharp tongue, not even good looks or strength or a particular portion of courage or goodness. Naturally manhood gleamed; it wrapped a playful, quick, dangerous manliness around a core of integrity. Roland had always been older, handsomer, and smarter; wasn't it he, after all, who'd been called to the front of the class to sight read a passage of Pliny the Younger, when the Vice President came to Philadelphia, having wagered a friend that no nigger could really read Latin? But Roland had lacked Tyree's humor. Roland had had little love in him, and never any give.

That's why Roland went so hard after the Africa scheme. That's why once he'd decided, he'd given no one, not even his wife, Blanche, time to get used to it. It was why he badgered Manny for money to go, and why Blanche had run away from him, taking their baby daughter, Africana, as he'd insisted on naming her, but had broken down into a tiny bundle of tears outside Zilpha's whitewashed home in West Chester. It was why they had sent for Tyree to come get her instead of her own husband. Roland would have beaten her something awful. Roland had no give.

But that had happened a long time ago. Tyree wished Mercer had known him then.

He wished she had known him before he'd followed Blanche on an impulse into the basement and made her his own. Tyree remembered how he'd gathered up her skirts with one hand and then pulled down her drawers with the other. He felt again the shocking softness of her thighs and the curve of her buttocks and, more shocking, her easy submission. He felt again that handful of buttery flesh. He remembered how he squeezed and rolled it in his hand before he took her, there, in the basement, his brother's wife, from behind, and how shocked she'd been when he bent her over for it. Roland must always have taken her from the front. He'd laughed to himself. Roland had no imagination.

Tyree wished that he'd met Mercer before all that. She made him yearn to be more virtuous. It was an old-fashioned idea, quaint. He had to smile at himself. She made him wish to be a political man again: the man with notions, who never veered from them. She also made him feel lusty, as if lust for integrity went hand in hand with the violence and thrust of his body. Tired of thinking, and tired of yearning, Tyree slipped into his house and up the stairs to Blanche's room.

The lamplight slanted in on her. She was bent over, sewing a bit of gray fur onto the brim of a large gray hat, and wearing her chemise, as he'd known she would be. Coiled on the top of her head was her braid. It was the color of creekwater, like her eyes. Coppery little naps rolled themselves into curls on the nape of her neck. Creek-colored puffs of wet hair peeked out from her armpits. The room was hot and close; she kept a little heater going. It smelled like Blanche and kerosene and the pelts. Outside, Nig-Nag could be heard braying and coughing in the alley. Tyree had paid him for the day's work. No doubt he'd used it for ale and now wanted some food.

Blanche looked up at her husband. "You sick?"

"No, I'm not sick."

"Oh," she said, looking out at the last strands of angled sun. "You're early."

"No, I'm not," he said. "You've lost track of the time."

"I'll be down directly."

"I'm not going down." Tyree sighed. "How are you this afternoon?" he asked.

His wife looked at him and coughed and laughed. "I'm quite well, thank you."

Tyree walked over to where she sat on her chair. He began to pick up the pelts and brushed leather.

"Oh, no," she said. "Please don't disturb those. I've just tacked them on—"

He sucked his teeth impatiently.

Blanche pouted and bent over the piece of hat she'd been working on. Tyree didn't look into her eyes. He knew that they'd be watery red from fur and fatigue. He did not want to see them.

Instead, he bent Blanche over so he could watch as he slid his fingers over the spiny tips on her back and around to her breasts. Mouse titties. That's what Manny had called them years before, and Roland had told his father never to say it again, because he was going to marry her. But the phrase had stuck in Tyree's head. He even teased her about it himself. He rubbed the chemise over the sweaty little mouse titties. The third floor was hot.

Blanche yielded as she always did. The yielding was subterfuge. He'd learned that over the years as he ceased to tremble with the larcenous thrill of having her, just having her, with her creamy skin and her creek-colored hair spilling over the pillow like a picture-book vision; just having her to take, as he had at first, two and three times in a night, whenever he awoke, hard and horny, reveling in her tiny cries; just having her to feel under the coverlet (the white coverlet she'd embroidered for months, then patched and quilted after Roland had come home and bled into it, like a stuck pig, as Della always said); just having her like this, strong-smelling, sticky, yielding. She yielded, but she retreated to some inner chamber of her most secret self, far away from him. She thought he didn't know, but he knew.

When he began to hate her for it, the year that Cyrus was born, it was his mother who took him aside to tell him that Blanche couldn't help how she was. It seemed as if she might, but she couldn't. Then Della reminded him that no matter how she was, she was his wife. She was family. She was doing her best, as Della had pointed out—Della who could barely abide her—and was it Blanche's fault if she failed to please him?

Tyree trailed his finger down the fine mist on her back and pulled her chemise up to her waist. Blanche said nothing. The lamp threw a gold glow onto her gold flesh. She preferred to do her duty, as she said, in the dark, but he liked to see it. He grabbed the tiny curve of her buttocks and took her there, from behind, as he'd done in the basement years before. He took her fast, and he felt the warmth from her heater on the backs of his thighs and her shaking flesh in front.

"Tyyyy-reeee." His father's voice drifted up the stairwell and slipped under the door.

"Unh-unh." He breathed it to Blanche. "Shhh."

She did not move.

His father called again, and then was silent. "Shhh. I'll go do for him," Tyree told his wife. "Just a little more. Gimme a little more. That's all I need."

He squeezed his hands around Blanche's waist and held her steady so he could get it right. He breathed deeply and got it going in good. He remembered Mercer's mouth and body, full and firm. It made him groan and push harder.

"C'mon, girl," he said.

Blanche answered: Um.

The air held hundreds of thousands of fine fur hairs; he swallowed them in big gulps. They tickled his throat and scratched at the back of his nose. His eyes itched. He felt himself finishing. So did Blanche. She whined, as always, for him to please be careful.

"Oh, for God's sake, Blanche," Tyree said. He always took it out before he made her pregnant. Without fail. "It's all right," he assured her to make her hush. "All right."

Tyree jerked Blanche's body to him a little tighter and closed his itching eyes and stifled a cough. Then he pulled out and held her to him while he came.

"Blanche," he said as he stepped away. "Want a rag?"

She heard him. His voice came to her from a distance.

"Uh-hunh."

Tyree sopped a rag in the basin and mopped at her crotch. He always did when he finished. It never failed to embarrass her, even after all these years, but she let him. He was gentle, after all. Then she pulled down her skirts and let her head fall to her chest. Her eyes closed, and although she could hear Tyree washing up, she let herself drift away, a long way, and she did not plan to pull herself back.

"You ready to eat?" he asked.

"Unh-unh."

Blanche had worked steadily that day—the light was good and her eyes held out—on an order of hats for Mr. Woodhouse; and she had prayed the while. She assigned herself prayers for stitches, as the priest had assigned her prayers when she'd been a child and still a devout Catholic, before Roland and his Protestant family had separated her from the Church. She prayed that God wouldn't blame her. It hadn't been her fault; she still loved the Church, still hailed Mary full of grace and blessed the fruit of her womb, Jesus. She prayed for her Jesus to come to her again, as he had before. She pricked her fingers and saw in the tiny drops of blood that dripped onto the pelts and disappeared into them the blood of Jesus as it dripped off the cross.

She had done her duty as Tyree's wife. She'd taken care of the children. She'd done her work. Now she asked Jesus to come to her. He was coming. Curious how he came when he wanted, not at her bidding, but at her need. She knew the peace that descended on the room before he appeared just as she knew the dimmed vision that preceded her headaches. She could feel her breathing change.

Blanche had borne the cross: Roland Quick lay on the pillow next to her, bleeding into the dowry sheets Della had given her because her father wouldn't; growling at her like a dog who's crawled home after a fight and snaps at his offspring; back from the streets she had asked him to stay out of, where he claimed to be working for the Africa Society but where he also prowled and gambled their money and drank and whored long after honest black colonists had gone to bed. Honest, God-fearing people bored him, and she'd bored him more than anyone.

"I have appetites," he told her, "that you have no idea how to satisfy."

"You know me, Lord," she said silently. And he knew how she had been scorned, how she had begged and been scorned.

Tyree pulled the door to. She did not notice him leaving, but she knew when he was gone.

"You know me, Lord," she cried.

He knew that after Africana, she'd gone to the Jamaican woman and got rid of Roland's next baby. Jesus knew it. Jesus knew how hateful Roland could be. He taunted her with Africa, knowing she was so afraid of it, afraid of savages and snakes, and more and more babies, with no doctors and no buildings, but tents like soldiers' and bare feet and bad food and headaches so bad they would go down her neck and make her see shapes and go faint and fall out. Jesus knew that Abby Ann had taken her to the Jamaican woman and brought her back, and threatened to tell whenever Blanche made her angry. Jesus knew it all. He'd seen how she rubbed up against Tyree in her black mourning dresses, because she had nowhere to go but back to her nasty father, and because Abby Ann insisted, saying that she'd have no prospects if they weren't a part of the Quick household.

Lord God knew that she tried to make good with Tyree. She'd borne him a child even though, after what the Jamaican woman did, it nearly killed her. She'd taken up the fur business to buy things for herself and the children and to give money to Abby Ann, who always threatened to tell. She worked hard and paid her debt and never told Tyree, because his family meant everything to him, and he'd never have understood about the baby and about how Roland was so hateful and pregnancy so hard for her. Jesus knew that she would keep on with the furs, even though they were making her sick. They were. She could feel it.

"Blanche!"

Della was calling her from downstairs. The family had gathered in the parlor for a formal goodbye to Mercer Gray. Aunt Zilpha was leaving. Tyree had taken Manny downstairs to see her off. Manny had come around to liking Mercer. Everyone liked her. They liked her children too. They liked them better than they'd ever loved Blanche. Dear God, she prayed, there are many kinds of bondage. Jesus, free me from my sin.

. . .

Mercer and her children sat together on the couch, with Mercer's
new leather travel bag next to her feet. Harriet played the piano
and they sang.

> God be with you
> God be with you
> God be with you till we meet again.

> God be with you
> God be with you
> God be with you till we meet again.

"Everyone should be here together."

"She's fallen asleep, Mama."

Della pursed her lips. "Can't you wake her? We talk about
the woman asleep as if she'd gone to meet her maker."

Tyree pursed his lips back at his mother.

"I'm just sayin if she's alive, she can be woke."

Tyree shook his head. "She's not so well this evening." He
did not want to get her. It was simpler like this. Abby Ann was out
at Ephraim's church for some service, and without Ephraim to
pontificate, Della would say a simple family prayer and they'd
leave quietly.

"This, just us, like this, Mama, this is fine."

His mother knew it but refused to let him alone. "Well, I
can call her, can't I? Is anything stopping me from calling her?"

Tyree shook his head.

"Blanche!"

Blanche smiled at the teeny tiny voice so far away.

"Almighty God," she whispered, "unto whom all hearts are
open and from whom no secrets are hid . . ."

The words floated to her. She praised and blessed God in
her heart. She felt lifted off the bed, where the bloodstain

showed through the scrubbed and sunned white linen. Sweet Jesus, had to be, lifted her gently, just so, just as black nursemaids lifted little white babies out of their carriages into the breeze.

Downstairs, Della gave up with a snort. She looked at Mercer. "I wish I had a nickel for every time that heifer sits up there and doesn't answer me."

Then she stood in the middle of the floor with her arms open. "Come on."

The Quicks linked arms. Mercer and her children joined the circle. Tyree put his arm around her waist. Having just taken his wife, he felt no less lustful. Mercer's shoulder was broad and solid against him.

"Lord, God," Della said, "you know these are wicked times. It pleased you to bring us this far by faith. It pleased you to wake us up this morning, Lord, and in our right minds. Be with the men in jail for doing your will. Be with them. Be with us. Be with this woman who you have brought to freedom within our midst. We thank you for Mercer and for these children who are free.

"God bless us and keep us while we are absent, one from another."

It was dark enough to leave. Tyree would drive them. For half an hour they hugged and wished farewells, until Zilpha stood by the door and ordered Tyree and Mercer to come with her.

The remaining family and Mercer's children shuffled into the kitchen. They did not bother to set the table for supper. Instead, they ate with their fingers from bowls lined with old linen. Zilpha and Tyree and Mercer, they knew, would soon be eating the same supper out of the basket that Della had packed for them (and nagged Tyree not to forget): boiled eggs and biscuits folded over Zilpha's spiced peach preserves or honey or filled with shin meat, bacon, or cheese.

"Blanche. Nobody's gonna bring you your supper tonight."

Della poured a glass of sherry for her and Manny, as if this were a holiday or a funeral.

She winked at Manny. "I just don't want her to think I forget so easy." Then she yelled: "You hear me, Blanche!"

Blanche heard, but she wasn't hungry. She lay back on Jesus, lay right back on his chest. He held her in sinewy, olive-skinned arms that smelled of hot sand and sun, and he kissed her with lips that tasted of wine. Then she saw herself sitting at the well, and she heard the singing:

Jesus met the woman at the well
Jesus met the woman at the well
Jesus met the woman at the well
And he told her everything she had done.

He said, "Woman, Woman, where is your husband?"
He said, "Woman, Woman, where is your husband?"
He said, "Woman, Woman, where is your husband?"
And she told him, Lord, she had none.

The voice moved up and down her spine, and Jesus looked into her eyes as the voice moved. He looked into her dark and dirty hiding places until he found her naked, cringing soul.

Then she was in the church. (*She went runnin, runnin, all through the city / She went runnin, runnin, all through the city . . .*) She lay on the floor by the altar, her face to the floor. The floor was cold, and she lay on it until the cold worked into her skin. She waited for a simple lash to give her stripes and pain, but he knew her too well. The lash was too easy. A force like a hurricane blew her body back, ripping her hands off the altar, and casting her, spinning, toward the darkness, down to where she deserved to fall, toward chaos and confusion and death.

Jesus caught her.

He caught her before the darkness swallowed her up and held her in arms that smelled like fresh sweat and sun and did not let her fall. From far away she heard herself crying. He was letting her touch the side where they'd pierced him.

"Why," he asked, "dost thou doubt me?"

The night was cold and black and fine. Mercer sat bundled in a scarf and shawl beside Tyree, Zilpha in the back. The soreness that had scratched at the back of her throat was gone. She felt stronger than she had since her escape.

"Road feels lonely now," Mercer said.

"It is lonely, isn't it?"

"So to speak." Lonely wasn't quite it. She felt alert, excited, secret. He felt the same. She knew it. It had caught her off guard that afternoon. Now she was ready for it.

"I thought Mr. Sharkey was going to drive us."

"He was."

"How come you're drivin instead?"

Tyree laughed into the darkness. "Because my Aunt Zilphie is a naughty old woman."

"Oh."

Mercer said nothing for a long while. Then, softly, "Getting free has cost me dear. I didn't do it just to be somebody's piece o' brownskin. And I'm not blamin you. I'm not saying this is all you and not me. I'm just telling you what I told myself this afternoon after you left."

"And I didn't get married to break my vows, either."

"You ain't broke nothin. Not with me."

"Not yet."

Mercer humphed.

"There. We've made our statements of intent. We intend to be virtuous," Tyree said. "Now may we enjoy our ride together?"

"You're laughing at me."

"I'd never laugh at you."

"Yessir, you would."

"Call me Tyree."

Mercer shook her head. "You don't care, do you?"

"Life is short. My folk live longer than most, and life is still short. Call me Ty."

She humphed. "I couldn't. What'll you call me?"

"Well, now that we've made promises to be good, I've decided to call you Sugarplum. What's the harm?"

Their shoulders touched as the carriage jostled. "Tell me about Canada," she said.

They arrived in the middle of the night. Zilpha led the way into the shuttered cottage. She and Mercer slept in her bedroom, Tyree on a chair in the front room.

At dawn, Zilpha made a fire in the stove and went outside to check her garden. On this trip to Philadelphia she'd been gone only a week, so she knew directly that a thief had been through. The few heads of cabbage at the end of the garden nearest the road had been snapped off and three pumpkins stolen. Zilpha would deal with the theft later that day. First, she'd see Tyree off and open up the house again, with Mercer's help.

Tyree left early, with only a wave and no more teasing. Sad and relieved, Mercer watched him go.

"Feels dull when he leaves, doesn't it?" Zilpha asked.

Mercer agreed mildly, remembering what Tyree had said about her and wondering why she'd make mischief in her own family.

Then it was time to work. They aired and dusted and scrubbed the small house and then went to the garden. Zilpha had planted carrots earlier in the month and now set Mercer to separating them and covering the bed with straw. Over the winter they'd rest, Zilpha said, then first thing in the spring, with luck, they'd grow again, and she'd have carrots by April. Toward the end of the day, she sent Mercer out with a bushel basket and wearing an old pair of trousers, to pick apples. They stored them in rows separated by straw in a tiny cellar under the front room. By evening, Mercer ate her boiled dinner gratefully. After they washed, Zilpha made up Mercer's bed just across from her own in the little whitewashed room with crooked walls.

"My husband, Shadd, and I built this on," she said proudly.

"I don't need that many," Mercer said as Zilpha piled on three, then four, then five pillows. "I can just sleep on my arm, and we'll save the linen."

"No, you don't sleep flat. Not here. You sleep on an angle. Too much congestion of the lungs here in the North. Cold weather'll set in any day, and you need to be propped. Now come on into the front room."

Zilpha closed the door to the bedroom, led Mercer to the kitchen, and made them a tonic of vinegar and honey, diluted with water. After they drank it, Zilpha sat down by the stove to smoke a small pipe. She said it helped the breathing passages. Halfway into the bowl of tobacco, Zilpha closed her eyes.

"Gabriel was a good father," she said, "far as that goes. But mostly he were away on ships, in service to Captain Dandridge. Captain's dead now, like Gabriel, but his family live up in that house. I were a slave in the family until I made twenty-eight years old. That was the freedom law."

"Then you married Shadd?"

"Naw. Time I got free, me and Shadd been married five years and I'd had my two boys."

"Two boys?"

"Yep, two baby boys. Measles took 'em both at the same time. Thought I'd lose my mind. Measles. That's why I hate to see Christmas come. That's when they died, in December."

"Never had any more?"

"I couldn't stand to." She let out a hard little sigh through her nose. "See, good thing you came in the winter. Keep me company."

Zilpha set down her pipe and went into the bedroom. Mercer heard bumps and thuds. When Zilpha came out, she carried an old gun in her arms.

"Have I thanked you for having me here?"

Zilpha barked out a laugh. "What? Think maybe I'm needin some thanks, huh?"

"I was thinkin while you were gone. I didn't expect you to come out loaded up, though."

"They shamed me into taking you, you know. They did. I'll tell the tale on my own self. After I spend a week or two with Little Black Bea, and her drinkin that stuff every chance she gets, and Della shoutin all the time, and my poor little brother half crippled, and the damn fleas and the noisy, dirty, stinkin streets, I tell you the truth, I don't want no damn company. I just want to be right back here all by myself. Tyree, maybe. He comes to visit, but the rest of them niggers can stay right there. . . . I don't mind, though. I likes livin with women if they know how to work. Can't stand no lazy women."

She sat down again with the gun and a handful of rags and a can of oil. Then she commenced to clean the gun as she talked.

"I tell you, over there, when I were a girl, they had a whole bunch of servants." She motioned in the direction of the Dandridge house, a mile away. Mercer knew where she meant. Tyree had pointed out the house on their way in and told her that Dandridge had deeded four acres to Gabriel, and Gabriel left it to Zilpha and Shadd.

"Mostly girls, so we all lived together, naturally. Then they got this indenture man, and they tried to put him in our wing of the house. Well, they locked him in his room at night, the headman did, the man who was in charge of all of us, him and his wife. They put the new man in the room, and they buttoned the door. And we could hear him in there at night, half the night long, rockin the bed. Humpin like he had a woman in there. He tried to be quiet, but we could hear him. We could even hear him breathin hard. Nasty old he-goat. And we had to change his nasty old bed. After a while nobody would do it. I likes living with women. You don't have none of that."

Zilpha proclaimed it sleeping time, but she did not get into her bed when she ordered Mercer to go. Instead, she reassembled her shotgun and dressed in four layers of clothes, including Mercer's shawl.

"This is good wool," she said, wrapping it around her head over her own hat and shawl. "Where'd you get it?"

"Miss Harriet brought it to me from the secondhand man."

"That Harriet's a clever woman, ain't she?"

"Yes, ma'am."

"Go to bed. I'ma be right outside."

Propped on pillows, Mercer slept fitfully. She went into and out of sleep, forgetting each time where she was. The gunshots, two of them, sounded as if they'd gone off next to her ear. She sat straight up and heard Zilpha's heavy step in the front room. Zilpha came into the bedroom, holding her gun. She took off her outer layers and lay on the bed in her clothes.

"I got a piece of him," she said into the dark. "We'll see in the morning did I get any hide. Come stealing food offa my table. Snappin off cabbages. Pickin my damn pumpkins."

She grumbled and fell asleep.

Mercer covered Zilpha and waited on her pillows until dawn. Just before light, the birds began their noise. Cardinals whistled, crows cawed, and innumerable brown songbirds warbled in the woods. Mercer dressed and went outside, steeling herself for the sight of a corpse in the pumpkins. Bluebirds, blue like nothing else in nature, swooped among the tall branches of the ash trees on the edge of the wood behind the garden. Frost covered the stubble grass. The earth looked cold, but also furry and friendly.

In the weeks that followed, Zilpha found laundry for Mercer to take in, and said that she should give Zilpha a quarter from every dollar to pay for her room. Zilpha herself returned to nursing jobs in the neighborhood. In the afternoons and evenings, they prepared for winter. Mercer delighted in Zilpha's ample provisions. Her appreciation confirmed Zilpha's opinion of her sensibleness.

"Look at these gooseberries."

"I'll tell you about those gooseberries," Zilpha said. "I went to whitewash the fruit trees for insects in the spring, and I look and see when I finished I have some left. So I poured it in that ditch that drains right along the gooseberry bushes. And this year—the best gooseberries you ever tasted."

Together, the women put up jars of gooseberry jam, applesauce, and spiced peaches with cinnamon and sugar that Zilpha had brought in quantity from Philadelphia. They smoked grouse that Zilpha shot ("The Lord made grouse so old women could hit") and a quarter of a hog that she bought from a German farmer who lived nearby. Mercer chopped and bundled kindling and stacked it a short distance from the house. She split logs and chopped them in quarters to fit into the stove.

In a week, Zilpha heard that the son of a woman in town had been shot in the back of the leg. She hurried home to tell Mercer.

"Said they were out hunting. He was huntin for some more of my pumpkins is what he was huntin for. What he got was a hole in the leg. I hope it learns him. The whole damn family is lazy. They so lazy they keep their firewood indoors. No wonder they boy likes to steal. Well, he won't steal from me no more."

Twice a week, before the vinegar-and-honey tonic, Zilpha would announce that it was time to write letters. Dutifully, the two women labored to write to their families. Besides the shooting, little happened. Their lives went according to Zilpha's unvarying routine.

After a couple of weeks, Mercer felt as if the world had become quieter—and more vivid. One afternoon, as she sat in the kitchen peeling carrots, the color of them struck her, as if, until now, she'd been peeling carrots through a veil. Gorgeous and simple and rich, orange stained the tips of her fingers. Zilpha's frugal fire danced delicately in the stove. Mercer's pleasure spread through her, splendid and thorough. It trickled through her like the streams that watered the Delaware Valley, flowing from hills far away and washing down to the city, into the high reservoir and waterworks, and down through locks and cast-iron pipes that fed the hydrants behind the houses where her children now lived.

"Looka this, Miz Zilpha. Look at the color of this one here."

Zilpha did not turn her head. Mercer waited. She'd learned that Zilpha never did two things at once, that she stopped one activity completely in order to give even brief attention to another. It was one of the reasons she did not like the city or children. Zilpha rolled her dough on the pin and set it perpendicular to the edge of the board.

"That one there?" She pointed with a floury finger.

"Yeah."

"Uh-hunh."

But Zilpha was looking instead at Mercer's fingers as she held the knife in one hand and the carrot in the other.

"Look how strong and straight your fingers is," she said, spreading her own hands for comparison. "And looka these."

The tips of her fingers turned toward the pinkie, and the knuckles were swollen with arthritis.

"Looks like they been out in the wind, don't they?" She laughed mirthlessly. "How long you think they'll serve an old woman who lives by herself?"

There was no answer Mercer could make.

"Cut me off a piece o' that," Zilpha said into the silence. "Now you've showed me how pretty it is, gives me a taste. Still got teeth. That's a blessing."

A month passed uneventfully. Harriet wrote to tell them that the children were well and learning faster than all their schoolmates, and that Etta seemed to have an aptitude for playing the piano. Then she wrote to ask Mercer to please visit her abolitionist friend Eliza Ruffin. She also sent a copy of a slim volume called *The Narrative of the Life of Frederick Douglass, An American Slave,* and she outlined briefly Douglass's career as a writer and lecturer.

Mercer sat down next to Zilpha, who handed her the lap board Shadd Nelson had made for her to do fine work. Mercer turned Harriet's letter upside down and began to write in careful indigo scrawl between the lines. Harriet used black ink.

"Harriet says Miss Ruffin has an abolition group, and I should visit them. Since somebody helped me, I should help too. I think Harriet is right."

"Like I was thinkin'," Zilpha said as she combed her hair, "could get took back yourself."

It was Friday, the day she aired her hair in the sun, weather permitting, like white women. Having aired it earlier, Zilpha now combed and plaited it. She was vain about her hair—she dyed it with a blacking brush and wrapped it in a navy-blue cloth in the rain to keep it from running—but she kept her vanity, like most things, to herself. Mercer couldn't help but feel sorry for Bea, the much younger sister, whose hair had fallen out during a childhood fever and never grown back.

"And once they're onto you, they might well come after me too."

Mercer stopped writing. "Do you think so?"

Zilpha smiled. "Probably not."

Seven / Make Your Mark

Mercer and Zilpha rose at dawn. The sky promised a fine day: dry, at least, with only a gentle wind. Walking weather, Zilpha called it, and good thing too, because Mercer had walking to do. Miss Eliza Ruffin's house was almost five miles away. Zilpha cautioned Mercer to leave at least an hour and a half to get there, and not to be late, repeating one of her favorite sayings: "You wanna know the difference between a nigger and a Negro? A half an hour."

Zilpha stirred the embers in the stove. The fire crackled into life as they washed and dressed in the dark. After tea and bread, Zilpha left to do her day's nursing work and Mercer began hanging the clothes she'd left to soak the night before.

The linen was heavy and wet. Mercer squeezed it with numb fingers and shook it hard. It snapped in the morning's silence, disturbing the birds who, having finished their loud first-light singing, had flocked to the slanting sun on the east-facing eaves of Gabriel's whitewashed cottage. Mercer snapped again and again. Each time, a cold spray of water wet her face. At first she tucked her chin, but then it came to her that her face took water better than her head. So she blinked and let the water fly, as she listened to the birds flutter with each crack of the fabric. Mercer felt the solidity of the brown earth under her feet and the contrast between her cold face and hands and her body, warm with exertion. The muscles of her back began to pull each time she raised her hands over her head. She did not think about her meeting.

Before noon, Mercer ate a soup of onions and potatoes. Then she took in the laundry. She sprinkled it and put on the finger covers that Zilpha had cut from old gloves over the years to protect the white linen from snags where her skin cracked around her nails or stains when it broke open and bled. Mercer ironed half the load by half past one. Then she banked the fire, closed the shutters, and pulled on a gray wool cape Harriet had given her. She was warm from the iron and the fire, and her palms were smooth and shiny from the starchy linen. She did not wash off the starch; her hands were too sore and dry.

Mercer walked fast. Harriet's letter, which she had successfully put out of her mind, came back to her. It reminded her, after a brief few weeks of serenity, of the fragility of her freedom. She felt herself becoming anxious. One fugitive wrote that the price of freedom was eternal vigilance. The Quicks had read her these things, but Mercer was beginning to know them for herself. She looked at the green-and-brown valley with vigilant eyes. Fields dotted with cabbage and kale and bright winter squash suddenly lost their safety. She was no longer protected from her pursuers but made conspicuous for them. She felt foolish to walk abroad on the open road with her long stride and powerful thighs, as if she were a citizen. Neat stone farms, springhouses, ice-houses and smokehouses; corn cribs and barns; water wheels spinning in fast-running creeks; fat cows and black-and-white goats with teats full of milk, chickens and roosters and hens that laid tiny green-and-white eggs: these were other people's—white people's—resources, as they always had been, not a common wealth she could share. Behind the window curtains, slave catchers and kidnappers could be hiding; people who would aid and abet her capture; people who would watch and applaud, or would look on indifferently, or, pitying her, would only shake their heads, as they might if a neighbor's dog were hit by a dray. They'd shake their heads and suck their tongues through thin lips like a gash in their faces, and return, gratefully, to their money and milk-fed children, and even the most well-meaning of them would fall back on the rock-bottom fact of human intercourse: better you than me. By the time Mercer arrived at Eliza Ruffin's house, she was rigid with distrust.

A blond woman with a blunt face opened the door. Behind her came Eliza Ruffin, dressed in a brown dress cut simply from rich fabric. She was tall but slight. She advanced with both hands extended and took Mercer's cold and shiny bare hands in her own soft ones.

"I am very grateful to you for agreeing to meet me. We cast a wide net among our Vigilant friends, but we could not know whether you would respond—or even where you were," she said.

Eliza Ruffin led Mercer into the alcove of a dark-green parlor. They sat next to a small fire, and the housemaid took Mercer's cloak before going to make tea. After the bright-blue day, the parlor felt private and dark. Then Ruffin explained her interest, as president of the Ladies Anti-Slavery Society, in the welfare of fugitives, and especially female fugitives, and especially Mercer. But beyond that, Ruffin admitted: "I have another particular interest in your case, and it is this: Passmore Williamson is my dear cousin. He's been in Moyamensing Prison for close to a month now, and our lawyers cannot seem to get him out."

Mercer studied Ruffin's face for resentment or blame. She had clear brown eyes and lush, wavy hair. No doubt she was about to ask Mercer to do something to help Williamson. Mercer owed the man a great deal. But how much did she owe him? Was this woman with her clear-eyed welcome about to ask Mercer to go back? Maybe the anti-slavery people had had enough of doing good. Maybe Williamson had had enough of prison and figured it was time for a switch. Maybe it was Mercer's turn in the barrel.

"What we'd hoped," said Miss Ruffin, "was that the lawyers could have him purged of contempt. We'd hoped that by his asserting vigorously—and honestly, of course—that he was unable to produce you and your children in court, he would be freed.

"Well, but, naturally, he cannot make such testimony unless he is allowed to appear in court, and he cannot appear so long as the judge holds him in contempt. The legal complications go on, but that's the outline, the sketch of it all. The lawyers have been to the Pennsylvania Superior Court, but they've ruled against us, so there's an end to it. Or not really an end, as they always say, because lawyers never give up, like people with things to sell, I suppose."

She smiled a little.

Mercer smiled back warily. "What do you think I can do to help you?" she asked.

"Well, your Captain Pryor has said that you and your children were abducted—kidnapped, actually—and that Passmore and Mr. Still and the rest must stay to answer charges, and really, the charges are ridiculous: riot—riot, mind you—forcible abduction, assault and battery, that sort of thing. And for Passmore, it's worst, because he's white, and the law holds him more responsible than the others. Our lawyers, his lawyers, think that if you were to swear an affidavit, witnessed by some third or fourth disinterested party—we'd retain another lawyer for the purpose—that you left of your own free will and Passmore did not abduct you, why, then, that might help his case."

Flushed, she finished with an uncharacteristic flourish.

"What is an affidavit, Miss Ruffin?"

Eliza Ruffin seemed eager to explain that Mercer would not be required to do more than tell her version of the story to the lawyers, who would write it down and have her make her mark at the bottom. They would swear in court that it was she who had given the testimony and she who had signed it.

"It's a petition, really, that's all."

"But won't they want to see me in court?"

Impatience crept into Ruffin's voice. "At this point, as I've said, no one is asking you to do any more than file a petition."

"I'm not ungrateful, Miss Ruffin. I am very, very grateful. I'm grateful for what everyone has done. I'm grateful to you now for talking to me and for giving me this choice. But what I'm learning, Miss Ruffin, is that being free costs dear. Now, mind, it's not that I won't pay. I'm just trying to find out what all it's gonna cost this time."

"It is quite likely that having received your affidavit, the judge will want to see you produced. Passmore is in prison for failing to answer the writ of habeas corpus. In other words, he has to stay in jail because he cannot produce your body."

"Produce my body."

"Yes. So you're quite astute to see that at some point, the people who have claimed to have seen you may also be asked to—"

"Produce my body."

"Just so." Ruffin made a quick little sigh. "But at each step it is your decision. Filing an affidavit does not obligate you to appear in court sometime later. You must know that."

Mercer knew nothing of the sort. What she knew was that with this affidavit business, she'd be jumping onto a moving train. She might be on it already.

"I'll file the affidavit, Miss Ruffin."

Ruffin sighed again. Her clear eyes had been hiding the extent of her anxiety. "Excellent."

They drank their tea, and somehow, while they chatted, Mercer found that she had agreed to return the next day at the same time to appear at Ruffin's anti-slavery meeting. Nothing was required of her, Ruffin said, except to appear and, perhaps, to answer a few questions. The following day, some anti-slavery friend, as Ruffin described him, would come to transport Mercer to New York, where two lawyers would take her testimony. The men must be able to swear that they'd seen her in New York, Ruffin said, in order to keep Pryor and his agents from combing through Philadelphia's anti-slavery coalition and finding her and her children. Mercer agreed.

Refusing Ruffin's offer of a servant and gig to take her home, she walked briskly in the gray-and-blue dusk. Pryor had done what he could. Now she would make her next move. The thought of action made her feel less at his mercy and less at the mercy of courts and judges and laws and marshals and officers who played by rigged sets of rules.

He run, he run, he run his best. He run right into the hornets' nest.

Could happen, she thought.

The Ladies Anti-Slavery Society meeting took place most weeks in a room off the Quaker meetinghouse that the Society shared with a temperance group. But because the temperance people had planned a special event for this afternoon, the Ladies Society agreed to meet at Eliza Ruffin's house. Harriet's letter had explained the group to Mercer, by way of convincing her to visit Ruffin. The Ladies Society was not just an outgrowth of a men's group but their own proper organization. They were Negro and white women together, and one of the colored women was a co-chairwoman (not, as Harriet explained often happened in mixed groups, the helper). In principle, they occasionally met in one of the members' houses, because they believed that women who worked together should not be ashamed to entertain each other in their homes (although in practice, they met at Eliza Ruffin's, and no one protested, or even took much notice, that they did not alternate). As opposed to many groups that abhorred slavery but cared little for equality, the Ladies Society believed that achieving the "elevation of the freemen" by fighting discrimination in the North was inseparable, as the promoters of the year's colored national convention put it, from "the great work of the slave's restoration to freedom." They sponsored lectures and informal talks and fairs like everyone else, but mostly they liked their abolition radical.

By the time Mercer arrived, a dozen women, four of them

colored, were assembled in the upstairs parlor. They had arranged themselves in a half-circle around the table where Eliza Ruffin sat pouring tea. The late afternoon was sunny and cold, but Eliza Ruffin's fire was just the slightest bit warmer than the one she'd had lit the day before in the downstairs parlor. Two ruddy-faced women shared a large chair and talked loudly about the virtues of not eating red meat. They moved on to the subject of vigorous exercise; then, in genteel language, and with giggles, to moderation in conjugal relations.

"Mr. Graham has worked out quite a specific regimen, and he says without question that it will relieve debility."

"The Mr. Graham who makes the crackers?"

"The same, yes."

"Relieve or prevent?"

"Excuse me. Prevention, of course—as in all matters of health, our first concern—but the system relieves as well."

"Priscilla is a wonderful advertisement. You are the picture of health."

"She always was."

"Well, yes, I've been blessed. But this regimen—"

"This regimen, my eye. Beth put her finger on it. Priscilla has never been sick a day in her life. I know, you see, Priscilla. I was there when your mother, my aunt Ruth, fed your family a lovely, rare chop every morning, noon, and night. I never saw so much meat. Red, quite red. And kept you in the house by the hour. You were the picture of health then, and you're the picture of health now."

"Well, I say like Sojourner Truth said: 'Is God dead?' What I mean is: Do Mr. Graham and these other people who presume to keep one alive forever, do they talk about the restorative powers of prayer. I've seen it, you know." She slapped her thigh several times. Merriment sneaked shamefully out of the room. The women, all but a couple, hung their heads or else looked reverently at the speaker's ample thigh and the pudgy hand that patted it.

"They said I'd never walk. Some of you here prayed for me. Don't you remember? And I didn't have to give up meat to do it. The tender hand of God touched me right here."

Again she whacked the recovered thigh, harder. Mercer began to think it was taking a little too much punishment for a limb that had been ailing.

Eliza Ruffin moved to stand next to Mercer's chair, and the stout woman's hand settled in her lap. Then she introduced Mercer to the group, saying that she could not tell them Mercer's former name, or the circumstances of her liberation, or even how long she'd been out of the South. Some of them had guessed who Mercer was, and they would tell the others later. It pleased them, however, to strike a note of secrecy in their meetings and to remind themselves of the gravity of their actions.

"I can say, however, that this woman's courage has made an indelible impression on me, and I think I can also say that she'd be willing to inform us—from her own experience—about the institution we've all sworn to erase from this country."

They clapped, surprisingly quietly, and began to fuss over Mercer's chair and her tea and what to put into it and whether or not she wanted a cake.

To Mercer, these women were a curious lot, at once girlish and old-ladylike. A small copper-colored woman spoke to Mercer through teeth and lips that she barely moved as she talked, as if not to disturb them: "I think you'll find a dear, good friend in Eliza."

Then, for no apparent reason, she continued. "I was just telling someone the other day that the greatest wish of my life is quite simple: only to live quietly and modestly with a few dear friends and to do good in the world and make others better and happier."

Mercer smiled at her. So what? she thought. I like rhubarb pie. Who the hell asked you? Her sudden irritation surprised her.

"Do you do this often?"

"Beg pardon?"

"Do you often come to talk to groups like ours?"

"Oh, no, I've—"

Eliza Ruffin cut her off with an apologetic look. "Mercer's just begun this sort of work, and"—she looked toward her deferentially—"if I'm not incorrect, Mercer, you're deciding whether or not the work suits you."

Mercer nodded, realizing that she was supposed to go along with this cloaking of her identity. But if these women were truly friends of the slave, why should she have to be so secretive? She turned back to her tea. It was milky and sweet. Mercer sipped out of a cup so thin that she suspected she might bite it through if she didn't take care.

"Well, I think it most important to make others better; and if they are happier in the process, so much to the good," said the copper-colored lady.

Mercer could tell that her sips were too noisy. She could tell that from how they looked at her.

"Of course one is happier if one is better."

"Well." It came from the redhead who'd earlier refused to moderate her red-meat consumption and had laughed loudest about limiting marital relations. "I must admit that I am very, very happy in the summer at the seaside, when I'm not engaged in any work at all and I'm not being of any service to anyone. Is that wicked? It is, isn't it?"

"Of course," said the colored woman from behind those taut lips, " 'happy' is too simple a word. Being at the seaside makes us happy. A child eating a candy is happy. But making others' lives better, such as work with the downtrodden, brings a joy that is longer lasting and more profound."

The women shook their heads and moaned softly together. Well, Mercer guessed that that set her straight. Happy sneaked out of the room and joined merriment down the hall.

At risk of shattering her cup, Mercer finished her tea. Eliza Ruffin promptly refilled the cup.

How, then, did she go from sitting in their midst drinking

tea to standing before them, turned, with her skirts raised to let them see the scars on her thighs? She would look back, just days later, and be unable to recall. She did remember how they strained with attention, how they asked her one question after another: Who had done this to her? For what transgression? How long was she beaten? With what object? How old was she when it happened? What had she done about it? What did other slaves do to help her? Did it bleed? How had she healed? How much of her body did the scars cover? Were all her people treated likewise? Was that why she'd run away, to avoid more beatings?

The room darkened as evening approached. They closed the shutters and lit the lamps. The lamplight bounced off their faces and onto her legs, still bared, suffusing the room with the glow of their curiosity.

Had a man done this to her? Had he done it to take her virtue? Had he forced her?

They filled their eyes with her. They rubbed their clean, white fingers against each other impatiently, as men rubbed themselves, absently, when a woman walked by.

The skin of Mercer's forearm was mottled and shiny where she'd once been scalded. Maybe they'd like to have a look at that too. Or maybe the toe where the nail had dropped off that winter before she'd started working in the kitchen with Suzy, when people lost whole toes from being out tending to the animals, but she'd lost only a nail and a tip.

They wouldn't want to hear about that, though, she figured. They wanted the knock-down-drag-out. That much she could tell. They wanted the horse whip and pony whip, the green sapling branch, the leather belt and bridle cord. They wanted the old man with nubs for fingers standing in the circle of blows. *Did you bleed?* They wanted a crazy-ass overseer and her on the ground, twitching and calling for Jesus. Why? Why did they want it so? *Did you bleed?* They wanted her crying and snotting into the clay, dirty, filthy, violated. Why? *Did you bleed?* They wanted Jackson Pryor crooking his finger at her after dinner. Or better yet, beating her first. They wanted rape in the room with them—on her body, contained in her body, the better to keep them safe.

Did it hurt? Hurt bad? Did you bleed?

Mercer dropped her skirts. She had been looked at plenty.

Eliza Ruffin said, "I think we've asked enough of Mercer today."

They fetched her more tea and a little white cake with vanilla-butter icing. She ate it slowly and sat wanting more while they concluded their other business.

That night, Zilpha finished reading aloud the first book of Samuel. Mercer dreamt that God was calling Bennie, but Bennie did not know who was calling him.

"When're they taking you to New York?" Zilpha asked. The two women lay propped on pillows in their beds, as Zilpha had prescribed. The sky outside their small, square window had begun to lighten. Zilpha reached for the glass of water she left for herself on the nightstand each evening. She gargled two mouthfuls loudly and swallowed hard.

"Today."

"Well," Zilpha said, "I'll be sorry to see you go. You been good to have around, Mercer, and that's the God's truth."

"I thank you for having me." Mercer wondered where she'd be going after New York. "They might offer to bring me back here. It's only a day or two that they need me."

"You're welcome back anytime. I don't have no trouble outta you. You're clean, and you know how to do things right, and you know how to talk and how not to talk."

Mercer laughed. "Yes, ma'am."

Quiet and clean. Zilpha and Pryor liked her for similar reasons.

She forced herself out of the warm bed and into the cold room and cold clothes, and then outside into the colder thin stink of the privy, where she emptied Zilpha's chamber pot. She laughed to herself again. Zilpha would no doubt miss her. When she came back indoors she washed, and the two women ate oat porridge that had steeped overnight in the well of the cook stove. Zilpha had no job that day, so she sat in her chair and directed in minute detail Mercer's travel preparations.

"Take some food, now. Take enough for two and don't forget to offer it."

Mercer packed biscuits, a square of cheese, four strips of cold bacon, two boiled potatoes, and some pickled cucumbers and apples in a basket. At six, a sallow-faced man in burgundy-and-black livery called for her. He led her to a carriage and helped her in. In the corner sat an older white woman. She wore a gathered white cap on her silver hair, and a brown cape over a heavy brown frock.

"Come in," she said, looking accustomed to command. "My name is Mrs. Eugenia Pitts, and I will escort you to New York."

She did not ask Mercer about herself, or about what Mercer might know. Instead, she told her, in a pleasing voice, about Congress and the Senate; the Fugitive Slave Law and the case of Anthony Burns in Boston; the bloody confrontation in Christiana, Pennsylvania, not far from where Mercer had been staying, in which a master, hell-bent on reclaiming his slaves, was shot and killed by them as he attempted to enter their house. Mrs. Pitts told Mercer about her own private meetings with Frederick Douglass and nodded her approval on hearing that Zilpha and Mercer were reading his book already; she told her about Mary Shadd Cary, who edited a newspaper in Canada; and without asking whether Mercer could read and write, she urged her for her own and her children's sakes to learn to do so. Given her pleasing appearance and natural speaking ability, reported to Mrs. Pitts by the Anti-Slavery ladies, Mercer ought to consider speaking to groups of abolitionists and potential friends to the cause, just as she had done yesterday.

"You made a deep impression on those women," she said. "A few of them had never seen a former slave, or talked to one, and I am afraid that the propagandists from the South have so

thoroughly dominated the arguments that many perfectly reasonable people in the North think all Negroes quite degraded, inca-
pable of ever governing themselves, and as senseless of their
bondage as horses."

Later, when Mercer would hold in her hands the precious
copy of Douglass's *Narrative* given her by Mrs. Pitts ("You, of all
people, should have your own copy to keep, not a borrowed one"),
she'd reread a couple early sentences and remember that precise
moment in the carriage. "I have no accurate knowledge of my age,
never having seen any authentic record containing it. By far the
larger part of the slaves know as little of their ages as horses know
of theirs, and it is the wish of most masters within my knowledge
to keep their slaves thus ignorant."

She'd remember how they warmed their feet on hot bricks
on the floor. She'd remember Mrs. Pitts's musical voice, her vehement ideas, and her call to action. And Mercer—Mercer who
as Virginia had dreamt of freedom and acted upon it, Mercer the
daughter of Virgil, the runaway man, and Lily, the beautiful and
broken woman—this same Mercer would read Douglass's words:
"And behold, a man made into a brute," and recall how often she
had thought of herself as a mule, an old mule pulling uphill,
wanting nothing more than a mat to lie on and slop to eat.

But for now, the mention of horses merely made Mercer
vaguely uncomfortable amid her carriage-riding comfort. The
words stuck in her craw and in her memory, and the sound of
their own horses' hooves droned rhythmically in her ears as if to
mock her.

Mrs. Pitts ended her lecture abruptly. "Well, that's enough,
I think. That's as much as one body can take in for a morning. But
I do want to be of help to you, Mercer. I'd like to think of some-
thing else I can do for you, or maybe your children." She looked at
Mercer and then away.

"Can you think of anything offhand? Well, we'll come up
with something."

After a while, she settled into gossip about the men and

women in the abolitionist circles in New York. Mercer could hardly follow, because she did not know any of the people.

"Naomi Rutledge, whom you'll be sure to meet, was once the director of the New York Society for the Encouragement of Faithful Domestics. Can you believe that? Well, her own domestics, it seemed, were leaving at a frightful rate, and everyone except poor Naomi knew it was her husband. Changed her mind about the servant class, and that led her to abolition. Funny, the paths people take to this work."

She smiled indulgently, rested her head on the cushion, and closed her eyes.

"Would you care to share my lunch?" Mercer asked.

Mrs. Pitts opened her eyes and took her time observing Mercer. "You are quite natural, you know. It's delightful."

Then she closed her eyes again. "You should rest now," she advised Mercer. "You'll want all your strength in New York."

They crossed into New York on a ferry. Mercer could smell the city halfway across the river. She remembered that Tyree did not like New York. As a young man, he'd heard accounts of the anti-abolition riots there in the thirties. One colored woman reported seeing a mob of five white men going into an apartment where a colored woman had recently given birth. They raped the woman and threw her three-day-old baby out the window.

"I see New York," Tyree said, "and all I want to do is keep going north."

At the dock, hack drivers shouted at them. Eugenia Pitts seemed undisturbed by the commotion. She raised her hand and waved at a man half a block away. Jumping down from his seat, he ran to them. He had long arms and a limp. He loaded their bags in his hands and under his arms until his torso was hidden, and then he bustled them back to the trap.

"This is my brother's driver," Mrs. Pitts said by way of introduction. To him she said sternly: "There's not enough room."

"I'm sorry, Mrs. Pitts."

"You know better than that. I left word to bring the carriage."

"I'll sit in the back," Mercer said.

The driver nodded gratefully. "Yes, yes."

"You can't do that."

Mercer shrugged. It was silly to argue. Mrs. Pitts wasn't sitting in the back.

"Well, then, let's get out of the filthy street."

They'd picked their way through excrement: from stray dogs and cats, and from horses, and, in alleys, from outdoor people. Pigeons picked the droppings for corn; rats scurried from the sewers in broad daylight to raid the graying carcass of a dead horse and piles of garbage waiting for collection. And from every dark corner, under every stone archway, wafted the smell of urine.

Then, on the main streets, away from the wharves, Mercer began to see the size of the city—and the number of people. Bunches of New Yorkers waited on corners. They rode in every kind of public and private conveyance and pulled all sorts of carts. They ran and walked and dodged the cars. They went into and out of hundreds of shops. They ate on the street and spat onto the ground and yelled and bought and sold. Dirty, poorly clad white children hawked their wares on the streets too, faces red and pocked, noses running snot. Look what they do to their own, Mercer thought. No wonder colored orphanages got burned down.

New York made Philadelphia seem modest by comparison. The buildings were taller; the streets twice as wide. Here Mercer felt safe from detection, yet vulnerable to dangers she couldn't even imagine.

They stopped briefly at the home of Eugenia Pitts's brother. The street had been swept and the steps washed. Only a few carriages clattered past. The house was a large gray-stone town house, empty of the family but full of servants. They took Mrs. Pitts to one room and Mercer to another. Mercer washed self-consciously in a blue-and-white china bowl with soap the color and shape of an eggshell. Then she dried herself, changed her blouse, and put her hat back on. The water and towel were so dirty that she looked for a place to empty them, and ended up sloshing her skirt.

"I'll take that," the maid said from behind her.

Mercer was glad that Eugenia Pitts had already gone downstairs to wait for her.

"Hurry," she called. "They're expecting us."

In the lawyers' New York office, in the muffled quiet of green baize and dark wood, Mr. Henry, the lawyer, gave instructions to the clerk who would take her statement. Then he spoke to Mercer.

"I will take this statement into a court of law," he said.

His voice was full of importance. Clearly he doubted whether Mercer understood the gravity of the situation. "You must assure me that every word is true and that the overall meaning given is completely true; nothing included that need not be and nothing wanting."

Mercer said, "I understand, sir. I understood when Mr. Williamson and Mr. Still were good enough to come to my aid in Philadelphia."

Mr. Henry turned abruptly to leave the room. "Begin," he said to the clerk, whose name Mercer never caught.

"State of New York, City and County of New York." The clerk read as he wrote. "Virginia Pryor, being sworn, makes oath and says . . ."

He examined her with pale-blue eyes behind thick spectacles. Mercer would have to use her old name. It no longer fit.

"Now you," he said.

"My name is Virginia Pryor, and I was the slave of Captain Pryor of Virginia; he received me from his father, who owned my parents. I have two children, the youngest between six and seven years old, the oldest between twelve and thirteen; and one more child in Virginia, between two and three, who I never expect to see again in this life."

Mercer paused to collect her thoughts and tell the story.

"If I may," said the clerk. "Not who you are but what happened on the afternoon of October first, 1855."

Mercer ignored him. She was talking, and Mr. Clerk-Without-a-Name would have to wait. He puffed his cheeks and blew out. "I'm losing my thought," Mercer said blandly. "I'll have to think some more."

She began with Pryor's bringing her to Philadelphia, and the hotel, the chambermaid who would not help them, and Nig-Nag, who did, and the boat and the rescue. At the end, the clerk nodded his head, as if to signal that she'd finished, but she hadn't.

"Please," she said, pausing again to think how to make an end to her story.

The clerk made a show of looking restless. Too bad, Mercer thought. He'd have to wait before it was time to run to Mr. Henry with the big voice and get himself another job to do. He'd have to spend more of his precious time writing down the words of a Negro woman. Too bad.

"I don't want to go back," she said.

"Of course not," the clerk said.

"No, sir, please write that down too."

"What?"

"I don't want to go back."

"Oh." He pressed his lips together hard and wrote.

"I could have gone in Philadelphia if I had wanted to. I could go now, but I had rather die than go back. I wish to make this statement before the . . . magistrate, because I understand that Mr. Williamson is in prison on my account, and I hope the truth may benefit him. . . . There, now. Thank you."

"Put your mark above your name here."

"I can write my name."

"It's already written. Kindly make your mark."

Eight / Hard Swearing

The judge did not release Williamson. He was to produce
Mercer's body, and the bodies of her children, or else the
court must know why not. His earlier statement, that Mercer and
the children had never been in his "custody, power, or posses-
sion," was not good enough. Months later, in his final opinion,
Judge Wells revealed his pique at Mercer,

> a person who informs the Court that she is one of the
> Negroes who escaped from Mr. Pryor, . . . and presents to
> me certain reasons, founded as she supposes in law, where-
> fore I ought to quash the writ heretofore issued. . . . Were
> she a party, to abide the action of the Court, she would have
> a right to be heard according to the forms of law; were she a
> witness, called by a party, her identity ascertained, she
> might be examined as to all facts supposed to be within her
> knowledge. But our records cannot be opened to every
> stranger who volunteers to us a suggestion as to what may
> have been our errors, and how we may repair them.

After they presented their surprise affidavit and their arguments, the lawyers returned to New York, convinced that they
had made a difference, although not an immediate one. Indeed,
though he still tended to favor the rights of the United States'

distinguished, slaveholding ambassador, Judge Wells began to negotiate with Williamson's lawyers more willingly. "They want him to come back contrite," Mr. Henry said to Mercer and Eugenia Pitts, "or the original ruling will be shown to be bad and Williamson to have been imprisoned for two months without cause. Whatever the legal merits, that's what you see happening."

The New York lawyer was paid for services and travel expenses by Williamson's friends in the anti-slavery community, and the case in Philadelphia droned on, the lawyers and judge now arguing minutely about what testimony the court would accept from Williamson as a request to be purged of contempt.

Mercer followed the news in New York through abolitionists. The lawyers had asked that she remain in the city for a couple of weeks following the filing of the affidavit. Eugenia Pitts put her up at a boardinghouse run by a couple named Brooks. He was tall, thin, and dark; she was short, plump, and pale. They informed her that they were temperance people, Baptists, and special friends of Mrs. Pitts. Then they laughed, as they did frequently, and when the woman laughed, she snorted. They were members of the Underground, had obviously known Eugenia Pitts for years, and took seriously her admonition to watch Mercer. Aside from a few trips to the market with Mrs. Brooks, Mercer did not go out. She saw the other boarders in the halls, but the Brookses brought her to their private quarters to take her meals with them. Mrs. Pitts stayed with her brother's family and came in hired hacks to collect Mercer for abolitionist events.

One took place in the schoolroom of an African Methodist Episcopal church and featured the famous ex-slave speaker William Wells Brown. He was a nattily dressed, handsome man with tan features and shoulder-length black hair. People who liked colored people called him proud; others called him arrogant. In an expressive voice, he described preparing older slaves for auction. His job was to black their hair, dress them, and make them dance so that they'd look younger and fetch a higher price. He said that as they danced, tears ran down their cheeks.

Tears flowed in the schoolroom as well. Mercer watched the audience. She wanted to feel what they felt, but she did not. She felt numb. Wells Brown took notice of her. He let his shiny brown eyes sparkle at her. What a shame, she thought, to have done it. Then to stand in front of all these people and tell the tale.

After the talk, Wells Brown made a point of coming to speak to Mercer. She thanked him politely for his message.

"You have a story, don't you?" he asked.

Conversation around them quieted.

"Not like the stories you've told, sir."

"Stories? I'll tell you a story. Last year in Pennsylvania, a waiter in a Wilkes-Barre restaurant was approached while he was working by three United States deputy marshals. They tried to arrest him. They scuffled. He was injured, but he managed to break away. He ran to the Susquehanna River, and when it appeared that the officers had him cornered there, he jumped in. The officers, I am told, tried for the better part of an hour to shoot him dead in the water and pelt him with rocks, until finally the local people drove them off, because the entire affair was too brutal, too inhuman, for even a black man to endure. With the help of his neighbors, William Thomas escaped."

Wells Brown stopped. He had seduction and anger in his eyes. He challenged her. He measured her, his eyes combing her unashamedly to assess and appraise her. Had she gotten the point?

"Stunning as that story is, how much more stunning would it be if William Thomas himself were not safely in Canada, serving someone his coffee right now, but were here, telling it himself?"

"Not many of us have your style, sir."

"You don't want my style, Miss. You have style all your own, and stories too."

Mercer smiled and nodded and looked at her feet.

"We need you. Our people get free and then disappear. They get free and go start a . . . a restaurant."

Mercer looked up, surprised by his vehemence. Then he laughed. She laughed too. She found herself liking him.

"I'd like to start a restaurant," she said with a grin.

"Oh, you would?"

"I cook. A man I know up North here told me good cooks are always scarce." She was being coy. He knew it.

"So I've heard."

"Yes, sir. Restaurant'd be just the thing. Stay warm and never go hungry."

"That would be nice, wouldn't it? Just stay warm and keep our bellies full."

"I done more than that," she said.

"Of course you have," he said warmly. "You've been through the storm. All the more reason to bear witness."

Then he turned away. People were spread out like a fan from his elbow, wanting to talk to him. Mercer stood silently, looking around her, when she heard Williamson's case mentioned.

"Honestly, I worry for his health. Have you ever been to Philadelphia? Do you know where the prison is?"

"No, I can't say I do."

"It's in a section called Moyamensing, which is notorious, even in Philadelphia, for disease and bad air. They've had awful outbreaks: typhus, smallpox, cholera. And the inhabitants are depraved. It's the worst place they could have put him."

"Were you one of the pilgrims?"

"To go visit? No, I'm afraid not. I haven't seen the jail itself, but I can't imagine it would be much better than the surrounding neighborhood. Have you been?"

"No, I haven't, but look, here's the next-best thing."

A man with a bald head and bushy orange-and-gray sideburns reaching under his chin was displaying a small copy of a daguerreotype, while he and a tiny woman debated whether Williamson had allowed or caused the picture to be distributed.

"Either way, it was brilliant," said the man. "Look at him.

Just look at the face. That's what these daguerreotypes can do. They capture the heart in the eyes. This man's eyes shine with integrity, which I'm sorry to say is in short supply on the bench in Philadelphia County. Integrity. Now, to publish this image as the picture of a man in *prison,* well, it's brilliant. Don't you agree?"

He passed the daguerreotype around. Mercer put out her hand to take a turn. At the sight of Williamson, she smiled immediately. There he was: the same steady eyes that had encouraged her, the same slender face and unsmiling mouth, rounded, nearly feminine, resolute, that had told her that the law would protect her.

"You see," said the man. He pointed to Mercer. "You see it, don't you? Integrity, I tell you."

"Yes, sir," Mercer said, handing him the picture. "Integrity most certain."

"He'll help free more of your race with this"—he held the daguerreotype in the palm of his hand—"than he did rescuing women from ferries."

"Although he couldn't do the one without having done the other first," Mercer shot back.

"Of course not." A small woman said it. She put her hand on the elbow of the man who'd been talking. "You just set this man straight," she continued cheerfully. Obviously the two knew each other well.

"You always want someone to set me straight."

"Well, if you'd stay straight, I wouldn't have to keep imposing on them."

The woman introduced herself as Prudence Randall. She was a curious creature, with the dual air of a highly moral woman and a naughty teaser. On her chest she wore a stickpin on which was pictured a white hand clasped over a brown one. She gripped Mercer's fingers in her own; they were small as a child's. Her voice, too, was tiny. It poured out in a thin stream from the back of her nose.

"The last colored woman Eugenia brought around went off and wrote her story, and what a story it was." She mentioned the name. "Have you read it?"

"No, miss, I haven't."

She held fast to Mercer's hand. "I'll send it round. Or, I'll send it by Eugenia. So, are you writing too?"

"I'm still learning how to write a proper letter."

"So are half the people I correspond with."

Mercer smiled. She noticed that Eugenia Pitts was coming toward them and looking displeased.

"The reason I ask," said Prudence Randall, "is because one of the things I do is suggest speakers, when I find them, to talk to meetings organized by New England anti-slavery societies. Just now they've begun to accept more colored ladies. I would like to encourage them to continue. Do you think you might be interested?"

"Prudence, this is my special new friend," said Eugenia Pitts in a tone of voice that sounded like a warning.

"I think I know who she is," said Prudence. "And I hope that when she's at liberty, she'll join us."

Mercer was not sure: Who all was "us"? And what was she to them? Was she what they wished they could be or prayed they were not?

"Your cousin is in the parlor."

Mrs. Brooks snorted a laugh and flounced out of the room.

Tyree opened his arms wide when he saw Mercer. She quick-stepped to where he stood in the middle of the room and reached out her hands. He pulled her to his chest.

"My dear cousin," he said into her ear. "How we've missed you."

Mercer rested against him for a moment, taking in again the feel of his body against hers, the smell of his clothes.

"Here," he said. He pointed to a parcel. "From the family."

He'd come to New York, he explained, to bring Mrs. Becker to her son's funeral. Mercer remembered Mrs. Becker, the widow who rented the Quicks' large and commodious house on Addison Street and shared it with Harriet. The house was quiet, chaste, and clean.

"I'm sorry to hear she lost her son," Mercer said.

Mercer untied the twine and folded back the sheets of canvas. Inside were two books, a pair of new black wool stockings, letters from Etta and Mattie, and a handful of rock candy.

"Thank them all for me," she said, handing back the canvas and twine.

"I have just three hours before I must go collect Mrs. Becker. So come out with me. We'll walk and go to a restaurant for a meal. Your landlord and landlady have given their permission."

Mercer went upstairs for her wrap. She took time to pull the new woolen stockings over her old ones, too, before she left. Two pairs made her shoes tight, but the additional warmth felt good.

Tyree smiled playfully when she came down.

"Luckily I'm your cousin, or else I'd never have been allowed to take you out. They're quite conscientious."

"Did you tell them you are my real cousin?"

"Cousin with a wink. I told them that you'd stayed with us in Philadelphia. They're on the New York Vigilance Committee, and they know Uncle Sharkey. I brought a note to them from him, telling them that I am who I claim to be. So they'll let me take you away, although I could see that they'd have preferred us to sit right here under their noses."

Tyree and Mercer walked along the snowy streets until they came to a small, black-owned restaurant that the Brookses had recommended. Mercer asked in detail about the children.

"How are they eating?"

"They eat."

"How's their digestion?"

"Well, I tell you," he said. "Must've been something not quite right, because Mother's put them on a regimen."

"What's a regimen?"

He told her that Della gave the children enemas once a week to clean their systems.

Mercer frowned. "I don't see no call for that."

Tyree shook his head. "Well, there's not much you can do. Mother swears by those things. If it's any consolation, Merce, we used to have one every Saturday night before our baths. She decided to make a clean sweep of it. Africana and Cyrus too."

To change the subject, Tyree told Mercer that Etta had blossomed. "She's a different child. Not a child, really. Every day she comes to practice piano. I've never quite seen a girl so determined. She's like a grown woman that way."

"Always was," Mercer said. "She was like a little old lady. She'd come over to me if I was frowning—you know you catch yourself frowning and didn't even know it?—and she'd pat my arm and say, 'It be all right, Mama.' She would. Just like a old lady. And she was always so scary."

"She had a lot to be afraid of."

Mercer did not like Tyree to point out her lack of compassion for her own daughter.

"Being scared couldn't help her none," she muttered. She'd wanted Etta to be stronger. Etta had not become stronger; only her circumstances had improved for the time being.

"About Etta," Tyree said brightly. "Harriet has a lady mentor, so to speak, in mind to guide her and help educate her."

"How so?"

"The lady is going to England, and Harriet seems to have reason to think that she'd be happy to take Etta along."

"Why would she be happy to take Etta along?"

"Sort of as a lady's maid on the passage, to help pay her way, I suppose—although if she hired a maid, she'd still have to pay her fare. But really, I gather, as a former slave, to testify to the

British anti-slavery people, who I'm told are very strong against slavery and contribute plenty of money to the cause."

Mercer pursed her lips and then slowly pulled them down on the sides. "I don't know," she said. "Seem to me Etta do just as well to stay at Miss Harriet's school and learn her lessons."

"Not many of us get to travel abroad. Harriet thinks the world of your daughter, Merce. I think she just wants to keep a top eye open for every advantage."

"How often do they lose those ships?"

"Very seldom these days, Merce. Look, you were going to go to Nicaragua, weren't you?"

"You see I'm not there."

"Hah. You win that one. But shall I tell Harriet to look into it? If the invitation is made, and you still feel the same way, you can say no then."

"I suppose."

The restaurant—Mercer had never been to one—was plain but clean. Tyree ordered bowls of oyster stew for them and pie and coffee.

"While the lawyers haggle," Tyree said, "Williamson is becoming famous."

"I saw a little picture of him here this week."

"You've seen that? His friends have had to make up more, there's such a demand for them. Can you guess how many visitors he's had? I'll tell you: more than three hundred so far. Frederick Douglass himself came, and Harriet Tubman."

"Doesn't she have a price on her head?"

"Oh, a big one, but I believe they're afraid to take her by now. Most of 'em wouldn't want to touch her. They're right. She carries a gun, and I'm sure that little black woman would use it."

"I hear about these people at the meetings Mrs. Pitts takes me to."

"Do you like them?"

Mercer stared at the table and puckered her lips. "Hard to say, Cousin Tyree."

He smiled. "No, it's not hard to say. If it's so hard to say, then you must not like them in the least."

"Well. The people have been kind to me. I cannot ever forget when people have been kind."

"Good. Now, that said . . ."

"But . . ." Mercer's handsome and usually somber face turned mischievous.

"But what?"

"But, well, you know I've had some crazy conversations."

"For instance?"

"For instance, this one very nice lady, very nice lady, came up to me and told me that she had been to a wedding last year where the bride refused to serve cake, as an example to Negroes."

Tyree laughed. "An example of what?"

Mercer raised her eyebrows and opened her palms. "I don't know. I thought I'd pass it on, though, so it could serve as an example to you."

"Hah," he said. "I'll tell Ephraim. Let's see if Abby Ann will forgo cake at her wedding. . . . What did this lady do? Did she give the money to the anti-slavery society?"

"I told you, I don't know. 'Nother woman took my hands between hers and looked me right in the eye and said to me"—Mercer pulled back the muscles around her mouth and spoke in a nasal twang—" 'No matter what they say, my dear, no one can tell me that your people have not been chosen by God to lead us to righteousness.' "

Tyree shook his head. "I've heard that one before."

" 'Your people will be raised. You shall be raised right out of the dungheap.' Out of the dungheap. And smiled at me just as nice and patted my hand."

They laughed and ate their stew and crackers.

Then Tyree became serious. "Do they want you to appear at Williamson's trial?"

"Yes."

"I thought so."

Mercer inspected the linen and cutlery. It looked as if they'd bought it secondhand.

"Mr. Wells Brown says that when you get free, you shouldn't just be selfish and go start a restaurant."

"Is that what he says?"

"Yep. I told him I would like to own a restaurant."

"What else would you like?" Tyree asked it with abrupt seriousness.

"I would like you to be in that courtroom when I appear."

"I'll be there. And I'll bring our men."

They did not say, either of them, what they were thinking: that anything could happen; that mobs had formed in other cities, even in Boston; that the government might deploy soldiers; and that the police were not on their side.

They finished their meal and drank their coffee in silence. Mercer sighed. Then she shook her head in an uncharacteristic gesture of helplessness. "You've done so much for me, and I can't do anything for you."

Tyree looked at her as he fished money out of the purse in his breast pocket.

"Love me." He said it so quietly that Mercer couldn't be sure she'd heard him.

Then, in response to Tyree's nod, the man who had served them came to the table. He satisfied himself that they'd enjoyed their meal, asked them to come again, and walked away from the table with the money. Tyree said nothing as he pulled out Mercer's chair and helped her with her cloak.

Outside, they picked their way through the dirty patches of snow on the sidewalk. Mercer felt as if she had traveled a long way since they had kissed in Bea's kitchen. He was wooing her now, but gently, and with respect. She loved Tyree, and she knew she owed him. That was plain, and she'd be a fool to forget. And yet this time, this precarious, wobbly, innocent time with him, had been sweet, and she hated to lose it. His whole family too. She'd put her feet under their table and accepted their regard.

She swaddled herself in it until it was safe to know how deeply she'd been despised before. How could she bear to earn their contempt?

"I'm not a whore," she said.

"Oh, Mercy."

"I know I owe you. I know that. And whatever you think about me and my children, Mr. Tyree, or what I might have did before I met you, I am not a whore."

"Neither am I, although when you put it like that, you make me sound like it. Listen, Merce," he said. "Listen to me. What I said was: love me. That's all. If I want more, I will say so."

"And if—"

"And then it's up to you."

He grinned and pulled a silver toothpick out of his pocket.

Relieved, Mercer said, "I always did like that toothpick of yours."

"Yes?" he asked, taking off a glove to work it. "I shall get you one."

"Oh, no."

"Oh, yes. I've decided to flood you with presents. First a secondhand traveling bag, and then a toothpick. Good God, where will it end?"

At the boardinghouse, Tyree said goodbye in the foyer. He brushed her cheek with a cousin's kiss, winked, and left. She watched him walk fast, breaking into a loping run halfway down the block. She made herself chat with the Brookses, and then went upstairs.

In the next few days, she read the books Harriet had sent. One was the autobiography of Henry Box Brown, who had had a friend mail him north in a box to escape slavery. Box Brown made a point of writing that his master had not beaten or starved him. His master had been what people might make the mistake of calling kind. But: "Heaven save me from kind masters," he wrote, "as well as those called more cruel; for even their 'tender mercies' are cruel, and what no free man could endure for a moment."

Mercer had difficulty understanding him on the first, second, and even third reading. By the fourth time through, however, Brown's prose, with its flowery, ironic rage, gave itself up to her. She felt proud of him for writing what he had, proud of herself for being able to read him. Mercer memorized passages, as Tyree and Harriet had advised her:

> . . . therefore, reader, allow me to inform you, as you, for aught I know, may be one of those degraded mortals who fancy that if no blows are inflicted upon the slave's body, and a plenty of "bread and bacon" is dealed out to him, he is therefore no sufferer, and slavery is not a cruel institution . . . far beyond, in terrible suffering, all outward cruelties of the system, are those inner pangs which rend the heart of fond affection, when the "bone of your bone, and the flesh of your flesh" is separated by embrace, by the ruthless hand of the merciless tyrant, as he plucks from your heart of love the one whom God hath given you for a "help-meet" through the journey of life. . . .

Her children hated memorization. Mercer understood why. Children wanted the whole passage learned, done, over with, in order to recite without squirming in front of their teacher and classmates. So did Etta describe the daily ordeal. But Mercer reveled in the luxury of sitting in Mrs. Brooks's tidy bedroom, saying one line over and over to herself, becoming familiar with the words, pulling meaning from intricate grammar, hearing the ragged whisper of her own husky voice. For the first time she could remember, she did not have to work. The time felt fat and rich, like sweet butter and cream. Besides, no one had assigned Mercer to memorize. She picked the passages she needed.

She needed them because a zoetrope of violence had begun to spin in her head, and a gap opened up between the careful language she was learning in these stuffed velvet parlors and the memories her indefatigable mind dredged up each day and stored like the pickled animals on Harriet's shelves. She'd thought she hated collections of things, fussy little glass cups and saucers or guns or ships. But she had her own collection of bones and blood that stood up and spun around. She remembered a black man on a farm in Culpeper who'd been drowned for revealing a plan to kill the master in his carriage and drive on north, with him propped on the cushion "asleep." The driver was hanged, but the others in the plot surrounded the telltale by the creek and held him down.

She remembered seeing a woman who had lost the skin on the sides of her neck when three white boys stuck her head between the slats of the hog fence to poke her.

She began to look from hundreds of miles' distance and through this newly memorized and half-absorbed language at the circle she'd once lived within. She stored up facts; she made a collection of facts; and each time she remembered one, another tumbled into view. She saw in her mind the mistress who'd beaten her. She saw Pryor in his dressing gown. She saw them taking her father away on the back of the dray. She saw her mother sewing and cursing in the corner. She saw Bennie running on the tips of his toes, leaning forward, laughing, his legs and feet splashed with pee and dusted with dirt.

"Don't cry."

She wrapped him in light like a garment and prayed for mercy. Then she memorized some more. She did have work to do. God had never come to Lily or sent her even the briefest of heavenly visions, but He had placed Mercer in the heart of anti-slavery America, and she could not fail. When they told her that Still and the five porters—Glover Trueheart, Robbins M. Boyd, Zachary Samuel Holloman, Jordan Jones, and S. Whitaker Ince—were about to go on trial, she was ready, she had made herself ready, to appear before all the world, to speak and be heard.

· · ·

In the three months since the beginning of Williamson's imprisonment, Mercer's case had gained notoriety. Several newspapers carried articles whose main interest seemed to be that a white man of some standing had been jailed on behalf of fugitive Negroes. The colored men who were charged with riot and assault and battery were mentioned secondarily. Mercer and her children were noted as the occasion for this drama between white American citizens, Pryor and Williamson. Mercer's sworn affidavit had been judged beside the point. The testimony of a white man was what the court respected. White men's words were what the law required.

"I wonder what you're thinking, my dear." Eliza Ruffin regarded Mercer with her straightforward brown eyes. She had taken great interest in Mercer and had arranged to meet her and Eugenia Pitts and ride on the train with them from New York to Philadelphia. Mrs. Pitts was dozing, so Eliza Ruffin whispered.

Mercer decided that Miss Ruffin would not have cared for her thoughts. Or else she would argue her down and show Mercer, gently, that the same was true in the case of women. They'd had such talks before.

"You know, I haven't seen my children in two months. When I left, I had no idea I'd be away from them this long."

Eliza Ruffin smiled politely but without much interest.

"I like the train," Mercer said. Out the window she could see farmland partially covered with a few inches of snow. The land was brown and white. It looked clean and peaceful. Mercer did miss her children. She missed the country. The train rocked gently. She removed her hat in the overheated cabin and set it next to her. Although Eliza Ruffin made a point of telling people that Mercer was traveling with them as a companion, Mercer knew that they appeared to passersby as white gentlewomen and a servant. Mercer was safe that way.

"Yes. Trains are nice."

Eliza Ruffin's face relaxed, and she looked like a little girl. Then she picked up her book and began to read. After a few minutes, her brows knitted just enough to make wrinkles between them, her lips pushed together into a straight line, and the little girl with brown eyes enjoying the rocking train was gone, replaced by the political woman. Mercer wished she had Ruffin's learning. She wished she could speak French. Etta would, no doubt. Mattie might.

Mercer stared out at the winter fields and felt fear begin to churn in her mind and her belly. What if, despite their work and planning, she was taken at the courthouse after all and sent back to Virginia, no doubt to be sold? What if they were laying for her, waiting to do to her what they did to that black man in Boston? The United States government had piles of money. What if they were prepared to spend some of it to make an example of her?

They were. When Mercer arrived at the courthouse, surrounded by her female guard—Eliza Ruffin, Sarah Stern, Mary Sterling, Eugenia Pitts, and Prudence Foley, the famous New England suffragette—the secretary of the Pennsylvania Anti-Slavery Society came up to their carriage and whispered to the women that they must walk close together, briskly, and be stouthearted: there had already been a contretemps inside the court. The district attorney had sworn he would detain Mercer; the commanding officer of the Pennsylvania State Militia swore he would not. A United States marshal, alerted to Mercer's appearance by the district attorney, was waiting inside, armed with a warrant for her arrest and a dozen men to execute it. Officers of the court were also on hand, to protect the witness and enforce the laws of the state.

State officers dressed in dark blue came to the carriage. The Anti-Slavery secretary stepped to the side and let them escort their witness and her female protectors up the steps to the District Court for the United States in and for the Eastern District of Pennsylvania. The ladies followed the first officers; the rest closed in behind them. They ascended the steps in a body and entered a brick building that had once held the U.S. Congress. Four of the five lady escorts were Quaker. They wore gray cloaks and shawls, and, under their shawls, quaint white caps over their hair. Only Eliza Ruffin was as tall as Mercer. The others were quite short. Mercer could not imagine how they must look, with her in the middle, towering above them, veiled in black.

Light poured into the courtroom through tall windows, onto the crowd of spectators. Through her veil Mercer searched the backs of heads for Tyree's. She could not find him. Crazily, unjustly, she decided that he would not bother to come. Why should he? He was free after all. And he'd already done so much. Too much, maybe. Maybe he'd had enough of doing for her. Maybe his goodwill had worn out.

Breathe.

William Still's voice came back to her. Her breath fluttered the veil, and her strength returned. She needed strength. She needed to pay attention. It wouldn't do to go feeble in front of all these people and in front of Pryor. She wouldn't give them the satisfaction. Besides, she owed it to Still and to the other men to perform in this court as well as they had performed on the dock.

The judge's bench, the jury box, the gate between the judge and onlookers, the benches for the spectators: everything was made of waxed and painted wood, worn smooth. Throughout the room, a chorus of soft wooden squeaks grunted and moaned underneath the hard voices of truths and lies. She bent her head to rest her eyes. Quite distinctly, as if he were calling her name, Mercer heard Tyree clear his throat.

She breathed again, deeply and with relief. Then she cleared her own throat, her eyes closed. She wondered at how quickly she'd been ready to give up on him. The man said he would come, she told herself, and he's here. And he'd promised to bring friends. Mercer looked again at the backs of heads. No doubt some of the black men seated in front of her were here with Tyree, ready to stand as others had stood before. Their presence gave her hope that Pryor would not have to win. She needed the hope as she needed breath, because the room seemed to be full of his presence, and full of the power of the marshal and his men. They had a warrant for her, and they had deputies. Mercer doubted that she'd be allowed to walk out the same way she'd walked in. She put blinders on herself.

Just do right by Mr. Still. First that, she thought, then the rest.

In a room just like this, Pryor's lawyers had argued that Mercer had been coerced and kidnapped away. A judge sitting on a bench had pronounced the sentence of contempt on Williamson. Here in this building somewhere—a new site, moved just four years before from its old location to make way for the railroad, and now just across the street, as Tyree liked to say, from the hall where the founders of America had written slavery into their most sacred national documents—Mr. Henry had presented Mercer's sworn affidavit. That judge hadn't cared a damn for it. Would this one care when she herself appeared to say the same thing?

But Tyree had come, and others too, she could see now: Harriet, Sharkey, and Little Bea. She would tell the story again. She'd tell it no matter the consequences. She'd tell it, and then, when the U.S. marshal stepped up to take her, she'd make her next move. She looked at the tall windows, too tall. She measured the distance from the witness stand to the two doors. She had no idea what she might do, but experience had taught her to take note of the lay of the land.

Then there was Pryor, who'd put off going to Nicaragua to see the trial through. He sat up at the front table, serious and imposing, as if he were the aggrieved person, as if he had been badly used. His justice had already prevailed. Weren't they all assembled? Hadn't he and the devilish judge caused men to be held in prison? Hadn't they caused her to have to hide and sneak like a common criminal, as if getting free were a crime? Hadn't he caused a whole passel of anti-slavery people to spend money and time defending themselves and their agents?

Goddamn you, she thought.

Breathe.

Through her veil, Mercer observed the other spectators. The blacks among them were well dressed. She recognized Quakers by the outstanding plainness of their clothing and supposed them to be friendly to her cause. With the other whites she couldn't guess. She'd been told in New York that cases were not won or lost because of the crowd. Someone, she forgot who, said that given the right man as judge, and the right lawyers, and the blessing of the Spirit, a judge could sit in his robes and on his bench and decide against a mob of a thousand. They claimed it had happened. Mercer didn't believe it. They respected their men of authority more than she did. She couldn't see how being a judge made a man just. Just a man seemed more like; and how many men would not be affected by numbers? And the jury were sure to have brought with them God knew what ideas about fugitives and colored folk. How would they judge differently, Mercer thought, if the courtroom were full of black men, with only a few whites scattered here and there? How would it be, as Wendell Phillips wrote of Douglass, if the lions told history?

But the government that went to lengths to keep as many blacks working (as cheaply as possible) would also go to lengths to keep too many of them from gathering their forces. They'd arrested ninety in North Carolina the month before for learning to read, and fifty in Maryland for daring to assemble together. White abolitionists said any number of things, and white jurors judged as they did because they were themselves protected by law. She was not.

The defense called two witnesses before her. One was a man who'd been sitting on the hurricane deck when the escape took place. He swore that Mercer and the children had not been coerced. The second witness testified that he had been on the avenue and that he, too, had seen that the woman and children appeared to have been going of their own free will. He amended his statement to say that the younger child was being carried, but the woman was walking straight ahead, next to William Still.

"Now, sir," said Mr. Baker, the lawyer, "perhaps you know that just yesterday, in this very courtroom, a Philadelphia policeman, Officer Robert Brown, swore that at first glance he thought he was witnessing a fight, and that he saw several Negroes forcing along a colored woman who was holding back with all her strength."

"No, sir, I didn't know. An officer said that?"

The lawyer looked at him.

"The policeman was paid," whispered Eliza Ruffin.

Mercer could not tell Mr. Baker's expression, because his back was turned to her, but she did hear the hint of chill in his voice. "Yes, Mr. McBride, an officer said that."

"Oh."

"But you saw no such thing."

"No, sir. She wasn't holding back a'tall, far's I could see. She were striding fast as a body could stride."

"And the Negroes around her?"

"Well, the one, like I said, was carrying the boy, and the rest, I suppose, were tryin to keep up with that colored woman. She's tall, you know, and look like she was puttin some ground atwix' her and that ferry as fast as she could."

The man grinned, showing a mouthful of black and missing teeth. People near Mercer sniggered or tripped their tongues.

"So there did not appear to you to be any coercion."

"Well, no, sir. That don't sound like coercion to you, do it, sir?"

"Certainly not. And Mr. Pryor?"

"Well, sir, he was comin along behind them fast, and he were carrying on at her and at them."

"And then what?"

"Then, you know, a hack'll come down that way now and again, 'specially when they know a ferry's comin, now that Delaware Avenue is opened up. So look to me like they flagged one down that was comin that way, and they got in."

"Who got in, sir?"

"Why, Still, there, and the woman and the children. And then that hack rode away."

"Thank you, sir."

The man grinned again as he got down from the witness box.

Mr. Baker walked to his table. He put down one set of papers and picked up another. Observers in the courtroom used the break to shift their weight in their seats and cough. Mercer could see Eliza Ruffin cringe when a consumptive-looking man next to her took out a handkerchief, stiff and crumpled from use, hawked and coughed into it. When the room settled, the judge told Mr. Baker to call his next witness. As before, Mr. Baker handed a piece of paper to the clerk. In his shrill voice, he cried out: "Virginia Pryor."

Courtroom observers gasped out loud and turned in their seats. They craned their necks for a look at the door in the back of the room; the sounds of their rustling rippled through the dead cool air, like a flock of heavy birds surprised into flight.

Mercer stood. She lifted her veil with gloved hands and threw it back over her head.

"I am here," she said.

Then, deliberately, she nodded to her protectors and made her way to the witness box. She moved slowly, because she felt her knees shaking and she wanted to walk steadily.

Pryor was looking at her, and she met his eyes. He looked as she figured he'd look: so reasonable, such a reasonable man, such a kind master, such a big, important man, and can you believe the nerve of that black wench and the Northern bastards challenging him on her account? He looked righteous.

You never had me, she thought. And you don't have me now.

Then she looked at the other table, where the defendants sat: Still, in his well-tailored suit, looking just as she remembered him, watching the proceedings with shrewd and shining eyes, and the other five, dressed in plain dark jackets, a row of deacons in their own tiny liberation church, prosecuted together to save the taxpayers' money. Only one, a powerfully built, pockmarked man, looked frightened. The others sat straight as schoolmasters, hands clasped together on the table, eyes revealing nothing.

Pryor was inspecting her. She wouldn't let him stare her down.

You don't have me.

She made herself look at him long enough to say the words in her mind, but not so long that she'd be noticed. Great big ambassador, she thought, running down one slave woman, two children, and six colored men who never hurt you a'tall. Big man. And one white man in jail for contempt. She couldn't tell whom he wanted to punish more.

And yet she was still tied to him as long as he had Bennie.

She masked her eyes with calm. They went as still as those of the defendants, and as black as well water. Her anger lay on the bottom, cold and deep. She walked real slow, so as not to disturb it. Somewhere in the corner of her mind, she heard the tune:

> *If I could*
> *If I could*
> *If I could*
> *I'd tear this building down*

It came up in her own voice from far away. She heard it rise up from the bottom of the well, as did the memory of Suzy's old story about the driver.

How'd his face look? How you think he looked? How'd 'e look? Just before the driver slit his throat, I mean. Just the tiniest little second before. Good ol' Ned. Just how you think he look?

She decided not to give them her new name. This trial was about the runaway, Virginia Pryor. She was more than that now. But for the trial, that's who she was. The rest of it was none of their business.

After the gasping and oohing and aahing, the spectators fell silent. Mercer walked the short aisle from her bench to the front of the courtroom, not looking for the familiar faces, but seeing them: Tyree's, Harriet's, Sharkey's, even Reverend Ephraim's. None acknowledged her. Mercer walked past them without blinking. Her petticoats rustled prettily as she walked up the aisle, and her new black shoes clicked on the waxed pine floor. She sounded like a lady. That was good. Let this colored woman make some damn noise as she went by.

The bailiff swore her in. Pryor had lied plenty, but they asked her to tell the whole truth and only the truth.

"My name," she said, less than truthfully, "is Virginia Pryor."

Having spoken to so many lawyers in New York, she knew her own story well. And having talked to so many gentlefolk, she knew how to speak slowly, clearly. She let her voice roll out of her chest, low and musical. The spectators were silent.

Mr. Baker asked her to tell her story, in her own words. She began telling it as she'd told it in New York. It was different this time. No voice urged caution. She'd done away with caution.

She caught Tyree's eyes. No one would be carting her out of this courtroom, back to Pryor's kitchen or his bed.

Pryor stared.

Take a good look, she thought.

"Mr. Pryor brought me to Philadelphia on the way to New York and to Nicaragua, where I was to make things ready for his wife before he sent back for her. I didn't want to go without my children, and he consented to taking the older two but said that the youngest, being an infant, would be too much of a bother; so I had no choice but to leave him.

"We came to Philadelphia by the cars from Washington, then went to the Swift Steamer to New York at one o'clock but were too late. Mr. Pryor took us to Bloodgood's Hotel, and then he went to dinner. He had told me in Washington to have nothing to say to colored persons and that, if any spoke to me, to say I

was a free woman traveling with a minister. We stayed at Bloodgood's till a quarter to three o'clock. Mr. Pryor kept his eye on me
all the time, except when he was at dinner. He left his dinner to
come see if I was safe, and went back again. While he was at
dinner, I saw a colored woman and told her I was a slave, that my
master had told me not to speak to colored people, and that if any
spoke to me to say I was free. She said she pitied me but could
not help me. After that, I saw a colored boy and told him the
same thing, and he said that he would try to get word. In a few
minutes, a colored man came, telling me that he would see what
could be done, but that the best they could do might be to telegraph New York, and if that was so, then two men would come
meet me there and take me with them.

"After that, we went on board the ferry; Mr. Pryor sat beside me on deck. I saw a colored gentleman come on board. He
beckoned to me. I nodded my head but could not go. Mr. Pryor
was beside me, and I was afraid. A white gentleman then came
and said to Mr. Pryor: 'I want to speak to your servant and tell her
of her rights.'

"Mr. Pryor rose and said, 'If you have anything to say, say it
to me—she knows her rights.'

"The white gentleman asked me if I wanted to be free. I
said, 'I do, but I belong to this gentleman, and I can't have it.'

"He replied, 'Yes, you can. Come with us. You are as free as
your master. If you want your freedom, come now.'

"I rose to go. Mr. Pryor spoke, and said, 'I will give you your
freedom,' but he had never promised it before, and I knew he
would never give it to me. The colored gentleman held out his
hand, and I went toward him. I was ready for the word before it
was given to me. I took the children by the hands. The younger
one cried—they were both frightened—but stopped when we got
on shore. A colored man carried the little one, and I led the girl by
the hand. We walked down the street until we got a hack.

"Nobody forced me away. Nobody pulled me, and nobody

led me. I went of my own free will. I always wished to be free, and meant to be free when I came North; I hardly expected it in Philadelphia, but I thought that I might get free in New York. I have been comfortable and happy since I left Mr. Pryor, and so are the children."

"Thank you, madam," said Mr. Baker. He stood and walked toward her. Then he breathed deeply, let out a dramatic sigh, looked down at his feet and up again. He grabbed his waistcoat in one hand and frowned.

What a show he puts on, Mercer thought. His black hair shone. How different he was from his stern and modest clients.

"Madam, were you abducted?"

"No, sir."

"Madam, did you leave Mr. Pryor of your own accord, under your own power, and through your own will?"

"Yes, sir."

"I see. Were you going to visit friends in New York, as Mr. Pryor said to Mr. Williamson?"

"I had no friends in New York, sir."

"Had you ever been to New York?"

"No, sir."

"Had you ever known anyone in New York?"

"No, sir, I hadn't."

"Thank you. And when did you next see Mr. Williamson?"

"I have not seen Mr. Williamson from that day on."

"Not at all?"

"No, sir."

"Corresponded with him? Asked others to correspond with him on your behalf?"

"No, sir."

"And the people you have encountered since then: were they his agents, following his direction?"

"No, sir. Only I once heard Mr. Williamson was kind enough to ask if my children and I were well, and that he was pleased to hear that we were. But that wasn't a message, just by the by."

"Thank you, Miss Pryor. You may step down."

Jackson Pryor had not expected to have to endure sitting through a court trial of black men. His desire at the start of this debacle had been simple: to get Ginnie back. He'd expected, and his well-compensated lawyers had led him to believe, that the porters would be taken care of quietly and that Williamson, who really did deserve to be punished, would be brought to court.

Philadelphia was of two minds about slavery, and Judge Wells, along with a majority of the gentry there, understood that slavery was business, and business was good for everyone. The Wells family had connections in the South; and his uncle imported cottonseed oil. As a promising young lawyer, Wells had handled many Southern clients and successfully defended slavery interests. As superior-court judge, he'd seldom been overturned. But Wells figured mistakenly this time: the contempt decree had not frightened Williamson into compliance. The self-righteous little bastard had proved more obstinate than anyone would have guessed, and months frittered away.

Editorials in the Northern papers began to portray Wells as a dupe, defending Southern greed over Pennsylvania law. Hundreds of visitors made the pilgrimage to Williamson's prison cell, and Northerners, who loved nothing so much as to feel aggrieved, got themselves worked up on his behalf. Williamson holed up in jail so damned long that the state brought the colored porters to trial first. That was unfortunate. Instead of appearing before United States court, where they'd be liable for a one-thousand-dollar fine and six months in jail for "harboring or assisting" a fugitive, the conspirators came before a Pennsylvania court, where, just seven years before, the legislature had passed a law repealing age-old permission for men to "bring and retain . . . slaves within the commonwealth." The best Pryor could hope for was that the niggers who'd accosted him would draw penalty for assault.

And to beat it all, Ginnie swished by him pointedly, wearing a rich suit of clothes and a sheer black veil pulled back over her hair like armor. She made herself into a colored Joan of Arc before his eyes, and he could not stop watching her. She'd always been a proud girl. That had been her appeal: she held up her head; she worked to perfection; and she kept her own counsel. He'd seen these qualities and appreciated them. He'd treated her well and taken her with him. He'd cared for her. Now she had the nerve and the gall to walk by him like the goddamned Queen of Ethiope: haughty.

When she'd stood up on that boat and yelled out that she'd always wanted to be free, Jackson Pryor had felt as if she'd kicked him in the stomach. It was probably his own fault, he'd told himself since, and no more than he deserved for treating her too well. But still, he couldn't have been more shocked, or, to tell the truth, more hurt. Hurt. He had said he'd free her. Surely she knew that; she'd asked him every six months. He'd promised already to free the boys and settle them with a little something. Would it have killed her to give him just a few more years? Give him a little more before wanting everything handed to her on a platter?

"I always wanted to be free."

Of everything that had happened, that was the sentence that most galled him. It still rankled. He remembered her young and pregnant, tall and strong—she was lush when she was pregnant, with big, full breasts pointing through the homespun—and arrogant even then, stinking up his study after they dragged her back from the freewoman's place. He knew she'd tried to follow that no-good Willie and his brother. He knew.

". . . But he holds me."

He remembered how sick she'd been with Mattie, sick as a dog; how she tried to render lard and was ill out by the slaughter-house, and he got someone else to do it for her.

He remembered how she had pleaded for the children to come to Nicaragua. Hadn't everyone tried to warn him? But after all he had done for her, he just couldn't believe it.

Jackson Pryor could have slapped her face.

Now she sat surrounded by the white women, as if by a circus troupe. The district attorney's assistant told him their names and what they did, but who the hell were they, really, and why didn't they go home and mind their business?

The district attorney had seen to it that the U.S. marshal came to court with a warrant for Ginnie's arrest. But now, Pryor saw, the state had lined the hallway from the court with its own militia. He'd wait and see.

Ginnie looked him straight in the eyes and poked out her lips in triumph. The whole situation was nearly intolerable.

Mercer descended the shiny wooden step and permitted herself a triumphant look at Pryor. The court clerk and the newspaper reporters had scribbled every word. Through his own agency, Jackson Pryor had embarrassed himself a hundredfold more than he would have had he simply got onto his stupid damn boat and left her to go free. Thousands would read about his humiliation. (Later Williamson would collect every scrap of documentation of the legal proceedings, including her own affidavit, into a book called *The Case of Passmore Williamson*. Seventeen years later, Still would write her story into his own book, which he would title simply *The Underground Railroad*.)

As for Mercer, she settled gratefully among her diminutive protectors. The court was with her. The judge had nodded his head kindly. Mercer felt handsome and well dressed. She felt Tyree's presence with her. Although she owned no money or property, she felt suddenly prosperous and strong. She understood now that she had helped make herself and others safer by speaking than by remaining silent. Whatever they might do to her, no one could pretend it had never happened.

Pryor's face was red with the effort to keep still. Good, she thought. Fine.

Before the judge dismissed the court for the day, he called the bailiff to him and spoke in his ear with quiet emphasis. The bailiff left the court and returned with half a dozen of the state militiamen to escort Mercer from the court. They marched into the courtroom from the hall in formation. Mercer and the women stepped into the aisle, and as before, the officers walked in front of, behind, and on either side of them. They held their guns at the ready and walked past the marshal and his deputies, out the door, and down the steps. On the sidewalk, Nig-Nag stood where he had waited all day for a look at the woman he had helped liberate. He jumped toward her, and the men nearest him thrust their guns like cudgels with two hands and knocked him down.

"Please, sirs, please."

When they saw that Mercer knew Nig-Nag, they did not hinder her from bending to help him up and then shaking his hand.

"They wouldn't let me in," he said.

Mercer nodded her head sympathetically. "Thank you for comin."

"Ma'am."

The officers guided the women into a carriage at the curb. Two militiamen got in with them; another sat on the driver's bench; and the rest followed in a state carriage that trailed close behind. They drove to Mary Sterling's house, because Mercer did not want to endanger the Quicks or her children.

Pryor's lawyer leaned toward him. "There's a man named Keller wants to have a word with you. I told him not to bother you here. He might show up at your hotel."

"What for?"

"Well, let's say business."

"What sort of business?"

"What sort of business? Well, the kind of business that would have kept you out of court here if you'd chosen to go to him before you came to me."

Pryor thought for a moment. Lawyers irked him. All clever and no spine. His own lawyer irked him even more. Maybe Pryor should have chosen a slave catcher. But he didn't like them. They were not fastidious about how they handled their freight. Pryor might have sent them after a man, but not a woman and children. Besides, he'd wanted the proceedings to take place in the light of day. Surely it wasn't so wrong to seek a just and honorable end to the whole nasty incident.

"Reward one theft with another? As if we are not governed by law?"

"You've never heard me say it," the lawyer said with a smirk. "Not me."

"I don't want to see this man."

"Well, he's a businessman and nothing less. If you tell him to, he'll leave you alone."

When Pryor returned to his hotel, Keller came walking toward him. Pryor knew it was he before he spoke. He had a red nose and a sharp little face that managed to be ingratiating and contemptuous at once. "Can't hang on to your own slaves," his face seemed to say. "Too bad. Let's make a bargain, shall we?"

"Captain Jackson Pryor? I'm Reginald Keller."

Pryor's eyebrows shot up. "My lawyer said you might be here, but I have no use for your services," he said. "As you know, this case has caused quite a stir. I don't need to have her disappear now; I have an embassy to run. You see, it's quite useless."

God knew she'd cost him already. He didn't even want to calculate how much.

"My men, the men I hire—they're freelancers, really, and we all like it better that way, if you know what I mean—my men have reclaimed a-plenty of men's property. Got a couple they're lookin for right now. It's like casting a net. Never quite know who you might catch by mistake, if you take my meaning."

"No, sir. I do not take your meaning. Now if you'll excuse me—"

He did not like this insinuating man, whose breath smelled of bad digestion and cheap tobacco.

Keller looked at him with mock thoughtfulness. "I know quite well that your old gal is a great celebrity now and she'd be missed. But there was those that helped her, and not all o' them would be missed. . . . Our men, you see, get ten dollars for every black the U.S. marshal says is a runaway and five dollars for every one he says is not. And we got a-plenty of them saying they're missin someone, if you take my meaning."

"I see," Pryor said.

Pryor reached into his breast pocket and pulled three twenty-dollar bills from his wallet. He was sick of being a Christian gentleman. Everyone's eyes mocked him for it. He gave Keller the money. If the man ever named him, he'd deny it.

"Then get one of those who helped."

Nine / Waiting

A fter the rigid order of Zilpha's cottage and the spare richness of the tended homes of the New York abolitionists and women's rights people, Mercer looked forward to the rowdy welcome of Little Bea's house. Sure enough, Bea wrapped her arms around her and hugged her at the door.

"Well, look at my old friend."

She talked fast and loud; she bounced as she spoke. Etta had written about Bea's anxious periods, but Mercer had never seen one.

At first frost, Bea said, the fleas died off, thank God, but "didn't those damned rats come back, or one at least, the Indian scout, we call it, looking for a place to settle. And my famous dogs performed—well—famously." Bea laughed and then pouted. "At least Old Standby did. You know Standby, of course. You know he'll go after anything—"

"I remember."

"But that other damn dog," Bea said, missing Mercer's smile, "that younger one with the torn ear—'member I called him Simple Simon? He *was* kinda simple, wasn't he? Well, once again he showed no interest in hunting. No interest whatsoever. Standby was all over here after the damn rat, actually a couple of 'em, and one ran right in front of Simon, and he laid there, just as stupid."

They were still standing in the vestibule. Mattie and Etta came running through the house from across the alley and yelling for Mercer. Mercer steered Bea out of the way and opened her arms. Mattie jumped up onto his mother. She held him on her hip as she had when he was two, and Etta threw her arms around them both.

Mattie grinned. He'd lost a tooth in the front.

"Looka this. Looka this tooth you lost."

"And look," he said, wiggling the one next to the space.

"Gimme here," Mercer said. "Lemme pull it. I ain't pulled me a tooth in years."

"Miss Della said you wasn't comin back," Mattie said.

"Aw, honey," Mercer said sadly. "I'ma always try to come back."

"And if anything happens, you got your sister," Bea said. "That's what happened to us." Bea said it with a terrible forced brightness, as if having been orphaned and raised by her sister had been a delightful adventure. Then her face collapsed like a glove, and she stood next to them, appearing conspicuously left out.

"Aw, don't be like that." Mercer motioned for Bea to take two steps forward.

The older woman looked pleased as she came into the circle of their arms. They stood together for as long as Mattie could stand. When he wriggled, they went to the parlor to sit down.

Mercer could not worry about Bea anymore for the time being. She pulled the children's warm bodies close. They felt robust in her arms, and they smelled like Della's baking. Mercer gobbled their faces with her eyes, and they soaked in her attention. Their eyes were clear. They showed good color and smooth skin. Mercer wanted to do nothing more than sit still with them by the stove, but Mattie jumped up.

"Here, hold on. Look what I brought you," she said. Suddenly she felt almost too tired to keep her eyes open. "Go fetch me that bag by the door."

She gave Mattie a second-hand toy boat. Mr. Brooks had made a new sail for it. "I saw boys float little boats like that in New York. Doesn't need much water. I saw one boy sail it in nothin more than a puddle."

She gave Etta a black silk hair net and a tartan plaid hair ribbon.

"Where'd you get the money?" Etta asked.

"I did laundry out at Miss Zilpha's."

"She worked you to death, didn't she? I saw your hands when you came in, and I said, 'I bet Zilphie worked her to *death*,'" said Bea. "Leastwise she'll let you keep your own money. Did she make you give her anything for board? You're too good to tell, but I bet she did. . . . Hunh. You better be glad it was Zilphie, 'cause Manny'll work you to death and then take your money too. And I tell you, he'll say you can't leave 'cause you owe 'im more."

"Here, Miss Bea."

Mercer handed Bea five sticks of lemon candy.

"Oh, I love lemon candy. You knew that, didn't you, and you remembered."

What Mercer remembered was how Bea scoured the house for candy when her mysterious supply of whiskey ran out.

Mattie raced through the back door to find a puddle to float his boat in.

Etta moved the footstool to the other side of Mercer's chair.

"Fire too hot?"

Etta nodded.

"Makes me so sleepy." Mercer laid her head on the antimacassar. "You got somethin to recite for me?"

"Yes, I do. But you suppose to read while I recite, to see do I get it right. I'll get my scrapbook."

"Oh, have you a scrapbook now?"

"Miss Harriet made us."

Bea had dropped off to a doze. Mercer sat listening to her

snore while Etta ran upstairs. Mattie and his boat had collected a small group of boys at the puddle under the hydrant in the alley. Mercer could hear them shouting.

Etta came back with her scrapbook. A thought occurred to Mercer.

"You knew I was comin back, didn't you?"

Etta nodded her head but dropped her eyes. She'd seen plenty.

"I tried to make Pryor let me bring Bennie when we came north, but they wouldn't. And once he took us to Nicaragua, Etta, there wasn't no telling when we'd have another chance at freedom, or when we'd get back to Bennie, either. I'm not gonna leave you if I can possibly help it. But I'm not gonna lie to you, either. Things could happen. God only knows what could happen. In the meantime, if somethin was to happen to me, I'm tryin to make sure you two have friends in this world who'll do right by you."

Mercer stopped to collect her thoughts. "You been keepin an eye on Mattie, haven't you?"

"Yes, ma'am."

"Anything happen to me, you keep y'all together, if you can, sugar. See how the Quick family stays together? That's the way you two stay together; put your money together; work together. And pray for your brother Bennie. Aunt Suzy's raisin him now. Pray for him."

They sat in silence, the magical wonder of reunion gone.

"You're old enough now so I can talk to you," Mercer said, with a hint of apology in her voice. "So, show me your book."

Etta's scrapbook was actually a used copybook whose pages were mostly or partially blank. Harriet bought a dozen or more for a penny apiece from a Quaker school at the end of the year and taught each of her older students to keep a scrapbook. She insisted on it, as she insisted that they write in them each day one passage she assigned and one of their own choosing.

"We must make a record of ourselves," she told them. "Record yourself, children, because no one else will do it for you. And learn from the greatest minds that have gone before."

Harriet required that they include French and Latin quotations in their books after their fifth year of study. At least once a week, they had to find a passage from among the abolitionist and black-owned papers donated by parents and sponsors: they read *The Liberator, The Anglo-African,* and the A.M.E. Church's paper, *The Christian Recorder.*

Etta showed Mercer the cross-stitch cover she'd sewn for her scrapbook. On it were an oak and a maple leaf, her full first name, the abbreviation for Philadelphia, and the date on which she'd begun the book. She'd chosen the design in homage to Mary Ann Shadd Cary, the black author of *Forest Leaves,* a book of poetry Etta admired.

"And they're red and yellow, like they were when we came north and got free. I put my name, but not my last name, so in case I lost it, it wouldn't help any slave catchers find us. And I put the date because Miss Harriet said you always date things. . . . When was I born, Mama?"

"In the fall, just after harvest. I told you that."

"Do you know the day? Or the month?"

"I don't know exactly. After I got older I started taking notice of the dates of things, but not before. I told you that." The question irritated Mercer. It made her remember her resentment of Pryor. She knew when Mattie and Benjamin had been born, because he told her. Willie had not been able to.

Etta turned to the first entry, which she'd attached with a straight pin. It was an article from the *New York Tribune.*

"There," Etta said, pointing. "Now I'll recite it, and you can follow and see do I get it right.

"As the public have not been made acquainted with the facts and particulars respecting the agency of Mr. Passmore Williamson and others, in relation to the slave case now agitating in this city, and especially as the poor slave mother and her two children have been so grossly misrepresented, I deem it my duty to lay the facts before you, for publication or otherwise, as you may think proper.

On Wednesday week, 2½ o'clock, the following note was placed in my hand by a colored boy. . . ."

Etta recited the article. Mercer had seen it before but did not say so; Eugenia Pitts had shown it to her in New York. Mercer felt bad that she hadn't thought to save it for the children herself. She was not recording herself. When the hell had she ever had time to record herself?

"Mr. Still wrote it to the paper," Etta was saying. "Miss Harriet gave it to me for my reading lesson."

"How long it take you to get to read it so smooth?"

Etta grinned shyly. "A long time."

"Is this Mr. Douglass?" Mercer asked.

A short passage had been copied on a diagonal in Etta's handwriting. Etta nodded yes and read it self-consciously:

"By far the larger part of slaves know as little of their ages as horses know of theirs, and it is the wish of most masters within my knowledge to keep their slaves thus ignorant. They seldom come nearer to it than planting-time, harvest time, cherry-time, spring-time, or fall-time."

"October, most likely," Mercer said to her daughter. "I did tell you that before. I made sure to tell you that. And I told you that it was a warm autumn. 'Member? That first night I sweated so bad?"

Etta looked peevish. She had asked for a date, not sweat.

"I told Miss Harriet it was probably October."

"Then what else do you want from me, Etta?"

Etta shrugged.

"You want a number, don't you? I'm sorry, sugar. I don't

have a number to give you. Don't make no never mind anyway. I don't have a number."

They sat awhile longer without speaking. Bea's head had tipped backward. Her mouth opened wide. Mercer got up and laid her to the side. The wig slipped over one eyebrow.

"Dammit." Mercer spread her fingers, placed one hand on each side of Bea's wig, and shoved it back up Bea's forehead.

Etta laughed behind her hand.

"All right, girl. Listen. What if I gave you a day, close as I could come, but it was the wrong day?"

Etta stopped sniggering. She sat straight, stubbornly holding aloft her new pressed hair and tartan ribbon and her sprouting breasts. She shrugged again.

"I'm tryin to work with you, dammit. You done come up here and start your schoolin, and now you want to pretend you know things you don't. And you want me to pretend for you. Why not make up your own day?" Mercer wanted to slap her, except that she had nearly decided to be done with slapping her children.

Etta collected herself enough to answer. "If you gave me a day, and there wasn't any other record of any other day, then that would be the day. I was just askin you to try to remember." She looked as if she was going to cry. "I don't want to make up a day. If you were to suppose, that wouldn't be the same as me makin one up."

"I'll think hard, then," Mercer said with a sigh, "and I'll give you a day by the end of the week."

Mattie came in, clutching his boat.

"Did it float?"

"It floats."

"Come here. I want to tell you somethin."

"Look, Mama."

Mattie reached under the chair and brought out a newspaper, rolled and tied with string on either end.

"Close your eyes," he said.

He put one end of it to Mercer's ear and the other end of it to his lips. He spoke in a whisper. "Mama, can you hear me?"

"I hear you."

"You gotta put your hand over your other ear." Then he spoke even more softly.

"Can you hear me now?"

"Now I can hear you fine."

He began a chant in a tiny voice. It was almost as if his voice were inside her own head.

He whispered: "I love my boat. I love my mama. I love my sister. I love my eyes. I love my ears. I love my mouth. I love my arms. I love my hands. I love my stomach. I love my legs. I love my feet. I love Mr. Ty. I love Aunt Bea. I love my God. I love my shoes."

Mercer pulled the newspaper tube from her ear. "Lemme see your shoes."

He held up his foot. "Mr. Ty got 'em for me and some for Cyrus."

"I want you to love your brother Bennie too, even though he's not with us," she said.

Mattie didn't answer. He fiddled with the newspaper tube and looked at his shoes.

"I had to leave 'im, Mattie, but we gotta pray for him. You feel bad we left him?" Mattie nodded. "Then pray for him whenever you feel bad. Say: 'God, I miss Bennie, and I wish we could've brought him.' "

Prudence Randall wrote Mercer in care of Eugenia Pitts. Mercer met with her at the home of one of Harriet's friends. It did not surprise her when the lady proposed that she make a lecture tour in New England, but it did surprise her when Mrs. Randall told her that the Anti-Slavery Society would pay her. The money she could make in one springtime tour was more than she'd earn in a year of doing laundry.

She'd make enough to pay toward the children's room and board, and then to get them to Canada and settled there. But first she'd have to leave the children again.

"I'm not sure what I have to say that other folk aren't saying already." She had seen and heard excellent speakers. Then she remembered the man with the stumpy fingers and her afternoon with Eliza Ruffin's group.

"You'd tell your story as you did in the courtroom," said Harriet.

"And then," said Mrs. Randall, "you have more to tell: what it was like in bondage; what you heard and saw; and of course, we in the Anti-Slavery Society want you to tell people how important it is for them to support the Society, which is working to bring an end to those wrongs. You could do that."

"Yes, ma'am," Mercer said. "I could do that."

"Do you need time to think about it?"

"Do you, Merce?"

Mercer looked gratefully at Harriet. "Yes, I do."

"Of course you do," Harriet said. "Among other things, the case has not been decided yet." She turned from Prudence Randall back to Mercer. "If it's in their—and your—favor, you may be delighted to go around New England."

"And if it's not . . ."

"If it's not," Randall said, "all the more reason, I say, to stand and fight. And if the judge is against you, he becomes that much more reason for your celebrity. I don't mean that in any vulgar way." She made a motion with her tiny hands as if she were brushing dirt. "I only mean to point out how the outrage of bondage may be used to foil slaveholders and not enrich them. Mr. Frederick Douglass spoke with a price on his head for some years."

"Speaking with a price on one's head. That helps make quite a draw," said Tyree that evening. "I suppose that she did not invite

you to speak on the stigma of color here in the North, or the reluctance of even devoted anti-slavery people to go beyond abolition of slavery to equality."

"Nope," Mercer said. "She didn't say none of that."

"I'll wager she didn't. And she didn't mention that when
one of Mr. Douglass's friends offered to buy him out, some other
so-called friends made quite a stink."

"But why?"

"Because they said it would go against his principles. They
were shocked to hear that Mr. Douglass wanted to be free more
than he wanted to be a symbol of Southern immorality."

They smiled tight smiles, as if it were funny. But Mercer
felt unsettled. She'd thought only about the money before. Now
she imagined herself in front of a promiscuous audience, men
and women, mostly white. She felt their eyes: curious, incredu-
lous, appraising. She saw it, she knew, because Ty saw it. Colored women speaking in public were not as bad as white women
speaking in public, Mercer knew, because black women weren't
considered ladies in the same way. Only now did it occur to her
that Tyree might disapprove.

"What do you think I should do?"

Mercer had been back with the Quicks only a day, and already she felt as if her feelings for Tyree had grown while she'd
been gone. He'd asked her to love him, and now she did.

Tyree examined her face. He picked up one hand and held
it for a moment. "I don't know. When you're away, I'll have to find
some excuse to see you."

She sucked her teeth.

"Just see you, that's all. And talk. Give you advice you
haven't asked for."

"I'm asking for advice now."

"About this speaking tour?"

"Yes."

"My advice is this: Let it wait a few days. You can think it
over. We can think it over, and then, if you decide not to do it,

you've lost nothing, and if you decide to do it, well, no doubt, by
having waited, she'll be willing to pay more."

"More? My God."

"Yes, more. They've got money. . . . All right?"

Tyree stepped back from Mercer. They were alone together
in the parlor. He signaled that the conversation was over, but
Mercer wasn't finished.

"Ty?"

He inclined his head curiously, warily. She'd never called
him anything but Mr. Tyree.

"My mother used to have to clean the old Pryors' latrine. It
was a indoor latrine. Mother said they bragged about how they
had it shipped from someplace, and how expensive it was. On
Sundays, when they went off to church, she was supposed to
clean up everything before they came back. So she'd clean up,
and then she'd use it. It was blue-and-white china, like dinner
plates. I'll never forget it."

Mercer paused and thought. Tyree watched her eyes move
from side to side. Her forehead worked with concentration. "You
know and I know I can't stand up in front of some people with
lace caps and tell them that story.

"My mother is dead, and the picture I have of her—the one
that comes to my mind when I call her name—is I can see her
sitting on that latrine, laughing. That's what I have left of my
mother.

"And I can't even see my daddy. I can't bring his face to my
mind. You know when you know a word but you can't quite think
to say it? That's how his face is to me. Am I gonna tell 'em that? I
said that to somebody in New York. She said to me: 'My dear
father died when I was three.' What do they care?

"And I left my baby, Ty. I left my baby in Virginia. Oh, God
help me." She groaned, and she began to tremble. "I can't tell
them that. I can't tell them that. I can't, Ty. I can't bear it. I had to
tell it in court. I can't bear to say it again."

The groaning turned to sobs. Harriet came running in from

the dining room. She checked Tyree's eyes. He inclined his head, and Harriet held her. At her touch, Mercer began to roll her head from side to side. The sobs nearly choked her. Della appeared from the kitchen. Then the children, and Blanche and Abby Ann. Each one touched an arm or a space on her back. Tyree stood at the edge of their circle: tight, noisy, cooing, shushing. When Mercer quieted, Tyree told them to sit down. They sat.

"No speaking tour." He said it to Harriet, then turned to Mercer.

"Merce?"

She looked up at him over her handkerchief. "I'll talk to some of the Railroad people about your little boy. Let's see what we can do."

The next afternoon, Harriet came to tell Mercer that she'd heard from the Anti-Slavery lady who was going to England.

"I thought we'd have better luck, frankly."

"She didn't want to take her? Well, it's just as well. I never did like the idea of Etta on the big old ocean." Mercer sighed. She didn't want to scatter her family any more than was necessary.

Harriet humphed with uncharacteristic irritation.

"It's all right," Mercer said.

"No, it's not."

"Why not?"

"Because Eugenia had the nerve to say that she expected the British to pay too much attention to her, and she'd get petted and spoiled. God forbid a colored child would get attention. For all her work with us, you know, that was the problem. A young Negro girl just couldn't have the character to withstand a little petting."

"Eugenia? Eugenia Pitts?"

"Yes. She wrote me saying that she wanted to do something for the children."

"She wrote *you?*"

"Yes."

"I wouldn't want to be beholden to her. I'm beholden to you and your family, and I don't mind being in your debt, but not her. I wish you'da told me."

"Well, I am sorry."

"Etta's learnin here so beautiful, like I told Mr. Ty. I tell you, if anybody goes to work, it ought to be me."

"Don't you go out until they settle the case."

"I wish you'd told me it was Mrs. Pitts."

As if to make up for the Pitts affair, Harriet asked Mercer to move into her rooms in Mrs. Becker's house. Mercer accepted, grateful to be out of Little Bea's shed. During the day, Mercer worked with Della at the Quicks'. Within a couple of days, she was also drafted to help sew Abby Ann's wedding dress. In order to pay them something for her room and board and the children's, Mercer took on all the work she could manage.

Sometimes during the relentless days, she smiled ironically to herself about her current schedule. In Virginia, people complained that they worked like mules. The Quicks worked more like insects. They understood work and respected it. In slavery, she'd worked because everywhere, and in every facet of her life, force pressed in on her. She hadn't given work. Just like she hadn't given birth. The pressure squeezed and squeezed and work came out, and there was not a thing she could do to stop it. Here comes. Pop. She worked for the big man. She worked for the boss lady. But she worked because it was in her, and to keep it in would have killed her. If she was making a gravy, how could she not, at least now and then, on a good day, when the sun was fine and the air was cold and clear, how could she not watch the flour fry in the grease until it was brown, just a little browner, just right, just deep brown and rich, one moment, half a moment, before it burned, and then pour in cold, cold water that jumped around in the pan and steamed and misted and greased her face and neck?

How could she not stir with all her might to get it smooth, smooth, and salty and rich? How could any man or woman resist doing some thing, some one thing, well and with joy? They took away the joy and sold it like they sold everything, but she'd given work as she'd given birth.

In the Quicks' household she gave work willingly. They worked alongside her, and they knew its worth. They knew it in aching backs, tired eyes, and stiffened fingers. They accepted her work like friendship in coin.

At night, Harriet directed Mercer's reading. She gave her lists of words to memorize, irregular verbs to conjugate, and complex sentences to dissect. Abby Ann complained that Mercer would never finish the fancy work for her wedding, so Tyree volunteered to read to her in the Quicks' parlor at night while Mercer sewed under a lamp. Manny demanded to be brought down most evenings too. They read the Bible, but also, at Harriet's urging, the black autobiographies of the day.

Blanche sat on the ottoman by Tyree's chair. By evening, her eyes were too weak to sew anymore, so she'd sit quietly, with her eyes closed and her head back. Sometimes she'd knit with her eyes closed. After fifteen or twenty minutes, she would put the knitting aside, rest her head on his lap and fall into a cough-racked sleep.

Abby Ann came down with Blanche and sat in the shield-back chair next to Mercer. They shared the lamp and the relative quiet of the far corner. There, Abby Ann chatted at Mercer while they worked on the wedding dress.

"Today, oh, my, what a fuss on Walnut Street. The people coming toward us started an awful commotion."

She paused.

"They did?"

"Oh, an awful commotion. And why do you suppose?"

Mercer looked at the felt cap that sat jauntily on the top of her head. Abby Ann had told Mercer to stop wearing her bonnets perched on the back of her head like country folk. She knew why the people on Walnut Street had made a commotion. Even if she couldn't have guessed, she'd heard enough of Blanche's stories to know where most of them aimed.

"They thought you was—"

"They thought," she said, refusing to let Mercer take her line, "that Ephraim was walking with two white women. And my heavens, I feared they would come after us."

"They would have ten or twenty years ago," Della said.

"Then they got up close on you and saw that bad blood come through, eh? Hah, hah." Manny laughed at Abby Ann. Then he said to Della, "Did you get the book?"

"Here." Della handed a book to Tyree. "I sent the girls to the lending library for it. You know how your daddy likes these stories."

"Not another one of those women?"

"That's good stories," Manny said.

"My father's favorite stories," Tyree said to Mercer, "are about white women who get caught by the Indians."

"*Real* white women," he said pointedly at Abby Ann. "I'm tired—nothin personal, but I'm tired of hearing about slavery, slavery, slavery."

"Is this one where she won't come back?" Tyree asked.

"Read."

Tyree read the title: *"The Narrative of Mrs. Mary Jemison, Who Was Taken by the Indians in the Year 1755 When Only About Twelve Years of Age and Has Continued to Reside Amongst Them to the Present."*

"I love those stories."

Tyree said to Mercer, "We were the only children at school who dreamt about being captured by the Indians, because Mother and Daddy only read the ones where the people chose to stay with their adopted families rather than come back to civilization."

"Can you imagine?"

"Great-Grandmother was a wild Indian."

"Used to take Grandpa Gabriel and his sisters and brothers into the woods for weeks. He said that's why he couldn't stand to be cooped up in a house and took to the sea."

"That was Mary, Gabriel's mother."

"Seems to me a ship would coop him up worse."

"What happened to his sisters and brothers?" Mercer asked.

"Consumption. Each and every one but him."

Etta came from Bea's to practice piano. Africana came down, as she was required to do, to sit and practice with her, although she wore her reluctance like a heavy burden. Etta played quietly, so that Tyree's reading could be heard over the music. She repeated troublesome musical phrases relentlessly, each one again and again until she mastered it. Africana fidgeted.

"You hear how she does that over and over?" Della said to Africana.

"Uh-hunh."

"What did you say?"

"Yes, ma'am."

"That's what you have to do to be good. See, you want to play, but you aren't willing to do the work."

Tyree stopped reading and looked from his mother to the girls at the piano.

"When I was a boy," he said, "they tried to make me do that on the piano, and after three or four times I would throw myself on the floor and scream and kick like the devil."

"And I came in here," Della said, "and I would beat him with anything I could get ahold of. Didn't do much good."

"Finally, my father said music was for girls, so Harriet had to continue, and I never did learn to play."

"Harriet didn't pitch a fit like you did," Della said. "But I'll tell you this: she never sat down and went at it like that child there, either."

Etta's practicing continued, ditties and chords and simple folk tunes from Europe, running under Tyree's voice and through it as he read. Mercer stopped every now and then to admire her. She wondered whether or not black churches ever employed women to play their music, and if so, how much they paid.

Winter kept them in. Snow had fallen; the air was damp; and the insides of houses and schoolrooms were stale with the fumes of coal dust and lamp oil. Cyrus and Mattie caught colds. Abby Ann came down with the croup. Della mumbled that it was Abby Ann's ambition to lie on her back and let someone take care of her. The others agreed.

When Ephraim came to visit, he greeted the patient by saying: "How you find yo'sef dis hot wedder, Miss Chloe?"

Delighted with his minstrelsy, Abby Ann responded in kind: "Pretty well, I tank you, Mr. Caesar, only I aspire too much."

Mercer learned from Harriet that they were quoting from a series of etchings and lithographs by Edward Clay that had become popular not just in the United States but also in England in the 1820s. The prints caricatured successful blacks—people like the Quicks and their ilk—as if such a professional class of Africans were hilarious in and of itself; Clay's blacks were bumblers and quacks, aping their betters, and doomed to incompetence. Now, thirty years later—years in which blackface minstrel shows had become so popular in America that Irish performers took to using the Africans' banjo for their own folk music— framed copies of Clay's caricatures hung on the walls of Manny's and Della's customers.

"I hear that shit in here again, they're both gettin out," Manny shouted from his room.

They giggled softly and lowered their voices.

"Bes' you stay inside, anyhoo," Ephraim whispered. "Colored people can't hardly go out widout being 'sulted."

Ephraim also did not endear himself by leaving fresh daily orders for Abby Ann's care. He pulled Mercer aside and asked her, as if he were sharing with her some secret that only she was worthy to receive, to change Abby Ann's linen, to bring broth, to wash her. Because the Quicks put up with the couple, Mercer did likewise.

She did permit herself to complain to Tyree that it was a good thing for their souls that Ephraim and Abby Ann had never had a chance to own slaves. It would have ruined them. They laughed together and then sighed and moved apart, as they did when they found themselves standing too close in the tight hallways.

Ten / Strong as Death

T hen came the judgment. In 1847, Pennsylvania's legislature
had clearly repealed slave owners' permission to carry slaves
through the state. About that there was no question. And from
the testimony, the jury agreed with the defense that no abduction
had occurred. All six men, therefore, were acquitted of riot. The
two who had restrained Pryor from grabbing Mercer were found
guilty of assault and battery—but just barely. Although as a rule
blacks drew severe prison sentences, these men received one
week in jail.

Judge Wells, meanwhile, found himself more and more
amenable to discussing terms with Williamson's lawyers. Although the Vigilance man offered no fresh information, Wells,
after a show of demanding specific new language in his petition,
purged him of contempt. He was never tried.

Mercer and her children were free.

The abolitionists and the suffragettes held small, temper-
ate celebrations for Williamson and Still. Leery of too much public display in Philadelphia, Mercer declined to visit her rescuers.
Instead, she bought two white handkerchiefs, embroidered them
with the date and her old initials, and sent one to each man. The
Quicks held their own small party and invited Nig-Nag. Mercer
served him his dinner and thanked him heartily.

"If it hadn't been for you, boy, we could still be slaves to that man."

"You'd be over in Nicaragua somewhere."

"With the distinguished Captain You-know-who, United States Minister Plenipotentiary near the island of Nicaragua."

"Hah."

"Could have fever and plague and God knows what else diseases."

"Probably one of y'all'd be dead."

Della served ham and duck and fish. They ate and drank until all they could do was sit back and digest. Nig-Nag left just as the sun went down. There was no moon. The Quicks had given him some money. He stopped on Locust at a place he knew, and the man threw him out. Then he walked back to Juniper Street, next to the alley where he stayed, to a whorehouse to get a drink.

The owner of the house, Cherade, would not let him in the fancy parlor, but sometimes she gave him a drink on the back porch, where he could get in out of the weather. She did tonight, handing him a quarter-full bottle of watered gin, since he had brought money. He drank some until he felt nice and easy. He had to pee and he could still walk, so he weaved his way toward the alley and let his body do what it wanted. Someone in a yard was saying "train" as he passed, and he let out a high-pitched "Choo-choo" and laughed because it felt so good and there was no one to stop him. Back on the porch, he took deep swigs from the bottle. He thought about Mercer serving him dinner. She bent over him. The door to Cherade's kitchen was closed. He was alone in the dark, and no one could see him or hear him.

He slipped his hand inside his pants and began to rub himself. Then he grabbed with his fist and pulled up and down. Mercer's nearness had excited him this night, but his mind jumped back to Abby Ann, whom he really wanted, always. She was so pretty. Her butt bustled up high, and she swung it when she walked, and her skin was so white and smooth at the neck. And her mouth was so pink. Suppose he could make that pink mouth suck anywhere he wanted. He stiffened and came in his pants and passed out immediately. In an hour, the boy who cleaned up for Cherade came to kick Nig-Nag, take the empty bottle back, and send him on his way.

Nig-Nag felt so good that he didn't even notice the slave catchers, one white, one black: a cynically matched couple, salt and pepper.

Keller knew better than to send two white men into the alleys where escaped slaves lived with free blacks, and he did not trust two Negroes, no matter how hardened, on this mission, alone together. Usually Keller kept these two men apart and chastised them to keep them from damaging the merchandise. But this time he'd told them to rough up the idiot boy and take his more valuable friends, Jack and Bo-Bo, who'd been out bragging about Nig-Nag's unlikely service in the Underground Railroad. Nig-Nag himself wasn't worth smuggling South, and he was too easy to identify. But his beating would send a message from Pryor. That's what the fastidious ambassador would get for his sixty dollars. And down in Georgia, Jack and Bo-Bo would go for a thousand dollars wholesale.

In the room, Jack lay tied and gagged on the floor, and two men held Bo-Bo in the corner. Nig-Nag wanted to turn fast and run. He saw himself hitting his butt and laughing, as he did to leave a room quickly. But he couldn't move. Shame on him. He'd drunk too much whiskey again.

Two men held tight to Bo-Bo, wrestled him to the floor, and tied him. Then one rushed at Nig-Nag with something. What? It hit him and he fell down. The man stepped on him. His foot caught in Nig-Nag's clothes, and he rolled over. Man tripped and rolled over him like a train.

"Choo-choo." He didn't mean to say it.

"Aw, shit." That was Bo-Bo. Nig-Nag knew his voice.

The man kicked Nig-Nag to make him be still. Dull, hard pain.

"I'ma tell." It burst out.

The man kicked him again. Sucked out his wind. Nig-Nag couldn't breathe. Then he breathed a little and it hurt so bad, so bad, he cried. The floor sloped. He was rolling toward the wall.

"Leave 'im alone."

"I'ma fuck you to shut you up."

Who said? Nig-Nag couldn't see. He hurt so bad inside. He heard the heavy thuds of their bodies.

"No marks, nigger. I'm not gonna leave no marks."

Thuds and thuds. Old Bo-Bo was crying. Couldn't be, 'cause Bo-Bo was a bad man. They couldn't make Bo-Bo cry.

"Choo-choo. Chug-a-chug-a-chug-a-chug-a." Nig-Nag couldn't stop. Nig-Nag. Shhh. The hurt was so bad. He crawled to the door. He had to get out. They dragged Jack and Bo-Bo toward the door and banged into Nig-Nag.

"What's this?"

They banged his head in the door. Old rotten wood door. It gave way. They were gone. Nig-Nag kept crawling.

They were padding upstairs to their bedrooms when Standby began to bark. Tyree heard him from across the alley and opened the back door. Nig-Nag lay on the ground, sticky with blood that had dripped from his nose onto his shirt. He was covered with mud and dirt, and his face had been hit badly. His eyes were shut. He could not talk much. It hurt too much to breathe in. He told them what he could. Ephraim, who had been on his way out, suspected Nig-Nag of lying.

"Are you sure that it was slave catchers and not just some of your friends who wanted your bottle?"

Nig-Nag rolled his eyes at Ephraim and rolled them back again to the ceiling, too hurt to be afraid.

"Kick, fuck, shit. Fuck 'im, Bo-Bo. Fuck, fuck." He began to cough and sputter.

"Oh, no," Della said. "Oh, no. I can't have that in my house."

"Get 'im out," Ephraim ordered no one in particular.

"Wait, Ephraim," Tyree said.

"Yes?"

"I'll help you take him over to the church for safekeeping."

"Hah."

"Slave catchers. Slave catcher men," Nig-Nag said. "They made Bo-Bo cry."

"We've never had slave catchers go into one of our houses. They wouldn't dare," Della said.

"Why not? What's to stop them? They don't even have streetlamps there," said Tyree.

"Look at him." Mercer put a wet rag to his lips and squeezed in a drop.

"Shit, fuck, fuck, fuck." Nig-Nag could only whisper and spit.

"Oh, Lord," Mercer said. "Is that blood comin outta his mouth?"

"Probably busted his tongue or something." Tyree took Nig-Nag's jaw in his cupped palm and squeezed open his lips. Two teeth had been knocked out. "So, come on, we'll take him to church."

"He's had his time living off the church," Ephraim said. "Reverend Brown let him live there for months, and he defiled the sanctuary. He stole things—"

"Just for a while. Christ, man, look at him."

Mercer watched bloody saliva bubble from the side of Nig-Nag's mouth.

"Fuck, fuck, fuck, fuck."

She could barely hear him now.

She washed his face. The water seemed to revive him.

"Choo-choo. Shit."

Della's head snapped around. "Oh, no, sir. Not here."

Mercer asked Della for some ale and water. Della inclined her head to the basement door. Mercer went downstairs, drew some ale from the keg, and added water. She offered it to Nig-Nag, who sucked at the cup noisily.

Tyree, meanwhile, had cornered Ephraim. He leaned against the wall, with his elbow next to Ephraim's head.

"So?"

"For another thing, we really need permission from the reverend."

Other ne'er-do-wells and idiots whom the church lodged routinely in the basement went to sleep and stayed put. But not Nig-Nag. He had sneaked around and climbed up through a loose board. He broke the board. Then he curled up in the choir loft and masturbated there and fell asleep. It wasn't something to say in front of women.

"Let me talk to you alone," Ephraim said to Tyree.

"No, no," Tyree said. He stepped into the shed kitchen and brought back Roland's old coat that hung by the back door.

"Tyree," Della said, "I like that coat."

"We use it for the privy."

"And doesn't it come in handy?"

Abby Ann entered the kitchen, trailing her shawls and rubbing her eyes. "We gave him Roland's old clothes before. I'm sure he got the brown coat with the black patches."

"Might as well throw it down a rathole," Della said irritably. She could see Tyree was determined.

"Well, go ahead, take it."

"You must go back to bed," Ephraim said. Abby Ann smiled with ostentatious wanness and left the kitchen.

"Ephraim," said Tyree. "You'll see to it that my mother gets her coat back, won't you?"

"If I have to rip it off him myself, Mrs. Quick." Ephraim laughed and took the old coat with a flourish.

"Will you call a doctor for him?" Mercer asked. Every now and then a new trickle of blood dripped from Nig-Nag's nose or mouth. She kept thinking of how the boy had grinned at her when she'd hissed out her story to him at Bloodgood's Hotel. Ephraim did not answer. Instead, he bent to wrap Nig-Nag in the coat.

"Don't fret about this boy," Ephraim said to her. He was using his Reverend Ephraim voice. "I'll take care of him."

Mercer appealed to Tyree.

"Very few white doctors you can trust after a thing like this," he said.

"If it really was slave catchers, you mean."

"Did they take Bo-Bo and Jack too, you say?" Tyree asked Nig-Nag.

"Fucked him. Beat 'em up. Bang my head in the door."

"But why do all that," Ephraim wondered, "if you want to sell people back into slavery?"

"Bo-Bo and Jack can take it. You'll notice they left Nig-Nag. Probably thought he was dead."

"There's no reason we couldn't send a note to John Oliver, the doctor's assistant," offered Harriet. "He'd come, I suppose."

"And charge for it too."

"I'll pay him," Mercer offered, to their surprise.

"I shall hold you to that, then," Ephraim said with an amused smile. "Ty, help me to the curb."

Harriet went to her desk and wrote a note to Dr. Wilcox's longtime assistant, a black man from Jamaica named John Oliver, and stuffed it into Ephraim's pocket as he and Tyree carried Nig-Nag out to the trap Ephraim had accepted as a loan from one of his parishioners.

Ephraim drove to the rectory, borrowed Father Brown's key, and lugged Nig-Nag into the sanctuary.

"You polluted this place once before," he said. "This time you'll sit here in the entryway. You'll be safe, you hear me, boy, and you'll be warmer than you'd be outdoors, so just be grateful."

In a slurred voice, Nig-Nag asked, "Jesus died for me?"

Ephraim was caught off guard. "What's your Christian name, boy?"

"Wilfred."

"Jesus died for all our sins, Wilfred, yours and mine."

"He died for me?"

"He died for you."

Ephraim expected Nig-Nag to ask what he needed to do for forgiveness, but he did not.

In the dark entryway, lit by one candle, which Ephraim would soon snuff out, Nig-Nag looked almost girlish. Ephraim felt a sudden compassion for him. He went to the basement, where they kept blankets for the poor. Nig-Nag was the poor, after all, so Ephraim tucked two blankets around him. He put his hand on Nig-Nag's forehead and recited the beatitudes. By the time he finished, the boy was asleep.

Ephraim looked at Nig-Nag, who was sitting with his knees drawn to his chest. He made the sign of the cross over him and hurried to return the horse and rig. As he was finally walking home, he felt a piece of paper in his pocket: the note to John Oliver. The Christ Church bell tower had gone eleven. It was too late to disturb the old gentleman. He'd send a boy in the morning.

Ephraim awoke early and went to church. Mercer stood on the steps, waiting for him; she carried a small parcel of food. He felt a wheedling irritation. Mercer was a celebrity now and, to Ephraim's mind, getting uppity. The Quicks, who regarded themselves as quite a special family, no doubt encouraged her to think of herself as quite a special fugitive.

"Morning, Reverend," she said sternly.

Good Lord, he thought, what a tone of voice. He looked at her squarely. "We've come a long way since that first psalm in the cemetery, haven't we?"

"Yes, sir, we have."

He opened the door. In the vestibule, Nig-Nag had fallen over sideways. He was dead.

. . .

Mercer insisted on accompanying Tyree to Nig-Nag's room. She'd never seen the kind of filth she found in his alley. A man with empty eyes opened the door. The wood was rotten and warped at the bottom. Inside was dark; it stank of old sweat and waste. A woman huddled in one corner on a horse blanket, clutching a newborn baby. A man and a young woman sat on the floor with four children. Next to the window stood one chair, obviously the place for the man who had opened the door for them.

"Mr. Quick," he said, sounding afraid. "Mrs. Quick, how do?" He nodded his head and shuffled.

"I'm not Mrs.—"

"Listen, we was comin right over to ask you about the place, and to pay you. But since it were empty, I let my family get in out the cold. You don't mind that?"

"Who came and got Bo-Bo and Jack?" Tyree asked.

"I don't know much about the men who was kidnapped," he said. "They tol' me they was kidnapped. I don't know. I didn't see it. Except that one of 'em was a bad nigger. Beat my boy, there, for no reason while I'm out workin and my wife were sick."

"Well, you tell anybody you know who knew Nig-Nag—you know the boy?"

"The skinny one, used to bark?"

"Yes. Tell 'em he's dead, and he's gonna have a service tomorrow afternoon, just past quitting time, over at St. Thomas."

The man rolled his eyes and nodded as if he were paying careful attention, and yet Mercer was certain that when they left, he would do nothing but go back to sitting by the window. She'd seen his face when they walked by.

"Mr. Quick, sir? You got any work, you let me know. I'm handy with tools."

"The rent is half a dollar a week, and I'll come for it on Saturday," Tyree called over his shoulder.

"They probably told the kidnappers just when to come," he

said after they'd stepped out of the alley and onto the street. "You know these catchers employ colored men to go out and scout."

"Because the man beat their boy?"

Tyree shrugged. "Could be. Could be he didn't beat 'im, but they wanted the room bad enough, and that's their story."

"Then they don't know how bad a thing they did."

"Could be."

A man with a limp called after them, and they stopped and waited for him to catch up. His name was Jim Freeman. Tyree knew that he lived in the alley and had taken Nig-Nag in now and then in winter. He'd been beaten and routed in the raid too, he said.

"Did they do that to you?" Tyree indicated his bad leg.

"No, sir. That been that way for a couple, three months. That's why I'm still here. The other two was middling: middling brown, middling height, middling weight, ever'thing, see. No limps, no marks nor nothin. You describe them, could be describing anybody. Easy to steal; easy to sell. . . . Well, sir, did I hear you right? The boy's dead and the funeral's tomorrow?"

"Such as it is. At St. Thomas."

"Thank you. It's decent to do it for 'im. Good day, ma'am."

Nothing could be done about the kidnapped men, but Ephraim volunteered to give Nig-Nag a funeral. It turned out to be a sorry affair. The undertaker wanted ten dollars to wash and dress the body and pump it full of formaldehyde, so they bought the cheapest box he had and paid him a dollar and a half extra to come break the body where rigor had set in and stuff him into it. They kept the coffin closed.

In addition to the Quick family, Jim Freeman showed up with four men from the alley. So did a handful of elderly church members who never missed any funeral. George from Bloodgood's came late, dressed for work, and left early.

Ephraim read from the Song of Solomon: "Who is this that

cometh up from the wilderness, leaning upon her beloved? I raised thee up under the apple tree: there thy mother brought thee forth: there she brought thee forth that bare thee."

He had developed a habit of stopping in the middle of the text and looking meaningfully at the congregation. When he did this time, his last words hung in Mercer's mind. She had no idea what the passage was that he was reciting; she knew only that Nig-Nag had no mother or father to mourn him, nor any family, either. Who knew who had borne him or where? Who cared? What apple tree?

Ephraim continued: "Set me as a seal upon thine heart, as a seal upon thine arm: for love is strong as death; jealousy is cruel as the grave: the coals thereof are coals of fire, which hath a most vehement flame."

Then he spoke about Nig-Nag, referring to him as Wilfred and calling him "eager to help," "cheerful," and "sometimes full of mischief." He mentioned in passing that Wilfred's willingness to please had made him an agent of God's work through the Vigilance Committee.

Poor Nig-Nag, Mercer thought. What would she have done without him? Love might be as strong as death, but who of the sparse group of assembled mourners had loved this pitiful young man? Had anyone washed his body or laid him out to cool before they busted him up and shoved him into his box?

Then Ephraim admonished them to take the eternal life that Jesus offered, "because he is coming and we do not know the day, because death comes to us all and we do not know the hour; because he is coming, because he is coming—he promised us he'd be back—commit yourself to him. Happy, I say, are those who die in the Lord."

He didn't dwell too long on what happens to people who don't, because no one suspected the broken body in the box at the rear of the church of serenity at the end, and they knew besides that he might not be dead had he not spent his last nickel getting drunk behind a houseful of whores.

Poor Nig-Nag, Mercer thought. Poor Wilfred. God bless his soul.

The public cemetery for paupers lay a few blocks away. The men hoisted the box onto a carter's dray, handed him half a dollar, and told him they'd follow on foot. Earlier that day, Tyree had stopped to pay a bribe to the city caretaker, who muttered about digging the hole, and then muttered again because he wanted a larger bribe than Tyree had given him. Ephraim closed the church. They heard the doors bang behind them as the dray clattered away, bobbling the cheap coffin under carelessly tied ropes.

Harriet took the children back to the schoolroom to help her clean up for the night. Tyree, Blanche, Della, Mercer, Sharkey, and Jim Freeman, with two of the men who'd accompanied him, walked behind the dray. At the pauper's graveyard, they helped Tyree hoist the box off the wagon and across the frozen ground to the shallow hole the man had dug. The box had no handles; they jostled it and felt the awkward weight of the body. The men took turns shoveling dirt in, just so that they'd be sure Nig-Nag would actually get the hole Tyree had paid for.

"He looks so alone," Mercer said.

"He is alone," Tyree answered. He took his turn at the shovel and passed it on. "And he died alone, poor soul, like a dog. But we are here now, and I suppose that's something. Not much, though, for the powerful thing he did in a powerless life."

The Quicks and Mercer shook hands with Jim Freeman and his friends in the bleak gray. On the way home, the Quicks met Manny.

"Oh, Jesus," Della said. "My husband is losing his mind."

Manny wore two cravats and no overcoat. Della had not drawn on his mustache. His face looked naked, the gray hairs of his natural mustache wispy and frail. He walked unsteadily.

"Aren't you goin to the funeral?" he asked.

"Funeral's over, Mr. Quick," Della said.

Tyree stood still, frowning. "Why are you wearing two cravats, Daddy?"

"Huh?"

"Oh, don't, Tyree," Blanche said.

Tyree frowned at her too. "How'll he know if we don't tell 'im?"

"He fell again last night, and his eyes were just shakin back and forth somethin awful, Ty. Don't scold your own father," she said.

"He got himself out here, didn't he?"

"That's it," Manny said eagerly. "That's it, Ty. Now run home. I'll be along."

"Go on," Sharkey said to the women. "Tyree and I'll stay with him. Go on home."

They left. Behind them they heard the three men arguing.

No one spoke until they arrived at the Quicks' house. Abby Ann was sitting in the parlor, waiting for someone to make tea, when they came home. Blanche told her in detail about the service. Abby Ann became furious when she heard that Ephraim had used the Song of Solomon verses.

"That was for our wedding," she said before stomping upstairs.

That night, Mercer and Harriet took out each other's hair, as was their custom, brushed and oiled it, braided it tight to make it straight, and then tied it with kerchiefs.

"Miss Harriet," Mercer said into the dark, "if I write to Miss Randall tomorrow, will you read my letter and correct it for me?"

"You're going to speak?"

"Yes."

"Just because Nig-Nag died, you don't have to, you know."

"Yes, I do."

Once Mercer committed herself to the tour, Tyree and Harriet accelerated the pace of her studies. And one night Tyree announced that he would take her to hear a lecture given by his friend.

"Not that man Silver, I hope," said Della.

"Yes, Silver, Mother."

"Oh, no. He's the most arrogant thing."

Blanche looked worried. Roland and Silver had been friends too, and Silver was for emigration to Africa. Tyree had threatened before to take Mercer to hear him, but hadn't had time. "She doesn't need to hear them, Tyree."

"Yes, she does. I'll take Sharkey to protect her from pernicious ideas."

At a quarter past seven, Tyree, Sharkey, and Mercer stepped out of a light rain into one half of the parlor of Mrs. Sadler's boardinghouse. Mrs. Sadler's husband, now dead, had created a large-capacity boardinghouse years before by punching an archway in the common wall of two adjoining houses. The parlor was so large that groups that chose to avoid the cost of a hall would come to Mrs. Sadler with a few dollars and a date. The African and Caribbean emigration groups chose Mrs. Sadler's because she was a democratic lady, and unlike the proprietors of most privately owned residences, did not mind sponsoring groups she disagreed with—so long as they paid promptly.

Tyree spotted the evening's speaker, Wayland Silver, through the doorway in Mrs. Sadler's dining room, drinking something before he began. He put his cup down and strode toward Tyree with open arms. They embraced without words and held each other. Sharkey explained to Mercer that Silver had attended Thetford Academy in Vermont with Roland and Tyree, and together Roland and Silver had decided that they were going to Africa. They'd had a falling-out just before Roland was killed.

"How do they look?" Silver asked Tyree, referring to the people who were assembling in the parlor.

"Stiff."

"Hah. They always look stiff," Silver said in a whisper. He shook Sharkey's hand and stood in front of Mercer while Tyree introduced them.

"I am honored to make your acquaintance, Miss Gray. I have followed your story with interest and sympathy. You'll never know how many people you've inspired or how many prayers you've received."

Silver looked at Mercer appraisingly with his small, black, mischievous eyes. He exuded health and charm and critical judgment, sharp and active.

"We've brought Mercer to hear your brand of speechifying, Wayland," Sharkey said, "because the abolitionists have engaged her to speak in New England in the spring. Have you any advice for her?"

"Take your winter clothes," he said. His smile remained as engaging, but Mercer thought she saw him taking her measure with his own personal tape. "What they call spring there isn't. And I hope you'll not be too offended by what I say tonight. There's freedom, and there's freedom."

"I don't understand what you mean," Mercer said.

"No. I shouldn't think you would."

"Don't be Delphic, Silver. We brought Miss Gray because we thought that she'd be interested in your views."

Silver raised an eyebrow. He took a deep breath and spoke wearily, sometimes looking at Mercer, sometimes looking through the doorway into the parlor, which was almost full by now.

"I'll tell you the truth," he said. "The Negro Emigrationist Society has sent me, has paid me (or will pay me, and soon, I hope) to convince African-Americans to return to Africa. I know, of course, that this scheme will be of greatest benefit to those who had money to make the greatest investment. Not these people here but the businessmen who've sent me, and are paying me, or will pay me, soon. I do not approve of the situation, but I accept their money. All of us, Miss Gray, are working for someone.

Most lecturers are too vain or too naive to keep that in mind, but it's true.

"What I want to do is keep giving these men facts, and facts and more facts, such as few of them would read in *The Liberator,* or *The Anglo-African,* or *The Christian Recorder*—those few of them who can and do read. We are a thinking people, capable of pride and strong feeling, but we have so few alternatives for our moral and political thoughts except for the word on the street or the word in the pulpit."

Silver's eyes narrowed to slits, and his carved lips sneered under his mustache.

"Preachers, literary societies, Freemason groups—all of them, Miss Gray, like to give their poorer brothers the predictable uplift harangue: frugality, temperance, modesty. And yet they know good and well that these men out here are heading back to their alleys, as soon as we finish speechifying at them, for a belt of whatever they can afford.

"Know what I call it? Race pudding. Negro speakers spoon it out and Negro audiences suck it up, night after night, in parlors from Boston to the Mason and Dixon line. It is that and a pious, churchy mandate for gratitude that will enslave the rest of us as surely as our brothers in chains are enslaved in the South. Our leaders, you see, don't want to be embarrassed, so they must keep us nice and quiet.

"So, there, Tyree. Have I been a beast to your lady speaker?"

"No, sir. I've been through plenty enough." Mercer answered him in an even voice, making sure, as Harriet had drilled her, not to say "I been" to this man. "You don't scare me."

"Well, good," he said.

He seemed sincere. Mercer was confused.

"So," Tyree said, "you got more speech left, nigger?"

"Go to hell," Wayland said.

Tyree and Sharkey laughed. They wished Silver well and went to claim seats at the back of the room.

Three dozen people, mostly men, shifted in Mrs. Sadler's motley collection of wooden chairs, castoffs from the deceased Mr. Sadler's many white employers. Much of the stiffness Tyree had noticed was caused by the unpredictability of their mounts, which besides being old and wobbly were likely to give off splinters.

"They *have* come for uplift," Tyree whispered to Mercer. "Or at least for comfort. I think we do come hoping for some comfort, at least, or hope. Silver may have a hard time selling them."

"Hope," Mercer said, her eyes bright. "I never thought of that."

Wayland Silver smiled, but not too broadly, as he walked to the front of the parlor. He'd dressed that evening in simple clothes, but they were well made and of rich fabric. If he were poorly dressed, they would doubt his credibility, and if too well dressed, his sincerity. As it was, the men calculated the cost of his waistcoat, and they were alert for insult. They knew that Wayland Silver had had everything a colored man could want in life and was not satisfied; in a moment, he would become, in their eyes, an educated Negro speaking treachery. They were uneducated and poor, despised by the common white man and hemmed in by law and custom. Men who lined their shoes with hot pepper to ward off the cold did not need to be told that they'd done a bad job of shoeing themselves.

Silver proceeded slowly and cautiously, invoking divine providence. He was determined to touch the folk who resisted him. Their eyes warned him to begin gently as he attacked the good white folk who gave blankets to colored widows and ran homes for colored orphans. But he would attack, not because he expected any of them to pack their bags for Africa tomorrow, but precisely because they never dared to dream of it.

He started by thanking Mrs. Sadler for the room, thanking the people for coming, and giving honor and glory to God. That done, he launched in:

"Twenty years ago, when my father and my uncle and several people here began their work on what some people like to call the Underground Railroad, the New England Anti-Slavery Society decided to build a school for colored men and women to receive manual training. Now, that same year, the National Negro Convention met, with colored delegates from New York, Ohio, Illinois, New England, Pennsylvania, Delaware, and points south. Perhaps you remember. They voted support for the school, and Mr. Lloyd Garrison, that most famous abolition leader, took off for England to raise the funds. But the next year, when Mr. Gerrit Smith opened his school in Peterboro, New York, or when the Institute for Colored Youth was established here in Philadelphia, did Mr. Garrison hail them? Did he mention them with pride and admiration? Did he run out and raise money for them? Two new institutions carrying on the good work that he has said must go on throughout this country?

"Well, you'd think he would, wouldn't you? You'd think he would, but I'm afraid you'd be wrong.

"Mr. Garrison would have nothing to do with them. Not a thing. And why not? Because they weren't *his* schools. You hear what I'm saying, ladies and gentlemen? Here were places where our people would be able to receive the education that Mr. Garrison claims to want to see us get. It's just that he wants us to come to him for it.

"We have some friends, my brothers and sisters, who enjoy helping us so very much that they don't want anyone else to have the pleasure. Why, some of our so-called friends have got so used to caring for us that they don't even like it when we take care of ourselves. Some of our friends—this is a terrible thing to have to say, but it's true—some of them would rather see us sink in ignorance and despair than find our own way to freedom.

"We must open our eyes and see our friends. God knows the abolitionists are our friends; they do toil mightily in our cause. But we must know our friends for who and what they are.

"Now, ladies and gentlemen, it is clear that we have friends who love us, some too well, some not well enough. We have friends. But they cannot do for us what we must do for ourselves. They cannot decide our destiny for us; nor can they push us there.

"I forgot, by the way, to tell you what happened to Mr. Garrison's school. You know that the Institute for Colored Youth right over there on Lombard Street is thriving, and the Peterboro School is growing too. Mr. Garrison's school, however, ran into some difficulty, I'm afraid."

He had them. The people in the adjoining parlors began to shake their heads.

"Oh, Lord," said an albino preacher, an itinerant who came to court Mrs. Sadler each time he passed through Philadelphia. "Well, tell it."

"Yes, sir, I will," Silver responded. "I'll tell you that at first they were going to build a separate colored school, and then they changed their minds. But once the Negro students enrolled with the others," he said, shaking his head, "once they were enrolled, I say, and just as they were about to begin the school year, it became clear that Mr. Garrison et al. had misjudged the situation.

"Now, this was happening in New Canaan, New Hampshire. But nobody had talked to the New Canaanites. The fact was they didn't like the plan. Didn't like it at all. So when the young people were all set to begin school, the townspeople hitched a team of oxen and pulled the building down. Just like that. Tore it down. So there was no school. There is no school."

Silver watched the bitter half-smiles. Sharkey nodded his head and raised an eyebrow. Mercer frowned slightly with concentration. The story had twists and turns. She was trying to follow.

"We need to know our friends. We need to study those who would free us from slavery only to deliver us into second-class citizenship. They sold my granddaddy as a quarter hand when he was six, then a half hand when he was ten, and a full hand when he was eighteen and able to earn another man's fortune for him.

"Where in America can we earn our own fortunes?"

Silver paused. Rain was falling hard now and coming in the windows. A few men jumped up to close them. The parlor became suddenly quiet and steamy.

"You see," Silver said, "there are no Garrisons in Liberia. They do not ask, 'Mother, may I?' in Haiti. In Yorubaland and the Niger River Valley, where the butterflies travel in clouds of color, or in the gentle rolling hills of Central America, black men and women do not have to *buy* their aging parents out of slavery or hire out their children to do the work of grown men."

Mercer could not stop watching him or listening to him, even though every word he said made her feel exhausted, as if she'd come so far and paid so dear for nothing. But the phrase about buying old parents stuck in her head. Yes, yes, yes, it was a scandal to have to do it, but could it be done? And would he and the others help?

"A young man asked me the other day," Silver continued in the hushed room, "how I could possibly trust the whites in the American Colonization Society to have our best interests at heart. Well, let me tell you: I do not. I do not trust them.

"I do not trust the *New York Herald*, which urged the government to encourage us to emigrate to Liberia because our 'racial inferiority' makes us a burden on the United States.

"You know as well as I do that when the American Colonization Society made its first overtures to Africans here in Philadelphia in 1817, before many of us were even born, three thousand men and women thronged Bethel A.M.E. to protest. Since then, of course, most of us have even refused to call ourselves Africans, so afraid are we that someone might notice and send us back. . . . Although no matter what we call ourselves, I'll wager they still know an African when they see one."

They laughed.

"I see. Folks have noticed you all too, eh?"

"But as I was saying, I do not trust the state legislatures that have given upwards of thirty-five thousand dollars each toward schemes to send colored Americans to Africa. I do not trust the

Virginia politicians who have levied a tax on the free colored men of their state for the purpose of raising emigration money. Huh. I do not trust any of them at all, and I say to you, my brethren, neither should you."

From inside the kitchen Mercer heard the rattling of cups. Silver had said that they had paid Mrs. Sadler extra to pour a tea for the audience after the talk. It made people feel a part of something prosperous.

Silver wiped his face and breathed and went on. Mercer could see that he was winding up. She could not tell where he was going.

"But I do trust our own, gentlemen and ladies. I do trust Dr. Martin Delaney, graduate of Harvard University Medical School and Pittsburgh's most prominent colored citizen, who just last year considered the issue of Negro emancipation in his excellent work, *The Condition, Elevation, Emigration, and Destiny of the Colored People of the United States*. Dr. Delaney advocates what he calls a Negro Promised Land in South America.

"I do trust the Reverend Samuel Williams of Johnstown, Pennsylvania, who took a party to Liberia and has returned so deeply impressed by the sight of free black men on free black soil that he has organized the Liberian Enterprise Company to encourage us Pennsylvanians to consider—just consider, mind you—that there might be an alternative to the fractional-hand status we endure in this place that we can only advisedly call home."

The men clapped and shouted. The few women clapped too. Silver mopped his face. A sycophantic writer from *The Christian Recorder* shook his hand. Even those who were appalled at the thought of sailing farther than the mouth of Delaware Bay pumped each other's arms.

Mercer thought she knew what Tyree had wanted her to see. She made a bow toward Silver; he nodded back with a weary smile.

Eleven / Her Father's Tooth

No more than two dozen people, three of them black, came to the church in the Massachusetts town where Mercer was to give her first talk. It was a Methodist church, homey, with wooden pews close to the pulpit and red leather stretched over the top of the altar rail and stained brown by the hands of supplicants. The wooden cross that hung behind the pulpit was unadorned except for a crown of thorns. Mercer noticed the cross and noticed, too, that it would hang over her head like judgment when she stood in the pulpit to speak.

The people came in promptly, just before seven and a half o'clock. They nodded and chatted in whispers. Mercer could see them from the pastor's office, where she was waiting with her caretaker and guide, Prudence Randall, who held her hand and patted it at regular intervals.

Prudence was a hand-holder. Mercer wished it were not so, but there was no getting around it. The white woman had held her hand on the cars, in carriages, and, now, it appeared that she was going to keep hold of Mercer in churches and halls and schoolhouses up and down New England.

"What good fortune to begin our tour here, Mercer," Prudence said. She insisted they call each other by first names. "These people are, for the most part, quite sympathetic to our cause."

Mercer felt nervous. Her hands and knees shook. She reminded herself again that she was not merely a display, but she felt like one: a bearded lady, a snake tamer. Look, look: a shackled ostrich, pet, statue, slave. The bent-over gal with her head stuck between the gap in the pig fence by the pasture with her skirt torn off and stuffed in her mouth.

On your knees, boys. Now I lay me. Hah-hah-hah.

Look, look, look.

What, in Christ's name, did she have to tell *them*, people with schooling and homes and businesses? What did she have?

The pastor, a tall, thin man, led her out onto the pulpit's platform and directed her to sit down while he introduced her.

"My dear," he said quietly, "you must remember to breathe."

Mercer felt herself smile broadly at him. "Yes, sir. I've been told that before."

"And here I am telling you again. Well, we learn through repetition, don't we? . . . Just breathe and ask the Lord to breathe His word into you. A minister told me that in seminary."

He looked at her mildly. Mercer breathed in slowly through her nose and prayed. The minister smiled.

"Are you ready?"

"Yes, sir."

He took his own breath, the air pushing against nostrils as sharp as slits, and began. He praised Prudence Randall's work and the New England Anti-Slavery Society, and said that he'd heard excellent things about Mercer Gray.

Then he motioned for her to stand. She put out her hand for him to shake as she'd seen other speakers do, but he seemed not to see it. Was it that she was a woman, a black woman? Or maybe he didn't see it. She hoped the awkwardness might have been hidden behind the pulpit. Now the hand that she'd extended was shaking badly. The minister stepped behind her and sat down. Mercer turned to the people.

She began her talk with thanks to the pastor and Miss Randall, the Society, and the church, and followed her thanks with apologies for presuming to come before them, in her ignorance, and press them to listen to her talk. She claimed to do it not for herself alone but for the thousands of her sisters and brothers who were still in bondage.

It had seemed the right thing to say when she'd prepared the talk and delivered it to the assembled audience in Manny's and Della's parlor, but now it fell flat. She felt that she'd lost something by apologizing for her ignorance. Her own voice answered: Well, don't *be* ignorant. Or else don't stand up behind the pulpit, and under the cross, cryin poor-mouth. She had planned to apologize for presuming to come before them, a woman, but she left that part out. She'd known she was a woman before she came. Her ears burned. Fear flexed and curled in her belly. She bore down to keep from peeing.

"I was born a slave. My parents were slaves. I had an older sister, but she died in childbirth with no doctor to attend her, and my brother died of disease when he was a boy. My father was sold when I was four or five years old, and my mother died when I was about ten. I have never seen my father since. I have wondered many times why I was left, but now that I stand here before you, I suppose I have been spared to tell the tale. I will try to tell it as best I can, ladies and gentlemen, and let truth be its own adornment.

"People up North here often ask me about whippins. They want to know if I was whipped, and how bad, and how often. The only really bad whippin I received was at the hand of my master's mother. When my mother was sold, you see, I was set to the task of carrying delicate laundry things and ironing them. That would be the ladies' lace and bobbin lace and special garments. I was given the job because my mother had been a seamstress, and she'd taken to have me with her to wash and iron the fancy things she sewed, so they figured that was work I could do.

"On this particular day, I slipped in the mud while I was carrying the laundry basket in from outdoors. Some of the clean things spilled on the ground and got dirtied. Well, I'll tell you that I was so angry with that basket I didn't know what to do, and sad too, I think mostly sad, since my mother was gone, and most of these things in the basket were dainties that my mother had made. So when these one or two things dropped, I just stomped my foot in a temper. But that was the wrong thing to do."

Mercer stopped and shook her head. To her surprise, a small chortle of amusement ran through the audience. Well, of course, she thought. These people had worked. And who had not had the experience of being young and careless? Who had not lost his temper?

"Like I say, it bein so muddy, stompin was the worst thing. I stomped, and my foot—'cause we didn't have shoes until winter—my foot, I say, went right on out from under me. I slipped and fell, and next thing you know, the whole basket went down, and instead of me havin dirtied two or three fancy things, I done ruined the whole batch. Worse yet, one little piece o' one got tore.

"Nobody was around, so I thought to make up some lie about how a snake jumped out from under a rock and nearly bit me.

"It's a terrible thing, but truth is, I learned early to lie. In this case, though, when I commence to tell the lie about the snake, the grandmother of the master's household was standin listenin at the top of the steps, and told 'em to send me on up to her, and she'd do the job herself. What I didn't know was that she had been watchin all the while out the window. She sent somebody to get her one of them short little buggy whips, and she whipped me first for carelessness, and next for temper, and finally for lying."

Mercer felt as if she were watching herself and hearing her own words. She sounded utterly unremarkable. Same ol'. Here she was all tricked up to give a big speech, and what did she say? Same ol'. And the story she was telling: how did she get there, claiming a whipping whose scars she had no intention of showing; revealing her own young practice of lying? They didn't understand that sort of outright lying, these people. When they lied, they believed themselves, like children do.

"And right here, now, I've got to take a moment and point out how one of the worse things about slavery is that it makes people lie. This is no excuse for my lying. It's not an excuse, mind you, but only to try to help you God-fearin and upright people understand what an evil influence this kind of living is. I lied, and it seemed the most natural thing in the world.

"Masters sure enough lie every day, too, and there's no help for it. Either they have to look us in the face and say the truth: You a human being just like me, and I'm still gonna keep you down; or else they gotta lie and say: You a human being, but not like me and mine. You don't feel things like I do. You don't grieve like I do for your family. You don't need anything of your own to have and to keep, to feel like a man or woman. You don't need a proper marriage, 'cause you don't have no shame."

Mercer did not want to sound pathetic. Who the hell would want to free liars and whores and thieves? Wretches who could not care for themselves? That's what white America suspected of them, and here she was giving them proof.

She saw herself in her mind, a big slave puppet dancing to a fiddle, and the white folks standing around in a half-circle, tapping their feet. *Oh. Oh. Oh. Loves to dance dance dance.* Then she saw the puppet where she was, in the pulpit, jerking and jumping, yelling like a fool:

> *Yep. Drop them clothes in that mud, and the old bitch*
> *come down on me like a owl on a mouse. Beat me bad.*

Then the puppet flings a scarred wooden leg out from one side of the pulpit, undergarments pulled way up. *Looky 'ere, y'all.*

> *Puts me in mind of another old woman I know did that*
> *once too many times—uh-oh—and this mulatto woman, crazy*
> *yallow gal with blue eyes, honey, throwed her right off the back*

*steps. Boom. Y'all know what I mean? Knocked her ass off the
damn steps, I tell you. Boom. Broke her neck too. Dead. I bet
she didn't never worry nobody about no devilish laundry again.
You know what I mean?*

Mercer trembled. It was like the trembling that takes hold
of a woman toward the end of labor, as if her body were a piece of
linen, pinned to the clothesline to flap and crack in the wind.

She forced her face to be still. She forced her voice to stay
low and calm. She steered her mind back to the faces in front of
her. She looked at them, not too hard or too long, but directly.
There they sat, willing to listen or to dismiss her, equally capable
of affection or scorn. She hadn't known that she might have to
lead them.

Mercer felt suddenly weary and alone. It was clear to her
that she had to gather her strength and go on. She had to carry
these people with her and drag them along like a plow for this one
night, for three quarters of an hour, at least; or else she had to
give up and let them watch her jerk and dance in the pulpit. If she
did not make them feel something, they'd pull back and leave her
alone in their midst for daring to open her blasphemous black
mouth in a white man's pulpit. They'd crap on her and call her
stink. They'd hate anyone who tried to lead them and failed, and
they'd hate a black woman more. She was supposed to bring un-
expected, but wished-for, hope.

"So we were practiced in lying on both sides. We learned
not to see what we saw, and not to know what we knew, and not
to feel what we felt. Some folks among us, though, taught us to
see. And said we should remember and hold on to a tiny scrap of
hope, even when there was nothing to hope for.

"My husband"—so she called Cooper in their presence—
"ran away to the North before our first child was born. I was to go
with him, but I got caught. I did not try to run away again until I
was presented with the opportunity fourteen years later."

She listened closely to each word out of her mouth. "Ran

away" wasn't good enough. That made Cooper sound like a child or a dog. But what else would they understand? A man in Clayton County was hanged for biting off an overseer's ear. I'n't leaving better? He left because he had to. 'Cause it would have killed him to stay. 'Cause the law's a lie, so he broke it. And who cares? He beat the owners at their own game. He said: To hell with this, and catch me if you can. Pay the cost to be the boss.

What Cooper would have said, of course, was: Y'all can kiss my black ass.

The church was warm now. The stove had heated up, and the people's bodies filled the front half of the building.

"Run away. . . . Some parts of slavery I'll never run away from. Slavery touches the body like the devil did to Job. It gets in your belly with bad food. It gets in your feet with the frost. It gets in your blood with the fevers and comes out in crippled-up fingers and bad hearts and weak lungs and sour stomachs. Sometimes people's minds seize up like a rusty engine. Slavery is death-dealing.

"But people do live, don't they? Folk say that, as if to say, 'Well, if it's so bad, how come you all keep on living? If you weren't made for slavery, whyn't you just die like the Indians?' And I don't know the answer to that.

"What I do know is that easy as slavery can kill the body, it can kill the soul. It was killing me, so slowly that I almost couldn't tell.

"I did run away. Call it that if you will, but much as I was runnin away from slavery, I was runnin toward freedom. The men from the Underground Railroad had their hands out, beckoning me. People in the crowd were no further away than we are right here. And I felt as if a voice was saying to me: If you want your freedom, stand.

"I wanted my freedom, and I stood."

That night, Mercer and Prudence slept at one of the parishioners' houses, in a dusty upstairs room. They sneezed.

"They got dust on top of dust, don't they?"

Prudence opened a window. "Is that better? Does that give us a breath of air," she whispered, "or does it blow the dust around?"

"I can't tell." Mercer thought she saw a face form itself in the leaves outside. She was too tired to look, or to tangle with her mind. Though the room was quiet and the audience gone, her mind continued to chatter and chuck like a family of squirrels. She propped herself in bed as Zilpha had taught her, closed her eyes, said a prayer for her children, and fell quickly into shallow sleep.

She dreamt of a city. In it, lions, such as the ones in Harriet's picture books, sat like dogs behind wooden fences. She could see them in the yards as if she were flying over them. One lion lay in the sun in a brickyard, shaking his mane. He was straw-covered and hot, so heavy that the pads of his paws sank into the cracks between the stones. Mercer could see his ribs as he panted, could even see the fleas and flies flurry and then settle again as he shook his mane. He yawned, and as he did, Mercer realized that inside the lion's mane was the face of a dog. The dog's face was a deception. He looked gentle, but he was deadly. He was waiting for someone to come down the alley or out the back door, and then he'd lure him with doglike movements and devour him.

A man walked through an archway. She could barely see his face. When he smiled, his teeth leaked blood.

She awoke suddenly before dawn. Her nose and throat were congested, and her eyes scratchy and dry. She wanted warm weather, safety, Bennie, Mattie, Etta, Tyree. Prudence coughed in the bed next to her. She, too, was awake. They left the house gladly at first light. Mercer said a muted thanks in a raspier voice than usual.

"I know we told you to make sure not to talk too long," Prudence said as they rode in a light coach to the next town. "But you can actually speak a bit longer this time. You held your audience the entire time. I saw no evidence of restlessness."

"All right," Mercer answered. The countryside was bare, mud-brown with snowy patches.

"Now, then," Prudence said with gentle wariness; she seemed frightened of Mercer sometimes. "Would you like my help to do that?"

Mercer shook her head. "No, thank you." She knew she'd sounded abrupt, but she didn't care. They rode for a few minutes in silence.

"There's no shame in collaboration," Prudence said. "Accomplished people inevitably bear the stamp of others' help."

Mercer wanted nothing so much as to be left alone. She said to Prudence: "You met my friends in Philadelphia. Before I left, they sat me down and worked with me. Every evening. They've helped me compose many talks, of several lengths."

"Oh, that's good," Prudence said. She tried to conceal her relief, but Mercer noticed, and Prudence knew it. She smiled mildly. "It doesn't do to be too sensitive about such things, does it?"

They arrived at the next town in time to settle into the guest room at their sponsor's home, wash up, and prepare to eat a light supper with four Anti-Slavery people from the area. Before she knew it, Mercer was in the hall, this time the back room of a meetinghouse. She stood in front of the people, and it was as if time between the two speeches had collapsed. She felt she'd been speaking, displaying herself, talking with her husky voice, forever.

". . . Now that I've told you some of the circumstances that have led me here tonight, I'd like to talk for a moment about what happens to people's minds under slavery. Black and white, both. No one is unharmed by this.

"To you people who honor honesty and truth among yourselves, let me tell you what happens to honesty and truth when men and women live next to each other and work and live and die under the great and terrible lie that is slavery. . . ."

Her mind boiled, and the mulatto on the back porch

floated to the top again. But she did not skim the story off the top and ladle it out.

Let me get real honest here. The fool came down the steps. The woman was already evil. Anybody could see that. And there's a point where you can't push people. You can push 'em far, I'll grant you that. But you could look in this woman's funny blue eyes, and you could tell: just walk on around her and leave her be. But no, this white woman wanted to meet the devil. Must have been. 'Cause like I was told, and like I'm tellin you, she laid into her about some stupid damn laundry, and that yellow woman just snapped: threw the bitch off the porch, she did. And the woman died dead. Broke her neck. By evening, every nigger in the county had laughed about it.

Now, isn't that terrible? Woman was dead, and people laughed. But that's what happens, isn't it? You live under slavery, and it makes you dead sometimes. It kills you off by degrees, and then it kills you off for good.

Can you hear me? Or am I too damn black for you to hear?

She had to get closer to them; that was a problem. They had come into the building and sat down, and they weren't coming any closer. But how was Mercer to make a bridge? How was she to speak to them with an honesty she knew to be impossible? They could not abide to hear the ill will that had grown up in their American soil. They didn't want to know that it was woven into their sheets of cotton picked by black fingers, as surely as it seeped into their dreams. So what could she say?

Mercer could feel the short hairs at the base of her scalp escaping from their bun and curling into little black peas. "Looks like dirt on your neck," Della would say to each woman in the house whose naps did not stay straightened. As she stopped to breathe and pick her way toward her conclusion, Mercer felt her hand reach up to smooth her hair, but it was no use. She put her hand down.

"I know that many of you here have lost parents, and some might, at this very minute, be separated from dear ones—children, aunts and uncles, sisters and brothers. I understand that these are the trials of life, for which we should thank God as well as for our joys. But what slavery does, ladies and gentlemen, is take the regular trials of life and hang 'em over a man's head, like a hatchet, waiting to fall. That's what it does. That's the honest truth.

"And when will it fall? Well, the threat is that it will fall whenever he fails to please the man who calls hisself his master. It'll fall if he's ill and can't work, or old, or has an accident. It'll fall if the master has gamblin debts, or a death in the family, or a costly wedding. It'll fall just because the master decides to move somewhere else for his health. That's worse than any whippin and as bad as all the other punishments that men can think up.

"They tell me a story that is taught to schoolchildren, that President George Washington left provisions in his will for all his personal slaves to be freed but that none of them would go."

They recognized the story. She could see it.

"Can I ask you for a moment, if you've known indenture, or known someone who had to bound out himself or his children, can I please ask you to imagine yourself *not* accepting freedom handed to you? Can you imagine that those poor wretches, Mr. Washington's people, each and every one, had become so degraded that they would not even stretch out a hand to take the gift of freedom when it was offered? The chance to live out from under the hatchet, suspended by a string, thin as a cat gut, from the ceiling, worse than shackles, and always there?

"That's a awful story we tell our children, ladies and gentlemen. A awful story. Stories like that are the kind of lies that grow up from the big lie we got going in slavery. The big lie just sits around making babies. And the lies don't stay down in the South. They move all over the country. They travel on the rivers and the cars, and in the wind, and the whole country is full of 'em, like a enemy that hides, and we can't even see. Like poison in the water.

"Some friends of mine, people who helped me in Philadelphia, they say that running away is like being one foot soldier in a army. Some of you sittin here have helped that army, and God will bless you for it.

"I'ma tell you, ladies and gentlemen, it's a mighty army, a terrible army, with banners flying and little children marching right alongside, playing their drums, and men and women all ready to do their duty and ready, if they need to, to die."

They clapped for her, and the pastor smiled, and Prudence Randall grabbed her hand and squeezed it and held it.

At the entrance to the church, people waited to talk to her. Their eyes drank her in close up. One woman said that she was sorry to hear about the beating. Another asked whether she had scars. Then they inquired about the family and so on. They wanted her, Mercer, to be all right. But they did not want to have to take in her view of their world and see themselves with her trembling terror and bitter condemnation. Their sympathy extended to draw her into the circle of people who deserved to be cared about, but they were not ready to include others of her complexion, as they liked to say to avoid the unpleasantness of calling Negroes Negro or black people black. It was still us and them, but now she was with us.

When they returned to their room, Mercer was hungry. She discovered as the tour progressed that she was usually hungry after talks. Most often, the groups who sponsored her invited her and Prudence to share a meal before the talk. There they told her all about themselves and asked her their questions:

What was it like?
Were you whipped?
Did they teach you the word of God?
Did any of you learn to read?
What kinds of clothes were you given?
Did you ever hear of our efforts?
Do you have children?
Do you prepare your own speeches?

What of those who think abolitionism un-Christian?
Have you ever met Sojourner Truth?
Have you heard Mr. Douglass?
Do you write? Will you write your story?
Now, honestly, did you think these thoughts as a slave?

Mercer ate as best she could, but Prudence Randall had impressed upon her the importance of entertaining the local people who'd made arrangements for the talk. So Mercer spoke and smiled and listened, and she could never eat enough.

At night, she'd lie awake in bed, her hungry body buzzing and alert. Even her skin tingled. She worried about how she had looked and sounded. Why couldn't she keep the buttons on her bodice from pulling when she gestured? Once they were pulled, and the puckers and wrinkles spread over her chest, how could she smooth them back? How could she keep the short hairs around her face and neck from going into a fuzzy halo? How badly did she sweat? Harriet had given her gutta-percha dress shields. Had they done the job? Had her face shone, greasy, greasy like a pan? Had she remembered to speak slowly enough, and clearly?

Am-is-are-was-were-be-been-being. I am, you are, he, she, it is, we are, you are, they are. She said them over ten or fifteen times. Harriet had joked that the first thing to go in black speakers was the verb to be.

Each night, Mercer thought about the questions people asked before and after, and she changed the talk as she lay in her bed, trying to push it, at once, in opposite directions, closer to her heart and theirs, trying to nudge the people farther, past comfort, and yet hold them with her.

What had started as a job had become a mission. How could it not have—now that she had walked through their green valleys and shuttered houses; their mill towns perched on green-and-brown riverbanks; their whitewashed churches where they received blessed assurance of everlasting life because they wished to be good? How could it not be a mission, now that she

had seen their men use tobacco, their women wear cotton, and
their children eat rice? She could not let them sit unmoved
before her, boxed up in their certainty, letting her words bounce
off them like rain and splash in puddles at their feet.

Prudence Randall said that the talks were going better than
she'd dared hope. She told Mercer not to change a thing. But as
Mercer lay in the borrowed beds at night, her body too stiff and
her mind too full of words for her to sleep, she gave herself new
instructions. It was not enough to make a good showing or to assure herself that she'd done more good than harm.

Shadowy faces of black people outlined in the trees caught
her eye, at dusk or dawn or in the night. Unlike the gray cat, they
did not move by themselves; but wherever trees grew and buildings clustered, they swooped in like swallows, sometimes the
same faces, sometimes different ones, to look down at her, or to
look at her through windows when she'd left shutters open, or to
wave at her through the windows of trains or carriages. They had
dark circles around their eyes and mouths like O's, as if they were
yawning at her performance or singing in the wind. Spring in
New England was muddy and cold, and the faces that watched
Mercer on her tour shivered in the frosty, shiny black nights and
floated over black ponds by the edges of white clapboard towns.
They were regular folks, who'd lived and died slaves, free people,
runaways. She heard them in her head at night. The mulatto
who'd killed her mistress was there. They were prophets and liars
and lovers and collaborators, traitors and wise men.

Mercer tried not to look too long into those faces, because
they looked back. They frightened her with their demands and
their needs. They hinted that they were her blood. Why did that
make it worse? She closed her eyes in the strange beds and
turned her back toward the windows. They helped give her her
voice, and they threatened to take it away. What could she say
that would be worthy of their suffering? What could she say, now
that words spoken called up other words, and each story fetched
from the well made room for another that bubbled, cold, cold

cold, perfect rage and perfect grief, fresh and cold, splashing from the bucket right into her dreams and thoughts, into her head and bowels and throat. Cold and pure as hate.

Babies laid in a trough at the end of a row of cotton. Jesus have mercy.

Words she'd heard twenty years earlier became pictures in her mind, brown-and-gray dreams where people moved again and again, slowly, through the same fields.

Don't leave them.

Again and again, men and women come to the end of the row with the trough and sing loudly to the babies, some sleeping, some crying, all laid out in the trough in the relative shade of a few mulberry bushes.

> *Baby, sleep,*
> *Don't cry, don't cry.*
> *Baby, sleep, don't cry.*
> *Baby, sleep,*
> *Don't cry, don't cry,*
> *Mama gonna get you by and by.*

Don't leave them.

Again and again, they turn back along the rows.

Don't go.

Again and again, the squall comes up from the east, big and dark and sudden, and the parents walk farther and farther away— "Rain comin'"—used to rain, used to sodden cotton like lead in the sacks dragging them down to the ground, dust to dust.

Drop your sacks and run.

Rain plops and pours. Women scream. Their clothes cling to their skin. Ditches turn to streams. Wind pushes them back. Their bare feet slip in the mud.

Babies sputter and cough and turn over in the water. She

hears the plump of their bodies against the wood. Little thuds. Ten-pound dumplings. Roll over. Roll over. No time to catch their breath to cry, they swallow and snort, alive still, still alive.

They drown too fast to cry.

Their parents come running, running, running, the men first, with big strides, the women just after them, screaming, falling, their breasts leaking at the thought of babies who are just now drowning. They scream because they know it's too late. The row was so long, and the sky just opened up.

They're drownded.

And where was Jesus as the water went up their brown button noses? And where was sweet, sweet Jesus who they called on for mercy, and called on in bed at night? Was he harvesting babies to make into angels before their lives of troubling? Before they had time to lay their own babies in a trough, before their own breasts swoll up hard and shiny with undrunk milk?

Don't ever leave them.

Mercer stood on pulpits and stages and risers, talking her talks, and she never forgot that as she spoke, two of her children lay warm and healthy between clean sheets and underneath striped blankets and one lay next to Suzy's pallet in Virginia. She never forgot that Nig-Nag lay dead in his cheap box in the pauper's grave. What could she say to be true to Etta and Mattie and Bennie, to Nig-Nag, and to the babies who floated in the rainwater and sailed on the wind like swallows, to look down on her in the cold Massachusetts night?

"Before I remember anything at all, I remember my father's tooth," Mercer began. The more she talked, the more she remembered.

"I was three, maybe four years old, a slave, as you know, the daughter of slaves. My father received a whippin such as people here in the North never tire of hearing described. It was such a whippin, ladies and gentlemen, done by the overseer of the place where we lived in Virginia, and done with a whip that cut his flesh after a few strokes, and then cut deeper and deeper, until the whip was wet with his blood and clotted with flesh. And the bits of blood and flesh dirtied the overseer's shirt as he whipped.

"The overseer did it out in the open, on a place where they used to call us together to hear announcements. It was mostly flat, dusty earth there, with a few rocks in the ground.

"I don't remember whether or not my father made a noise. But I do remember that they tied him to the ground, and toward the end, his head jerked up and down with the force of each blow, and he hit his mouth on one of the rocks. I remember hearing his tooth hit like a chink when you break a piece of china. And I saw his tooth fall right out, just like that, and roll to the side. There it was, somethin that had been part of him; they'd just beat it out of him, so it seemed.

"The overseer gave us leave to help carry him back to our shack. I stood next to him. I remember that I wanted so badly to cry, but somehow or 'nother I knew that I should try not to, and I was tryin so hard not to cry that I almost missed it when my father said to me as he passed, carried along by the other men, and my mother comin along behind, he said: 'Fetch me my tooth.'

"So I sat under a tree nearby, and I watched the patch of dirt where his face had been. The overseer cleaned his whip, but they never did sweep the ground after a whippin. They wanted to keep the dirt all disturbed and the bloodstains and let the flies come, just so to remind people as they went by. Just to show 'em.

"After everyone was gone, I went and pushed around in the dirt till I found my father's tooth. It were just fine, the whole thing knocked out in one piece, the root and all. You ever seen a whole tooth? Well, they're long, ladies and gentlemen, just like pullin a plant out the ground, as much below as there is above. I recollect how it was pointy on the end.

"Now, while I'm standin there, the overseer sees me and asks me what am I doin. Somethin tells me to hide that tooth, and the only way I can think to do it is to pop it in my mouth to keep it safe. Somethin told me—and this is the sort of thing a slave child learns while other little children are learnin their rhymes—somethin told me that if my daddy wanted that tooth, that the overseer would take it away. So I put it in my mouth, ladies and gentlemen, and go back to suckin my thumb like always and head for our shack.

"I remember walkin in the dust, and keepin my father's tooth up against the front of my mouth so I wouldn't swallow it."

Mercer told them how her father planted the tooth back in his own mouth, and tied it in place with a rag around his head, and left the next day. She told them about the runaways and the work slowdowns and the people who vowed never to be whipped again, and weren't. She told them about the white family who worked alongside them for little money, and about midwives and schooling at church meetings.

She asked them what they thought people like her parents might have done with freedom. Her mother, the seamstress, she said, would have sewn beautiful dresses for their daughters' weddings. Her father would gladly have fought for this country in a war, or learned a trade, or opened a business. Everyone she knew in the North looked at the slaves and said: Isn't it terrible what bondage does to people? And yes, it was. But Mercer asked another question: Wasn't it bountiful and glorious grace that some of these people even live at all? That they live and dare fight back, or dare to resist, or dare to hold the line where they would be forced no more.

"More than I can recall, people have asked me how anyone who has ever been in bondage, or anyone who has ever been despised, could betray his own people? I never know why people would ask me, but they do. And then I'm asked to explain how someone could pretend to be related to a fugitive, only to cheat some well-meaning anti-slavery folks out of money. How could they do that, knowing, as they must, the harm they've done to the cause?

"I'm asked how collaborators in the South could be so low as to turn in a fellow African when he's plannin to escape. How could others get pleasure out of overseein their brothers and sisters, and doing the master's whippin for him?

"And the first thing that comes to my mind is not why some of us, some few, have been made into wretches by this widespread and powerful evil, but why, through the grace of a good and powerful God, more of us haven't, why all of us haven't?

"There was a man, I am told, who stood up at one of the Negro conventions and called for all slaves to rise up in violent revolution. Yes. Yes, he did indeed, and there were plenty to shout, Hear! Hear! to it, just as the patriots and founding fathers of this country shouted, Hear! Hear! when their number decided on rebellion."

They gasped—she had underestimated their horror at the thought of a black uprising—but she went on.

"But I say to him and to all who would brand us cowards because we have not joined together in bloody revolution, because we have not righted the situation ourselves, all unarmed and ignorant, I say to them, ladies and gentlemen, that it's only by the grace of God that we have lived at all, that it's grace that some remain to resist, some to fight—and die, as surely as we sit here—some to escape, some to live on in that system, and not just live like brutes but try to live Christian lives, giving love to someone along the way."

Mercer was breathing deeply and steadily now, as if she'd been walking hard and strong.

She felt it burning inside her like fire. Sweat ran down her spine and under her arms, into the gutta-percha dress shields. Her face glistened with it. She dabbed at her top lip with her handkerchief and let her forehead shine. She was nearly finished. The noisy mind that had chattered at her throughout the tour like squirrels was running efficiently. The squirrels zipped back and forth, quieter, faster, carrying ideas and information and laying them out for her at the bottom of an oak tree. What became clear to Mercer as she spoke was the fear in these people's eyes. They were afraid of any hint of blacks rising up and giving back the gall they'd received. They were afraid of her father and his tooth, afraid of her mother's perfect skills. They were afraid to hear that the world was not as they'd thought it, divided up neatly with stone rows between—them up here safe and sound and loved by their special God; the Southern whites evil and greedy; the Negroes like hired horses, worked too hard but made to be worked nonetheless.

Mercer was beginning to talk about freedom. These feisty, hardworking Americans: did they want freedom? Or did they want to be warm and dry and loved and fed. Did they just want more freedom than someone else? Surely they didn't want freedom for all slaves: black people free to roam the country and beat them at business and pan for gold and preach the gospel and build homes and educate children. They just didn't want them treated so bad. They wanted to sleep easier at night.

Mercer was going too far now. She'd switched from herself to them. She'd stopped blaming the evil Southerners and begun to show them their own involvement. Their faces began to close against her. Too bad.

Still, she spoke. Voice was what she had; it was all she was: her skin and sinew and bones and flesh and sex and power turned into voice and breathed through her, her voice breathed through them. America called her big and black and separate from them. Other. They drew their wagons in a circle and fought the others to the death. Well, she would live. She became voice like mist and settled into the pores of their skin.

"We are all in this thing here together. I have been told, since I've been North, that slavery keeps prices down. I have been told that we in the North live better because three millions of black people toil without wages in the South. I am not an educated woman, ladies and gentlemen, but I know that no one in this room would subject his sister or brother or his friend or neighbor to bondage, but we here let it go on, and the North lives better. How much better is better? Would anyone here in this room, if they saw slavery for a day, or lived it for an hour, have the heart to say: 'Let it go on, just so the price of cotton stays at four pounds to the penny. Let it go on, just so sugar stays at half a penny a pound'?

"How much better? Would anyone here say: 'Yes, sell that baby away from that mother just so I get my snuff for two bits and not two and a half'?

"Well, suppose we were free. What then? Would your children's bellies still be full if all the empty bellies cryin out for food were fed? Would there be land enough to house us? Land to farm and graze? Schools to educate us? Enough police to keep us safe? How could there be enough work in the cities?

"I am an uneducated woman, as you see, and know as little about business as most of my people, but it seems to me that there's enough work for us to do now, and there'd still be work to do if we were free. It seems to me that if men and women in bondage were suddenly paid to work and let loose to build their own homes, that the man here who sells lumber would be made richer, not poorer; and the shop owner would sell more meal, not less; and without the expense of housing and feeding Negroes, without the expense of overseers to beat us and keep us from trying to escape and rebel, the slaveholders would be not too terribly impoverished—and God forbid they should want for anything.

"In Philadelphia, where I gained my freedom, colored people, I am told, contribute hundreds of thousands of dollars to the city's business. And as much as any people, they look to themselves to care for their sick and old and orphaned.

"We have enough. We have plenty in America.

"And Negroes are capable. I come to assure you of that, and to assure you that our freedom is nothing to fear.

"We're living in a big house. Jesus said that in his father's house are many rooms. Every day, in a bedroom at the back of the house, the master takes one of the servants in and beats him to death. Everybody sees them go in. Everybody hears his cries. Everybody hears the body fall to the ground. We all see 'im drag out the body. But no one says a word. Think of the soul sickness in this house.

"Slavery is to be feared. The misery of millions of people is to be feared. Their unanswered prayers are to be feared. The soul sickness of a country that allows murder and mayhem and pretends not to notice is to be feared.

"Rich and powerful men will tell you to fear my people free. I tell you, I fear for all of us so long as we are not."

They didn't believe it, but they didn't close down, either. That night, for the first time on the tour, Mercer slept soundly.

Twelve / Fire and Sword

"W ell, wouldn't you know that while we were away yesterday he fell." Della, at the kitchen table, addressed Tyree as he came in the door. "He can't talk this time. He means to say one thing, and seems like he can't find the word, and then he forgets altogether. He can't lift his head, Ty. He can't hold his water."

Tyree hadn't seen his mother since he'd left Ephraim and Abby Ann's wedding the previous day. Having helped with Mercer's escape, Tyree now worked regularly with the Vigilance Committee. This time, he'd taken two young men to a New Jersey farm owned by a colored farmer Tyree had never met before. Tyree had liked the man and his family and accepted their offer of a bed.

Manny had wanted to go to the wedding, but the entire family had argued against it.

"I thought Zilpha stayed with him."

"She did stay with him. This happened when she went downstairs to fetch his supper. She had a terrible time getting him back into bed and sending someone for us."

Della spoke faster now, words tumbling toward tears.

"I've done washing three times today. Harriet's worked like a dog. You know Harriet's faithful; thank God, Harriet's faithful, but she's got the school to look after. How're we going to keep this up?"

"How's Blanche?"

"What do you mean, 'How's Blanche?' She's your wife. I mean to say, how's she supposed to be, with you running over the county after stray Negroes? Seems to me they got all this way by themselves, they could find the way across a little further."

Tyree shook his head.

"Charity begins at home. We needed you last night. We needed you today."

"I was repairing the roof on 1637 today."

She shrugged. "Bea has got worse than useless, you know. Same thing she did last time your father took sick. Zilpha has been there, and I swear that's the only thing that'll keep her in check. But when Aunt Zil comes over here to be with your father, Bea goes back at it, her and that old black nigger across the street from her.

"Abby Ann and her pious yellow self is so busy counting her new linen, she can't even be bothered to call and see if the people who practically raised her need a glass of water."

"Aunt Zil still here?" Tyree asked.

"Zilpha's here, thank God. I asked if she would stay, 'cause you can see I'd have no help, no help at all, except for Harriet and that dear child Etta."

"Where is she now?"

"Who, Etta?"

"No; Aunt Zil."

"She got your father washed and dressed this morning and sat with him. I think she's gone to Bea's to sleep. She'll most likely come back after supper."

Della wiped the bread around her plate. "I'm just eating to be eating, you know. You hungry?"

"No, thanks."

"Sit down," she said. "Remember that ham I made?" She jumped up and went to the pantry. Returning, she said, "That was the one Aunt Zil brought. It was sixteen years old. I had to cut the crust off it. The crust had worms, but the ham: you have never tasted such a one in your life. You left yesterday before we cut it."

Della held out a slab of ham to Tyree.

"Mother, you always have good food in a crisis."

"Why not? Would I do better to get drunk and cry out the window or go up in my room and sew some old arsenic pelts until I go batty? . . . So, how is it?"

"The ham? It's extraordinary."

"It's gorgeous, isn't it?"

Tyree poured himself a glass of water from the pitcher and sat next to his mother.

"You used to be hungry all the time. Not Roland. Roland was fussy. He was a fussy baby and a fussy boy. I admit it now, he was the oldest son, and we favored him. We did. But he was fussy. He's dead and gone, but I can say it anyway. Roland was a fussy baby. There was nothing you could do for him but hold him. A bad old spoiled baby. But you were a different story."

"Who spoiled him, Mother?"

Della patted his hand and smiled at him. "Little black Bea. Your daddy. I spoiled him too. But God knows I've paid for it. You have no idea how I've paid for it."

She paused, as if she had been running at a gallop and then slowed to a walk. "When I was nursing you," she said, "you just grabbed on like I don't know what, like a . . . like a . . ."

"Like a leech," he said. It was what she always said.

"Just like a leech." Della fastened on the word as if she'd never thought of it before. "Just like a leech."

Then she made big sucking sounds with her mouth and laughed. She pushed on his hand as if to encourage him to stop holding back his own amusement.

Tyree knew she was trying to distract herself. He held her hand. It was the best he could do.

"Seems like every time I nursed you, you'd break the skin, and then it was blood running with the milk."

"Uh-hunh."

Della shrugged her shoulders. She raised her eyebrows and sighed.

"So what did you do?" He had never asked before.

"What could I do?" she said. "Didn't have money to go out and buy some woman to come in and wet-nurse you. Couldn't take you out to one of the cheap heifers nursin five at once, and each and every poor little baby ends up gettin two drops of milk and a case of the croup. Right? Couldn't take you to one of those baby farm places and pay some she-devil by the week to feed you sugar water till you swoll up and died. Right? I'n't that right? Humph."

Della pouted. "You know why the mothers—shouldn't even call them that, although God knows what some of them haven't been through—you know why they pay by the week, don't you? I mean, 'cause you'd think they wouldn't want to come back again and again and again, right?"

"Never thought about it."

"Well, you wouldn't. They pay by the week because they know their poor babies won't make it through the month, and they don't want to waste their money. They won't let you pay by the day, or else they wouldn't make no damn money a'tall. . . . So I nursed you. And look how big you are now."

Tyree sighed. "I'll go on up now."

"Carry some of this broth I made. Maybe he'll take some from you."

"If he didn't want it from you, Mother, you know he won't take it from me."

"Just try," she said. "Just carry it up, will you just kindly do that for me, please? Can't I ask anyone for anything without them telling me why it can't be done or how they don't want to do it?" She looked as if she would cry.

"Here, here." Tyree stirred the broth and ladled some into his father's large china cup. "And if he doesn't drink it, I will."

Tyree smiled and kissed his mother's forehead.

. . .

Upstairs, Manny was tied into his chair with two lengths of sheet, across his chest and around his waist. Tyree stood in the doorway, looking at him. He was turned toward the window. His head drooped forward. Spittle hung from his lips in a fine white thread. Tyree knew that Manny was keeping watch. He'd done the same thing before. He refused, as he had said the first time, to lie down and die. So he'd sat up, day and night, strapped into the same chair, until he felt certain that he would live and, to a great extent, recover. Now he was strapped in again, as if posture would work magic.

Tyree stood watching for a long time. He did not want to go in. Now and then Manny would dig his heel into the carpet and push. Or he'd reach into the air with his left hand and wave. He'd made the same movements before, only stronger. In fact, after his first seizure, he'd succeeded several times in tipping himself over. Everyone had come running, and he'd looked up at them with impatience. Now he did not have strength to tip himself.

Tyree stood in the doorway, sipping the broth. Della made soup according to a recipe Bea had taught her back when they'd all catered together. She cooked bones and vegetables in water one whole day, strained the broth, and cooked it again with new bones and new vegetables the next day. For a moment, he did not think but only tasted the broth and smelled the steam and felt the cup's warmth in his two hands. Tyree knew that he was deciding to find a way to have Mercer. He'd dreamed about her at the farm and awakened making plans. He'd offer to find her a situation— maybe have colored farmers put her up in a cottage in New Jersey. She liked the country, and she could have her own little cabin and a garden. The Negro sections of those towns were relatively safe, and the children could go to school. That would be much the easiest for Tyree right now, what with Manny going downhill so fast. But Mercer might balk. In that case, he thought he'd leave. He'd take Cyrus and Mercer and her children and go to Canada, and that would be that. The family could keep their money. Blanche and Della were used to each other after these many years, and they would unite in their anger at him. It would be all right, he thought. He could leave.

Manny coughed and gagged. Tyree walked into the room even as a voice within suggested that he might continue to stand in the doorway instead. Perhaps his father would choke, and perhaps he should. Perhaps they should stop snatching him back from his destiny. Despite the voice, Tyree picked up the rag that hung on the side of his father's chair, put it over his mouth, and slapped him on the back, hard, three times. Manny coughed phlegm into the rag and drew a deep breath. Tyree sat down opposite him.

Della's claim that Manny had been waiting for Tyree was ludicrous. It did not flatter Tyree, as he supposed she meant it to do, and he doubted that it comforted her. Why did she say such things? Manny didn't hang on for anyone. He hung on for sheer meanness, for himself, or maybe, Tyree thought, simply from habit.

"Say," Manny said. The word came out as clearly as it ever had, with his old intonation. "Go for a walk?"

Tyree raised his eyebrows. "Who go for a walk? You?"

Manny nodded.

"Where to?"

Manny's eyes lost their focus. His head sagged. Tyree could see that it took all Manny's strength to keep his eyes looking up at him. He felt the same surge of compassion toward him that he had felt toward his mother. He felt it even as he wanted to escape them. His house and life were cramped: tight, stifling, crowded, junky. He wanted space and sky and room. Junked up. He wanted a woman his own size and work for which he was suited. He wanted Mercer—her silences and her voice; her mannish shoulders and her womanly bosom; he wanted her gulping, racking sobs and her big, throaty laugh.

Manny had slumped to one side in his sling.

"Here," Tyree said. "Want to sit up?"

Manny nodded. He made an attempt to sit up, but he moved his hips rather than his torso. The chair moved with him. Tyree explained to him what had happened. Manny nodded his head, cutting Tyree off impatiently.

"Try again," Tyree said. "And keep that left hand on the arm of the chair, see. Try to steady yourself."

Manny rolled his eyes, as if he'd deduced the hitch and had it figured out.

"Go." Tyree held the chair to give his father some resistance.

Manny did not try again.

Tyree noticed that he was unwashed and unshaven. "Sit up."

Manny made a face such as older children make when they refuse a command and are perfectly willing to take the blow.

"So what?" he said.

Tyree hated him for not trying. All his push, all those years, and now he would sit in his own filth, hanging off the side of an old chair?

"Goddamn it."

Tyree sat back in his chair and sipped some more broth. Manny reached out his hand. "Mine," he said.

"Mother says you wouldn't drink it."

Manny rolled his eyes. "Mine."

Tyree placed the cup in his father's outstretched left hand, but by then Manny's burst of energy was spent. He spilled the broth onto his lap.

"Goddamn it," Tyree muttered again.

He could no longer tell what his father could and could not do. Behind the bedroom door sat a wash bucket and a bushel basket filled with clean, folded rags. Tyree doused a clean rag in soapy water and daubed at the puddle, but it had soaked in.

"Goddamn it."

Manny echoed him. "Goddamn."

Tyree untied Manny, stood him up, and took off his trousers. Under the trousers was a diaper stuffed with rags. His mother had told him that Manny could not hold his water, but Tyree hadn't remembered.

"You wet?" he asked.

Manny looked insulted.

Tyree changed the undergarment, trying to pack rags in front, as the women had done. He put fresh trousers and a shirt on Manny and then sat him down in the chair and began to tie the restraints. Manny groaned and fought. He flung his arm as hard as he could and kicked out his leg. He succeeded in scratching Tyree's neck and cheek with his nails.

Tyree let Manny go; he slid down in his chair. Tyree grabbed him with both hands by his shirt. He spoke from behind clenched teeth. "I'm gonna pick you up and shake you, old man. You remember how you used to shake us? I'ma shake you. Now, the same way you spoke to me when I came in this room, you talk to me now. You want something, goddamn it. Talk to me."

"Fuck you."

Tyree gave his father a little shake. "I just want to see how it feels."

He shook him again.

"My walk."

"Your walk?"

Manny nodded his head indignantly.

"You thought you were going on your walk?"

Manny nodded again.

"I didn't say we were going now, Daddy. I asked you *where* you wanted to go, and you never answered me." Tyree put him down but could not resist giving him an extra shake.

The seizures had pulled Manny's face out of line, like a devilish sculptor. Every emotion registered larger and more crudely than before. Now he was pouting, and he looked like an old child. The pout enraged Tyree all the more. But he knew that he had to settle things. Weak as he was, Manny was not dead or dying yet, despite Della's fears. Tyree could have wrestled him into the chair, but he did not.

"Listen," he said. "If something happened to me, how would you and Mother be fixed for money?" He put his face close to Manny's. "Now tell me: All our lives you've been working; now I'm working. Where's the money, Daddy?"

Another exaggerated expression crossed Manny's face, this time one of contempt. *"You* tell *me,"* he said quite clearly.

"Well," Tyree said, "you think about it, and we'll talk tomorrow." He picked up one of the restraints.

"No, wait." Manny didn't say it clearly, but that's what it sounded like to Tyree.

He pointed a finger at him. "Ask Roland."

"Roland's dead."

Manny shrugged. "Roland was a thief. Ask Mother."

He waved his hand dismissively. Once again Tyree picked up the restraint.

Manny put his hand out to stop him. "Shelley." Then he leered with his new puppet's slipped-to-the-side face, inviting Tyree into the joke.

"What?" Shelley was Manny's name for Rachel, whom Roland and Tyree had called the Shed Kitchen Woman. She'd been Manny's woman for as long as Tyree could remember. Tyree bent down again, this time hooking his arm around his father's middle and pulling him sharply back into the chair. He tied him quickly.

"If you can't sit up in your chair, what the hell are you going to do with her?"

Manny nodded his head with crazy earnestness, as if to say that he *could* make use of their time.

"Just gemme there."

"I told you a long time ago," Tyree said, "that I didn't want to hear about her. What did Roland steal?"

"Get Bea."

"I'm not going to get anybody. My mother is downstairs, working like a nigger for you," Tyree said.

"She gave Roland my money."

Tyree left the room. His father's calls came after him. He called Tyree's name over and over and over again. Tyree closed the door and stood in the hallway, listening.

"Tyyyy-reeee. Tyyyy-reeee. Tyyyy-reeee."

With the door closed, no one else could hear. Manny's voice went on, getting lower, more ragged. Tyree leaned against the wall and let the hallway close in on him. He felt trapped in the steam from pots cooking food other people would eat; trapped behind doors where once he called for his father and now his father called for him, with each, in his own time, determined not to answer; trapped in a marriage as confining as the house, with a wife working her needle into arsenic-poisoned pelts and pricking her finger like the girls in fairy books, as if trying to put herself to sleep; putting ex-slaves and Irish immigrants and destitute black families into stinking shacks without privies for half a dollar a week; hemmed in by decisions he'd made when he was a boy and wanting to appear a man. And now that he was a man? What had he done besides dream of putting another woman in a house for himself, just as his father had done? A thought came to him. He opened the door. His father was still calling his name.

"Did you buy that house for Rachel?"

Manny's mouth hung open. He looked at Tyree, seemingly confused.

"You bought her that house. With our money—*our* money. Didn't you?"

Manny laughed at him. "Go get your own woman."

Tyree left the house by the front door to avoid his mother. He walked around the corner and knocked at Bea's door. Bea leaned out over her windowsill. Her wig leaned too.

"Where is everybody?"

"Gone to your house to get you."

"Why?"

"To make me behave."

Tyree went inside. Making Bea behave had been Manny's job. Upstairs, Tyree stood in the doorway of Bea's room, looking at her back. She balanced a china cup on the windowsill.

"Did you take Daddy to see Rachel this past year?"

He startled Bea. She screamed and upset the cup. It fell off the sill and crashed onto the ground.

"I loved that cup," she lamented. "The saucer broke ten years ago. Your father broke it. . . . Don't mind, sweetie pie, just step around it," she hollered down to a neighbor passing by. The woman made a face when she smelled the alcohol.

"That'll give the old cow something to report to her temperance committee." At that Bea laughed outright. Then she looked frightened.

"Manny died?"

Tyree shook his head. "Nope."

"Good," she said. "Good for him. Good for the old bastard." She reached under her stool for a small bottle of gin. "He got aaaalll the money. He got aaaalll the papers. I ain't got nothin. Your mother don't even have nothin."

"You've got this house," Tyree said.

"Nah, I don't have this house. I was supposed to have this house, but he kept the damn deed, so what do I have? . . . Well, I tell you a secret. I got *something.*"

"Why doesn't my mother have anything?" Tyree asked irritably. Then: "Aunt Bea, were you taking Daddy to see his woman, Shelley?"

"Who's Shelley?"

"Why?"

"Why not?" she said with a dramatic sigh. "Now, who do you want to go see?"

"Did he give you money?"

"You know what?" She used her coy face. "You have

become the new Manny, Tyree. That's what you are. I was afraid we might not have somebody to sit on our necks and tell us what to do and keep all the money to himself."

Tyree took the bottle of gin from her table.

"Don't do that to me," she said. "Don't be Manny. Be my Tyree. Be my little ray of sunshine."

"Oh, Auntie Bea," he said sadly. "I'm taking Etta across the way."

"Oh, Auntie Bea," she mimicked. "Oh, Auntie Bea." She said it again, in a small voice. "I'm lonely, and all my high-and-mighty family can do is take away anything that gives me pleasure. I love that girl."

"Harry says you work her so she can barely finish her lessons."

"Children are lazy by nature, Tyree. You know that."

"Zilpha'll be with you."

"Oh, Christ, not her. Don't take the girl and leave me Zilpha. Naw. Take Zilpha and leave me the girl."

"Your boarders are still here."

"They're no help. They're ninnies, both of 'em. The parents pay you a pittance, and they figure they should have their name in the newspaper. I need help."

"What kind of help do you need?"

"I need the help you're taking away. I need somebody to look after me. I need some damn money. They make me beg for it." Bea began to cry. She looked sorry for herself.

"Well, Aunt Bea," he said, "they make me work for it."

"I worked before you were born," she said derisively. "I worked, I tell you. My brother worked me until he couldn't work me anymore. If I'da been a whore, they woulda wore a hole right through me."

Tyree tripped his tongue.

"Too bad," she said. "And then, when I couldn't work anymore, I did their dirty work too. Yeah, I took my brother to that woman. I did. I ran messages to her from him for years. So what? . . . I'll tell you something else, Mr. Know-Everything. I'll tell you something you don't know. Your mother don't have anything because she gave Roland his Africa money and she never got it back."

"How do you know?"

"She's cryin now, ain't she?"

"What Africa money did he have?"

"That's how she always was. Came into this family with nothin, and look like she gonna leave it with nothin."

"How much Africa money?"

"Enough for him and Blanche and the baby to go and buy land when they got there."

"Did you get any?"

She waved her hand in the air. "I don't have anything, Ty. Where's *my* money? Huh?"

"Aunt Bea, you spent your money on whiskey."

"I don't touch whiskey." She grinned, showing her top gum. "I drink gin."

Tyree couldn't imagine why he had bothered to come and ask her about the trips to Shelley's. Bea took Manny to Shelley's. Manny gave Bea pocket money. Bea bought her gin. And the gin made her talk foolishness. Roland had boasted about his Africa money—a small fortune—but Tyree hadn't believed him. And neither Manny nor Della had given any indication that the family's savings were missing. None at all.

"You must stop again," he said.

She looked at him curiously. "Stop what?"

"Drinking, Aunt Bea."

"No, Tyree, I don't think I can."

Tyree turned and walked out of the room. There was no way to breathe in this family, and no reason not to leave it. All its members had a catalogue of hurts that excused their own behavior; willfulness reigned unchecked: his mother had handed the family savings to Roland, his father bought his mistress a house; every few years, Bea fell into her drinking again.

Tyree refused to believe that one of them did not have the money. Roland would not have trusted anyone outside the family to hold it. Sharkey was the best bet, since he could be trusted not to tell Manny and not to spend it. Tyree brought to mind his several conversations about the Quick finances with Sharkey. Perhaps he'd been trying to decide whether or not it was time to tell Tyree about the nest egg, or maybe he was holding it until the family needed it. Maybe Sharkey liked the idea of claiming the money as his own. He might even have it in mind to distribute it in his will, in order to keep Manny from giving any more of it to his woman or—Tyree wondered he'd never thought of it before—any other children Manny may have fathered.

In any event, Tyree felt easier about leaving. It would be as selfish and willful as anything any of his relatives had ever done, but at least he would not try to make excuses. Besides, he felt sure now that they'd be provided for.

Bea sat alone, listening to her nephew's footsteps.

"Oh, well," she sighed aloud.

She reached under the mattress until she found the hole. Stuffed into it was a bottle of gin. Next to the bottle, deep in the padding where her hand could barely reach, was a bundle of money wrapped in an old schedule for a steamer to Africa. She wouldn't think of disturbing the bundle. It wasn't like money anymore. It had acquired its own properties and power. She could no more spend it than she could have spent the diamond ring Gabriel wore on his finger when they buried him. Nor could she separate even one dollar from the sum: seven thousand two hundred and thirty-four dollars. Now and then she'd tear the numbers from a newspaper and drop them behind one of Manny's bottled ships, just to fuck with him. It was the fortune they'd built from her working like a nigger. They'd broken her health, and had it not been for the strain, she would never have developed this terrible thirst for gin. So she kept the ransom and slept on it every single night.

Dear Mercer:

We see from your last letter that Miss Randall has scheduled you to speak in a few towns upstate of us in Pennsylvania. The news has caused much discussion here on Pine Street. We all agree that so far as slavery and race issues are concerned, Pennsylvania lags behind the New England states in tolerance. In short, we are concerned for your safety. Perhaps Miss Randall's group has assurances that the towns you are to visit are particular pockets of anti-slavery sentiment. We hope that is the case. In any event, we are sending you part of a recent letter written to *The Christian Recorder* by an itinerant preacher who traveled and preached just recently, so far as we can see, quite near to where you and Miss Randall plan to go.

Please send us, very specifically, the dates and places of your talks in this state. We may be able to be of some help. Now I will give this over to Etta, who has been assigned to copy out the article. You are asked to admire her handwriting, which I am told is excellent these days.

As always,
Tyree Quick

P.S. Ephraim and Abby Ann were finally married. Quite a show. Bells and smells. Harriet no doubt will give you all particulars next we see you.

Dearest Mama:

I hope you are well. Mattie and I are lerning our lessons. Mattie cifers as good as me alredy, but I have lernt a good hand and sevral tunes on piano. Here is the letter from the Christian Recorder.

"During the last presidential canvass, I felt it to be my duty to make special efforts to instruct the people, in regard to their duty, on political questions. To do this, I visited many places in the surrounding county, preached and delivered anti-slavery lectures . . . I dwelt at some length on the evils of slavery, tried to show what we had to do with it, showed the position of the two old political parties, spoke of the fugitive law, etc.

"At the close of my 3rd effort, a minister of the Brethren Church got up full of excitement and wrath, and commenced a tirade of abuse on the anti-slavery party, and particularly against the sentiments of the foregoing discourse. He said 'we had nothing to do with slavery, that it was none of our business, that we had better preach the Gospel and let slavery alone, that it was nobody's business how men voted, that this thing of preaching politics was all of the Devil, that he would be ashamed to open his mouth on that subject on the Sabbath Day, that his conference had forbid the agitation of that question, &c.'

". . . We find in them bitter, malignant and ignorant opposition.

"To my mind they are wrong, *deeply* and *damningly* wrong, and that it is our duty to call loudly on them to repent on their wickedness."

Pls. be careful, Mama. The town where this minister said these things is only a few miles from you. Uncle Sharkey and Uncle Ty say that sometimes people hurt speakers that come to thier towns. Uncle Ty might come to make sure your safe, but him and Mr. Manny had a big fight about it. So I don't know.

Your loving daughter (and son),
Willietta Gray and MATTIE

After she'd read it, Mercer gave the Quicks' letter to Prudence. They were in an alcove in the parlor of a New York State sponsor, who'd gone to see about a snack for the women. Mercer had been carrying the letter with her all day, reading and rereading it. She had had some cool audiences, but none so hostile as the preacher reported in *The Christian Recorder*. Prudence Randall handed the letter back to Mercer without comment. They finished their sandwiches of brown bread with butter and honey and drank tea with their sponsor. Not until they were going to bed did Prudence ask Mercer in an offended tone:

"Were you going to withdraw from the commitment?"

Mercer said, "I wouldn't just 'withdraw.' But we shouldn't let it go without even giving it some thought, don't you think?"

Prudence's tone was arch. "To what purpose? To withdraw? At the first inkling of conflict? The very first, Mercer?"

Mercer poured water into the rubber bucket Bea had given her. She washed her stockings and dress protectors in it and hung them over hooks on the side of the armoire. Prudence Randall had her things washed every week by local women. She'd offered to pay to have Mercer's done too, but Mercer had declined.

"I suppose we're bound to look at things different ways sometime," Mercer said.

The bucket was too small for both Mercer's feet, so, as was her custom, she eased the right foot in first. The water was cold and soapy.

"Look like I could use a bigger bucket," she said, knowing that she said the same thing most nights.

"Haven't we, haven't I, Mercer, made certain that you have been safe?"

Mercer saw how the conversation would go. Prudence would think that the whole thing was about her. Mercer sighed. She took out the right and put in the left foot, wiping the clean one with a worn cloth.

"This little piece of rag," she said. "I brung this from Virginia. Doesn't look like nothin, but I always did like the cotton. . . ."

Of course you've made certain. And I never would say otherwise."

"And well cared for?"

"Yes."

"And well received?"

Mercer looked at her and nodded her head. "You have, and that's a fact, and I'm grateful. . . ."

Prudence Randall climbed into bed and turned her face to the wall. Mercer knew that she was more than offended by the letter; she was personally hurt. There was no remedy for it. The next day, Mercer wrote back to the Quicks, thanking them for alerting her and assuring them that she would finish the tour promptly and see them soon. She also sent her schedule. Prudence would just have to pout if Tyree appeared. Mercer hoped he would.

That night as she fell asleep, she thought of Virginia and food. She could almost taste blackberry dumplings and blackberry buckle. It was silly to remember it with such fondness. She'd never eaten buckle till she was a grown woman cooking it, and then only in the kitchen, fast, with the butter dripping down her fingers, eating handfuls before anybody saw how much. But the sickly-sweet images came back sometimes when she drifted off, like old people's memories of loving parents who never loved them at all.

He came. Mercer saw him standing at the back of Justice Hall, which, for all its grand name, was a simple wooden structure in a small Pennsylvania town near Harrisburg. Justice Hall held no more than fifty people. On their way to the town, Prudence had described with pride how Justice Hall had come to be. It had been built a few months before by the members of the growing local universal reform movement: temperance, anti-slavery, women's rights. Mercer had only half listened. They had ridden hard through New York State, and she was tired of the road, and tired, period. She made an effort to save her strength for the lectures.

Later she would tell Tyree how frightened she'd been to go ahead with this, the last lecture.

"I almost took sick, you know what I mean, so that I wouldn't have to go through with it," she'd tell him, "except that we'd done all right at the others, and I hated to let them make me back down." She humphed. "And after I talked so bad about how white folks lied, I hated to pull up lame like that."

Later they would shake their heads together, wondering and rejoicing that he had come to this town and not the one before, and how she knew he was near even before she saw him.

But at the time, Mercer stepped out onto the stage, smiled mildly, looked people in the eyes, as she'd made it her habit to do, and took in their tension. They were supporters, or at least, most of them seemed to be, but nervous supporters. So far, her reception in this town had been cold. There'd been no dinner before the lecture, no friendly, well-meant questions, no embarrassed requests for her to bare her scars. She and Prudence had eaten alone in a farmer's kitchen, while the farmwife, who had served them, went outside to rig the horse to a wagon. Unlike the New England schoolteachers and businesspeople they'd stayed with earlier, the Pennsylvania farmers received pay for the hire of the room and for their meals. The farmwife had behaved well toward them, but like the audience now, she appeared watchful. She'd driven them and their suitcases into town for the lecture and told them emphatically that the way she understood it, it was not her job to come get them.

"Well, certainly," Prudence had said. "Preacher Winston has it arranged."

Prudence Randall had written to Preacher Winston, and he had written back, but Mercer noticed that he had not met them at the coach, nor had he left any message for them at the farm.

The woman told them that the front door would be latched when they returned to spend the night and that they should come in by the back. Then she turned the cart and drove away.

. . .

"Before I remember anything," Mercer told her skittish audience, "I remember the feeling of carrying my father's tooth in my mouth.

"You know, that's a feeling a child doesn't forget. There's a long root on one end of it, like it was clearly something that was meant to be planted. And yet here I was, carrying it around in my mouth, holding it for him, the safest way I knew how.

"How it came to be there, and what it means to me, tells one story of one woman's bondage in America, this land of freedom, where there ought not to be such stories. . . ."

She had worked hard on that last sentence, too hard, she realized now, to get it to flow off her tongue. It sounded hincty, as Zilpha would say. Her voice, at least, was right. It was quieter now than when she'd begun her talks. She had learned that she didn't have to shout to be heard. She didn't have to rush to get everything in before they began to look out the window, or close their eyes and doze. Her voice, one woman had told her bluntly, was worth all the words she said with it. Mercer had been insulted at first, but she'd learned from it. She could depend on her voice when her mind wouldn't cooperate. The voice came from its own place and passed through her, like water, and she came to trust it.

Still, she felt alone. For some reason Tyree had slipped out of the room, and without him the aloneness ached in her bones. Mercer did what she needed to do. She breathed as William Still had told her those many months ago, and as the gentle minister had told her, and she called to mind the beginnings of other talks, when she'd felt alone and too tired to fight them or woo them, too tired to force herself to go on. She reminded herself, as she'd remind a three-year-old who says she can't walk any farther, that she's on the way home—almost home, sugar pie—and she'll see to it that she gets there. She held her own hand. Then she told herself that she didn't have a choice. So there.

The strength trickled into her again, like groundwater, and she tapped it. She smiled at them because she felt it, and it felt good, and the aloneness didn't ache. She smiled because the trickling within had nothing to do with them. They couldn't take it away.

Mercer took her time. She described her father to them. She told them how he used to put her feet on his and walk with her like that. She told them about the naughty laughter in her mother's eyes, the cleverness and precision in her fingers, which loved and petted her children when she could. Mercer had never said or seen it that way before. She recalled, but didn't mention, how good it had felt to hear her parents moan together in the dark, and laugh now and then, and sleep, and how her parents' bodies warmed her and her brother when they brought them into bed with them in the cold winter.

Grief filled her chest and dropped heavily into her stomach. Her father would have been about her age now when they whipped him that last time; her mother, younger.

By the time Mercer returned to the tooth, the people had stopped holding back so hard. They weren't with her yet, but they'd stopped pulling so hard against her. They seemed less eager to see her fail. Tyree stepped into the room again. He caught her eye, but she could not read his expression. From outside the hall, she heard whispers and rustling feet.

Then a brick came in through the window. Glass flew in, and a woman screamed. People gasped. Some of them jumped up. That's all it was at first, one brick. A man near the front stood and called for order. The people quieted each other. The man said that the mischief makers wanted to create confusion. He raised his hand in the air. "But we'll show 'em, won't we?"

"Yes, indeed."

"Sure."

"We'll show 'em."

Then he called for a group of men to go outside with him to see about the commotion.

Tyree began to walk slowly to the front of the hall. He hugged the walls. Mercer tried not to draw attention to him by watching him. No more than five other black men were in the hall.

As soon as a dozen men had gathered at the door to go out, a second brick came in through the broken window, then another. The third brick struck a woman in the head. Mercer could see that, but she could also see that few people in the audience could tell what was happening. The woman screamed when she was hit, and her scream broke the audience's resolve. Other women screamed. Men and women jumped up and began pushing one another to get out. Tyree was nearly to the stage.

Stones, bricks, and pieces of wood came in at random now. Shattering glass made a desperate sound. People who had been waiting their turn began to push; people who had been pushing pushed harder. Mercer heard them screaming at one another to hurry for God's sake and to wait for God's sake, to stop it and to go. They cursed and cried and moaned. Someone fell, and a struggle broke out between those trying to pick her up and those trying to step over her to get past. The crush was brief. Mercer was left onstage, along with Prudence, who cringed in her seat and looked, as Mercer did, to Tyree.

"Come," he demanded. "Don't get separated from the crowd."

Mercer and Prudence held hands and followed Tyree. They were just behind the last of the audience pushing out. The night was cloudy. Some people were running home, some crowding onto their neighbors' conveyances. Alerted by runners, a dozen or more men had mounted horses and ridden to the hall, and were grabbing up their women.

"Wait."

A man wearing a minister's collar came riding up at the rear.

"Come on," he said, holding out his hand to the three of them. "I'm Preacher Winston."

Mercer had seen him slip into the hall a few minutes late, looking distracted, and he'd gone out with the group of men who tried to quell the commotion. He sat perched on the red leather seat of a shiny black trap, ridiculously fragile-looking and small under the circumstances. Tyree opened his palms.

"Well, I can take somebody," he said desperately.

"Go ahead," Mercer said to Prudence.

"I'll stay with you." Prudence clasped Mercer's hand in both her own.

"No." Mercer said it as firmly as she could. She bent over Prudence and tried to find words to convince her.

"God has sent us each a helper. You and I will be safer apart. You must get away. Besides, this is the man who came to my aid before."

"We must rendezvous," Prudence said, looking expectantly at Winston. "Where?"

The preacher mentioned a town with an inn, halfway to Philadelphia.

"I shall wait for you." Prudence let go of Mercer's hand. She climbed up onto the seat next to the preacher, and he drove away.

Tyree pointed out a grove of trees near a barn, several fields in front of them. "That's where we're going. I've got a horse and wagon behind the trees." They were at least half a mile away.

Mercer lifted her skirt to clamber over a fence and trot around the edge of a field of new corn. They could hear noise behind them. The men on horses had galloped to the hall. They were shouting. Tyree waved at Mercer to run and stay with him. Together, they ran from the sound of the men. More glass shattered. At the edge of the field, where two trees grew together, Tyree stopped running abruptly. Mercer stumbled into him in the dark. He held her to keep her from falling and motioned for her to crouch down low next to him in the darkness.

Justice Hall was on fire. The men on horses pranced in front of it, whooping and yelling. Smoke billowed into the spring night, and no wind blew it away. Low clouds pushed toward the ground. The smoky fog curled low over the land and burned their eyes. A stench like ruin attached itself to the mist and coated their clothes and skin. They breathed it in until they tasted it on the backs of their tongues. One of the arsonists fired a gun into the burning building. The gunshots exploded with dry pops into the smoky air.

"Why shoot," Mercer whispered, "if it's already on fire?"

"They're making sure no one will come put it out," Tyree responded.

By now, three or four dozen men on foot had joined the men on horseback. Others appeared to stand in a wide half-ring. Some had brought buckets. But the fire brigade did not come with its tank on a wagon, and the men with buckets did not form a line to the creek. The hall burned, and they watched.

The fire commanded Mercer's attention too. Even from half a field away, she could hear the draft it created, sucking new fuel into the flame with pops and thuds and gusts. Flames crawled out from the windows. After a while, the roof began to collapse. The men on their horses yelled each time a section of the roofing crashed and a billow of black smoke rose into the grey fog.

Mercer could see their lust. They wanted to be able to set fires and not get burned. They wanted to shoot guns in the air, with no paybacks. This was the freedom they wanted.

If I could
If I could
If I could
I'd tear this building down

Every time a barn burned in Virginia, whites went about with pinched faces, and Negroes with sidelong grins. She could understand that. What she hadn't expected was that people who had homes and families of their own, men with money and the franchise, would need to burn up and tear down too. It had been naive. Rich folk who wanted for nothing would still steal from each other—or from the lowliest man or woman on earth—so why wouldn't these men long to destroy?

Sure they wanted to tear the building down, and they were doing it. Negroes provided the occasion. *If I could.* Forty timid souls huddled nervously inside Justice Hall were no match for these men; no sheriff or policemen or citizens' vigilance committee would stop them. *If I could.* Mercer was the excuse.

And there had to be one. God was good, and the devil was evil, and there had to be someone to hate, some other within their border, in their homes and fields and beds, so that when they lay them down at night, their fear could have a shape, and they would never be alone.

"Next time fire," Tyree said.

God had promised it. Mercer looked at the men and saw two score little God-men trying to burn away their own sin.

"My parents were unbelievers," Mercer said in response, and she could see why now, watching the flames dance and the smoke roll and the men dance and thinking of the God above, force, pure force like fire, burning up the world with displeasure and revenge. And even Jesus, have mercy, mercy Jesus, promised to come back with a sword. Mercy she'd named herself. Mercy.

In the beginning was the Word, and the Word was with God, and the Word was God. He was infinite mercy, and yet He'd come back as a lion. He'd carry a sword.

Mercer shivered against Tyree. She was cold and exhausted from holding herself up like a lightning rod in America's race storm. Boom. Hate like thunder rolled within her and crashed around her and her trying to speak freedom to power. Mercy without a sword, tricked out in righteousness, and who cared a good goddamn?

Tyree and Mercer sat very still. If they could, if they could, Lord, if they could, who knew what they'd do with anti-slavery instigators and especially black ones. Runaway or free made no difference to the flame.

One man held up the long stick he'd brought with him and shouted.

"What'd he say?" Tyree whispered into her ear.

"I couldn't hear."

Someone yelled back, and men with sticks ran along the side of the building and began clubbing at the ground. The men who'd lit the fire were drunk. They needed more. They'd found it: smoky death riding on wind with dry leaves and soot; sneaky death swooping from the trees on owls' wings; soft, wet death settling dewy on the cornfields; death sitting quiet on their foreheads, resting patient on their chests in the morning before dawn. Close as veins under the skin. Death in the bowels like sickness and fear.

Thank God for the rats. They whined and whistled and bit and snapped. Finally, they died.

Tyree and Mercer were stiff with sitting and filthy with soot. They did not get up from the shadows of the trees until long after the rats had died and run, and long after the men had thrown their clubs into the fire and gone home. Justice Hall smoldered into a smoking black hulk on the green.

The horses had pulled the steering mechanism away from Tyree's wagon and stood motionless under a tree twenty yards away. The wagon tilted on its wheels and rested on its back.

Mercer gasped. "Oh, my God. They busted it."

Tyree shushed her. "Look here," he said. He opened his palm to reveal the kingpin. "Sharkey told me to take it."

"So no one else could."

"And so that anyone who tried would think we'd already been done."

It took them half an hour to prepare the wagon and the horses. Then they waited another half hour, just so that they would not meet any of the rioters. It was late and dark and close. Mercer sat close to Tyree but said little.

"I'm afraid," she said.

"No wonder," he said. "That was some show."

"Recite something, won't you?" she asked. "That story you used to recite about the men in the war?"

Happy to distract himself, Tyree began to whisper the story of *Henry V*, stopping to recite King Harry's speeches. Mercer grunted appreciatively into the darkness, falling asleep as the king meditated on the responsibility of kingship and the empty comfort of ceremony.

They reached the inn before dawn. Rather than alarm the household, Tyree pulled the wagon behind the barn. He put his arm around Mercer, laid his head on top of hers, and fell into a restless doze.

At dawn, they awoke and went into the inn. Soon Prudence Randall came downstairs to meet them; she appeared at once weary and radiant.

"Thank God you're all right," Mercer said.

Prudence answered, "I don't think I've ever been better."

Mercer realized that Prudence had probably been wanting a confrontation on this tour. They ate a breakfast of fried scrapple, biscuits, and coffee. Then they fed and watered the horses and headed slowly toward West Chester, where Prudence could stop at Eliza Ruffin's house before returning to Boston. Tyree and Mercer would spend the night at Zilpha's before going on to Philadelphia.

Eliza Ruffin was waiting for them at the head of her road.

"We've been watching for you," she said. "Come in."

Tyree declined. "No, thank you. We'll keep moving. If we stop, we'll fall over."

He also refused her offer of fresh horses. He didn't want to be obligated to come back and exchange them. Instead, he watered and brushed his own tired animals.

Prudence held Mercer's hand and patted it. "What a time we've had." Mercer patted her hand in return.

They promised to write. Prudence would send Mercer's payment in care of Tyree.

"Where will you be?" Prudence asked.

"I don't know," Mercer said. "But the Quick family will have my address."

They embraced. Then Mercer mounted the wagon's driver's seat.

"What're you doing?" Tyree asked.

"I'm drivin you, Mr. Tyree Quick. How about that?"

"You mean it, don't you?"

"Yes, I mean it," she said. "You've been drivin and drivin."

"Well," Tyree said, laughing, "I'd be delighted."

Eliza Ruffin clapped her hands. Prudence Randall, who was crying unashamedly, dabbed her eyes and waved.

"You'll have to give her a handkerchief," Tyree called as he climbed up beside Mercer. "Mine is unfit, I'm afraid, and their things got burned up."

"Burned?" Eliza reached into the pocket of her cape and produced a handkerchief.

"Yes, burned. Miss Randall'll tell you the story."

Mercer flicked the reins on the horses. They pulled forward slowly, barely moving the wagon.

"They're tired," Tyree said.

Mercer snapped the reins harder. "Walk on," she said. "I'm sorry you're tired, but you gotta pull anyhow."

"You're going to get the last measure out of these poor nags, aren't you?"

Mercer did not look at Tyree, but she smiled and sucked her teeth. "Ain't but five miles more, horse. Walk on."

Thirteen / The Land of the Living

As if agreeing to one final effort, the horses broke into a rhythmic walk. Tyree laughed.

"I'm giddy," he said. "Just five miles, you say, Merce?"

"Yes, Mr. Tyree, just fives miles more."

"That's good, 'cause I'm like these horses. I don't think I could make it much further."

Tyree put his elbows on his knees and let his chin drop toward his chest. In a few minutes, he fell asleep. His body swayed with the wagon until he finally slumped against her. The solid weight of him felt good.

Mercer looked around her at the well-watered valley. Deerskins hung to dry on a fence in a south-facing field. West Chester, where she had stayed hidden that winter, felt familiar and welcoming. It brimmed with game and birds, vegetables and fruit trees, and gentle weather over gentle land. Unlike city wealth, this was prosperity she understood; she could imagine it for herself and her children. But Pennsylvania's lovely valleys also harbored patrollers and enemies. Vigilance was the only way to stay safe, or stay free—constant vigilance. After less than a year, she felt weary of it, and weary of her false attachment to Tyree Quick. She loved and trusted him; she enjoyed his company. That was true and very nice. But she had to leave, because she also wanted the comfort of his body. That had been so, she admitted to herself, for many months now.

Mercer watched Tyree's bent head bob with the ruts on the road. His breath came slowly now and deep. His black hair curled in tight rounds at the base of his neck. It came to her to run her fingers over the line where the hair stopped. She held the reins firmly instead. Her speaking tour was over. It was time to pick up her children and go.

Zilpha had the place shut up. It looked just as it had the day Mercer had come with her from Philadelphia. The whitewashed shutters were closed and latched. Tyree walked down to the old springhouse, where Zilpha kept the key in a bottle.

"Where do you think she is?" Mercer asked.

"Gone to the city to help with my father."

"Is he worse?"

"Yes," Tyree said irritably. "He's worse. . . . I'm going to take these horses up to the Dandridges' stable. Shouldn't take me more than half an hour."

Inside, the house was cool and dark. It gave off its characteristic smell of dried tobacco and lavender from the rolled rugs. Mercer started a fire in the stove and fetched well water and put on the kettle for tea. Tyree washed in the tub outside. Then he slept. Mercer made soup and corn bread, then sat down in Zilpha's chair by the stove. The cottage felt safe and abundant. Next to the chair, some mending sat folded and waiting in Zilpha's basket. Mercer picked it up, put it down again, and dozed. When she awoke, late in the afternoon, Tyree was sitting in the other chair, watching her. On the east side of the cottage, the side that faced the road, he had pulled the shutters. Sun slanted in from the west.

"What time is it?" she asked.

"Five," he said. "Time to eat."

They ate together.

"Tastes like Aunt Zilphie's," Tyree said.

"Well, I'm sure." Mercer laughed. She had made the soup exactly as Zilpha would, with Zilpha's vegetables, Zilpha's cured pork, Zilpha's pot, just as if the older woman were standing next to her, telling Mercer, who had cooked for five dozen people at a time, how to twist an onion off the braid and how to cut a carrot.

Then Tyree suggested that they walk along the edge of the woods to the west, to look for blackberries. Mercer stared at him quizzically.

"It's too late to start back to the city," he said, "and it's not safe to keep riding around at night."

They stopped at the mulberry tree on the way. Mercer held out her basket, but Tyree put two berries to her lips.

"Don't save them," he said. "Here, eat them now, while they're still warm."

At the edge of the woods, past a spray of wild lilies leaning toward the sun and bunches of blue cornflowers, they found the blackberry bushes. After the thin sweetness of mulberries, blackberries tasted rich and dark. The tips of Tyree's and Mercer's fingers stained purple.

Back inside the house, they settled in the chairs on either side of the stove. Sunset threw gold shafts in the west windows and along the pine floors. The shafts climbed up the wall and faded. They did not speak for a long while. Then Tyree pointed to the footstool next to his chair.

"Come, sit here," he said.

Mercer smiled crookedly and hesitated.

"Come on," he said. "Come sit here."

Mercer moved and sat on the stool, facing him. Tyree lifted her hand between his two. He held her violet-tipped fingers next to his and compared them.

"This is what we did as children," he said.

"Us too."

He held their two hands in his free hand and swiveled them like a dancing puppet. Mercer's fingers, square and blunt, were nearly as large as his. He examined them in the orange half-light. He rubbed his hand over her hair and cupped the nape of her neck with his palm. "When I was eight years old, I'll never forget, I discovered my first love. I thought she was the prettiest thing I'd ever seen."

"And what was her name?"

"Name was Lizzie."

"Did you tell her about your love?"

"No, but I sat behind her and picked the lice out of her hair."

"That was some kinda love."

"It was almost as good as this."

"What? Well, I'm sorry. I don't have no lice."

"I've grown beyond that now," he said, and laughed. Then seriously, he asked her: "May I?"

"May you what?"

He tripped his tongue and looked at her and held her face with his hand. Then he traced her eyebrows with his thumbs, and her temples and cheekbones. He did it over and over, with gentleness and pressure. Each time he rubbed her temples, she felt close to tears, as if they'd been collecting in pouches behind her eyes and he could run his finger alongside them and loosen their hold.

"You gonna make me cry."

"Shhh."

Mercer closed her eyes and let the tears overflow her eyelids.

"Aw, Merce, Merce," he said, kissing her forehead. "Aw, Mercy, are you sad?"

"I suppose," she said.

He did not stop rubbing. "Am I making you sad?"

"Sure you are."

He kissed her spilling-over eyes and then her mouth.

"Blackberry lips," he said. Then he asked: "Do you want me to stop?"

She shook her head no. He stood, pulled her up, and turned her around to begin to undo the buttons down the back of her dress.

"I've wanted you," he said, "since I first saw you on that ferry."

She felt his fingers on each button. She liked a dress with a lot of buttons. In a moment, she answered him.

"I remember that first time you picked Mattie up outta the wagon at the cemetery. 'Member, he was asleep?" She paused and shuddered as the air tickled her back above her camisole. "You been carryin my children ever since, and I owe you."

"You don't owe me anything. I owe you for bringing me alive again. I want to take you to Canada, Merce—you and the children, yours and mine. Shhh. Listen to me, now. And I want us to live as man and wife and family."

"Wouldn't be a real marriage?"

"It'd be as close as you can get, Mercer."

"You wouldn't leave your family."

"I'd have a new family."

"Like Job."

"No, not like that. My children haven't died."

Something had died for him, though: the illusion that kin transcended will, that when push came to shove, the Quicks would sacrifice anything for their clan. He'd leave, and someone who'd been holding their secret money would pull it out, and they'd sell a house or two and evict Mrs. Becker and stuff her house with three families, and they'd tell bitter stories about the son who ran away. Harriet would move home. Bea would sober up for another two years. Blanche would remarry, and Zilpha would convince Della and Manny to hire a man to do the work Tyree had been doing. They'd done fine without Roland. They'd do fine without him.

"Will you do it?"

Mercer felt his mouth on the nape of her neck where he had rubbed earlier. The spot was still warm. Her dress slipped down. She held it from falling off by crossing her arms. Then she felt his hands on her shoulders.

"Will you come with me?"

Tyree caressed Mercer's shoulders. They were wide, wider than they seemed in her clothing, and he could see the muscle under the smooth chestnut skin. What was boyish about her was her frame. He'd thought it just her movements, her absence of coyness, or the way she lunged when she rushed; but now it seemed to him, as the ancients had said, that temperament might indeed arise from the body. It was her body that had held such power as she sat atop the steamer. He rubbed the ample shoulders and remembered the admonition of adults when he was young: to pick on someone your own size. He'd never thought to love someone his own size. No one had told him that. He'd never felt such plenty under his hands, rubbing warm and alive against his body.

She turned to him, tears still sliding from the sides of her eyes.

"Merce," he said. "My Mercy. Will you come?"

"I want to come."

They made love on the living room floor, on a quilt Tyree grabbed from the cedar box in Zilpha's bedroom. Tyree went fast and greedy and hard and fell asleep. In a couple of hours they awoke and lit the lamp. They boiled water and washed themselves. They were hungry again.

"You're looking at me," she said.

"Well, of course I am looking at you."

Mercer heated the soup and biscuits and made coffee while Tyree lit a small fire in the old fireplace. It was a gorgeous luxury, like the cottage and its ample store and its privacy, like the blackberries, like kissing his mouth or eating cream.

"I never had a whole place like this all to myself," she said.

"I never had you all to myself."

"Zilpha would have your hide if she saw you buildin a fire at this time of year."

"But you were chilly, weren't you?"

Mercer laughed, delighted, for the moment, with their playacting. Tyree spread their quilt by the fire.

To bed, to bed, said Sleepyhead.

But instead of lying down, they stood by the table where they'd eaten, and kissed until he turned her back to him. As he pulled down her bloomers, Tyree's hand felt a scarred patch of skin on the backs of Mercer's thighs. It was leathery skin, with welts that had raised up once and never gone down. Tyree drew in his breath. Mercer heard him.

"You didn't feel that before?"

He did not move his hand. "No."

Mercer pushed his arm away and began to pull up her bloomers. "That's the difference between us," she said.

She didn't like feeling scarred and ugly with him of all people. She didn't like the hesitation of his fingers, just enough to signal disgust.

"No, no, no, no," he said. He clasped his hands under her buttocks. "Please, no."

"Life is short, Tyree."

"Come on, Merce. Come on now. I've been with you this far, haven't I?"

He turned her so that her back was to him again, and she did not resist. He pushed down her bloomers, and although she listened warily for a hint of repulsion, she did not stop him. He drew his hands up to hold her around her waist and then to touch the surprisingly small black nipples.

"Life is short," she repeated.

"So kiss me before you go."

It was a joke, but they didn't laugh. He turned her face to the side to reach her mouth, and they kissed as gently in the alcove of Zilpha's kitchen as if they were making up for their adultery, or were soon to renounce it.

Mercer held on to the chair, and finally got up on tiptoes and bent her knees to get just right for making love. He held her thigh and under her belly.

"I'm gonna take my time," he said.

Wait a while, said Sloth.

Then she laughed. It felt good to have him, and to laugh and to forget everything but this moment and this pleasure. She'd never had such pleasure: it was rich, fat lovemaking, like gravy. This pleasure did not make her want to please. It did not make her worry about his delight. It did not make her afraid to enjoy, because the joy would be added to her account and taken out, double, sometime later. This pleasure made her greedy.

Put on the pan, said greedy Nan, and we'll have a bite before we go.

It made her groan and stretch with him. It made her feel for his tongue. Then Mercer let her belly go flat on the table and arched up toward him.

"You take all the time you can."

Greedy, greedy. Open your mouth. Lick the pot.

"Slow?"

She couldn't believe herself. Open. Everything open. Open wide. They took their time. They stopped and talked. They rubbed and kissed and fondled. He called her name like a rumble in her ear and said he loved her.

"Don't leave me," she said.

They finished, and Tyree bent over her to kiss the back of her neck and the side of her mouth. Then he stood and rubbed his hands up and down her back. Against his thighs he felt the mottled flesh. He ran his fingers over it lightly, determined to accept it as part of her, and finding the determination less difficult to accomplish than he'd have thought. Now that his body was satisfied, his fingers made no judgments. They would remember.

"Looka here," Mercer mumbled sleepily into the crook of her arm. "My head is almost in the soup bowl."

"You're a terrible old thing, stretched out here on the table."

"Uh-huh."

"Didn't even clear the dishes."

She tripped her tongue. "Going with another woman's husband, and don't even wash the dishes first. That's terrrrr-'ble."

Neither of them moved. Tyree stood, pressed against her, absently fondling whatever came to hand.

"Tyree?"

"Yes?"

"Why'd you come out before you finish?"

"What do you mean, why?"

"I mean what for?"

"So that we don't make a baby."

"Oh."

"You didn't do that?"

"No, we never did that. Where'd you hear that?"

"It's from a book for married people."

"Hah." She began to laugh.

"You think that's funny?"

Mercer was laughing so hard she could barely breathe. "A book?"

"Yes, indeed, a book. Some married people we know lent it to us."

It was a lie, but the truth was too complicated to bother with. The couple had lent the ten-year-old copy of *The Married Couple's Handbook* to Roland when he and Blanche married. Tyree had read it before they gave it back.

"Besides, I'm not gonna have no more babies."

"How do you know?"

She shrugged.

"Well, I might," he said.

"Oho."

"Yeah, you go ahead and laugh, Miss Know-It-All. I feel like making one tonight."

"Oh, Jesus." His tone made her serious.

"Yes, I do. I feel like planting a baby and watching you get big. That's the kind of primitive brute you've made me into. I was a civilized man when I left Philadelphia."

Mercer went into the bedroom and found a nightgown to put on. It smelled of the leather bag Tyree had given her, and the lecture tour. She breathed deeply, grateful not to be traveling, not to be talking about herself to strangers, grateful not to be looked at. She went to the kitchen, where Tyree now sat silently with his trousers on, and she cleaned the table and washed the dishes in cold, soapy water left from earlier.

"So," Tyree said. "Why don't you go to Canada first, for the obvious reasons? I know some people we can write to find you and the children rooms for the time being."

Mercer said nothing. She finished the dishes and brought two spoons and half a jar of spiced peaches to the table.

"What do you think?"

"I suppose." Mercer did not want to leave without him. They'd convince him to stay.

She would have thought herself more hesitant, if only out of loyalty to the family that had fed and clothed and hidden her. But the fact was that Harriet and Sharkey were the only other Quicks for whom Mercer felt loyalty. So this is what it comes down to, she thought. She wanted him, and so what.

She had better sense than to make excuses to herself about deserving a chance for a love of her own, after Willie the Cooper's leaving and after years with Pryor had made her shut down inside like an empty house. Deserving had nothing to do with it.

"They'll have money enough to keep them, and Sharkey'll watch 'em, and Zilpha will come in and help Mother now and then."

"Are you convincing yourself?"

"You have not objected."

"I should object. If I don't, I'll be no better than the snake the people brought into the house and put on the hearth."

Tyree looked around the room. "It bit them, of course."

" 'Cause it was a snake."

"You're not a snake, Mercer."

"Well, I better look hard at what I am. Your family took me

in. Now I'm saying to you, 'Yeah, let's us go to Canada, and too bad for the rest.'"

He paused. "You know your abolitionist friends wouldn't want much to do with you if you take up with me."

"I know that," she said. "But I never meant to stay in that line."

"We've made up our minds, haven't we?" Tyree asked.

"I have."

Tyree led her to the quilt in front of the fire. Mercer lay down and closed her eyes. Her body had once been an unprotected field. Now it felt like a cool, green garden with high stone walls, such as she'd seen in Harriet's books. She fell asleep. Tyree lay next to her, propped on one arm, watching the fire glow play on her face and indulging himself in regrets for their good names and easy society, for the love and respect of his family and their houses and furniture and money. But he wanted Mercer. He wanted himself as he felt with her. As if premature grief would cut his loss, therefore, he let himself miss the house on Pine Street and its familiar inhabitants. Then he traced a finger along Mercer's jawline. Whore, snake, lover. Mercer's honesty could be mighty raw. He stanched the doubt that trickled through him.

Life was short.

"He's been holding on for you," Della said as Tyree stepped into the kitchen. "Can't really call it more than that. I told him that you'd be back, but I didn't know when, did I now?"

She'd been crying. Her eyes were red and swollen, and her voice sounded resentful and flat. He hated to see her suffer, but he begrudged her his sympathy. His own resentment reared up to meet hers. They felt sorry for themselves, and in that self-pity there could be no room for compassion. He knew this, and knowing made it the more distasteful.

Tyree's mind and body tingled with the thought and feel of Mercer. It made him impatient with the lies that held his family together. He didn't want it to hold together; he wanted them to fly apart. He wanted to put them into a sling and cast them across the water and free himself. He sighed.

"You sound tired," she accused.

"Daddy isn't waiting for me, Mother."

"You're like him, you know. You don't think you are, but you are. I told you he's waiting for you. I told you *your father is dying.*" Della's voice rose to a high-pitched whine.

Cyrus came whooping down the stairs, calling him. Della slammed her hand against the table as he appeared in the doorway. He stopped running and shouting but did not stop grinning. Tyree squatted on his haunches and opened his arms. Cyrus ran to him on noisy tiptoe, pantomiming silence. Scooping his son toward his chest, Tyree stood.

"Did you bring home Mattie's mother?"

"Yes, I did. She's over at Aunt Bea's."

"Good," Cyrus said. "Mattie was scared."

"Come on," Tyree said. "Let's go see your grandfather."

"May I show you something first?"

"What is it?"

"It's something I can do."

"Not in the house, jumping and jumping around like monkeys," Della said. "I cannot stand it. I cannot."

"Here," Tyree said. "I'll watch you out the back door." He turned to his mother. "He can do it in the yard, can't he?"

"Watch the clothes," she said wearily.

Cyrus put his hands up in the air and measured the ground in front of him with his eyes. Tyree found that he was holding his body taut, leaning forward, expectant. Then Cyrus rocked his arms back and shot them forward, pulling his body down in an arc. His two hands hit the ground solidly, fingers spread wide in the dirt. The right elbow bent more than the left, as if he had forgotten to push hard enough with it, or was afraid to. But he recovered and sprang the rest of his body over. His feet slapped the earth, and his torso flew up. The somersault wasn't perfect, but he'd done it.

"Look at that." Tyree grabbed his son's hand. Cyrus stood before him, flushed and jubilant. Tyree felt jubilant with him, for him. He saw again in his mind the moment when Cyrus committed himself to tumbling down and throwing himself forward. He'd thrown his head and his arms down in spite of his fear, and Tyree, who had often suspected that the boy would inherit the timidity that circumscribed Blanche's life, felt relief sweet as joy. He grabbed his son and held him tight to his chest.

"It felt good when you did it, didn't it?"

Cyrus grinned. "It was the best thing."

Tyree sent Cyrus upstairs. "Go tell your mother I'm home," he said. "And I'll be up to see her in a bit."

Then he turned to Della. "You gave Roland money, Mother."

She didn't deny it. Nor did she register any surprise that he knew. "I made a terrible mistake, Tyree, and I've paid for it; God knows. Emmanuel beat me—you know that, and thank God you stopped him. All I can do is cook, Ty. That's all I know to do. I didn't even know how to raise children till I had my own. You know my family's gone. You children are all I have."

"How much did you give him?"

"You don't know how your father did me."

"How much, Mother?"

"He bought a house for that heifer who use to sneak and sleep in people's shed kitchens."

"How much, Mother?"

"He bought a proper house for her all to herself, and we're crammed in here, and we cook out of here, and it's our warehouse, and he took her to the Academy of Music to see the Black Swan when she came to sing here. Tyree, he never so much as took me for a walk around the corner, and he took her to the Academy of Music."

"So you gave Roland the money."

Della's lips were pursed together and trembling. She jutted her chin upward to answer yes. "I never heard the Black Swan in my life."

"How much, Mother?"

"Everything."

Blanche smiled as he entered the door. "Look." She held up a hat trimmed in gray fur. "Isn't it pretty?"

"Yes."

Hello, he thought. Pretty hat. Goodbye.

"Cyrus," he said, "go on downstairs and see if there's something you can do to help your grandmother. I'll go in and see Granddaddy by myself."

In the rear room on the second floor, Tyree sat down at his father's desk and looked through the papers, including notices of money owed to three creditors. He thought he knew where the money was, but he had to put his hands on the deeds to the houses.

In the front room Zilpha dozed in the slipper chair next to Manny's bed. Manny lay still. Only his eyes moved. They glinted out of his face, startlingly alive. Tyree shook Zilpha and told her he would sit for a while. She stood, rubbed her back, and walked out slowly. It was as if the brother and sister had aged five years instead of three days. Manny did look much worse.

"Daddy," Tyree said without preamble, "you've got to tell me where you keep the key to the strongbox. It's time now."

Manny did not move his lips. He did not look in Tyree's direction.

"Mother doesn't have the deed to this house. Is it in your desk? And the houses for hire?"

Nothing.

"Aunt Bea's deed. Where's her deed?"

He paused.

"I've looked through your desk, and I can't find them."

Manny's voice rasped out in a whisper, and his words slurred so that Tyree could not understand him.

"Roland." Manny barely said the word, but Tyree caught it. "Roland?"

Manny indicated yes. His eyes resumed their glittering stare at the ceiling. Then he looked at Tyree and reached from under the blanket for Tyree's hand. His eyeballs began to gyrate. Tyree called his name. He didn't answer. His quaking eyes could not focus. Then he closed them and lay back. Tyree called his mother.

Zilpha returned. Bea arrived, drunk and resentful, and they sent her home. Cyrus and Mattie were dispatched to fetch Harriet from her meeting, Sharkey from his rooms over the stable, and Ephraim and Abby Ann from their carriage house behind the rectory. Blanche brought her sewing downstairs and sat in the hall, stitching in the semidarkness. Mercer and Etta came from Bea's to finish cooking the food that Della had begun.

In the kitchen, Tyree watched Mercer cook with her daughter. He watched the square deftness of her fingers as she kneaded dough for rolls. He watched the taut lines of her forearms and the movement of her lips as she licked them in concentration.

"I didn't think he was this bad," Tyree said. "He wasn't this bad when I left."

Mercer's behavior toward him, now that they were in the house, had become circumspect. He felt as if he were talking to himself.

The sun went down, and Etta lit the lamps. From habit, Tyree envisioned how much oil they'd use that night, how much they'd have left in the can in the basement, when he'd need to replace it, and how much it would cost. Where were the deeds? Tyree began to worry what tricks his parents had played with their real estate. And where was Sharkey?

"I'm going to get Uncle Shark," Tyree said.

"Stop and look in on Bea, will you, and send her back here if she's able," said Della.

Tyree cursed under his breath and went out the back door.

Bea was sitting on her bed when he came.

"What's that smell?" he asked.

"What smell?"

"Pissy."

Tyree followed his nose. Bea's customary chair sat beneath the open window. Tyree walked to the chair and put his head out the window. Below he saw a puddle. Bea laughed.

"I got me a pot to piss in and a window to throw it out of."

"Aunt Bea, this gin has taken your mind away."

"I got a pot to piss in and a window to throw it out of. He can go ahead and die if he wants to. God knows he's my brother and I tried to love 'im, but he just don't want anybody to have anything but him."

Bea's face, always on the verge of looking strangely girlish, reminded Tyree of spoiled children who gloat at each other after taking some advantage.

"You going to sit here in the dark while your family is across the way?"

"No," she said. "I'm gonna light a lamp."

She laughed again, a false belly laugh that Tyree would never forget. *Hah-hah-hah.* She fumbled with the tin of matches.

"Here," Tyree said. "Give me."

"Not giving you shit. I gave you already. I gave everything I had."

Tyree reached down in the dim room and took the tin of matches from his aunt's fingers. "Gimme." She lunged toward him and bumped into the nightstand. The lamp tipped over. Oil spilled out around the wick.

"Oh, forget it," Tyree snapped. He put the matches in his pocket, turned, and left the room. You didn't need a lighted room to drink gin in and stew. Maybe she'd have herself another half bottle and throw some more piss into the street. It occurred to him that he should have closed and locked the window. Most likely, however, she'd just fall back on the bed and sleep and wake up contrite after Manny had died.

In the backyard, Tyree passed the old laundry pot still full of dirty wash water. He filled two buckets from the shed and took them out front to pour onto the sidewalk.

"Thank you, Tyree." Mr. Chaz, an old neighbor, leaned out his window and spoke to Tyree. "What in God's name is wrong with your aunt? What in God's name? She's been bad before, but now she's completely out of hand. I am just glad you came."

"Me too."

"The girls still living with her?"

"Her boarders?"

Mr. Chaz was straining to see over Tyree's shoulder and into the window.

"No, sir. My sister Harriet took them around the corner with her to fill out their contract with my aunt." Tyree answered carefully. Unlike most parents, these had insisted on a contract. Bea had signed it, and she was liable to board the girls for a year. Who knew what might get back to their parents? And Tyree was sure Bea had spent the money already.

Other neighbors stood in the street, taking in the cool evening and the gossip.

"That's not what I think."

"Oh, yes it is."

Tyree wanted to shout in their faces: A pot to piss in and a window to throw it out. I'm looking for deeds to houses, and she's making jokes. Until my father dies, it's her window. After that, none of us knows.

The urine had seeped into the bricks. Tyree went inside for two more bucketfuls of soapy water. Above his head he heard Bea moving about slowly. It took him three trips to wash out the stink. Then he heard Bea fall and scream. It was as much a moan as a scream. Tyree was so sick of her antics he nearly left her. She fell plenty and never told anyone. He sighed. It was as if his entire family had heard his determination to leave and pulled out all their tricks. He replaced the buckets and went upstairs.

The fire had begun on the nightstand and quickly jumped to the bed. Bea lay on the floor, moaning. Tyree stuck his head through the open window and yelled "Fire!"

"Fire."

"Fire."

Neighbors took up the call.

"Close the window," Mr. Chaz yelled across the narrow street.

Tyree threw down the window and squatted to pick up Bea. She was on her hands and knees, pulling feathers out of the mattress. She threw handfuls of feathers onto the flames. They spread the fire throughout the room and made fumes that burned their eyes and throats. Tyree grabbed her from behind. She thrashed and screamed at him to let her down and not to leave the bedroom.

"It's on fire," he said.

"Goddamn it. The bed is burning. Get my money out."

"You said you didn't have any money."

"It's in there."

Tyree made a lunge with his arm into the hole exposed in the side of the bed. His knuckles hit a gin bottle.

"Shit."

Over her protests, he dragged her outside and thrust her into the arms of a neighbor woman. Then he went back through the short house for the buckets again. Standby and Simple Simon ran back and forth in the narrow yard, barking.

Other men had already gone in and were dousing the room.

There was terrible confusion, however; the room was dark. Tyree called for a ladder. He stood at the top, opened the window, and shouted in: "Two men. Only two men. Holden and Andrew, tell the other men there's no room."

They were wasting time.

"Bring water."

Tyree reached down for a bucket and passed it in. Smoke poured into his face. He bent down and breathed, stood up and heaved the bucket over the sill, took an empty bucket and bent down again and breathed. Inside, the men tore down curtains and wet the floor and the furniture to try to keep the fire from spreading. They fought the fire for an hour.

When he was satisfied that they'd saved the house, Tyree climbed down from the ladder. His back was sore and his lungs had filled with smoke. He went inside to thank the others and to tell them that he'd finish the job. He made a mental note to ask his mother to bake two large chickens. He'd take one to each man's family, with a bucket of beer.

As he surveyed the charred, wet room, he heard Mercer come up behind him. Neighbors had sent for the Quicks, but no one left Manny's bedside. They did not want him to die alone, as Della said, just because Bea had decided to show herself for what she was: an old drunk. Instead, they sent Mercer and Etta. Etta was talking to the neighbors.

Mercer came to Tyree and said into his ear: "Your aunt is over across the street, crying about all this money she had in the mattress. She said it was Roland's money."

"Jesus."

Tyree felt his stomach flop. He argued against the sudden dread. Sharkey had to have it. Who in his right mind would trust Bea with money?

But other knowledge spoke back: Bea would agree to schemes. Wasn't it Bea who'd taken Manny to see his woman when he could no longer walk alone? And didn't she always want a part in foiling him?

Tyree used his bowie knife to dig in the pile of charred feathers, wet and still smoldering. He hit the bottle he'd touched during the fire. The bottle was blackened. Near it were the curled remains of paper: a pile of burned dollar bills, the size of a small bread box. Next to it was a pile of longer, folded papers. He waded into the burned bed muck and used his hands to pick out what had been money and deeds. Of the Quick family's life savings, no more than five hundred remained. Tyree's gut tightened.

Five hundred dollars. What the hell could he do with five hundred dollars? How long would it keep the women in his family going? None of them could oversee the hired houses that generated their income. Della was too old to cater on her own. Blanche made some money, but she wouldn't be able to keep it up too many years longer. Harriet had her hands full with the school.

Mercer stood behind him. "Last year this time," she said, "five hundred dollars would've seemed like all the money in the world to me."

Tyree threw the bottle across the room. It shattered when it hit the wall. He turned suddenly and took her face in his hands. "I have never wanted anything so much as I've wanted you."

He pulled Mercer toward him and held her tightly. "Do you hear me? I never loved a woman like I love you."

"You're not comin with us, are you?"

"Shhh."

"Was it a lot of money?"

"It was enough to let me walk with a clear conscience. How much is that?"

"I don't know."

"I don't know, either."

Bea had fallen asleep in the neighbor's chair. Tyree left her there and returned to his own house. The Tobies crouched in the parlor, hats in hand, tears rolling down their freckled faces. They did not come up to the room.

Africana had been sent to fetch Ephraim. He arrived just behind Tyree and Mercer, too rushed to do more than nod at the living.

Manny stared at Ephraim, but he did not speak. His eyes looked desperate and afraid. Della held his hand and spoke soothingly to him. Tyree knew that his father hated to have his hand held. Della patted. Manny's body shivered and jerked.

Ephraim prayed: " 'The Lord is my light and my salvation; whom shall I fear?' " Frenzy and pain showed in Manny's eyes. He was afraid, all right. The terror jumped out of him like contagion.

" 'The Lord is the strength of my life; of whom shall I be afraid?' "

Death. Damn well ought to be afraid of death. The family who'd been afraid of Manny now feared to watch him die. He had no strength to offer them, no courage, no money. Only more fear. It was all Tyree could do not to grab him by the collar and shake what was left of him. "What shall we do with five hundred god-damn dollars?"

Ephraim rubbed oil on Manny's forehead.

Manny hated church and hated Ephraim even more, and this fool was anointing his head with oil as if he were one of the disciples. Tyree wished for the end. He wanted Manny to die and be done with it, so that they could wash him and mourn him and put him in the ground, and Tyree could hunt through the papers and strongboxes to see whether he might still take his handsome Mercer away and start afresh and get it right.

" 'For in the time of trouble he shall hide me in his pavilion: in the secret of his tabernacle shall he hide me; he shall set me up upon a rock.' "

Tears ran down the women's faces. They cried for Manny's and for pity's sake; for the loss of babies and love; for the death that awaited each of them. Della sobbed loudest.

" 'I had fainted, unless I believed to see the goodness of the Lord in the land of the living.

" 'Wait on the Lord: be of good courage, and he shall strengthen thine heart: wait, I say, on the Lord.' "

Mercer repeated the words to herself. Had she believed to see the goodness of the Lord in the land of the living? Was that it? God-awful truths grew in the same soil as goodness and light. The psalmist knew it. Parents did forsake their children. They always had. Mercer heard herself sob. She had forsaken her boy. Lord take him up. Her own parents had been taken away. Lord take us up. She had been willing to take this man from the family who'd cared for her. They had been God's pavilion for her, this row house on Pine Street her tabernacle where God had hidden her. And he'd been willing to go. All this she knew, and yet she had believed—she knew it now that she heard it said—she had believed to see the goodness of the Lord in the land of the living. Virgil and Lily had known that.

Rub the angel wings. Make'm grow. Lily breathed her love to Virgil at night. Angel wings would not grow later. They sprouted when he touched her. When he was gone, he took heaven too.

I had fainted
Mercer cried for her parents.
She cried for her brother.
unless I had believed
She cried for her little son.
She cried because Willie had left her alone.
to see the goodness of the Lord
She cried because she'd lived under Pryor's domination, a living woman, dumb as a tree.
in the land of the living

Tyree would not come with her now. She could not have her own way. No safety lasts. The price of freedom is vigilance. The only thing for sure is stay black and die.

Tyree would not come. Not if his family had no money to

take care of themselves; not if he was the man she loved. She could see the goodness of the Lord in the land of living, and this last love taken away would become the cornerstone of her new life. She could see it as soon as she turned her back and headed north. She'd see it in her memory: the sight of the man she loved waving goodbye.

Manny's breath went away. It was terrible to see. He strained and jerked to breathe. It seemed as if they had always been in this room. The health and the good times, the rich foods and good clothes, his rare laughter, even the oppression of him, had been an illusion. He began to void himself, and the room filled with his stink. They were sick with the sight and smell of him. It was time for Manny to die. His body jerked again, and his bubbly snarl gurgled up in his throat. He coughed and tried to breathe in. He couldn't. Della jumped up to lift his head. She was weak and shaky. She fell onto the bed. Her breast pressed against his face. Ephraim grabbed her and pulled her back. Harriet helped her sit down again and pressed Manny's hand into his wife's. Manny's eyes did not see her. They were fixed, with muted terror, on the middle distance. Death was sitting on his chest, no doubt, showing him a terror saved up for him alone. Then the eyes stopped moving, and the rattling breath went dead.

After the Quicks washed Manny's body and wrapped it in clean sheets, they went downstairs to eat. Della insisted. They drank the beef broth that she had cooked for him and ate rolls that Mercer had baked earlier that evening. They heard themselves groan as they ate. It all made Tyree want to hold Mercer and kiss her mouth and make love to her and sleep, forgetting, on her breast. Instead he excused himself and went to walk outside until the yearning had passed.

When he returned, they talked about funeral arrangements and Bea's fire. Tyree took a screwdriver and forced the strongbox.

There he found another hundred dollars. He returned to the kitchen, not sure what to tell his mother, not sure what she already knew.

"He didn't say anything to me at all," Della was saying. "After forty years."

"Last words mean nothing," said Tyree. It was a lie.

On the Swift Steamer, Mercer watched Philadelphia fall away. This was the boat she was to have taken with Pryor.

"Mama, why don't you open the letter Mr. Tyree gave you?" Mattie asked.

"I was going to wait to open it."

"He said that it was for all of us," said Etta, anticipating her mother's objection.

Mercer took it out of her bag reluctantly. They'd kissed in the backyard in the early morning under slanted yellow sunlight and said goodbye. She would correspond with Harriet, they agreed, but not with him. The heavy, cream-colored envelope with "The Gray Family" written in neat black calligraphy looked like another goodbye. Mercer was exhausted from them.

She handed the envelope to Etta.

"It *is* for all of us, Etta. You open it."

Etta turned the envelope upside down to pull out its contents. A silver toothpick fell onto her lap.

"That's for you?"

"Yes."

Mercer slipped the toothpick in her mouth, then dropped it into her purse. "Read the note," she said.

"These men have worked with Mr. Still and others to help find and recover relatives."

Underneath that one sentence were two names and addresses. Folded into a separate sheet of paper were five slightly charred one-hundred-dollar bills: the price of a child Bennie's age.

A   NOTE   ABOUT   THE   AUTHOR

Lorene Cary was raised in Philadelphia and Yeadon, Pennsylvania. She was graduated from St. Paul's School in 1974 and received a B.A. and M.A. from the University of Pennsylvania in 1978. While studying at Sussex University on a Thouron Fellowship for British–U.S. student exchange, she earned an M.A. in Victorian literature. In 1992, Colby College conferred on her an honorary Doctor of Letters.

In the early 1980s Ms. Cary worked as a writer for *Time* and as Associate Editor at *TV Guide*. Since then, she has taught at St. Paul's School, Antioch University (Philadelphia campus), and the University of the Arts, and has written articles for such publications as *Essence* and *The Philadelphia Inquirer Sunday Magazine*. In 1992 she was a contributing editor at *Newsweek*. Her previous book, *Black Ice*, was published in 1991 and chosen by the American Library Association as one of its Notable Books for 1992.

Ms. Cary lives in Philadelphia with her husband, R. C. Smith, and their daughters, Laura and Zoë.

A NOTE ON THE TYPE

This book was set in Fairfield, the first typeface from the hand of
the distinguished American artist and engraver Rudolph Ruzicka
(1883–1978). In its structure Fairfield displays the sober and sane
qualities of the master craftsman whose talent has long been dedi-
cated to clarity. It is this trait that accounts for the trim grace and
vigor, the spirited design and sensitive balance, of this original
typeface.

Composed by ComCom, a division of The Haddon Craftsmen, Inc.,
Allentown, Pennsylvania
Printed and bound by Quebecor Printing Martinsburg,
Martinsburg, West Virginia
Designed by Robert C. Olsson